OWN GOAL

L.A. WITT

ARTIFICIAL INTELLIGENCE

No artificial intelligence was used in the making of this book or any of my books. This includes writing, co-writing, cover artwork, translation, and audiobook narration.

I do not consent to any Artificial Intelligence (AI), generative AI, large language model, machine learning, chatbot, or other automated analysis, generative process, or replication program to reproduce, mimic, remix, summarize, train from, or otherwise replicate any part of this creative work, via any means: print, graphic, sculpture, multimedia, audio, or other medium. This applies to all existing AI technology and any that comes into existence in the future.

I support the right of humans to control their artistic works.

OWN GOAL

Eight seasons ago, Jarek Badura made the biggest mistake of his career, earning him the nickname "Joke." He's been fighting ever since to prove that season was a fluke, and he's only just started to leave it behind, finally regaining some respect and securing his place as second line center.

But his team just made a new acquisition, and suddenly he's linemates with the man who was the unknowing catalyst for his fall from grace all those years ago.

After seven long seasons, Hunter Michaud is done carrying his disastrously managed team. An unrestricted free agent, he startles the hockey world by accepting an offer elsewhere, signing with a team that works together and builds on each other's strengths. And it doesn't hurt that one of Hunter's longtime idols is on the roster.

He just doesn't realize how much his career is already intertwined with Jarek's.

Or how much resentment is waiting for him in Pittsburgh.

Or how much chemistry is hiding under the ice between them.

Own Goal is a 127,000-word contemporary hockey romance that isn't currently part of a series, but the author doesn't dare declare it a standalone because that's just asking for it. For fans of slow burns, grumpy sunshine, enemies to lovers, and teammates to lovers!

CW: Verbal abuse (remembered and on-page), some physical violence (on and off ice).

CHAPTER 1

JAREK

"You know what would make this game more interesting?" I gestured down the green as Dima and I stepped out of our golf cart to join Ferns and Dolls at the sixth hole.

Dolls cocked a brow, glancing up from selecting a club from his bag. "If Ferns could actually stay under par once in a while?"

"Hey!" Ferns snarled something in Swedish, which only made Dolls chuckle.

"I mean, yes," I said. "That would help. But that's not what I was thinking."

My three teammates eyed me.

I smirked and gestured down the green again. "Goalies."

Ferns and Dima both laughed. Dolls looked like he might be considering it.

Dima must've caught the interested spark in our teammate's eye. "I dare you." He nodded back toward the parking lot. "You have your mask in car, don't you?"

Dolls pursed his lips and nodded. No surprise—we'd all been doing some light practicing at the training center lately, including this morning. "Pads, too. Should I get them?"

"Ugh, no." Ferns tapped Dolls' shoe with his club. "Just take your swing. I don't want to get kicked out because you tore up the grass with your skates."

"Fuck off." Dolls rolled his eyes and went to tee up. "I wouldn't wear my skates on the grass."

And with that, we were all off and running, working out what the rules would be for golf with a goalie, whether each golfer would have his own goalie, or if the goalie would be his own entity trying to fuck up all our scores. The conversation continued for the next three holes, with the usual pauses each time one of us teed up and took a swing, not to mention the chirping at Ferns for consistently being three or four over par.

"*We* should have goalies," Dima said sagely after the ninth hole. "The three of us"—he gestured at me, Dolls, and himself—"so Ferns has a chance."

The laughter almost drowned out the string of Swedish profanity.

The conversation drifted, the golf continued, and I savored this relaxed pace. We still had weeks to go before training camp started, and though we all religiously kept up our workouts on and off the ice, we took advantage of every opportunity we had to enjoy the downtime.

Ferns and Dolls—Rune Fernholm and Mikael Dalström, respectively—had come back two weeks ago from Sweden, and I'd been here for about a week after spending a month and a half with my family in Kladno. I was always exhausted after the long trip to Pittsburgh from Czechia, and I traveled either alone or with my sister; I had no idea how the two of them managed the journeys from Sweden with their wives and the five children they had between them. Maybe that was why the families always traveled together.

Dima—Dmitry Meknikov—usually went home to Yeka- terinburg, but his son was born early in the offseason, and Dima had surgery on his elbow three weeks after that. I didn't blame them for holding off on travel this time. Fortu- nately, his wife's family lived in Montreal, so they'd come down to help with the baby while everyone recovered.

Dima had been a little worried he wouldn't heal from his surgery in time for next season, but judging by his golf swing, he wasn't in any pain. Or, well, not enough to stop him from playing, anyway. With hockey players, that didn't mean much.

"Does your surgeon know you're golfing?" I asked as we rode in the cart toward the twelfth hole. "And does Coach?"

"I feel fine." He bent and straightened his arm as if to emphasize how fine he felt. "See? Healed!"

"Uh-huh. Like when Bauer's knee was 'just fine' when he came back for the playoffs?"

"Pfft." Dima rolled his eyes. "I'm *fine*."

Yeah, we'd see about that.

I just chuckled, and we continued after Dolls and Ferns. It had taken me a long time to find this chill vibe with some teammates. Wearing sweaters for four teams in three seasons didn't really do much for bonding with the other guys, especially when I'd been trying to claw my way back up from a spectacular fall from grace. Luckily, Pittsburgh had seen something in me. They'd claimed me off waivers halfway through that one season, and in the years since then, I'd found my groove.

Being reunited with Dima, my best friend from major juniors, had helped a lot. Through him, I'd become close to Dolls and Ferns as well. We were a tightknit group now, golfing together, working out together, eating together. I'd found my professional groove, too; working my way up from the fourth line to the second. I'd never see the top line as long as our captain and star center, Chase Mayweather, was still playing, and I could absolutely live with that.

Another season or two like this, and maybe people would forget about my third year. The one that still hung like an albatross around my neck, along with the nickname I'd earned that season: Joke Badura.

I shuddered at the thought, rolling my shoulders under my sun-warmed shirt. I wasn't going to think about all that. Not right now. It was a lovely day. I was playing some damn good golf. I was out with my closest friends. Everything was fine in ways it hadn't been for a long time, and the clouds of the past weren't going to close in and rain on it. No fucking way.

It was my turn to swing. I hit the ball and watched it sail through the air in a satisfying arc. It landed a lot closer to the hole than I'd thought it would, bounced twice, and then rolled even closer.

"Oh, that's bullshit," Ferns grumbled, following it with some Swedish curses.

"Eh, he could still blow it," Dolls said cheerfully as he teed up his own ball. "You could beat him if he goes..." He furrowed his brow. "Hey, Dima. How far over par would Yars have to go for Ferns to beat him?"

Dima picked up the scorecard. "Uh..." He furrowed his brow, lips moving as if he were mumbling to himself. Then he looked at us and announced, "Seventeen."

"Right." Dolls gave a sharp nod. "So if Yars completely blows this hole and the next—"

"Yeah, you'd love it if I blew a hole," I muttered, and

threw a tee at his head. It bounced off his baseball cap, and he flipped me the bird.

Ferns huffed with annoyance. "You all suck."

"Um, actually?" Dima held up the scorecard. "According to the numbers—"

"Shut up."

I snickered. To be fair, Ferns was a spectacular eight ball player, and no one on the team could beat him at soccer. He was just utterly snakebitten when it came to golf.

Dolls had apparently done enough chirping to warrant some karma from the gods, because his ball ended up in the weeds. Now it was Ferns snarking and joking while Dolls swore and grumbled. Dima and I just chuckled and shook our heads as we headed for the carts.

I was just teeing up to sink the ball when someone's phone went off. I turned a look on my friends. "What the fuck? I thought phones were off unless someone's wife might go into labor?"

"Yeah, yeah." Dolls pulled out his phone. "But it's Delphi."

That shut us all up. Ferns, Dima, and I exchanged wide-eyed looks while Dolls took the call. Delphi—Greg Torkelson to everyone else—was one of the team's scouts. He'd earned the nickname Oracle of Delphi because he was *scary* good at predicting which prospects would do well and who would tank. On three separate occasions, he'd urged our GM to pass on some top-rated draft prospects, insisting he use our first round picks to select some no-name kids from teams with tepid records.

Sports analysts had lost their minds over it, saying Pittsburgh's GM needed to be fired for pissing away the opportunity to grab potential generational talents.

As it turned out, all three of the coveted top picks had

flamed out after a season or two. The three nobodies? One was Ferns, who'd been paired with a useless D partner on an awful major junior team, but had blossomed under our coaches and had already set two League records for defenseman. Another was a goalie who'd been almost unstoppable for seven seasons, and he was now a nightmare to play against after he'd signed with Dallas as a free agent two years ago. The third sleeper had spent most of last season tearing it up in the minors, and would almost certainly be brought up this year or next.

This year's draft was over, but free agency had kicked off this week. Delphi had been tight-lipped about that, though. We knew there were a number of blockbuster players shopping around for offers, and after two of our forwards and Dolls' backup goalie retired after last season, Pittsburgh had cap space to burn. There was no telling what kind of talent our GM was going to sign, and I was admittedly on pins and needles now that Delphi was calling.

"Think they grabbed O'Brien?" Dima whispered.

"God, I hope so," I replied, watching Dolls for tells. O'Brien was a defenseman playing for Denver, and *everyone* wanted him on their team. I suspected Denver would re-sign him, though. He probably just wanted to see what he could get on the free agent market before he committed. Couldn't blame him.

Suddenly, Dolls straightened. His jaw went slack. "No. You're *lying.*" His eyes lost focus, but they kept getting bigger. "Are you—you're fucking serious? You can't be—are you *sure?* And it's a done deal?" Dolls murmured something I didn't catch, and he paced back and forth on the green. Goalies were high-energy and twitchy anyway, and Dolls could never stay still for long, but this seemed... different.

My chest tightened, and I again exchanged looks with Ferns and Dima. They had the same expressions on their faces—nervous excitement. The front office had landed someone big, hadn't they? Someone exceptional?

Maybe that centerman out of Los Angeles? Or that incredible right winger in Boston who could stick handle in a phonebooth? Hell, maybe they *had* snagged O'Brien.

Finally, Dolls ended the call and lowered his phone, turning a stunned look on us.

"Well?" Ferns prompted. "What did he say?"

Dolls glanced at the phone in his hand as if it might clarify something. Then he shook his head and faced us again. When he spoke, he sounded dazed: "We just signed Hunter Michaud."

Dima and Ferns were immediately calling bullshit and telling him that couldn't be true. A second later, they were whooping and hollering, celebrating our team's acquisition of one of the biggest generational talents the League had ever seen.

Me?

My heart hit the grass at my feet.

The clouds I'd tried so hard to keep at bay were dark and thick, swirling around my head as my teammate's words echoed in my ears.

Hunter Michaud.

My team had acquired...

They'd signed...

Hunter Michaud was going to be on *my goddamned team?*

Any team that wanted to win wanted Michaud. It was a no-brainer to snatch him up if the opportunity arose, even if it meant jettisoning half the roster to free up cap space. Our

GM should get a *medal* for wooing him into signing with Pittsburgh.

But that didn't mean I could stomach being on the same team as Michaud.

"Hey. Jarek." Dima nudged my shoulder. "You still here?"

I shook myself and forced a laugh. "Yeah. I'm... Yeah, I'm still here."

None of the guys looked convinced in the slightest. In fact, they were all studying me uncertainly.

My face heated, and I cleared my throat. "We should..." I nodded down the green. "We're going to start holding up other players."

"Yars." Dolls inclined his head. "We just signed Hunter—"

"I know we did," I snapped, and regretted my sharp tone even before my three teammates jumped. I exhaled hard. "Yeah, it's great. But we should..." I again gestured toward the hole. "Before we start holding up everyone else."

They weren't convinced and weren't trying to hide it, but they let it go. In awkward silence, we continued golfing.

Or, well... *they* continued golfing. I was extremely competitive at everything I did, but I couldn't play for shit now. My concentration was gone, and my enthusiasm wasn't far behind.

In the end, Ferns almost beat me after all. Came within a stroke or two, I thought. I didn't really pay attention.

I couldn't say I fucking cared.

CHAPTER 2

HUNTER

It had been a long, long time since the first day of training camp had filled me with something other than dread.

I was pretty sure I'd been excited when I showed up for camp my rookie season. Cautiously optimistic when I'd come back the second year. Every season after that, though? The ball of lead in the pit of my stomach just seemed to get bigger and heavier.

This year, as I pulled into the player parking lot outside the training center for the Pittsburgh Hornets, I couldn't help smiling. The ball of lead was long gone. I swore it had vanished the moment I'd finished signing, initialing, and signing my contract back in July. My mood had lightened with every call I ignored from my previous general manager and front office staff and with every text I closed without reading. Every box I'd taped shut or watched the movers carry out of my place had filled me with glee instead of stressing me out like it probably should've. I'd actually laughed out loud when my plane had taken off from Toronto, and I'd almost cried with relief when it landed here in Pittsburgh.

A new team. A new start. All the toxicity and pressure and bullshit were behind me now. I wouldn't have minded signing with another Canadian team—and Vancouver would've been great, since that was home—but crossing the border into the U.S. did make my old team and my old life feel farther in the rearview.

Good fucking riddance.

As I got out of my car and strode into the training center, I didn't feel quite the level of excitement I had my rookie year. I'd been in the League too long to be that naïve.

But this was a good start. And Pittsburgh was well-known for having one of the friendliest and most welcoming locker rooms in the League. There were some guys here I'd played with in juniors or during their stints in Toronto. Some I'd idolized to varying degrees since my early pro days and even my time in juniors.

The biggest attraction, though? Everyone running the team believed this was, you know, a *team*. Not a bunch of guys who could half-ass it while someone else—namely, me —carried everyone's weight. In fact, during negotiations, the general manager had issued me a warning that had actually been an enormous selling point:

"We know you're a star, kid," he'd told me. *"And we want your talent. But the Pittsburgh Hornets are a team. We don't put up with showboating and putting yourself above the team. This isn't going to be the Hunter Michaud show. You understand me?"*

Loud and clear, sir. Where do I sign?

Because that was *exactly* what I'd craved. I'd been fed up with the opposite in Toronto, and I was looking forward to being a member of a team instead of everyone's work-horse. Yes, there was pressure. Yes, expectations were high.

But a locker room where I was explicitly *not* to be treated any differently from my teammates?

Sign. Me. Up.

I strolled through the halls of the unfamiliar training facility, using both signs and memory from my brief tour to guide me to the general locker room. Being training camp, there wasn't room for everyone in the main Hornets locker room. By the end of camp, the roster would be whittled down enough that most of us would be in there, but for now, we spilled into the other rooms that were used by other teams playing games and tournaments in this building.

When I'd met Coach Henley here last week, he'd offered to get me a stall and a nameplate in the main locker room.

"No," I'd insisted. *"I haven't earned a place in there."*

Yeah, I had a feeling he and the GM had already written my name in ink on the team's season roster—no pressure or anything—but I wanted to start on level ice with my teammates. If I went straight into the main room like I owned the place, nameplate and all, then someone was getting bumped out here to one of the generic rooms with the rookies and prospects. Even if there was space for me—which there probably was, thanks to offseason trades and retirements—it would still send the message that I didn't have to prove myself like everyone else.

Don't give the team a reason to resent me before I've even put on my skates, Coach.

Fortunately, even if he thought it was ridiculous, Henley had taken my request to heart. When I'd come by yesterday to take care of some paperwork, I was told I'd been assigned to Locker Room B and to find an empty locker. Perfect.

The room had been deserted when I'd left my skates

and pads here yesterday. This morning? I was greeted by the familiar noise and smells of a locker room full of hockey players. There was a mix of kids who couldn't have been more than eighteen or nineteen (prospects, most likely) and some players I'd seen around the League.

I hadn't even made it through the door when someone in the hallway called out to me.

"Hey! Mish!" Gray Sawyer broke into a big grin, and then he strode over and pulled me into a bear hug. "Man, I thought they were lying when they said they signed you." He drew back, grin still wide and bright, showing off the place his leftmost incisor had once been. "What are you doing, slumming it here in the 'Burgh?"

I chuckled. "Eh, I heard they had you in the first D-pair, so I figured they needed all the help they could get."

He barked a laugh and slapped my shoulder. Then he slung his arm around me. "Come on, I'll introduce you to the boys."

I hesitated, gesturing at the locker room. "I, uh... I should probably get my gear on."

He blinked. "They put you in here with the babies? Seriously?"

Some warmth rose in my cheeks, and I shrugged. "I'm the new guy."

He eyed me. "You're Hunter Michaud."

I smiled brightly. "Aww, look at you! Remembering people's names!" I smacked his chest. "Next up, colors and numbers!"

"Oh, fuck you." He motioned for me to follow him. "At least let me introduce you to the rest of the team. We're still way early."

Eh, fair enough. I let him herd me into the main locker room. Being introduced as just one of the guys *was* something else I'd craved for a long time. People thought the whole star player thing was great—and in some ways, it was —but it was hard to make friends with guys who were already starstruck before you'd even shaken hands. That was kind of unavoidable, but it helped to have an old friend introduce me around as Mish, warning them about my penchant for pranks (which I argued was exaggerated) and how I sometimes knocked my teammates' teeth out (which was technically true).

It was crowded in here with both familiar players and younger guys, so we were hardly the only ones socializing instead of putting on our gear. Yeah, I decided a few minutes of this wouldn't kill me.

Sawyer might, though, if I kept chirping at him.

"Oh, come on." I smacked his arm. "Are you still salty about that? It was an accident!"

He glared down at me. "*Both* times?"

I huffed with mock exasperation. "Yes, both times. My shot is good, but it's not deliberately-knock-out-my-buddy's-tooth-while-he's-going-fifteen-miles-an-hour-in-the-other-direction good."

Rolling his eyes, he absently tongued the place one of those teeth had been.

Vincent, a freckle-faced prospect, laughed. "That'd be a hell of a trick shot if you could do it on purpose." He squinted at Sawyer. "How many do you have left, anyway? Looks like there's still plenty, so—"

"Ugh, fuck you, kid."

I snickered, gesturing at Sawyer's face. "I mean, I can try for that big one in front. Might be easier than the—"

"You know what?" Sawyer cuffed the back of my head. "Eat a dick."

I just chuckled, as did the other guys he'd been introducing me to. I could tell the other guys—three young prospects and a veteran player I'd met once before—were a little starstruck, but the casual introduction had made a difference. We were all bantering and talking like peers.

Thank *God*.

Don't get me wrong—I was proud of my skill, and I was glad I'd been able to play as well as I had. But there'd been a lot of lonely years in there, going all the way back to my 12U days when scouts and journalists had started sniffing around. That kind of attention didn't do many favors for someone trying to find a place in the social hierarchy. By all rights, it shouldn't have been such a big deal now that I was an adult. Every team had big name players.

But when your damn coaching staff and team management acted like you were the Second Coming, it cultivated a mix of envy and resentment from everyone else that didn't really bode well for being just one of the guys. It was hard to mesh with teammates who hated me because everyone acted like I was going to singlehandedly bring the Cup to Toronto, and who hated me for... not singlehandedly bringing the Cup to Toronto.

And yet people had been *shocked* when I didn't re-sign.

I eventually broke away from the conversation to return to the other locker room and get dressed. It was, after all, time to skate with my new team.

Pulling on a yellow practice sweater felt good. A new start. A clean slate. This was going to be amazing. Everyone else probably thought I was a dork, smiling like a kid on Christmas—or a rookie at his first pro training camp—while I got ready. Eh. They could think what they wanted. They didn't know the pressure that had been on my shoulders all this time, and how fucking liberating it was to be here.

Now it was time to prove I deserved a spot on this team

and in the main locker room. I grabbed my stick, gloves, and helmet, and headed out to the rink to warm up.

Before I reached it, though, one of the prospects fell into step beside me, his face so red, he looked like he'd just bag skated for an hour. I was pretty sure that was just a blush, though.

"Hey, you're, um... You're Hunter Michaud, right?" He recoiled timidly, as if he was terrified I was about to put him in his place. How dare this lesser mortal speak to me?

Ugh. Fuck that.

I smiled. "I am, yeah." I stopped walking, and he did too. Then I took off one of my gloves, tucked it under my arm, and extended my hand. "What's your name?"

He gulped, fumbling with his stick as he took off his own glove, and as he shook my hand, he said, "Kip Robbins. The, uh..." he stammered a little, but managed, "The guys just call me Robs."

"Robs. I'll remember that. Everyone calls me Mish."

His blush got impossibly redder. Then he cleared his throat and motioned toward the rink where our teammates were warming up. "Just, uh... I wanted to ask... If you've got time..." He chewed his lip as he met my gaze, and he shyly asked, "I don't want to bother you or anything, but I've been watching your backhand forever. Could you... like... show me a thing or two?"

"Yeah, sure." I shrugged. "Do you shoot right or left?"

"Right." He laughed softly. "Same as you."

"Oh, cool. I mean, I can show someone either way, but it's definitely easier when we both shoot with the same hand." I clapped his shoulder. "Come on. Let's go warm up, and I'll help you out when we have a few minutes. If we don't get a chance today, we will before camp is over. Promise."

Okay, I wouldn't lie—this was one of those situations where the starstruck thing was kind of fun: when someone looked like I'd made his whole day just by existing. *This* was the good shit.

And I was always happy to help out young players. I'd been *livid* when I'd found out that prospects in Toronto had been expressly forbidden from approaching me. That clearly wasn't an issue here. The young guys were often shy about talking to any of the veterans, but at least here in Pittsburgh, they were allowed to. With any luck, after I'd worked with Robs a little, word would get around that I was as approachable as the next player. How the fuck did anyone build a team if players were afraid to talk to each other?

Looking at you, Toronto.

We warmed up for a few minutes, just skating easily and shooting lazily at the goals. When I was good and loose, I found a few pucks and searched for Robs in the crowd. That was easier said than done—there were a *lot* of new faces on this ice. At least the practice jerseys we wore at camp had numbers and names on them, unlike the blank ones we'd wear during the season. I was pretty sure Robs had worn number eighteen. Or was it sixteen? I scanned the crowd and found number eighteen. No, that wasn't him. Too much scruff on his jaw. So he must've been—

Ah. There.

I called out, "Hey. Robs!"

His head snapped toward me, and a second later, his cheeks colored again. He'd been talking to another young prospect, and he said something to him as he gestured at me. The other kid's lips parted and his eyes went huge. They exchanged a few words, and then both skated over.

"Do you mind showing him, too?" Robs gestured at the

other prospect, a tall Black kid with the beginning of a goatee. "This is Ouellet. We played together in juniors."

I took off my glove again and extended my hand. "Mish. Nice to meet you."

Ouellet blinked a couple of times, then shoved his stick into Robs' hand, took off his glove, and accepted the handshake. With a heavy French Canadian accent, he said, "Nice to meet you."

I motioned toward the goal as I put on my glove. "You working on your backhand, too?"

He again took on a shocked expression, but then nodded vigorously. "Please?"

"Sure. Okay, so to start with, let me see how your backhands look..."

We only managed about fifteen minutes before Coach Henley blew the whistle.

Ouellet's shoulders fell. "Damn. I was just starting to get it."

"Nah, don't sweat it," I said as we skated toward where our teammates were gathering. "Next break, we can do some more."

I swear, he almost tripped. "Really?"

"Of course." I flashed him a quick smile.

Then we joined our teammates and everyone took a knee so Henley could get everyone started. I had to fight a smile the whole time. I'd been on Hornet ice for less than half an hour, and I already felt a million times better than I had in Toronto.

Best. Decision. *Ever.*

Training camp kicked off as it usually did. Every team was

different, but this was fairly predictable. We were divided into three color-coded groups. I was in the yellow group, and the coaches ran us through drills, line rushes, board battles—everything imaginable to get a look at our abilities, strengths, and weaknesses. Later, there was a scrimmage between the yellow and black teams, which we won.

After that, we closed out with the part everyone loved to hate—conditioning. Which meant skating. Hard. In circles. For-fucking-ever. I kept myself in damn good shape during the offseason, but this part always kicked my ass. It was necessary. I could do it. But it *sucked*.

"Fair warning, kid," an older teammate—one who was long retired now—had told me when I'd whined about it my rookie season. *"It gets worse every year."*

He was so right.

But it was part of training, so I did it. And then the next morning, we were back at the training center to do it all over again.

The banter in the locker room was a mix of whining about sore legs and chirping at those doing the whining. I just laughed along with it. My legs were sore, but they'd be worse after today's session, so I'd save my complaining until then.

Out on the ice, I spent some more time with Robs and Ouellet, who were eagerly practicing everything I'd shown them with their backhands. It would take some time to perfect it, but they had the idea, especially Ouellet.

Then it was time to practice again.

And damn it, I'd almost started feeling like just one of the guys, but boy did that go out the fucking window when the skills coach paired us up for another drill.

We'd been working in various pairs since yesterday and into today, but the coaches were still figuring out who had chemistry with who. Some of the longtime pairs were kept together, like Mayweather and Cole, who'd been joined at the hip for like five years. Everyone else was shuffled around while the team settled into a groove.

So far, that had been fine, but this time…

Peering at his clipboard, the skills coach called out, "Badura. Michaud." He gestured sharply for us to join the other pairs by the dashers.

I didn't think anything of it in the moment. Well, okay, I did. My first reaction was to get a little giddy and maybe a tiny bit starstruck myself. Paired with Jaromir Badura? Fuck, yeah, even if it was just for a drill. I'd been following his career ever since his rookie season three years before I was drafted. He'd been an incredible forward back then, and those gray eyes and sharp features had intrigued me almost as much as his hockey prowess. The first time I'd seen him laugh in an interview had damn near broken my brain, and I must've watched that video a hundred times since.

When I'd been selected by his team, I'd been ecstatic… and then crushed when he was traded away less than a week after the draft.

Now we were on the same team, and the coaches were pairing us up for a drill, and I might've been feeling a little like Robs and Ouellet in that moment.

But one glance at Badura on my way to across the ice…

Fuck. If looks could kill.

It wasn't like I'd never seen him in person before. Hell, I'd played against him plenty of times. His mean-mugging was pretty legendary throughout the League, especially since it could intimidate the crap out of opposing players. I'd been on the receiving end of it because that was hockey. We all glared at each other like we were mortal enemies, but as soon as the game was over, we were fine. Friendly, even.

But the way Badura scowled as he joined me—dude, this was practice. Fuck, it was training camp. And we were on the same team! What the hell?

He stopped beside me and looked anywhere but right at me. The other pairs were chirping and jawing. The two of us? Dead silent.

And now that I thought about it, he was the only returning member of the Hornets I *hadn't* spoken with since I'd arrived yesterday. There'd been introductions, banter, casual conversation, strategizing during drills—all part of being teammates.

But not with him. Not a word. Not once. Somehow, even when he'd been around a group I was being introduced to, he'd suddenly just... not be there anymore.

Had he...

Had he been *avoiding* me?

For fuck's sake. Talk about a disappointment. Something, something, never meet your heroes.

To my surprise, though, as the drill got started, he leaned toward me a little and gestured across the ice at the defensive pairs waiting to play against us. "Watch out for Fernholm. Number ninety-three." He glanced at me, his expression colder than the ice beneath our feet. "You blink and he'll steal the puck right off your stick."

I knew that. Fernholm's ability to steal pucks was as legendary as Badura's glare, and I'd played against him plenty of times. In fact, he'd stolen the puck off my stick just like Badura described. More than once. But in the interest of making nice with my frosty linemate, I said, "Thanks. I'll keep an eye out for him."

That earned me a sharp nod and nothing more.

When it was our turn, we skated away from the dashers. The coach sent a puck to Badura, and he shot it to me as the defensemen came at us. To my surprise, Badura's cold shoulder vanished. We passed the puck back and forth, both dancing around the defensemen before Badura faked, passed, and gave me the perfect opportunity to put the puck behind the goalie. The goalie made a valiant attempt, but...

Sorry, pal. Nothing personal.

Most of our teammates would share a fist bump at this point before heading back to the dashers to wait their next run.

Us? Yeah, right.

It was like the polar opposite of how most hockey players got along. On ice, guys would throw down and throw punches, but as soon as the horn sounded the end of the game, they were laughing about it over beers.

With Badura and me, we meshed easily on the ice. Or, well, we had for one drill. As soon as the whistle blew, he wouldn't even look at me.

Well, this will be fun.

Please, Coach. For the love of God.

Pair me with someone else.

CHAPTER 3

JAREK

Unsurprisingly, Michaud was good.

What did surprise me, though, was that we were good *together*.

Over the second and third days of training camp, the coaches rotated us through different partners as they felt out all of our skillsets, strengths, weaknesses, and on-ice chemistry, but more and more, they kept putting the two of us together. By the end of day three, I wasn't paired with anyone else and neither was he. By day four, they were testing out different right wingers to round out our offensive line. I suspected it would be Dima, since he and I had been paired up for the past three seasons, and he and Michaud seemed to mesh well.

There was also the question of who would be center on our line, though I doubted it was much of a question. Michaud and I could both play center or left wing, but he was stronger... I mean, he was stronger everywhere. He was Hunter fucking Michaud. His faceoff stats were better than mine, too, so it was no shock that the coaches were leaning toward putting me on Michaud's wing.

Fine. I could live with it. I was irritated enough about being linemates with him. No point wasting energy bitching about where on that line we were. At least they weren't punting me back down to the third line or some shit.

I got it, though. We were good together. We read each other well. And there was a reason he was as famous as he was—he truly was a generational talent with an exceptional ability to maneuver the puck, his own body, his stick, and all three at the same time in ways no one should've been able to. He could score impossible goals from the most jaw-dropping angles through the tiniest openings. Playing with him was an experience even in practice, and being his linemate in a game would be mind-blowing.

I respected him. I admired him. I'd hoped and prayed for a linemate like him ever since juniors.

A linemate *like* him, as if any such thing existed. There was no active player like Michaud. Only a handful in the century-plus of League history. Watching Michaud skate, watching him stick handle, watching him play—it was awe-inspiring. People joked that he wasn't human, and it was hard not to wonder, because how did he *move* like that?

But it was a kick in the balls to watch him, too. An even bigger one to skate with him. To be his linemate, even for the duration of a single drill.

Every time one of the coaches paired us up *again*, I ground my teeth so hard they hurt.

Every time, I heard the echoes of the head coach and general manager I'd had in Toronto a lifetime ago.

"It'll all be worth it when we sign Michaud," the GM had told me.

"The two of you as linemates?" Coach Robertson had whistled, shaking his head. *"Fuck, son. You and he will be unstoppable together."*

I hated how much I'd hung on those—okay, they hadn't been promises. They'd seemed like it in the moment to my naïve young self, but they hadn't been. I'd hung on them like they were, though, and in the end...

Well, in the end, Hunter Michaud had put on a Toronto Shamrocks jersey, and I'd put on the nickname Joke Badura. I'd believed the men in charge, and they'd gotten what they wanted, and I'd been paying for it ever since.

Now the man at the core of that Faustian bargain was here. And I was here. And...

"Michaud. Badura." Coach Bancroft, the offensive coach, pointed to where other pairs were setting up for the next drill.

I bit back a curse and skated toward the wall on Michaud's heels. Glaring at his back—at the number forty-one and *MICHAUD* printed across perfect shoulders—I focused on my anger instead of the unexpected and unwelcome lump in my throat.

I'd been a wreck ever since I'd found out he was coming to this team. Was it too much to ask to be paired with anyone but him?

Don't you all understand how much this is killing me?

No. No, they didn't. They couldn't.

Because literally no one in this building knew.

Not my coaches. Not my teammates. Not the men who'd become my friends.

Not Michaud.

I gritted my teeth as I came to a stop beside him. I didn't look at him, focusing instead on watching Dima and one of the prospects taking their turn ahead of us.

It didn't help that there was a very unprofessional part of me that *wanted* to look at Michaud. It wasn't as if I hadn't seen him over the last several years. I'd played against him, and anyway, he was practically the face of hockey these days—there was no escaping photos and videos of Hunter Michaud.

But now that there wasn't a game to distract me—now that there were lulls in the action and opportunities to look at him from way too close up—I had to say the cameras did *not* do him justice.

He was white, same as me, and I had an inch or so on him. Six-foot, according to his stats, with an ass and thighs for days. He had a body to die for—lean and ripped like most guys in this line of work—and dark blond hair that was always either sweaty and tousled or arranged to look artfully mussed. He'd lost the soft babyface he'd had for his first couple of years. His jaw was sharper now, his cheekbones more pronounced. That once boyish smile had turned into something that made me wobble on my skates, especially when someone made him laugh and those hazel eyes sparkled just right.

Early on, there'd been a running joke around the League that he'd probably win two or three Cups before he could even grow a playoff beard. Now he had a respectable dusting of dark scruff on his jaw that made him unreasonably sexy. No one had ever seen him with much of a playoff beard, never mind kissing the Cup with a smooth babyface, because Toronto had been a mess despite his legendary play. Maybe this would be the year he finally had a chance to show everyone how thick that playoff beard could get.

If he could get past the second round.

Which he just might.

Now that he was playing with the Pittsburgh Hornets.

With my team.

Almost certainly on my line.

Oh, fuck me.

I *had* to get it together. My world had collided with Michaud's a lifetime ago, and I'd been reaping the results ever since. I couldn't blame him any more than I could blame Pittsburgh's GM for signing him. The resentment burning like hot coals in my stomach—that wasn't his fault, and I knew it. This was on me. All in my head. I *had* to get a goddamned grip. Pull it the fuck together. Yeah, it had taken me all these years to regain my equilibrium and reclaim my professional reputation, but I couldn't put that on Michaud no matter how much I wanted to. I sure as shit couldn't take it out on him.

But could I play with him? Could I function as his linemate?

For a hot minute, as he and I waited our turn, I debated blowing it. As much as this chemistry came naturally, it didn't happen on its own. If one of us decided to be lazy, or was distracted, or just didn't give a fuck, our performance would fall apart. Timing was something that took a whole lot of work to maintain, and very, very little work to unravel. A few disastrous or even disappointing drills, and the coaches would conclude that our first couple of days had been a fluke, and we'd each be paired off with other potential linemates.

I could do it. I could ensure this was where our partnership potential ended. Michaud could skate with damn near anyone, and I'd been linemates with half our forwards before. It would be fine, even if it meant going back to the third line.

Closing my eyes, I pushed out a breath through my nose. Yeah, I could botch this, but I wouldn't. Not when I knew all too well how something like that could come back to bite me in the ass and keep haunting me for years to come. Getting knocked down to the third or even fourth line was the *best*-case scenario.

A whistle signaled that the pair ahead of us was finished. Michaud and I skated away from the dashers—him toward the left faceoff dot and me toward the blue line, where Coach Bancroft was waiting to send me a puck. I caught his pass, skated around a defenseman, and fended him off with one arm while I passed the puck to Michaud. It landed on his tape, and he danced around Ferns, deftly avoiding his long reach and lightning fast poke check before passing back to me, executing it all in a blur of graceful movement. I almost missed his pass, not out of a need to sabotage our drill, but out of sheer awe over watching him move. Hockey was a dance when Hunter Michaud was involved, and being a part of that dance —not an opposing force, but a partner—blew my damn mind.

I recovered, fortunately, and the puck found the back of the net. Instead of a goal horn, I was rewarded with a bark of "Fuck you, Yars!" from Dolls just before a whistle announced that the next pair was ready to start.

Chuckling, I skated by and tapped my stick on Doll's pads. "Better luck next time."

"Eat a dick," he muttered, glaring up at me through his mask, and then he was laser-focused on the next incoming pair.

I joined Michaud at the boards. The first few times we'd run a successful drill together, he'd offered up a grin and a fist bump. This time...

Well, I didn't really blame him. I hadn't been all that receptive to it in the beginning, and I still wasn't now.

He didn't do anything. Don't be an ass.

Though it occurred to me that maybe if I kept my shoulder cold, this problem would resolve itself. Coach understood that even if two players kicked ass together, that would only last for so long if they didn't like each other. Animosity was corrosive, and Coach valued the team's overall vibe too much to risk it.

So if Michaud pulled him aside and asked to be paired with anyone but me, then this arrangement would be over before it started. Coach would put us on separate lines, and one of us would be gone by the trade deadline.

One of us. Yeah, right. As if anyone with a goddamned brain would trade Michaud away when the option to get rid of me was right there.

Thank God, we had a break a few minutes later. The scrimmage was next, and we'd be playing the black team after they'd finished with their training on the other sheet. We had about twenty minutes to catch our breath and hydrate.

Under the pretense of wanting to retape my stick—something I absolutely could've done out by the ice—I stomped back to the locker room. And thank God, it was deserted in here. The white team had just gone out to the second rink for conditioning, and the black and gold teams were getting ready for the scrimmage. No one needed to warm up—not two hours into training camp—but we usually skated, bullshitted, and just tried to stay loose until it was time to set up.

I'd join them all in a minute.

I put my gloves on a shelf in my locker, leaned my stick against the stall, sank onto the bench, and rubbed my neck with both hands.

Of course, I only had about thirty seconds before the distinctive scuff of approaching skates drew a curse from my lips. It was probably just someone coming in to fix some gear or maybe to use the restroom. But damn it, couldn't they all just... stay out there for a few minutes? Let me get my head together before I had to pretend I wasn't coming unraveled for reasons I couldn't explain to anyone?

Oh, but just my luck...

"Yars?" Dima's voice had me cursing under my breath a second before his skates clomped into the room. "You all right?"

I schooled my expression as best I could, then looked up at him with what I hoped was a convincing smirk. "Just trying to erase the memories of watching you skate."

He snorted and rolled his eyes. "I never knew you were so jealous of my skating."

I flipped him off, then reached for one of my gloves. Not to put them on—I just needed something to do with my hands as I avoided his gaze.

Dima's stall was four over from mine, but he sat down on the bench beside me. Damn him. And he hadn't just come in here to shoot the shit, either.

"What's going on with you?" he asked in that pointed way of his.

I thumbed the embroidered black logo on my glove. "I just needed a break."

"Uh-huh." No one could fit *"you aren't bullshitting me, you moron"* and *"I'm your friend—talk to me"* into two syllables the way Dima could.

That persistent lump in my throat grew. I wanted to tell him. I wanted to unload everything and plead with him to help me make it all make sense.

But I couldn't. There were things I could never tell anyone—not even my best friend—and there was no explaining my state of mind without that backstory. As much as I wanted to unload all this, it just wasn't possible. Not without causing headache and hell for more people than just me. Including people who didn't deserve to get swept up in it.

No, I had to keep this to myself, which meant I couldn't vent to Dima or anyone else.

I tried like hell to swallow that lump. No doubt my teammates had all noticed my sour mood; I didn't need to explain away tears on top of everything.

Dima's hand landed firmly on my shoulder, the weight unavoidable even through my thick pads. "Jarek. You've been acting weird ever since you found out Michaud signed here. What is going on with you?"

I stared intently at my glove, picking at a loose thread on the logo. I didn't even know where to begin. I doubted Dima or anyone else could begin to understand. I'd lose his respect, and God, if there was anything that could make me swallow my pride and get myself together, it was my refusal to lose the respect of Dima or any of my other teammates. I'd fought way too long and way too hard to earn that, and this fuckery with Michaud had already cost me enough.

"I'm good." I ducked out from under Dima's hand, shoved myself to my feet and grabbed my stick and other glove. "We should go skate before the scrimmage."

Then I started walking, shaky from the inside out because I was terrified my friend would sit me right back down and drag the truth out of me.

He didn't, though. He just breathed out a string of Russian curses before following me toward the sheet. Once we were on the ice, we skated in opposite directions, and I focused on keeping my feet under me.

This was the hand I'd been dealt. Michaud was on my team. There was a good chance we were going to wind up linemates. I could either mentally implode over it, or I could adapt and overcome.

I *could* adapt and overcome. I'd spent seven seasons clawing my way back from my biggest professional mistake, and I wasn't going to lose all that ground just because I was face-to-face with a reminder of my stupid, unchangeable past.

Nothing like that was going to happen again. *I* was the one pulling the strings this time.

Skating a lazy circle, I scanned the faces on the ice until I zeroed in on one.

Michaud was talking to a pair of prospects. He'd been working with them off and on since training camp started—helping with their backhands, I thought—but now the three of them were just shooting the shit as they, like me, skated enough to stay loose. Someone said something, and a laugh broke out on Michaud's face.

I damn near tripped, so I yanked my gaze away.

Even if it wasn't the best-case scenario for my sanity, the best-case scenario for my career was to be paired up with Michaud when the season started. I could cope with my frustration over the past. I could cope with my attraction to him.

But if I truly wanted to leave Joke Badura behind...

If I truly wanted my friends and teammates to stop wondering what the fuck was wrong with me...

My best bet was to play like hell alongside the man who'd unknowingly derailed my career.

So that was exactly what I would do.

CHAPTER 4

HUNTER

Badura didn't like me, and even when he seemed to be trying to hide it, he failed miserably. The more we were paired up for drills and scrimmages, the more his jaw worked. To the point I sometimes amused myself by wondering if someone should let his dentist know he was grinding his teeth down to nothing.

Funny—I'd always thought he looked hot when he was angry, particularly when he was at the jaw-clenching, nostril-flaring stage. It took a lot to set him off, and on the rare occasion he lost his temper and threw gloves, I was not above bookmarking that video and rewatching it when I was alone. Even when he was just simmering, his fuse burning down until the fists flew, he was *ridiculously* attractive.

But that was a lot less amusing or sexy when it was directed at me. Especially when I hadn't done a damn thing except show up and put on a Hornets jersey.

Leaning against the dashers beside him, waiting our turn for a puck handling drill, I stole a look at him. His mouthguard was half out of his mouth, and he was chewing on it furiously like so many of us did during games. As hard as his jaw was working, it was a damn miracle he hadn't gnawed right through the plastic.

And he didn't do it when he was working with someone else. Not that we'd been anything but joined at the hip since day three, but before that, I'd caught glimpses of him with the others. That, and whenever he was working with a prospect, which we all did off and on.

No, the angry chewing was only with me. Ditto with the pair of deep crevices between his eyebrows.

I rolled my eyes and turned my attention back to the pair running the drill in front of us. Today was the last day of training camp. Ever since we'd been assigned to each other for the duration, I'd vacillated between not caring what he thought of me and being seriously annoyed by his cold shoulder. He didn't have to like me. I had no idea why he didn't, considering we'd never exchanged two words before he'd decided I was persona non grata, but whatever, dude.

On the other hand, we did have to coexist. And by the last day of training camp, the coaches had made it clear we'd be paired up on the second line for the foreseeable future, likely with Dmitry Meknikov on our right wing.

"I feel like a heel," Coach Henley told me, "putting Hunter Michaud anywhere but the top line. But Mayweather's held that center spot for—"

"It's fine, Coach," I insisted. "Honestly. I'm not here to knock the captain out of his spot. And he'd probably go on strike if you suggested bumping Cole down so I could take over as Mayweather's winger."

That had earned me a grunt of agreement and a hint of a grimace, as if he couldn't even stomach the idea of broaching the subject with Mayweather and Cole. I didn't blame him—those two were magic together, and no coach in his right mind would separate them.

After that, Henley's worry seemed to be more or less assuaged, though he'd insisted repeatedly that the Hornets didn't really have a first and second line anymore. Instead, we had a 1A and a 1B. Both lines would likely play around the same number of minutes each night, and my line might start some games.

Whatever. I didn't care if he called it the second line or the 1B line; if anything, putting me there solidified what he and the GM had told me about not being able to skate in here and assume I was top dog.

That's a feature, not a bug, Coach. It's all good.

And it was. Except for that tiny tidbit where my left winger and I had potential to be as inseparable as Mayweather and Cole. If our on-ice chemistry at camp carried over into games, we'd be unstoppable.

Our *off*-ice chemistry was an issue, though. We went together like... like... Okay, science had never been one of my strong points in school (aside from physics, since that could apply to hockey), but Badura and I were like water and one of those chemicals that exploded on contact with water. Magnesium? Lithium? Whatever it was. Put them in the same jar as water, and *boom*.

For the moment, we didn't have to interact much off-ice, but that wasn't going to last beyond today.

Once training camp was over...

Once we didn't have all the prospects around anymore...

Once we were down to our twenty-three-man roster for the season...

It would be a hell of a lot harder to avoid him in the players' lounge, the bus, the plane. It was already getting awkward in the locker room since the roster had been pared down enough that the staff and our teammates insisted I should move into the main locker room. Badura and I weren't right next to each other, thank God, but the room was only so big. If our teammates hadn't picked up on the bad chemistry by this point, they would once we were all together more often than not with fewer distractions than we had right now.

Which meant that one way or another, Badura and I needed to unfuck this. Like... now.

Well, not *now*, because we were on the ice. After camp, though? We were having a conversation whether he liked it or not.

But first...

"Badura. Michaud." Coach tapped his stick on the ice. "You're up!"

Badura's mouthguard disappeared into his mouth, and we both pushed off. Per Coach's instructions, I skated along the blue line before trying to weave past one of the defensemen. Meanwhile, one of the rookie forwards passed the puck to Badura, who executed a beautiful dance around the other defenseman, then passed the puck between the skates of that defenseman and the one who was on me. They both lost track of it, and when it landed on my tape, I spun to my left, shaking off the confused defenseman.

At this point in the drill, I was supposed to shoot for the net, but both defensemen wisely collapsed in on the goal, blocking the lane while still leaving enough room for the goalie to watch me.

Outside my peripheral vision, Badura tapped his stick on the ice, calling for the puck. I wound back like I was going to slap it between the D-men, and as soon as they and the netminder reacted, I fired the puck to Badura. No one saw his one-timer coming—it sailed behind an oblivious defenseman and right over the goalie's shoulder.

Badura let a smile crack through as he did a little fist pump. A second later, before the coach had even started telling the defensemen what they'd done wrong, Badura's gaze locked on mine.

And the smile fell.

And once again, the ice beneath our skates had nothing on the chill between us.

Oh, for fuck's sake. What is your problem, dude?

I decided I was done waiting to find out.

My opportunity came a couple of hours later, after we'd all showered, eaten, and gone to a team meeting. I'd learned early on that Badura was among the first to leave as soon as he had the chance, and I was ready for him.

When he came out the back door of the training center, I said, "Hey. You got a minute?"

He jumped and did a double take, and as soon as he saw me, his expression hardened. Though it was much warmer out here—summer was hanging on by its fingernails despite this being September—the air between us was frosty.

He glanced back, then stepped out of the way of the door, letting it swing shut behind him. "I've got a minute. Why?" He sounded *thrilled.*

While I'd been waiting for him, I'd gone back and forth about how I'd do this. Aggressively? Diplomatically? I hadn't really landed on what I planned to do, so I just went with what came out, which turned out to be somewhere in the middle.

"It sounds like we're gonna be linemates, at least for the time being." Oh, it was so, so hard not to fold my arms just to deal with this nervous energy. I settled on sliding my hands into my pockets. "But I get the feeling there's some, uh... animosity here?"

His lips tightened and his jaw clenched, the muscles taut beneath the layer of dark scruff. For a moment, I thought he might spit something at me like, *"Oh, gee, you noticed?"* or *"There's nothing—it's all in your stupid head."*

But he didn't speak. He just watched me. And waited.

Okay. Apparently this was on me. Of course it was.

I took a deep breath and tried to keep my voice mellow. "Am I doing something wrong?" I showed my palms. "I'm just here to play hockey. If you don't want to be linemates, then I—"

"You'd love that, wouldn't you?" he snarled, startling me back a step.

"What?" I tilted my head. "What are you even talking about? We play great together! It's when we're *not* playing that—"

"That's the only part that matters," he snapped. "We don't have to be friends off the ice."

"No, but we do have to be teammates," I threw back, my patience slipping. "We don't have to be friends, but before this week, I didn't know you from Adam." I put up my hands again. "Where is this animosity even coming from?"

He laughed bitterly. "Of course you didn't know me. It's a little hard to see anyone else with the spotlight on you."

I blinked. "The spot—"

"Please. We all get it. You're the best. You're better than any of us. So you're here to—"

"Jesus Christ," I hissed. "Do you have any idea how much pressure I've been under? Since I was a *kid?*"

"No, I don't." He let the sarcasm drip. "I can't imagine what it must be like, everyone knowing you're God's gift to the fucking sport while the rest of us—"

"Are you going to say while the rest of you had to work for it? Huh?" I narrowed my eyes. "You really want to go there, Badura? Tell me I haven't worked my goddamned ass off just like everyone else?" I gestured at my face. "Do it. Look me in the eye and tell me I haven't, or that any of this shit was just handed to me. Do it. I fucking dare you."

Surprise registered, but only for a second. Then he looked away, and even through my own anger, I realized the emotions registering on his face weren't quite right. Anger, yeah. I expected that. But there was something else. A crack revealing something raw and vulnerable underneath, as if I'd stomped on a nerve with an ice skate.

What the hell?

I schooled my expression and my tone to something less confrontational. "Look, I'm not asking to be BFFs or some bullshit. But I'm here, and you're here, so we might as well—"

"Yeah, you're here," he growled. "Believe me—I haven't forgotten that since the day they signed you."

I stared at him. What did that even mean?

And maybe it was just fatigue catching up to me after five days of training camp and trying to settle into a new place. Maybe I'd just hit my damn limit. I hadn't done or said a damn thing to this asshole, and he still thought I was shit on his shoe.

"Ugh. You know what?" I threw up my hands. "Whatever your problem is—go fuck yourself."

He muttered something that made me quite glad I didn't understand Czech, and he turned on his heel and stalked away, leaving me standing there like a dumbass.

Well, that was... productive.

I closed my eyes and let my head fall back. Fuck. Trust me to go and make things worse. But I had no idea what "things" even were, except that this asshole—this *linemate* of mine—hated me because God only knew why.

A car door slammed.

Then an engine roared to life. I turned to see a deep red Jaguar backing out of a parking space, and when the glare of the sun shifted on the windshield, I caught a glimpse of Badura's face. Sunglasses on. Jaw still set. Pointedly not looking anywhere near my direction.

The engine revved again. The tires squeaked on the asphalt.

And then he was gone, leaving me with the late summer sun beating on my shoulders and no idea how to fix... whatever this was.

Were we going to be able to function as linemates? Should I just bite the bullet and tell Coach this wasn't going to work?

Except... no. There was no way to do that without anyone thinking I was throwing my weight around or making demands. They'd laugh me out of the office if I asked to be bumped down from the second line—they weren't paying me this much for third line minutes. The only way we were getting separated was if Badura dropped down to the third or fourth line, and I had no doubt that would make *everything* worse.

There was no fixing this without rocking boats I did *not* want to rock. There was nothing I could do except suck it up and pretend my winger didn't hate my guts for some reason.

Damn. And here I thought Pittsburgh would be an improvement over Toronto.

The squeak of hinges told me the door had opened again, and I looked over to see Dima and Ferns striding out in mid-conversation.

"I'm just saying," Dima was telling him. "As long as Dolls wears his gear, who's going to know?"

Ferns rolled his eyes. "You want to explain to Coach why our starting goalie is down because of a golfing incident?"

"Do you think he'd be surprised?"

Ferns actually seemed to consider that. "Eh, maybe not."

I eyed them both, not sure I wanted to know.

"Oh, hey." Dima gave me a clap on the arm. "How are you liking Pittsburgh?"

"I like it so far," I said. "I haven't really had time to explore yet. I've barely unpacked my apartment."

Ferns laughed. "Do as much of that as you can before the season starts. Or else it'll be boxes until the offseason."

"Don't I know it," I muttered. "I'm getting there, though."

"Well, if you need more hands..." He gestured at Dima. "He'll help you."

"Hey! Stop volunteering me for things, asshole!"

Ferns just snickered.

Dima rolled his eyes, but then he glanced at his phone and sighed. "I should go. Chloé probably needs break from the baby."

The teasing left Ferns' expression. "Rough night?"

Dima nodded. "I don't get why these things are born not knowing how to sleep. It's easiest thing in world! Come on!"

Ferns and I both chuckled.

"Lena and I have been asking that since Eva was born." He elbowed Dima. "The second is always worse, too."

Dima muttered something in Russian, which made Ferns laugh again.

We said our goodbyes, and they started to go.

But then I called after them, "Wait, before you go..." When they turned, I hesitated before I said, "I won't keep you. But... You guys are tight with Badura, right?"

I had no idea how to read the uncomfortable expressions or worried glances they exchanged.

"We are," Ferns said cautiously.

I flicked my eyes back and forth between them, hoping they might pick up what I was getting at and offer me some kind of insight without me having to dig it out of them But no, apparently much like in my conversation with Badura, I had to lead this dance.

"Look, I know I'm the new guy. I don't want to fuck up the team's chemistry, you know? But Badura?" I grimaced and shook my head. "I don't have the first damn clue what to make of him."

The way both guys avoided my gaze told me I hadn't imagined anything.

"Just throw me a bone," I pleaded. "If there's something I did, or something I can do—I don't know how I pissed him off, but I want—"

"You didn't do anything." Ferns sounded both sure and exhausted. "I don't know what's going on with him, but I think it's him, not you."

"Great," I muttered. "So is this just what it's like to be his linemate?"

Dima and Ferns exchanged looks again.

"No," Dima admitted. "It's not. I'll... Let me talk to him. He's idiot sometimes, but he's not bad guy."

"Thanks," I said. "Because I really want to stay here. But when your linemate hates your fucking guts..." I rolled my eyes.

They both grunted in agreement and nodded. And here

I'd hoped they might tell me this was just how Badura was with everyone.

Nope. It was me. No idea how or why, but the problem was me.

I couldn't say I felt better. If anything, my conversation with Badura had left me feeling sick to my stomach. As if I'd made things exponentially worse. And dragging our team-mates—his friends—into it didn't seem like a good idea either. Especially when one of those teammates was our third linemate.

But what else was I supposed to do?

CHAPTER 5

JAREK

Beer & pizza tonight. You in?

Dima's text made my stomach growl even as the thought of more social interaction made me tired. I'd had my fill of people the last few days. A quiet night in sounded amazing.

But Dima and Chloé made the most incredible homemade pizza, *and* they brewed beer as a hobby. Really, *really* good beer. That, and much like leisurely afternoons on the golf course and quiet nights in, homecooked food would become a luxury before too much longer. Most of us tried to get as much of it as we could this time of year.

Sure, I responded. *Time?*

I didn't ask if I needed to bring anything. I knew the answer—Chloé would have my head if I didn't bring one of the giant fruit tarts from the bakery down the street from my condo.

An hour or so later, fruit tart in hand, I walked up to the front door of their gorgeous Sewickley Heights home. There was tape over the doorbell and a note asking people to please not ring it because the baby might be sleeping, but that wasn't a problem. I'd texted Dima when I'd arrived, and I was pretty sure he could hear the Jaguar's engine anyway (I of course didn't rev it or make it loud when I came to their house these days, but it wasn't a quiet car).

When Dima came to the door, his baby was asleep on his shoulder. He gestured upstairs, then put a finger to his lips, and I nodded. He'd mentioned before practice this morning that the baby had barely slept at all last night, so Chloé was probably the one catching a nap right now. I didn't blame her.

After I'd toed off my shoes, we moved into the kitchen, and I put the fruit tart on the kitchen island.

As soon as my hands were free, Dima nodded at the baby. "Do you mind?"

"Of course not." I smiled as he handed his sleeping son off to me. Ilya didn't even stir as he settled on my shoulder. Keeping my voice soft, I asked, "He finally decided to go to sleep?"

Groaning quietly, Dima rolled his eyes. "Of course. Keeps his mother up all night and fusses all morning. The second I get home from camp..." He gestured at his son again.

"So is that your magic touch?" I asked. "Or does he have it out for Chloé?"

Dima huffed a laugh, turning to pull some things out of the refrigerator. "I think they're both adjusting now that my in-laws have gone home." He glanced back at Ilya and grimaced. "I hope they're better before I go on the road."

"Eh, give them time."

"There isn't much time." He pulled out some cheese and set it on the island, flicking his eyes toward the baby again. "She'd rather he wasn't sleeping right now, but he was so exhausted after last night and this morning..." Dima shook his head. "Tonight's going to be rough, though."

"Because he's asleep too early?"

"Mmhmm. Good thing we have tomorrow off."

I took that to mean Dima would be getting up with Ilya tonight so his wife could rest. That didn't surprise me at all. He was thrilled to be a dad, and he wanted to spend as much time with his son as he could before hockey demanded he be away from home.

That, and Dima worshipped his wife. All through her pregnancy, he'd fallen all over himself to make sure she was happy and comfortable. Whenever he could, he went with her to doctor's appointments, too, and he'd pleaded with his own doctors to schedule his elbow surgery so he could still help her out as much as possible, even with her parents in town. And as long as I'd known him, every chance he'd had while we were on the road, he was Facetiming or calling her.

Some of the guys teased him for being whipped, but I envied the two of them. They'd been together since he was sixteen and she was seventeen; she'd lived across the street from his billet family when he was in major juniors. He and I had been teammates, and it had been kind of cute, the way he'd all but forgotten anyone else existed once he'd met her. Back then, he'd barely spoken any French at all—just enough to sort of get by living in Quebec—and she still didn't know much Russian. Fortunately, they'd both been competent English speakers, and together, they'd become fluent.

They'd been through their ups and downs like anyone else, but they were—as many fans had declared—relationship goals.

Not for the first time, I wished I could find a partner as fiercely devoted to me as Chloé and Dima were to each other.

Except I had one. And I lost him. Because...

I tamped down that thought. I was feeling shitty enough without thinking about my own major juniors sweetheart. About the one who'd made me forget other boys even existed. About how the four of us had innocently fantasized about one day being in the same city while Dima and I played for the same professional team.

Most of that fantasy had come true. Three of us were here now. They were still together and would be until the end of time. But me... I was alone. I had no idea where Marc-Yves was now. Only that if things had been different —things he didn't fully understand to this day—then maybe he'd be here in Pittsburgh.

Maybe I wouldn't be alone.

God, I didn't need to go there tonight, so I forced those thoughts aside as best I could. "Is there anything I can help with?" I gestured at the various things Dima had pulled out for pizza toppings. Fortunately, he was used to restless hockey players who could get into trouble if they weren't kept busy, and he set me to work cutting up green peppers and mushrooms while he took the baby.

He put Ilya into a carrier, which he kept on the floor where he was well within sight but not in any danger of us tripping over him or dropping something on him. When the baby started fussing at one point, Dima left to change him, and right about then, Chloé was waking up, so she took over.

It was still kind of funny, watching them be so grown up and domestic after we'd all been ridiculous kids together. We were still glorified teenagers when we were with our teammates, but here was Dima, doing the whole father and husband thing. Here was Chloé, tired and smiling with their baby in her arms while she and Dima bickered over which type of sauce he was making and if one of them should cut up more olives.

Jesus. Next thing I knew, we'd all be talking about retiring from hockey and what we'd do next.

And I'll probably still be alone.

Again, I pushed those nagging depressing thoughts away. They'd been swirling around my head like storm clouds lately, and I didn't have to think too hard to figure out why. It wasn't an early midlife crisis. It was this uncomfortable feeling that came with finally getting to a point where I felt good in the present—felt like my world was firmly on its axis—and then finding out I'd have the biggest mistake of my life thrown in my face every fucking day for the foreseeable future.

God. Stop.

I was here to enjoy a relaxed night. One of the last I'd have for a long time. So, I concentrated hard on helping Dima with food prep. On chatting with Chloé when she came into the kitchen. On enjoying dinner with my friends while we all melted over their baby.

After dinner, Dima went down to the basement and returned with a couple of unlabeled bottles of beer. We settled on his back deck to relax and drink.

Just like anything he and Chloé brewed, the beer was amazing. I didn't know what their secret was, but everything I'd ever tasted here had been smooth with all kinds of amazing flavors. This one was an earthy IPA that I informed Dima had better be under my Christmas tree this year.

He pretended to be non-committal about it, but he knew if he wanted his annual cache of wine from my grandfather's vineyard in Morava, he'd better pony up a case of this IPA. The Christmas alcohol exchange was, after all, tradition.

After we'd talked a bit about the beer and what kind of wine he expected under his tree, Dima's tone shifted abruptly to something serious enough it made my stomach flip. "While we're here... I need to ask you about something."

"Oh. Uh." I sipped my beer. "Okay?"

He studied me, his expression as sober as his voice. What the hell? He put his bottle down, and as he sat back, he looked me dead in the eye. "What is up with you and Michaud?"

Any hope I had of playing it off as nothing went out the window when I sagged back against the seat and whispered, "Sakra."

Dima's eyebrow rose. "So there *is* something?"

Oh, there was. Nothing I could explain to Dima or anyone else, but...

"Yars." He leaned forward again, pressing his elbows on his knees. "What is going on? I didn't think you even knew the guy, but ever since we found out he was coming here..." He threw up his hand as if to ask, *What the fuck, dude?*

I stared into my mostly empty beer bottle as I tried to find the words. My pleasant mood was gone. I was already raw from letting my thoughts wander close to that never-healed wound Marc-Yves had left behind. The last thing I needed was to focus on Michaud. The two of them didn't know—would *never* know—how or why fate had played all three of us. Michaud didn't even know Marc-Yves existed, and Marc-Yves would never have a clue why Michaud mattered to the trajectories our lives had taken.

And Dima sure as shit didn't know anything about any of it. There was a part of me that ached to tell him. To tell *someone*. If I couldn't tell my best friend, then who could I tell?

No one, that was who. I'd kept my mouth shut all this time, and I wasn't about to stop that now.

"Yars," Dima prodded. "Is there something the team should know about this guy?"

My head snapped up. "No! No, it's—he hasn't done a thing. He's fine. He's good."

Dima's eyebrows rose as he inclined his head.

I avoided his gaze. I didn't even know where to start.

Taking on a more playful tone, Dima said, "Don't tell me you have crush on—"

"The fuck I do," I snapped, and instantly regretted it when my friend recoiled, his hands upraised.

"Hey, hey." He drew back and stared at me with wide eyes. "Take it easy."

I sagged back against the chair again. "I'm sorry. I didn't... I'm sorry. It's..." God, I wished this was simple as having a crush on Michaud. And on some level, I did have one. It was impossible not to. As a freshly drafted eighteen-year-old, he'd been cute. These days? Fuck me, but he was gorgeous. "I can't even explain it. He's... there's nothing wrong with him. And no, I don't have a crush on him. It's..." I rubbed my hand over my face. "It's me."

"Okay, but why? We have to function as a line. If the two of you are ready to kill each other..."

Shit. Fresh guilt pressed down on my shoulders. I'd already felt like an ass for making things awkward on the team, but it had to be uncomfortable as hell for Dima to share a line with Michaud, me, and my bullshit. There was no explaining it away or excusing it. And if it was bothering both Michaud *and* Dima enough to confront me about it, then it was only a matter of time before one of them said fuck it and got the coaches involved.

Right then, Chloé poked her head out of the sliding

glass door. "Dima, could you take Ilya for a moment?" She nodded over her shoulder, cradling her son in the crook of her elbow. "I'll clean the kitchen."

Dima's face lit up like it always did when he saw her, especially when she had the baby with her. "Of course." He got up. "In fact..." He jerked his head toward the house. "I'll clean. Yars can entertain Ilya."

Chloé looked past him at me. "You don't mind?"

"Of course not." Smiling, I rose, grateful for the diversion. "I can play with the baby while Dima earns his keep."

Dima rolled his eyes and flipped me off, which earned him a giggle from Chloé as she handed me the baby.

We went back inside, and I held and entertained Ilya while Dima cleaned up the kitchen, and Chloé hung out and chatted with us. I suspected she just needed to put Ilya down for a few minutes; she loved cuddling with him, and she didn't believe a newborn could be spoiled by too much of it, but sometimes she needed a break. Ilya was happier if someone was holding him, and I didn't think there would ever come a time when Dima said no to that. In fact, as soon as he was done washing the dishes, we settled in the living room, and in no time Ilya was asleep on his chest with Dima's hand splayed across his tiny back.

This whole family was so cute.

Fortunately, the subject of Michaud was dropped. Not forgotten—Dima wouldn't forget something like this—but on the back burner for now. I just hoped Dima let it go for tonight.

He was right that I needed to unfuck things with Michaud. Or at least stop being a dick to him, since I was too much of a coward to talk to him about it. Or talk to him at all if it wasn't about hockey plays.

Hopefully that would be enough for both Dima and Michaud to let it go and move on.

But I had my doubts.

———

There was no practice the next day, and I desperately needed something to keep my mind and hands occupied. Good thing I had an ever-present outlet for my need to be busy—helping my sister renovate her house.

It was an old Victorian I'd bought for her out in Squirrel Hill. One that needed a *ton* of work. I'd insisted I was happy to get her someplace newer, whether a house or a condo, but she'd fallen in love with it. We'd spent hours discussing all the ways she planned to fix it up, from refinishing the hardwood floors to gutting both bathrooms.

But there was a reason I'd joked that she was moving to Squirrel Hill because she had the focus and foresight of a squirrel. Case in point—she'd picked out the house last summer, somehow forgetting just how demanding medical school would be once classes picked up again in the fall. Between us, almost nothing got done on the house during the school year and hockey season, which had left the offseason, and I thought we'd made some pretty substantial headway.

"We're going to be working on this until we're dead," Eliška muttered as she glared at the bare living room floor.

I glanced up from prying the lid off a bucket of polyurethane. "Didn't you say that about medical school?"

"No, I said medical school would probably kill me. This?" She gestured around us. "This will just go until we're dead."

I chuckled, popped off the lid, and put it aside.

Today, we'd be refinishing the hardwood floors in the living and dining rooms. Before training camp, we'd started sanding the floors, stripping off the awful, scratched-up finish that had been there when she'd moved in. Today, it was time for the polyurethane. All the windows were wide open, as were all the doors on the ground floor. Eliška's cats were locked in her bedroom upstairs with multiple fans blasting toward the screen-covered window so neither of them got high off the fumes

We got started, rolling the foul-smelling liquid onto the wood in smooth, even strokes, both working toward the center of the room. From there, we could step into the hallway and move to the dining room, which was only about half the size of the living room.

Applying this stuff didn't require much brainpower beyond keeping it even and watching for bubbles. It was a slow process, and not the most exciting thing in the world, though it was pretty satisfying to watch the pale wood turn a richer shade beneath the finish. The polyurethane was clear, but it brought out a warm, dark color from the wood that was gorgeous. Much nicer than the near-black stain that had probably been ugly even before it had been scratched all to hell.

I was grateful for the somewhat mindless work. My brain hadn't stopped whirring since my conversations with Michaud and Dima yesterday. I hadn't slept well last night, not even after a couple of beers at Dima's place and thirty minutes on the bike after I got home a few hours later. I'd tossed and turned, reliving the past and wallowing in shame from back then, not to mention the guilt over being an asshole to Michaud.

One way or another, our next practice was going to be awkward as hell. I *had* to get out of my own head enough to function with him just like any other teammate. I'd had bad blood with teammates before, and we'd just swallowed it and stayed out of each other's way.

I didn't have bad blood with Michaud. All I had was—

"Hey. Jarek." Eliška poked me with the handle of her paint roller, and I realized we'd almost made it to the center of the room. "What's going on with you?"

I shook myself. "Nothing. Nothing. I'm..." I looked at the section of floor I'd finished. It was fine. There was a small bubble that I fixed without much fuss. I dipped the roller in the bucket again, and as I started on another section of unfinished wood, I said, "I'm fine. Nothing is going on."

I didn't have to look to know she was watching me skeptically.

Great. She'd picked up on my distraction. Best solution —distract her with something else so she'd hopefully forget. Or maybe convince her I had something else on my mind.

I cleared my throat as I rolled on the polyurethane. "I haven't seen anything from the university lately." I glanced at her. "Isn't there a tuition payment due soon?"

From the quirk of her eyebrow, it wasn't working. Still, she played along. "You already paid this semester. Last month. Remember?"

"But I thought there was going to be—"

"Don't, Jarek," she said in the same tone our mother had used when we'd tried her patience. "Something is on your mind. I can tell."

"How?" I waved a hand at the area I'd finished. "Are the bubbles like tea leaves?"

She snorted. "No, but your face is as loud as Táta's when he's not happy."

I rolled my eyes. There were few things Eliška loved

more than reminding me how much I was turning into our father.

And there were few things I wanted to talk about *less* than the black clouds swirling around my head, so I just muttered, "We should finish this coat before it starts to dry."

She huffed with annoyance and didn't push the issue.

I wasn't naïve enough to believe that was the end of it, though. Unlike Dima, Eliška was not one to let something go until she was satisfied the dead horse was *thoroughly* beaten. Once we'd finished the living and dining rooms, she went upstairs to check on her cats (who were enjoying the fresh air through the screen), and then we stepped outside to get some air for ourselves. She handed me a glass of water, and we sat on the brick steps.

"I still need to get some furniture out here," she muttered, shifting as if she couldn't quite get comfortable on the bricks. "Ugh. Maybe before next summer."

"Yeah, right." I laughed as I brought my drink up to my lips. "You'll forget. Again."

"Fuck you," she muttered, bumping her shoulder against mine.

I bumped her back. "Do I need to tell Matka about your filthy language?"

"Pfft." She rolled her eyes. "I'll tell her I learned it from you. Then you'll be in trouble."

I groaned. Such was being the older brother—I was always in trouble for something my sister did.

We drank in silence for a moment. Then Eliška did the same about-face that Dima had done last night, shifting from playful to serious so fast it almost gave me whiplash.

Eyeing me, she said, "Answer me truthfully—what's going on with you?"

I fought the urge to fidget uncomfortably. "What do you mean?"

She furrowed her brow. "I mean I've seen you like this before, and it wasn't good."

I shifted and focused on the water glass in my hand. "Seen me like what?"

She tsked, and an ice cube bounced off my head. "Don't be dense."

"I'm not being dense!"

"Then stop being stubborn." She studied me before she said, "You were fine last time I saw you. Before training camp started. But now... I mean, I swear, you keep going off into your own little world."

"I always do that."

"Not like this. It's... you seem like you're going back to the same dark place you were after Toronto." She paused before gently adding, "And after Marc-Yves."

I winced. Nobody was going to leave either of those nerves alone this week, were they? And Eliška had still been in Czechia when that had gone down, though we'd talked all the time. Trust her to notice even from thousands of miles away. There was no getting anything past her now that we lived in the same city.

"Seriously," she pressed. "What's going on?"

More and more, I wished I could tell someone. Before all this, I'd made as much peace with the past as I ever would, but having Michaud here and unavoidable had pulled all those wounds open again. The truth ached in my chest alongside a much colder one—the one that played like a mantra in the back of my mind, reminding me I couldn't say anything without destroying the careers and reputations of people who didn't deserve it.

Like it or not, no matter how much I wanted to unload

this years-old burden, I *had* to carry it alone. That task just hadn't been this difficult in a long, long time.

"Jarek." Eliška nudged me. "What's on your mind? You're worrying me."

I chewed my lip as I thumbed the condensation on my glass. After a moment, I turned to my sister. "What would you do if you got some coveted residency, and so did someone who'd edged you out of another program you desperately wanted early in your schooling?" I swallowed, trying to keep all the hurt and anger and God knew what else out of my voice. "Something that set you back for years? And then after you'd finally made up all that lost ground, you were partnered with that person? So every damned day, you had to look in the face of the person who was the reason your career went off the rails?"

It wasn't the whole story—not even close—but it was the best I could come up with that didn't show too many cards.

Eliška whistled. "Shit. That would suck."

"Mmhmm." I took a deep swallow to cool my anger, and I pretended anger was the *only* emotion that needed cooling right then.

She pursed her lips. "I guess that would depend on whether that person orchestrated the situation. Or if they even knew they'd played that role." She half-shrugged. "I know programs are limited, so if someone got a seat I wanted—I mean, there isn't much I can do about it, you know? But if they did something to sabotage me so they could have it..." She raised her glass in a mock toast. "Might have to cut some brake lines."

I laughed, almost choking on my water.

Some amusement twitched at the corners of her mouth, but she sobered. "Is this about Hunter Michaud?"

I flinched, probably answering her well enough.

Though she didn't know the whole story, she'd heard plenty of times how pissed I'd been to be traded away right when my team had acquired him. He'd been a sore spot for a long time, even if Eliška could never know why.

Wiping a hand over my face, I nodded. "Yeah. Having him here, it's—it's really been fucking with my head."

"I bet," she whispered.

"I don't know how to act like everything is fine and normal. He didn't do anything wrong. He doesn't have a fucking clue what's up my ass. But every time I look at him..." I trailed off as that damn lump climbed my throat again.

"But you're on the same team." Her tone was gentle now. "You can't change that. You guys have to get along somehow. Especially if you don't want to be traded again."

I closed my eyes and exhaled. Being bounced all over the League had sucked. I liked where I was, and I liked the place I'd found on this team. I liked being near my best friend. I was terrified of losing all that again. And this team valued its unity—no one would hesitate to send me packing if I screwed up the dynamic. Least of all over something I couldn't articulate.

I chewed my lip. "I know. I need to... I'm trying to figure out how, you know? And... It gets worse. We're *line*mates."

She blinked. "Seriously? The coaches stuck you two together when you don't get along?"

"I guess we hide it well enough." I sighed. "Or they like what they see on the ice enough to turn a blind eye to the rest."

"How long do you think that'll last?"

"Not long," I said dryly.

"Then do whatever you have to do," she insisted. "And don't push your teammates away this time. Including

Michaud, but also your *friends*. You succeeded in pushing away Marc-Yves, and we both know you were determined to push me away, too."

I wished I could make a joke about my sister's relentless stubbornness, but it hurt too much. Yes, she'd stuck by me even when I'd valiantly tried to shove her away. Sometimes I still thought that whole shitshow was the reason she'd decided to come to Pittsburgh for medical school—not just to take advantage of the excellent programs, but to keep an eye on me in case I fell apart again.

She'd never admit that under torture. The CIA could never make me admit I was grateful for it.

We were family, though. Family stuck by family even when family was stupid.

Marc-Yves... he hadn't stuck by me. He'd tried, but then he'd given up and bailed. I told myself more often than not that that was because I wasn't someone people fought for.

Other times, I admitted it was because I'd given him every reason to go and not a single damn one to stay.

And once in a while, when I could dig deep enough to scrape bone, I'd acknowledge that there was truth in both of those things.

For reasons I really didn't want to look at too closely, I way too raw to think about any of that right now, so I just whispered, "I won't push people away." I didn't know if I was lying or not.

Eliška, at least, seemed to take me at my word, because she nodded once and said, "Good." She watched me for a second. "Do you mind a little unsolicited advice?"

I raised my eyebrows.

"Okay, so, you said this guy didn't deliberately edge you out of anything, right?" she said. "Like he didn't have anything to do with you being traded?"

Dropping my gaze to the bricks between my feet, I nodded. "They traded me before he ever set foot in Toronto."

"Right. So maybe you need to separate him from your feelings about him."

"What do you mean?"

"Besides the fact that there's nothing subtle about you when something is bothering you?" Eliška bumped my shoulder with hers again. "I bet he knows something is up."

I chewed my lip as some warmth rose in my face. Oh, yeah, Michaud knew something was up. I hadn't left much to the imagination, and he'd confronted me about it. After yesterday's conversation, he was probably still wondering what the hell he'd done to earn my attitude, and the truth was that he hadn't done a thing. He'd been as much a pawn as I'd been.

I sighed and wiped my hand over my face. "God, I'm such an asshole."

"You are."

I snorted. "Kráva."

She punched my arm. "Kokot."

We both chuckled. Our mother would have our heads if she heard us speaking that way, least of all to each other. It was in good humor, though.

Sobering a little, I reached up to rub the back of my neck, wondering when those muscles had started getting so stiff. "You're right, though. I... He's done nothing wrong."

He just reminds me of what I *did wrong.*

"So be nice to him," she said. "You'll still have"—she gestured at her own head—"whatever's going on up here, but at least you and your team won't be as miserable."

I gave a little grunt of agreement. I hadn't even had to spell out to her how much this was affecting the team. That

Dima had noticed, and that I doubted he'd been the only one. She'd played hockey herself for years before she'd come to America. She knew exactly how quickly friction between two players could fuck up an entire team's dynamic.

"I will," I said, and I meant it. I had no idea how I was going to keep all my emotions off my face when I was around him, but for the sake of the team—and for my line-mate who really hadn't done anything wrong—I'd find a way.

"Good. And whatever is going on with you—don't push people away." Eliška squeezed my arm. "People love you. Let them in."

I nodded because that was easier than arguing with her.

I wished it were as simple as she made it. Yes, people loved me. And yes, I needed to let people in closer than I did.

But nothing could change the fact that at the core of all of this was a truth I couldn't tell anyone. Not my team-mates. Not my friends. Not my sister. Not Marc-Yves.

And definitely not Hunter Michaud.

CHAPTER 6

HUNTER

"Hey, Michaud." Coach Henley appeared beside me as I was pulling on my practice sweater. "Hang back for a second—I want to talk to you about something."

My heart dropped into the pit of my stomach. "Uh. Okay. Sure. What's up?"

He made a just-a-second gesture, then motioned at my teammates, who were gathering up sticks and gloves to head to the ice.

My heart dropped even deeper. Was something wrong? I'd made the team's final roster, and we were out of training camp and well into regular practices. I thought I'd been doing well, but... maybe not? Maybe I'd fucked up and hadn't even know it? Fuck, what was going on?

As I waited for my teammates to clear out so Coach Henley could tell me what was up, chilly panic crept its way along my spine beneath my gear. My ears rang with the echoes of another coach in another time and place.

"This isn't major juniors anymore, kid. You're getting paid way too much money to be putting up numbers that pathetic."

"I'm sorry, Coach. I'm... Maybe I'm not ready to be on the top line or—"

"The fuck *you're not!"*

To this day, I could remember the jolt of terror when he'd barked at me. The way the visceral fear had thrummed in my bones.

"I don't want excuses, Michaud." He'd been so close in that moment. Right up in my face. The locker room wall had been so cold through my base layer as I'd pressed back against it, all too aware there was nowhere to go. *"I want you to get out there and prove you were worthy of being the top draft pick. Or do you want me to go tell Wilcox to release you because you're clearly not?"*

"No," I'd said shakily. *"I'm... I can do this. I'm—"*

"Then get the fuck out there and prove it. Because between you and our last top ten pick, the draft is starting to look like diversity hire bullshit."

"Diversity—what? No. I'm good, Coach." I'd set my jaw if only to keep my teeth from chattering from a mix of anger, shame, and fear. *"I deserved that spot."*

"Yeah?" He'd narrowed his eyes. *"Then fucking prove it before I ship your useless ass off to the minors."*

"Yes, Coach. I will. I'll—"

"Mish?"

I jumped, sucking in a breath.

Coach Henley cocked his head. "You all right, kid?" His voice was even and calm, his face full of concern.

"I'm..." I glanced around, and I realized the locker room was empty except for us. Fuck. How long had I been mentally back in Toronto? I shook myself and met Coach's gaze. "S-sorry. Sorry." I cleared my throat. "You wanted to talk to me?"

He furrowed his brow. "You sure you're good?"

"Yeah. Just, um..." I laughed, hoping it sounded convincing. "I can get up in my own head sometimes. I'm good." *C'mon, heart. Slow down. Coach Robertson isn't here.*

Coach Henley studied me, but then he shrugged. "Right. Uh, anyway, the first preseason games are next week. I wanted to know how you feel about putting on an A for the split squad games."

I blinked. "Oh. Really?"

He nodded. "Normally, I wouldn't bother to ask, especially since you've been a captain before and it's just for a pair of preseason games. But since you're new to the team, I figured we should have a conversation about it first."

"It's fine. It's... Yeah, like you said, I've worn a C before, so..." I half-shrugged. "As long as the guys are good with it, so am I."

"All right." He gave another nod. "I'll let the boys know." He clapped my shoulder and flashed a quick, fatherly smile. "Why don't you get out there and warm up?"

I returned the smile, gathered up my stick, gloves, and helmet, and headed for the ice. Halfway down the hall, I paused to gather myself. The conversation with Coach Henley had been perfectly benign, but I was still queasy from mentally reliving one of countless verbal beatdowns I'd taken from Coach Robertson. There'd been *so many*. In his office. In the locker room. Anywhere he could get me alone. Or at least away from cameras. When he let fly in front of my teammates, it had been humiliating, but behind closed doors had always been the most terrifying. Though he'd never lifted a hand to me, there'd always been some instinctive fear that *this* time, he would.

I hated that he'd always been able to reduce me to that terrified nineteen-year-old rookie who was convinced he was failing everyone who'd ever bet on him. Even when I was twenty-five, the team captain with a handful of fights under my belt against players twice my size, he'd still been able to send me back to that scared kid who couldn't carry the weight everyone had piled on his shoulders.

And now I was twenty-six, five hundred kilometers from Toronto, and he could still make me queasy with panic when my new and chill coach wanted to ask me a simple question.

Yet he'd still had the audacity to be shocked when I'd high-tailed it out of Toronto the instant I'd been a free agent. Still had the absolute balls to tell the fans I'd been selfish and greedy. That I'd let down the team and the whole city. Fuck that guy.

I shook myself again and headed for the ice, focusing on the simmering anger instead of the nausea twisting in my stomach. I hated that Robertson had played the *"diversity hire"* card. That rookie me had let it show how much that stung. That he'd noticed, and he'd kept using it whenever he wanted to get under my skin. Those conversations—especially the earliest ones—were among the very, very few times in my career when I'd regretted being out as gay. I hated him still for making teenage me feel that way, even for a moment.

Stepping out onto the ice helped. Something about that first step always centered me. Even when one of Robertson's tirades had still been ringing in my ears, this made a difference.

The fact that I was stepping out onto Pittsburgh's ice today was *amazing*. As I skated around with my teammates, warming up for practice, I embraced the unfamiliar that was slowly becoming familiar. The banners on the walls. The ancient scoreboard. The puck-battered ads along the dashers—some for companies I knew, others for brands I'd never heard of.

Every comfortingly strange detail was a reminder that I was here now. Toronto and all its toxic leadership were still in the same League as me, but literally in another country. My teammates seemed to like me. The staff all seemed thrilled to have me.

Coach Henley's reputation was well-known throughout the League. He was a tough coach, but a fair and mellow one who didn't see any point in screaming at his players. There wouldn't be any more getting dressed down in front of my team. No more cowering against a locker room wall or an office door because my volatile excuse for a coach was yet again straining his vocal cords at my expense. It was all behind me now.

Sometimes players left toxic teams only to have their coach or GM eventually follow them. After every season, firings happened, as did retirements, and suddenly coaches and general managers were moving around the League just like the players were. As a result, sometimes the player wound up playing for that coach or general manager again. That had happened to a friend of mine from major juniors —he'd high-tailed it off an awful team, had one blissfully good year in another city, and then his new team hired his old coach.

I had some insurance in place for that. It was a highly unusual clause—one my agent didn't think the team would go for—but Pittsburgh's attitude had been, *"What Hunter Michaud wants, Hunter Michaud gets."* I felt weird about taking advantage of that, but this *one* time, I'd done it. In the end, my contract had an ironclad and confidential clause stating that if the organization hired Joe Wilcox or Hal

Robertson in *any* capacity, negotiations would begin *immediately* to move me out of Pittsburgh.

No one had objected to signing it, and the club's legal department had agreed it was irregular but not unreasonable.

"Either of those two come sniffing around for a job in this city," Andrew, the GM, had mused while we'd signed the paperwork, *"they're going to get laughed right out of Pennsylvania."*

Fine by me, so long as I never had to work with one of those two fuckknuckles again.

A whistle blew, pulling me out of my thoughts, and my teammates and I headed toward the bench to gather around the whiteboard. Everyone took a knee, and Coach Henley ran us through the plan for this morning. He also briefed us on the upcoming preseason games, including who would be the alternate captains on the split squads. No one seemed surprised by any of the assignments, though Jarek's lips tightened a little as our squad's leadership was read. I just couldn't say for sure if that was because I'd be wearing one of the As or because he would.

Possibly the latter, I realized, since things *had* started improving between us. Subtly, but noticeably. He wasn't so abrasive toward me, and while he didn't chirp or banter with me, we could communicate. The air was still awkward and weird between us, but less hostile. Hell, a couple of practices ago, he'd even told me to call him Jarek or Yars instead of Badura. I wasn't quite comfortable with using his nickname, and he apparently wasn't comfortable using mine, but the upgrade to first names—I'd take it. Though sometimes if one of us needed to get the other's attention in a hurry—during a drill or a scrimmage, for example—we'd shout out the nickname instead. It... well, it was better than skating on eggshells, so I tried not to think too much about it.

Of course the team would decide who wore the C and two As for the season, and I didn't imagine there'd be any changes from last year—Mayweather had been captain for like ten years, and Fernholm and Meknikov had each been alternates for a long time as well. I suspected Coach just wanted to use the preseason to see how well some of us could fill that role, and how our teammates would respond to us. Wasn't all that uncommon, and it made it a little easier if a member of the leadership went down at some point. Or, as had happened my fifth season in Toronto and my second year as captain, all three went down at the same time.

All I knew for sure was that no one seemed bothered by me wearing an A during the pre-season games (aside from *maybe* Jarek), and practice was getting rolling like normal. Like a normal team where the coaches didn't put the fear of God into their players, where all the players were expected to contribute, and no one was put up on a pedestal. Heaven, as far as I was concerned.

And as we got going on some special teams practice, Coach had me on the second power play unit along with Jarek, Dima, Sawyer, and Olson. My ego admittedly wanted to bristle at being relegated to the second unit, but I reminded myself I was the new guy *and* Pittsburgh already had an awesome top power play. Depth was important in special teams, and spreading the 1A and 1B lines between the power plays meant better depth and better consistency. That had been one of Pittsburgh's weak spots last year—a wildly inconsistent second power play unit, accompanied by a mediocre penalty kill. And part of being a regular member of the team—which I wanted—meant taking places besides the number one spots.

My ego would get over it.

Meanwhile, I joined my guys to practice against the number one penalty kill, which... Damn, whatever problems they'd been having last season seemed to be a distant memory now.

I wondered why Sawyer was on the second unit, too, but I understood after watching a couple of drills with Ferns quarterbacking the top unit. *Nothing* got past him. His passes were crisp and fast, and his one-timer—God, it was a good thing goalies wore pads. I swore that one shot he took from the blue line actually knocked Dolls back a little, prompting some loud swearing from Dolls along with some equally loud—but highly amused—chirping from Ferns.

Then it was our side's turn. The special teams coach sent the puck to Dima, and the battle was on. Three of the four penalty killers collapsed in on the goalie like a phalanx, each of them poised and ready for any one of us to take a shot.

This was where Toronto's power play had struggled—we'd pass and pass and pass and pass in hopes of wearing down the penalty killers, but no one would take a shot.

Dima passed to Jarek, Jarek passed to me, and I fired at the goal. The penalty killers weren't expecting it, but the goalie managed to deflect it. Jarek snatched the rebound away and set up like he was about to pass. The defenseman closest to him went in for a poke check to relieve him of the puck, but Jarek startled everyone—myself included—by firing right past the D-man and under the leg pad of the unsuspecting goalie.

All five of us cheered as the penalty killers swore and regrouped. While the other power play and penalty kill started their drill at the other end of the ice, we shared some fist bumps and helmet smacks.

"Nice job!" I told Jarek. "I swear I thought you were going to pass it to Sawyer."

Jarek actually smiled at me, and he shrugged. "One of their guys moved. I saw an opportunity."

"Good," Sawyer said as he skated up beside him and smacked his shoulder. "Keep doing that shit in games this year, all right?"

Jarek laughed. "Fuck you."

"He's got a point." Dima slung an arm around Jarek, almost knocking him off his skates. "Do fancy shit in games, not..." He gestured around us with his stick.

Rolling his eyes, Jarek shoved him away and muttered something that I assumed was both cursing and Czech. Dima responded in—I thought—Russian, grinning even as he probably swore right back at him.

We all settled down and watched the other special teams practicing. While Jarek's attention was fixated on the play, I caught Dima's gaze. His eyes flicked toward Jarek, then back to me, and we both shrugged.

So I wasn't the only one who noticed, was I? That things were... smoother? I mean, Jarek was clearly trying. I had no idea why it took so much effort to be civil with me, but it was better than the alternative, and it wasn't going unnoticed. Had Dima said something to him? Because I swore the shift had happened after I'd spoken to Dima and Ferns after I'd had it out with Jarek.

Well, whatever it was, I'd take it.

Though it was a double-edged sword, I realized as we set up to practice with the penalty kill again. Less hostility was great. Of course it was. The problem? Now that there was less animosity between us, I started seeing him the way

I had ever since he was drafted—professional admiration, and, uh, *not* so professional admiration.

Because when he wasn't being a dick, Jaromir Badura was both an incredible hockey player *and* a ridiculously hot man. Our rocky start hadn't taken away from either of those things at all.

And it was kinda hard to skate when this man—this gorgeous player I'd had a crush on since before I was a rookie—was right here on the ice with me. Executing those impossibly fast turns and controlling the puck so precisely it looked almost effortless. Sharp features taut with concentration, then breaking into a spine-melting smile when he fist-bumped Dima, who'd just scored.

It was...

Honestly? It was almost easier to play with him when he was scowling at me and giving me the cold shoulder. The seamless chemistry on the ice was exhilarating, and when he'd throw me a smile or a nod, when he'd give me a fist bump like he would any other teammate, it made my brain go haywire.

I had to admit, for as much as the young guys sometimes got starstruck with me, I was a little starstruck with him, and that only intensified now that he was being a decent human being. I'd followed his career from the start, even through that awful slump his third season, and I'd been so damn excited when I'd been picked by his team.

But then he was gone, off to another team. At least there, his performance had started to recover. Started to get back to the forward who'd been a top ten overall pick. Started to be himself again... only to be absolutely snakebitten for half a season. Hadn't he gone like fifteen, twenty games without so much as a point? It was bizarre.

Maybe things hadn't been great in Denver, where he'd

been playing at the time? Hard to tell. Whatever the case, they'd put him on waivers, and he'd been picked up by Pittsburgh, and after a season or so playing here, he'd been back in top form.

And I was here. And he was here. And he was playing like Jaromir Badura. On *my line.*

God, if we could keep this going into the season, especially with the way the other lines and the D-pairs were playing, there would be *no* stopping this team.

I couldn't wait.

After practice was over, I grabbed a shower, threw on a pair of gym shorts and a Pittsburgh Hornets hoodie, and went to see what the cooking staff had come up with for today.

About halfway there, though, I was waylaid by Dima.

For a second, I had the same jolt of *oh shit* I'd had when Coach Henley had pulled me aside before practice. Was something wrong? Had I fucked up? Was he going to—

"I just wanted to make sure I told you before you left," he said. "My wife and I—we're having barbecue this weekend. Before preseason starts." He gestured toward the lounge where some of our teammates were already eating and talking. "A lot of the team is coming. You're welcome to join us."

"Oh. Uh." I smiled. "Sure, that would be great. Should I bring anything?"

"No, no." He waved that away. "Just show up ready to eat. Trust me—there will be far too much food."

I laughed. "I can do that. And speaking of..." I motioned toward the lounge. "Food?"

"Oh, God, yes." He herded me in that direction. "You can sit with us. We'll tell you all about the shit Dolls and Jarek did at last year's barbecue."

Chuckling, I went with him. I was kind of grateful he hadn't brought up the different vibe between me and Jarek, and that he was moving on as if everything was normal. Maybe he knew as well as I was that the best thing to do was just pretend this *was* normal, because if one of us said something, the awkwardness would come back.

When I sat down with Dima, Jarek was at the same table. He glanced at me, surprise and something not quite readable flashing across his face, but he didn't say anything either. He just continued eating, and when Dima brought up the shenanigans from last year's barbecue, he joined in the chirping and laughing like nothing had ever been amiss.

I still had no idea what had been up his ass about me in the beginning.

But this?

I'd take it.

CHAPTER 7

JAREK

I took an Uber to Dima's place for the barbecue since he'd promised to break out a new beer today. I tried not to drink too much around my teammates, but Dima made good beer, and I felt like getting a buzz on today.

Plus Dima had told me most of the team would be here today.

Including Hunter.

"Do you mind if I invite Mish?" Dima had asked me in the parking lot yesterday morning. *"Chloé and I want you there, but we don't want you to be miserable if—"*

"What?" I'd laughed it off. *"Why would I be miserable?"*

Of course, Dima had given me one of those looks that said he saw right through me, because he always fucking did. He hadn't even had to say a word.

With a sigh, I'd shaken my head. *"Don't worry about it. We were fine today. We've been fine. Your barbecue—it'll be fine too."*

His skepticism stung, but I knew damn well I deserved it.

He let it go, though. He always did. Sometimes because

he took me at my word. Sometimes because he was giving me enough rope to hang myself. At least whenever it was the latter, he never rubbed it in my face. He just helped me untangle myself and move on.

I didn't deserve a friend like Dima. I was glad I had him, though, and even if things had been weird between Hunter and me, I wouldn't have missed one of Dima's barbecues for the world. So, after I'd thanked my Uber driver and started up Dima's driveway, I promised myself today *would* be fine. Dima had nothing to worry about. All the crap in my head where Hunter Michaud was concerned—well, I'd keep it in my head where it belonged.

If I was lucky, no one would suspect a thing.

I made short work of sampling Chloé and Dima's latest offering—a dark ale with what I swore was a caramel flavor. And it was somehow better than the version they'd made last fall. I knew a thing or two about winemaking thanks to my grandfather's vineyard and winery, but brewing beer? Not a clue. All I knew was what I liked, and these two had yet to create a beer I didn't like. Good thing I hadn't driven tonight.

As Dima was distributing bottles to some of the new guys—those over twenty-one, of course—the sliding glass door opened, and I glanced over, curious who had arrived.

Oh. *God.*

Hunter stepped outside in a pair of shorts and a plain gray T-shirt. Beneath the bill of a baseball cap from his major junior team, a pair of sunglasses covered his eyes, which was probably the only reason I didn't start openly drooling.

"Ah, Mish!" Dima gestured for him to come over to the cooler. "Do you want a beer? It's a dark ale."

"It sounds great, but..." Hunter shook his head. "I drove."

Dima nodded sharply. "Got it. Do you want some to take home, though? We made plenty."

"I won't say no to that." Hunter gave the beers a longing look. "I'd love to give it a try sometime. Didn't realize you homebrewed, or I'd have come in a cab."

"Next time," I broke in, slinging an arm around Dima's shoulders. "He's always got something new." I turned to him and pointed my beer bottle at his chest. "And you're still holding on to that case of IPA for my Christmas present, yes?"

Dima blinked, then shook himself and elbowed me. "You'll get your beer as long as I get that wine you promised me."

"What?" I rolled my eyes and shoved him away. "You say that like I have ever—*ever*—failed to give you a case of wine."

Hunter tilted his head. "Wait, you make wine?"

Something weird zinged through me when he spoke, and again when we made eye contact. I didn't think it was the alcohol. It was just... talking to him. That mix of emotions and attraction that was always just beneath the surface and tried to bubble up whenever I saw his face or heard his voice.

But, as I reminded myself the same way I did fifty times a day, that was my problem, not his. I schooled my expression and my tone, talking to him like I would any of my teammates. "My family owns a vineyard back in Czechia, and this one..." I nudged Dima with my elbow. "Is always demanding wine."

"I'm not *demanding*," Dima protested. "You're always

threatening not to give me any unless I give you beer. *Now* who's demanding?"

I tsked. "It's not a demand. It's setting the terms and conditions of a trade."

"For Christmas gifts."

I shrugged unrepentantly. "Well, if you'd give me some damn beer the rest of the—"

"Oh, this one." Dima groaned and said to Hunter, "He says I don't give him beer." He pointed sharply at the bottle in my hand. "Like he doesn't have some every time he comes over."

Hunter's laugh almost made me drop the bottle in question. It wasn't fair how good-looking he was. Did time *have* to be so kind to him while it was busy running me through the wringer?

I took a deep pull of beer before I said something to break this illusion that I was over my issues with Hunter. I needed to get a fucking grip.

As Hunter was introduced to some wives, girlfriends, and kids, I busied myself pulling my stupid head together and swallowing some more of Dima's amazing beer. I didn't want to get drunk—that would be bad—but maybe I could get buzzed enough that I wouldn't care that Hunter was here.

Was that even possible? Well, we'd find out.

I had a pretty solid poker face, I thought. As we both drifted in and out of conversations—sometimes hanging around the same people, sometimes not—I made sure I interacted with him the same way I would anyone else. Chill. Relaxed. A little bit of banter, but not too much familiarity. Those lines were harder to see after my third beer, so I slowed down; no point in getting drunk enough to say all the shit I was trying to forget about.

But as the day continued and we all fell into a groove of socializing and eating, he was tough to ignore. He always was. We had amazing chemistry on the ice. I'd dreamed of being this in-sync with a linemate like this. Did it have to be *him,* though? And if it did, did it have to be *now* instead of when I was a young player and he was a rookie?

Though it was hard to say if it would've been better back then. No, I wouldn't have been discarded by Toronto or bounced around before landing here in Pittsburgh, but that was only part of my complicated feelings about him. If he and I had been on the same team back then...

Fuck. That was a thought. Because though time hadn't tempered my anger and regret by much, it had tempered them a *little.* The fury and guilt I carried today had been so much more raw back then.

Back when, had promises been kept, Michaud and I would've been teammates.

"Hey. Yars." Dima elbowed me. "You still here?"

I shook myself and turned to my friend. "Of course. I was—" I thought fast, then grinned as I held up the bottle I'd been nursing. "This is stronger than the shit you usually brew."

He snorted. "The hell it is." One eyebrow went up. "You good?"

"I'm good." I sipped my beer. "Are we going to show these kids up at cornhole or what?"

Dima eyed me, but he let it go, and we headed down the steps from the deck into the backyard. There, several team-mates were talking shit while they tossed beanbags at the cornhole boards.

"How the hell are you so good at this," Sawyer was saying to Ferns, "but so bad at golf?"

"Oh my God." Ferns pelted him in the chest with one of the beanbags. "Fuck you."

"What?" Maxwell, one of the two rookies who'd made the roster, chuckled behind his soda can. "You can't play golf?"

Dolls started to chime in, but a pointed look from Ferns shut him up.

Dima, however, was undeterred. "He's terrible at golf. I'm with Sawyer—I don't know how he can be so good with puck and at"—he motioned at one of the boards—"but still so awful on golf course."

"I hate you both," Ferns muttered as he turned to toss the beanbag.

"They're not wrong," I told him.

He flipped me off, then threw the beanbag, which went right into the hole. Fist-pumping, he faced us. "Beat *that* score, assholes."

Sawyer pursed his lips. "Maybe we should make this score his handicap on the—" Another beanbag hit him in the chest, and he snickered.

Despite being heckled by most of us, Ferns still managed to soundly beat Sawyer. That wasn't difficult— Sawyer's cornhole skills were on par with Ferns's golfing prowess.

As the guys retrieved the beanbags from the last round, Dima said, "Yars, you playing?"

"Why not?" I had a nice buzz going—about the level where I'd either play pretty well or I wouldn't care how I did. Ferns handed me the beanbags he'd been using, and I looked around. "Who am I playing?"

"How about the new guy?" Sawyer shoved the other beanbags into Hunter's hands. "Let's see if you can aim a bag as well as you can aim a puck."

My heart skipped. Hunter shot me a deer-in-the-head-lights look.

Then, at the same time I said, "Sure, bring it on," Hunter said, "I'm in."

This would be... interesting. We took our places in front of the two boards, and when we exchanged glances, I could almost see my own thoughts in his expression: *Just play it cool and no one will notice a thing.*

I cleared my throat. "You know how to play?"

"Try to get the beanbags through the hole, right?"

"Or at least get them to stay on the board, but ideally through the hole."

Hunter shrugged a little too casually—like someone trying really hard to seem like he *wasn't* trying really hard. "Sounds easy enough." He cocked a brow. "Are you any good?"

"Depends on how much I've been drinking."

His lips quirked. "So... you get better when you've been drinking? Or...?"

I grinned. "Wouldn't you like to know?" I tipped my head toward the board. "Throw the beanbag."

I probably *had* drunk more than I should have because I liked that challenging look a little too much. I was also a little too interested in the way his T-shirt sleeve pulled up and revealed more of his ink; he had an elaborate tattoo sleeve on his right arm, and fortunately for me, I hadn't drunk enough to get caught ogling the intricate designs. I'd seen them in photos and stared at them long enough to know what they were, so I didn't need to figure out all their lines and curves. Just... couldn't stop staring at them. Him.

Oblivious to my drunk ass watching him, Hunter tossed the beanbag. It landed on the edge on the left side, and for a second or two, seemed like it would stay there. Then it shifted and dropped onto the grass with a muffled thump.

Hunter swore, the sound mostly masked by our teammates heckling from behind us.

"Ooh!" Ferns exclaimed. "Can we take him golfing?"

"What the fuck?" Hunter spun around. "I only missed once! Give me a chance to really fuck it up before you drag me *golfing*."

"You don't golf?" I asked, chuckling.

Hunter shook his head. "Nope."

"What?" Dolls scoffed. "How the hell are you a hockey player if you don't play golf?"

"Hey!" Norris, his backup goalie, threw a beanbag at his head. "I don't play golf!"

"I know, exactly." Dolls threw the beanbag back at him. "Like I said—how the hell are you a hockey player if you don't—"

"You know what?" Norris huffed with mock annoyance. "Get wrecked, Dolly."

"Don't call me that!" Dolls growled.

Norris shot him a pointed look.

Dolls rolled his eyes. "Fine. Fine! You can be a hockey player who doesn't play golf."

"That's more like—"

"Just not a very good one," Ferns chimed in.

"Or a popular one," Dima added.

Dolls snickered as Norris shook his head and headed for the cooler, probably for another beer.

I just chuckled and turned to Hunter "You sure you want to 'not play golf' on this team?"

Hunter eyed our teammates, then shrugged and turned a look on me that I liked a little too much. "I think I can handle them."

"But why not golf?" Dima asked. "With the way you hit puck, you'd be amazing at golf!"

"Definitely," Dolls drawled. "Just like Ferns."

"Hey!" Another beanbag sailed at Dolls's head.

Hunter's expression turned to confusion, and he asked me, "Okay, what am I missing?"

I nodded toward Ferns. "He sucks at golf."

"Fuck you, Yars!"

I chuckled and gestured at the beanbags. "We'll call that last throw a warmup. Try again?"

Hunter glanced down at them. Then he flicked his eyes toward Ferns. Toward the cornhole board. Toward me.

That grin made my head lighter than the beers I'd drunk. Holy shit.

And then, without warning, he chucked the beanbag at Ferns, catching him in the chest and almost knocking his beer out of his hand.

"What the fuck?" Ferns yelped. "Damn it, Yars!"

"What?" I said through my laughter. "It wasn't me!"

"Bullshit it wasn't!" The beanbag sailed past my head. "Dick!"

"It wasn't me!" I held up my own beanbags. "See? I still have four!"

Ferns eyed me. Narrowing his eyes, he looked around.

Who threw the next one, I couldn't say. All I knew was beanbags were suddenly flying in all directions, occasionally hitting a body with a decisive *smack*. Someone hit Dima in the ass. One beanbag hit my thigh. Dolls tried to throw one at Ferns, but Ferns ducked. The beanbag sailed away from where we were supposed to be playing cornhole, flying over by the barbecue pit... and catching Coach Henley right in the side of the head.

Everyone stopped like kids whose baseball had just gone through the kitchen window.

Henley picked up the beanbag, which had landed in his lap. He peered at it, then at us.

"That was Ferns," Dolls called out.

"Damn it, Dolls!"

Coach chuckled, rolled his eyes, and tossed it back. "Have fun, boys. Just keep it over there."

There was a chorus of, "Sorry, Coach!" and then the guys tossed some beanbags to Hunter and me.

I was still laughing as I caught the fourth bag. To Hunter, I said, "You going first, or am I?"

"That depends." He tossed one into the air and caught it, and there was that devilish grin again. "We throwing at the boards, or trying to get Ferns in trouble?"

Maybe it was the look on his face, maybe it was the beer, but I couldn't help considering the options. "I mean, we could try to get Ferns in trouble, but—"

"Just play the game!" Ferns barked.

Hunter burst out laughing.

Oh God, he was so pretty. *Too* pretty. Fuck, was I drunk? I mean, I was, but was I *that* drunk?

Probably.

Whatever. I liked it. I liked the way he looked, laughing as he chirped back and forth with our teammates.

As competitive as I was, I genuinely didn't care who won this game of cornhole. Or if we even got started playing at all.

I just hoped he kept smiling like that.

CHAPTER 8

HUNTER

As the barbecue wound down, those of us who remained—a few of the single guys and some of the others without kids—helped Dima and Chloé with some of the big cleanup. We tried to help with everything, but our hosts insisted they would handle it from there and refused to let any of us argue.

Chloé shoved take-home containers into the hands of the younger guys and even put a few aside for us veterans. As she cut up one of the remaining pies to divvy up between all of us, she looked at Jarek. "You need a ride home, yes?" She pointed at the mostly empty beer bottle in his hand. "I know you've had more than enough of those."

He laughed. "I'm not that drunk, but no, I wasn't planning to drive." He drained the bottle, and as he put it into the recycling bin, he added, "I came here in an Uber. I can take one home. Don't worry about me."

"No." She shook her head emphatically. "I'll take you home. Just let me finish this and get my keys." She paused. "Oh, I'll need to see if Ferns can move his car—he's in front of the garage, I think."

Jarek opened his mouth to speak, but I beat him to it: "I can drive him."

They both looked at me.

I cleared my throat and motioned toward the driveway. "I'm heading out anyway, and then you don't have to have anyone move their cars around." I met Jarek's gaze and raised my eyebrows. He had no idea how hard my heart was pounding, and I had no idea *why* it was pounding, but I tried to look and sound like this was no big deal. "Ready when you are."

"Uh." He glanced back and forth between us.

I instantly regretted floating the idea. Tonight had gone so well, I'd actually felt like his teammate instead of someone he wished would step into traffic. But now I'd pushed my luck, and he—

Jarek shrugged. "Sure. Thanks. I'll, um... Let me tell Dima we're leaving." Then he was gone, padding out of the kitchen toward the porch, where Dima was gathering empty cans and bottles.

Chloé watched him go. After he'd closed the door behind him, she turned to me and smiled fondly as she continued portioning out pie for the guys. "He's a little prickly sometimes, Jarek." She pushed a piece of pie into a container. "But he's a good man. Good friend."

"Yeah, he seems like a good guy," I said with what I hoped was a neutral smile. Not one that gave away my fear that he still inexplicably didn't like me, and definitely not one that gave away how much more I liked him after a relaxed day in the company of his much less prickly side. "Seems like everyone on the team is pretty chill."

"As it should be," she said.

I nodded but said nothing. God knew I'd spent my fair share of time on teams where people *weren't* particularly chill. Jarek wasn't the first to be a dick to me, and he probably wouldn't be the last. I was just glad he was the only one in Pittsburgh who'd apparently been less than thrilled to have me, though he *had* been a lot less of a dick. Even... nice to me. Today, he'd chirped and chatted with me just like he did everyone else.

I still didn't know what had changed—if our conversation had gotten through to him or if something else had flipped the switch—but I'd take it. It could've been space aliens or the Ghost of Playoffs Past. Whatever. At least now I had some hope that my linemate and I wouldn't kill each other before the season even started.

Though he might still be the death of me for entirely different reasons, because right now, surreptitiously watching him talking to Dima while he helped collect food containers, he was...

God, he really was gorgeous. Someone had done an article a few years back about the sexiest players in the League, and they'd described Jarek as having hypnotic gray eyes, cheekbones sharper than skate blades, and a grin that could turn a straight man gay. I didn't know about straight men, but his grin and his eyes and those perfect, sharp features could make *my* knees wobble. His face could be so serious sometimes, like when he was mean-mugging an opposing player, an intrusive camera, or, well, me. But Jesus Christ, when that man smiled... And especially when he let loose and laughed like nothing in the world could ruin his mood...

"He is pretty, isn't he?" Chloé said in a conspiratorial whisper.

I jerked my attention to her, my face suddenly on fire. "What?"

She laughed, rolling her eyes. "Please. We both know he

is." She snapped a Tupperware lid onto a bowl. "It's okay. I won't tell. Everyone drools over him."

"I'm not..." I cleared my throat, because let's be real... I was. I absolutely was.

Chloé had the good grace to let the subject go, and I was pretty sure my face had returned to its normal color when Jarek came back in from outside.

"—can at least put some skates on him and see how he does," he was saying over his shoulder to Dima.

Dima followed him inside and gave an exasperated sigh. "I am not putting my son on skates before he can even hold up his own head."

"I'm just saying." Jarek flashed him that wicked grin of his. "The sooner you start him, the better his odds of learning to skate better than his father."

An empty beer can bounced off Jarek's head before landing on the tile floor with a *clink-clinkclinkclinkclinkclink*.

"Boys." Chloé tried to look and sound stern, but she failed miserably. "If you get beer on my clean floor..."

"Sorry," Dima said, and grabbed a couple of paper towels.

Jarek picked up the can, but he didn't look nearly as contrite as he dropped it into the bin. "He started it."

"I did not!" Dima huffed dramatically and bent to mop up a couple of stray drops of beer. "*You* started it with all this nonsense about putting my *newborn* in skates."

"He *does* have a point, mon amour," Chloé said.

Dima rose, eyeing her.

She met him with a toothy grin. "Ilya deserves a chance to skate better than his father."

Dima huffed and tossed the balled up paper towel at

her. She squealed and batted it away, then picked it up off the counter and threw it at him.

"Jesus Christ," Jarek said melodramatically. "Get a room, you two."

They each said something to him—one in Russian, one in French—and I was pretty sure both translated to "shut the fuck up."

Jarek just chuckled. Turning to me, that playful laugh still on his lips and his beautiful eyes still dancing with amusement, he said, "Ready to go?"

Ready to—oh. Right. I was driving him home. In my car. Alone.

"Yeah. Yeah." I pretended not to be the least bit flustered, which probably made me sound *supremely* flustered. "When you are."

We said our goodbyes, both took some containers from our very insistent hostess, and headed out. I'd parked down the street in front of a neighbor's house, and the short walk felt like it stretched on for miles with Jarek walking beside me.

The silence felt weird, so I flailed for a way to break it. Finally, I gestured over my shoulder and asked, "Are they always like that?"

He chuckled. "They've been that way since juniors."

"Since—oh, you and Dima were on the same team, weren't you?"

He nodded. "Yeah. That's when they met, too."

"Wow." I smiled. "Seems like a lot of guys meet their wives when they're in juniors. Like the hockey equivalent of high school sweethearts."

At that, Jarek's humor abruptly faded. "Yeah. They do."

Ooh, shit. That was a nerve, wasn't it?

Fuck, fuck, fuck.

I had no idea how to salvage the moment, either. Mostly because I couldn't be sure what nerve I'd stepped on, though I could guess. Sort of? Either way, I went with the lesser of two evils: awkward silence until we were in the car.

I started the engine and glanced at him as he pulled on his seat belt. "So. Um." I cleared my throat and managed to croak, "Where am I going?"

"Get on the freeway going south."

I nodded and pulled away from the curb. The drive wouldn't be a long one, but it *would* be unbearable if this silence held on. And for that matter, Jarek was just buzzed enough to have forgotten he didn't like me, so maybe I could also make him forget about that moment on the way to the car. Might as well make conversation while I had the chance.

After I'd pulled onto the freeway and got up to speed, I drummed my thumbs on the wheel and glanced at him. "So, um. Can I ask you something about your major junior days?"

He looked across the console, eyebrows up as if he hadn't expected the question. Truthfully, it hadn't been my go-to conversation starter, but I'd jumped on the first thing I could think of that felt more or less benign. His pro career had been rocky, and I didn't know where all the landmines were. But he'd had an amazing and—as far as I knew— drama-free career in major juniors.

Except for that fucking landmine I'd stepped on while we'd been walking.

Way to go, Michaud. You're on a roll tonight.

But he cautiously said, "Uh. Yeah. Sure."

I swallowed. "Why did you play in Canada? I played in Toronto with a guy who was in major juniors in the Czech

Republic, but you came to Canada. I was... just always curious about that, I guess."

"Oh." He fidgeted a little more. "I mean, I had *planned* to play in Czechia. I wanted to play professionally in North America, but I always assumed I'd start in juniors closer to home."

I stole another glance at him. He was staring out the windshield, his expression unreadable but not defensive or uncomfortable as far as I could tell.

"My uncle lives in Kitchener," he went on after a moment. "He convinced my parents that if I came to stay with him and made it onto a juniors team in Canada, I'd have a better chance at being noticed by the North American scouts. So, I came over when I was fourteen to live with him."

I nodded as he spoke. "It, um... It sounds like it was a good move."

That prompted a soft laugh, and when I glanced his way again, I almost ran off the road. I was so used to Jarek's features being hard—especially when I was around—that the nostalgic smile was startling.

"At least it gave me a chance to work on my English," he said. "I was... eh, okay at it when I came to Canada, but by the time I was drafted into juniors, I was mostly fluent." He laughed. "So, of course, I ended up playing in Quebec."

"Oh God." I groaned. "That was my biggest nightmare."

"It was?"

"Uh-huh. I took French all through school, but I'm *terrible* at it. My dad's family is Quebecois, but we've lived in British Columbia for three generations, so..." I trailed off into a shrug. "We speak English at home, and I just... sucked at it."

"Really?" He sounded interested, but also amused. "Why's that?"

I cleared my throat. "Because it wasn't hockey."

Jarek barked a laugh. "I had the same problem when I was supposed to be learning English."

Grinning, I turned to him again. "Yeah?"

"Yeah. I was—oh, this is my exit." He gestured up ahead.

I signaled and got over, slowing as I approached the ramp.

"Go right at the end," he told me. "Then just keep going for a while."

I nodded.

"Anyway," he went on. "I knew I needed to learn English if I wanted to come over here, but it was just so fucking *boring*." He groaned. "I'd spend half of class counting down the minutes until I could put my skates on."

I chuckled. "Oh, yeah. I can relate. And I was... I mean, I can sort of talk to my grandparents, but then they just complain that my French is embarrassing."

"Really?" He sounded amused.

"Yep. My whole time in youth hockey, we all just prayed I didn't get drafted into Quebec."

"Right, and you played in..." He paused. "Calgary, wasn't it?"

It shouldn't have been surprising that he knew that. I was well aware that my name, stats, and every little detail had been practically put up on a marquee the instant I was drafted onto that team. That spotlight had been on me since my youth days, and I still sometimes met people who could quote my stats from juniors. It was weird, but it was a thing.

Still, it made my cheeks burn to realize Jarek knew anything about me. Why? No idea. Maybe because this was

Jaromir Badura, and nothing made sense when it came to my brain's reactions to him. Especially since he'd stopped cold-shouldering me.

I tapped my thumbs on the wheel again and tried not to fidget. "Yeah. Calgary. I had hoped to get picked up by Vancouver, but..." I trailed off into a half-shrug.

"Why Vancouver?" Beat. "Hometown, wasn't it?"

Yet another tidbit everyone and their mother knew about me. Yet another layer of heat in my face.

I nodded. "Yeah. I figured it wouldn't happen, but a boy can dream, you know? Would've been nice to be close to my family during that time." I rewound what I said, and winced. "That must've been tough for you. Being over here while your family was back in Europe."

His shrug was subtle, but my peripheral vision caught it. "It was. But this was my dream. My parents visited as often as they could, and I went back to Czechia during the offseasons. Now they don't travel as often—my father has some health issues—but my sister and I go home whenever we can."

"Your sister?"

Jarek nodded. "She lives here. I was traded to Pittsburgh while she was picking out medical schools, and one of the schools she wanted was here. So she applied there, got in, and came to live nearby."

"How is that? Having her in the same town?"

"It's good. We were always close, even when I lived far away, so it's good to have her in the same city." He turned to me. "You have a... brother, right?"

"Mmhmm. A year older."

Jarek gave a quiet chuckle. "Is it true he hates hockey?"

I snorted. "God, the press really won't let that one go, will they?"

"So it's not true?"

"No." I rolled my eyes. "He loves watching it and can quote stats going back decades. He just doesn't like to play. But when everyone was focusing on me when I was a kid, they kept hammering him with questions about why *he* wasn't playing. So he started making up answers to amuse himself. He told one that he couldn't put on skates because his foot was scarred to hell and back from the grizzly bear that attacked him when he was six."

Jarek laughed. "But that one didn't get as much press as saying he hates hockey?"

I shot him a look. "We're Canadian. Getting your foot mauled by a grizzly is nothing compared to *hating hockey.*"

The laughter that poured out of Jarek was so beautiful, I vowed to write my brother and that reporter a handwritten thank-you note as soon as I got home. And I was supposed to play hockey with this man?

Still chuckling, Jarek gestured ahead. "Up there on the left. That driveway."

I followed his instructions into a parking lot at the base of a condominium complex. The building was maybe five stories, with garages and stoops making up the ground floor.

"This is me." He indicated the second unit on the left. "Just pull up in front of the garage."

Why was I disappointed that we were here?

I kept my expression neutral, though, and I steered into the spot he'd indicated. I set the brake because I didn't trust myself to look at him and not have my foot slip off the pedal. With the car safely idling, I turned to him. "So I'll, uh... See you at practice?" Yeah, that was smooth.

But the way he smiled... ooh, hell. Was this really the same man who hadn't been able to look at me during training camp?

Yeah, it was, and my God, the way he was looking at me right then...

It was ridiculous, all things considered, but the sudden impulse to lean across the gap between us and kiss him was *almost* irresistible. The irrational certainty that he'd let me... that he wanted me to...

I cleared my throat and tore my gaze away from his as I tried to be subtle about sitting up, pretending I hadn't started leaning in like a dumbass. "Right. Uh. I should get home."

Nodding, Jarek sat up a little, and I realized he'd leaned closer to me too. What the hell?

"Yeah. Um." He unbuckled his seat belt. "Thanks for the lift."

"Don't mention it."

We locked eyes again.

One heartbeat.

Two.

Three.

Abruptly, we both turned away. He reached for the door and I put my hands back on the wheel because what else could I do with them? After murmured "good nights" from both of us, he stepped out of my car, and when the door shut, I exhaled.

Holy. Shit.

I watched him walk up the stoop, and I waited until he'd opened the door before I started backing out of the space. As I did, he turned back, smiled, and waved. I did the same, and somehow didn't hit his neighbor's motorcycle.

Get a grip, Michaud. What the hell?

I got out of there, drove until I was sure I was well out of sight, and then pulled into a gas station. My tank was two-thirds full, but it gave me something to do that wouldn't result in a crash.

As I put gas into my tank, I replayed the walk to my car and the drive to Jarek's place. The conversation. The perfectly benign but weirdly civil conversation, given how we'd interacted since we'd met. Was it too much to hope we'd keep going like that? Or... maybe dial it back a few notches so I could still remember how to play hockey?

God, I was a train wreck over him.

I reminded myself he'd also been drinking. Not a ton—he'd still been steady on his feet, and he'd hardly been slurring—but maybe enough to forget, if only for an evening, that I wasn't his favorite person in Pittsburgh.

I'd take it.

I wouldn't dare read too much into it.

But I'd take it.

CHAPTER 9

JAREK

Professional and sexual frustration were conspiring to drive me insane, and two weeks into the regular season, I was pretty sure they were going to succeed. He was always *there*. On the bench and on the ice. In the locker room and on the plane. At team meals and at team meetings. Always, always *there*.

Some days, the resentment held my concentration. Some days, it was desire and fantasies. Others, my brain vacillated between the two like a puck during a tic-tac-toe play. It was a genuine miracle I could remember how to play hockey, and even that was getting harder by the day.

Fortunately, about the time it was all coming to a head, the team had a night off. We'd practiced this morning and would again tomorrow, and we had a game tomorrow night, but this evening? All mine.

Time to find someone to distract me from everyone and everything in my world.

Apps made me nervous. I knew another gay player whose profile was screencapped and leaked all over the internet. There was nothing really scandalous about it, but it was fuel for the homophobes who thought queers like us didn't belong in sports. It had to be humiliating for him, too; the thought of it made my skin crawl, probably because I'd already had my fill of being gossip fodder and a punchline.

Clubs felt safer. I didn't run into a lot of gay guys who followed hockey, least of all well enough to recognize me. Those who did seemed to abide by the unspoken code of silence, and the rest couldn't figure out how to get decent photos in the low light. Or maybe that was just me rationalizing.

And anyway, if someone posted a photo or a video of me from a gay nightclub, it wouldn't matter too much. I was out. Marc-Yves had come with me to some red carpet events while we were together. There was no novelty in busting Jarek Badura being a gay dude, especially since when I was out in public, I always behaved like there was a camera nearby. No bumping and grinding. No blowing someone in a car. No screwing someone in a men's room. As long as I didn't give anyone anything scandalous to reveal, I was good.

So, clubs were fine. An app profile going public just felt too intimate. Too revealing. Catching me in public and making it more public? Oh well.

As it happened, there was a club in downtown Pittsburgh that I'd been to many times. Lanterns was high-end with a nice atmosphere and excellent bartenders. The place was always crowded with men who had the same idea I did, and I could usually find someone there to keep me company for a night. Plus there was a certain amount of discretion; the lighting didn't make for very good photos, and anyone caught photographing other people without their consent was booted out and banned for life. Just brandishing a phone in camera or video mode could get someone kicked out. This place didn't fuck around.

I drove in, since I didn't drink much if I was planning on hooking up. There was a parking garage around the corner that was secure, with both cameras and patrolling guards, so I was fine with leaving my car there. Then it was just a short walk to the front door, ID and a modest cover charge, and I was on my way inside.

As soon as I walked in, I felt better. Some of the recent tension melted out of my neck and shoulders as I let the disco lights and the thumping beat settle around me like a familiar blanket. It could get overstimulating and leave my ears ringing, but it was also a welcome break from everything else in my world. A fireworks show when I needed a distraction.

On my way up to the bar, I surveyed the crowd. Lots of men who were on the prowl, judging by the way they were all sizing each other up. Perfect.

At a corner table was a group that was clearly here for a bachelorette party. One of them wore a novelty bridal veil, and all six of them were drunk enough to probably make my hardest-partying hockey player friends say, *"Yo, it's only nine-thirty—you might want to pace yourselves."*

I wasn't crazy about groups like that in places like this. Lanterns kept an eye on them, since if anyone was going to push boundaries in here, it was almost inevitably the drunk straight people. Thank God the staff was pretty good about intervening if there were any issues, and they did not hesitate to throw people out.

We welcome people of all orientations, the owners had explained under a nasty review from a bride whose party had been kicked out. *But at the end of the day, this is a safe space for LGBTQ+ people. For the protection of our patrons, we enforce certain rules. Your party elected to break those rules and put our patrons at risk of being outed. You are therefore no longer welcome at Lanterns.*

That was one of the reasons I loved coming here. It was safe. I didn't have to look over my shoulder and sweat about being seen. Once in a while, someone would recognize me, and there'd be a little smile and a nod, but they were respectful and left me alone.

Tonight, as I sipped a rum and Coke and looked around the room, I couldn't quite get into the swing of things. I wasn't so sure this was what I needed after all. Sex, yes. All the games between eye contact and the bedroom? Maybe not.

I had a sudden pang of loneliness in the middle of that crowd. I wanted Dolls here, trying to calculate their blood alcohol content based on the bottles on the table and muttering that he hoped none of them were driving. I wanted Dima bitching about American beer while we all laughed at Ferns, drunk off his ass and dancing like no one was watching.

Ah well. I was here. Might as well make the most of it. I'd come to unwind and find someone to help me burn up the sheets, even if the meet-flirt-fuck dance sounded exhausting. All the fatigue and pressure of the regular season, coupled with being around Hunter Michaud all the time—I was going to dissolve it all in a drink or two, and then chase the rest of it away with another man's breathless cries.

I had my first drink in hand. Step two—a man.

And my God, there were plenty of men on offer.

That redhead near the edge of the dancefloor was sexy

as hell. I wondered if he did that thing with his hips when he wasn't wearing those skintight pants. Might have to find out.

Another guy had some interesting ink running up his sculpted arms and disappearing beneath his white tank top. Would his tattoos look hot with sweat rolling along their crisp, black lines? Probably.

And over by the bar, there was—

My drink almost slipped out of my hand.

You have got *to be shitting me.*

Really?

Then again, maybe I shouldn't have been surprised. This *was* a high-end gay nightclub, after all. I'd run into football players, the odd musician stopping in during a tour, and a few actors who were in town to film a movie. In fact, a few months ago, I'd come in here and hooked up with the pitcher from a visiting major league baseball team (turned out he played catcher pretty well too).

So if I was going to cross paths with another pro hockey player in a gay nightclub, it was going to be here. Especially another hockey player who lived on the same frenetic schedule I did and had the same rare opportunities for a night out.

But did Hunter Michaud have to pick *tonight* to come strolling into Lanterns dressed like *that?* In painted-on black pants that left nothing to the imagination and a black T-shirt that fit him more snugly than his base layer?

"*Sakra,*" I hissed into my drink.

I had a precious minute or so to think it might not be him after all. My eyes were playing tricks on me. That happened sometimes when the lights were flickering and I couldn't see very well.

But then he gestured for the bartender, and his sleeve

pulled up just enough to reveal the ink on his forearm. Only a little, but I'd seen that tattoo enough to recognize it from just the inch or so that peeked out.

Sakra, indeed. That was him. That was Hunter Michaud, on the goddamned prowl in the same club where I was desperately trying to forget he existed or how much I wanted that spectacular body.

Oh, fuck my life.

And as if that weren't enough, he glanced around the room, and despite all the lights and shadows and bodies and movement, he zeroed right in on me as if I were standing in the middle of an empty sheet of ice.

Our eyes locked. His grin faltered, but only for a second.

He acknowledged me with a sharp nod—a silent "hey" from across thirty feet of floor and crowd—and he held my gaze just long enough for me to respond in kind.

Then he turned his head, and the spell was broken in the same instant the eye contact was, and I was out of breath and off balance. What the hell?

Okay. I needed to pull it together. This was a big club. Not huge, but big enough we could lose each other in the crowd, and I *needed* to lose Hunter in the crowd.

I'd come here to hook up, so it was time to find someone who could hold my attention (among other things) and make me forget all about my teammate. Someone who could capture my focus and not let me track Hunter and that tall, broad-shouldered guy out onto the dancefloor. Someone whose hands and body and mouth didn't leave me any brainpower to notice how those two moved together.

Because, sakra, the way they moved together...

Was there anything Hunter *wasn't* good at? Probably,

but it turned out that dancing wasn't one of them. He moved with music and people with all the ease and grace he handled a puck or slipped between defensemen. And of course, there weren't any pads this time—just tight black pants and a shirt like a second skin, every stitch hugging perfectly contoured muscles like a damn dream.

I had to look away as I took a drink. It would be just my luck someone would slide a hand over the gorgeous ass or something right when I was swallowing, and I'd end up choking.

I pulled an ice cube onto my tongue to cool myself down. As I rolled it behind my teeth, I let my gaze slide back to the dancefloor. To them. To him.

Hunter was as media-trained as I was, and part of that involved being acutely aware of how we appeared in public. He danced, but he wasn't handsy, and even when he moved in close with someone, there was still some distance. No making out. No groping.

In that moment, for entirely selfish reasons, I was glad he'd had that trained into him like I had. I didn't think I could handle being in the same room while someone found out what that gorgeous mouth tasted like.

At the same time, though, I didn't know how much it was really helping. Especially not when Hunter moved on to a tall black-haired guy with a big grin and a visible hard-on. Half a song later, they were still within the realms of what PR would find acceptable but absolutely into each other's space. A hand on Hunter's waist. Hunter's on the other guy's hip, just below his belt. Barely any daylight between their bodies.

And those scorching looks passing between them?

Jesus fuck.

I pulled my gaze away again and went for another drink. Of course, it was as bone dry as my mouth. Damn it.

Well, at least that gave me something to focus on besides my teammate toeing the line of what hockey players could get away with in public.

I made my way to the bar. I was tempted to get another rum and Coke, but opted for just a Coke. My head was already light in ways that had nothing to do with the alcohol, and I was seriously debating getting out of here sooner than later. Might as well stay sober enough to drive.

For a few minutes, I hovered near the bar, letting the ice and the fizz of my refreshed drink hold my attention. There was a part of me—multiple parts, if I were honest—that wished I was brave enough to get on that dancefloor and see if he had any interest in me. I doubted it, given all the reasons I'd given him to think I was an insufferable dick, but that didn't stop me from imagining what it would be like to have those hands on my body. There were shadowy corners in this club where people could get away with a lot, and there were moments when I thought it was worth the risk of getting caught in a compromising position in one of those dark corners. This was one of those moments.

Probably because I could be sure beyond a shadow of a doubt that I had zero chance with Hunter. I'd blown it long before I'd ever seen how his body could move on a dancefloor. Long before I could ever get jealous of hands drifting over perfect muscles.

"Kurva." I pressed my glass to my forehead as if that had any hope of bringing down my body temperature.

There wasn't a man in this building who would satisfy me tonight, because fuck me, I wanted the only man who justifiably wouldn't want anything to do with me. Whether

I left now or later, the night was going to end with my dick in my hand and my linemate on my mind.

So why stick around?

I lowered the glass and sucked another ice cube into my mouth. Then, because I was a complete masochist, I slid my gaze toward the dancefloor.

Hunter's absence stood out more than the bachelorette party taking over the scene. Some guys had moved out of the way to avoid the flailing elbows of the drunk dancers, rolling their eyes and scowling from the sidelines while they waited for the party to get it out of their system.

Hunter wasn't on the sidelines, though.

He was gone.

Oh, thank God. Now I could focus on…

Yeah, who the fuck was I kidding? It was like seeing a spider and then *not* seeing it anymore—now I couldn't think of anything except *"Where the fuck is he?"* Why did I even care, anyway? Ogling him was just going to drive my dumb ass insane, so the sooner he went someplace else, the sooner I could—

Movement in my peripheral vision caught my attention.

There was movement everywhere because this was a nightclub—people dancing, walking around, tending bar, flagging down bartenders, talking—but somehow I zeroed in on that one flicker of movement.

Because of course I did.

And I looked.

Just in time to watch Hunter slipping into the hallway that led to the exit.

With that other guy's hand on the small of his back.

Exhaling, I leaned against the bar. It was probably just as well Hunter moved fast when he saw something he wanted.

Now I could...

Go home and jerk off while I imagined Hunter naked, that was what I could do.

Wasn't like I was going to get anywhere with anyone who was still in this club.

So, with a heavy sigh, I took out my wallet and flagged down the bartender to close out my tab.

CHAPTER 10

HUNTER

Lying back on my bed, I stared up at the ceiling.

The relaxed bliss from my orgasm had long since faded. Shawn's Uber had already come and gone. Hell, he had to be home by now, and he lived clear down in the South Hills.

It wasn't even midnight.

Exhaling into the stillness, I scrubbed my hand over my face. This had to be a new record for me. I never moved that fast with guys. When I went to a club, I wanted to actually dance and enjoy myself, not jump on the nearest available dick.

But tonight had been different.

Jarek had been there.

He'd seen me. I'd seen him. There was no pretending we hadn't made eye contact across Lanterns and acknowledged each other.

It wasn't just that one time, either. There were mirrors along a few walls in the club, and I'd found him again and again. Almost every glance... he was watching me.

I hadn't been able to look long enough to parse his

expression. The combination of heavy shadows and wildly flickering lights had made him difficult to see.

But he'd been watching.

A lot.

If Jarek hadn't been there, I most likely still would've ended up naked with someone before the night was over. Just... not *quite* that soon. And not with that guy.

But Jarek's gaze had prickled my senses as surely as the sweat rolling down my neck and Shawn's breath whispering across my skin. There'd been no avoiding my teammate's presence. No forgetting him. No ignoring him. Not even when he wasn't looking, but especially not when he *was* looking. Which he had been. A lot.

I hadn't been self-conscious or worried he was judging me. I didn't give a shit about that. We were both openly gay, so I wasn't showing him anything he didn't already know about.

I just couldn't ignore him, or the way his presence had hummed at the edges of my senses, and about the time that bachelorette party had main-charactered their way onto the dancefloor, I'd had enough.

"Want to get out of here?" I'd asked Shawn as we moved off the floor.

His eyes had widened. "Like go to another club? Or...?"

"I mean we could." I'd grinned and slid my hands up his chest. "Or we could skip that part."

His face had lit up like he'd just hit the jackpot. I didn't think he knew or cared who I was—he just knew he was about to get laid.

And he had gotten laid. I'd also learned too late that he didn't kiss hookups on the mouth, which was normally a dealbreaker for me, so the sex had been a whole lot less fun than I'd hoped. All because of my fucking teammate lurking in the shadows. I'd needed to get the hell out of Lanterns, so I'd bolted with the first man who was willing without making sure we were compatible, and the sex had been... meh. What fun was sex without kissing? Wasn't like he'd made up for it with anything else his mouth did. About the only thing he'd had going for him was his dick; he was average size, slightly bigger than me, and he'd fucked me until I'd come. But the whole not-kissing thing took an otherwise four-star fuck down to two stars *at best* as far as I was concerned.

What a waste of an evening.

Now Shawn was home, and I was here, and Jarek was still prodding at my senses even though he was probably banging someone else right this minute.

I wasn't ready for the flare of jealousy that thought ignited.

What did even I care if Jarek was with another guy? He was an asshole, and despite being civil on the ice and those moments of near friendliness, he clearly didn't like me. And, like, maybe getting laid would make him less bitchy. Beyond that, what difference did it make to me if he was in bed with someone right now? If those long fingers were tracing over sweaty skin. If he was disheveled and out of his mind, driving himself and someone else wild? If some other guy had his mouth around that dick, and—

"Oh my God." I rubbed my eyes. "What is wrong with me?"

And why was I getting hard? I'd already come once, and I had *not* been thinking about Jarek in the lead-up to that orgasm. There hadn't been a single brain cell devoted to his hot body or his sharp accent or—

With a groan, I rolled out of bed and onto my feet.

The cold shower didn't do much. Took care of the hard-on, yeah. Brought my body temperature down, sure.

Got Jarek off my mind? Not even a little.

With a defeated sigh, I turned the water back to hot. As the spray beat on my back, I pressed my arm against the wall and rested my forehead on it. I gave up and let myself imagine Jarek in here with me, which had my cock coming back to life in no time. With my free hand, I stroked myself all the way hard, and I closed my eyes as I kept going, kept rocking into my own fist, kept thinking about Jarek's hands, mouth, body...

I'll bet he kisses hookups.

That thought had me groaning into the near-silence and pumping myself harder. Jarek's slim lips were sexy as all hell. It would be a crime if he didn't use them to their full potential.

As if that man does anything halfway.

Oh Lord, that was a thought. If Jarek put even a *fraction* of his hockey work ethic into sex, he'd... Well, hell, he might kill me. Ride me so far into oblivion I couldn't find my way back.

I could... definitely think of worse things.

"Fuck," I whispered over the noise of the shower, and I jacked myself faster as I imagined him pounding into me. A toy would've made this even better, but I hadn't come in here planning to get myself off, so... my hand would have to do.

My hand, and my very vivid imagination when it came to Jarek.

I wanted him. Kneeling in front of me while he licked and teased every inch of my dick. Standing behind me and holding my hips while he plowed into me. Pinning me down on the bed and...

God.

Kissing me.

Kissing me deep. Hard. Gentle. Sweet. Playful. I couldn't imagine a plane of existence where Jaromir Badura wasn't a good kisser, and holy hell, I wanted to taste him. I wanted to know everything he could do with that gorgeous mouth, and I wanted him to send me into the stratosphere, and—

"Fuuuck!" I shouted, slumping against the wall as I came. And came. And... Jesus Christ.

My legs were still trembling when I stepped back under the rush of water. My head spun, and I didn't think it was entirely because I was out of breath.

"Oh my God." The sound of the shower swallowed my voice. I had to practice with Jarek tomorrow. Not just after we'd crossed paths at a gay night club, but after I'd jerked off while thinking about him.

Who was I kidding? After I'd been fucked by a stranger while thinking about him. Because I couldn't lie to myself: the whole time that guy—what was his name?—had been railing me, I'd been fantasizing about Jarek. My hookup had probably gone home thinking he'd rocked my world. And that was fine. Let him think whatever made him feel good.

But the reality was that it was the fantasy of Jarek that had made me tremble and shout like that.

Jarek, the man who'd be on my wing tomorrow.

God, I was so fucked.

CHAPTER 11

JAREK

I knew why *I* couldn't focus this morning. What the hell was up with Hunter?

Seeing me at Lanterns hadn't bothered him in the moment. Not enough to stop him from dancing or meeting someone to hook up with. Did he think I was going to out him or something? Or sneer at him because he'd managed to get laid?

Pfft. I was the one who'd gone home with my hand last night. I was hardly in a position to act superior.

But now he couldn't even look at me. He didn't seem hostile, just uncomfortable. Embarrassed, maybe? I had no clue.

Well, whatever the issue was, it followed us from the locker room out onto the ice. What had started as not being able to make eye contact quickly turned into barely being able to skate, never mind handle the puck. Any time we had to communicate—which was *a lot*—we'd both trip up a little. Hesitate when we couldn't afford to. Release the puck a second before the other was ready.

In short... we were a mess.

And we weren't the only ones who noticed.

Oh, I knew Coach Henley noticed from the start, and I kept trying like hell to pull it together. Though I knew he'd never tear into us—publicly or privately—the way Coach Robertson always had, that fear ran deep, and I fought valiantly to play better, if only to convince him I didn't need a post-practice lecture.

The damage was done, though. My concentration was shot, and all I managed to do was overcompensate, over-think, and make everything worse.

What worried me was that Hunter wasn't doing any better. His legendary stick-handling was nowhere in sight. His release was hesitant. Jesus Christ, he'd almost lost an edge like three times.

The whole time, Dima kept eyeing us both as if he wondered what in the world had gotten into us. He was a strong player, too, but the way our line looked right now, it was as if a top line right winger had been sent to play on the fourth line of a minor league team.

What the fuck? his eyes said all through practice.

Yeah, I'm wondering the same thing, Dima.

Because there was no way in hell last night had fucked up Hunter's head like it had mine. Except... what other explanation was there? He'd been fine yesterday, and he'd seemed fine last night, but this morning...

What the hell?

When practice finally—mercifully—ended, I doubted anyone was surprised when Coach asked Hunter and me to hang back. Great. We were bag skating, weren't we?

"You don't want to bag skate until you puke?" another coach's voice thundered in my ears. *"Unfuck yourself out there, Badura."*

My legs ached just thinking about it.

From the corner of my eye, I caught Hunter playing with his mouthguard. He always did that. Hell, we all did. But there was a difference between fiddling with it because we were high-energy athletes who were bored easily and the sharp, twitchy movements that came with being nervous. Scared, even.

Coach waited until our teammates and the rest of the coaches had left the ice. Then he turned and he glanced back and forth between us. "You boys want to tell me what's going on?"

There was an edge to his voice, but it didn't ignite my nerves the way I still expected it to after all this time. Coach wasn't a doormat, but he wasn't unkind either. He wanted respect and results, not fear.

One of these days, that would sink in.

I took out my own mouthguard and cleared my throat. "Just a little off this morning, Coach."

His eyebrow arched. "Both of you?"

Hunter and I exchanged glances that were equal parts uncomfortable and confused.

Before either of us could speak, though, Coach put up his hands. "Listen, whatever it is? Whatever's off between the two of you?" He gestured sharply at either of us. "I don't care. Just figure it out and unfuck it enough that it's not on my ice. Got it?"

"Yeah, Coach," we both said.

He looked back and forth between us. "You boys going to have it together tonight? Or am I going to have the media asking why two-thirds of my second line are healthy-scratched?"

"You won't, Coach," Hunter said. "Sorry. We'll..." His eyes flicked to me, and his face colored as he exhaled. "We'll be fine for the game."

Coach studied us both for a second, then nodded. "All right. Go hit the showers, and don't let me see any of this shit tonight."

Again in unison, we said, "Got it, Coach."

Then he headed toward the locker room. Hanging back on the ice, Hunter and I looked at each other again, and damn if his deer-in-the-headlights didn't echo what I felt in that moment.

What is going on? And how do we change it?

But he just cleared his throat, absently tapping his stick against his skate. "Yeah. Tonight. We'll be fine." His raised eyebrows added an unspoken, *"Right?"*

All I could do was nod. My mouth had gone too dry to speak.

Without another word, we followed Coach to the locker room. I shed my gear and stepped into the shower, rolling my shoulders under the hot spray as I tried to unwind some tension.

One way or another, Hunter and I had to have it together for tonight's game. And for every game. It didn't matter how distracting he was. I couldn't afford to be distracted, and neither could he. So what if I'd jacked off to fantasies about him last night? Being a gay guy surrounded by hot men all the time, I was used to interacting with men I'd thought about with my dick in my hand. It just kind of came with the territory of being a queer athlete.

But somehow, knowing I'd come *that hard* thinking about him while he'd been in bed with someone else, looking Hunter in the eye after last night was... way more difficult than I'd anticipated. Especially since he was still struggling to make eye contact with me, too.

This wasn't something I had any experience with. What the hell?

Well, it didn't matter. He was here. I was here.

And we *had* to get it together.

———————

Hunter was right—we did have it together that night.

The goal horn blared as the visiting goalie, bathed in red light, shook his head in defeat. I had about two seconds for a celly before both Dima and Hunter grabbed me into hugs, shoving me into the glass in the process. The defensemen— Ferns and Sawyer—joined in a second later.

"Way to go, Yars!" Dima slapped my helmet with his glove. "How about one more?"

I laughed, shoving him back. "How about you pull your weight for once?"

He rolled his eyes and muttered something I didn't hear.

"Aww, give him a break." Hunter chuckled. "He got a goal... uh... two games ago?"

Dima punched Hunter's arm, and all three of us laughed. Then we headed for the bench for fist bumps. Hunter had the assist on my goal, so he was right behind me. As we took our seats on the bench, I was grateful for the breather after an intense shift, and I caught his eye. And it was a good thing I'd already been sitting down.

What the hell? He's a teammate!

And he's... him.

I grabbed one of the iPads under the pretense of reviewing my shift. Mostly I just needed something to look at besides Hunter. Because I fucking wanted to look at Hunter. A lot.

My goal replayed on the screen, but I barely noticed

what was going on. My mind was on the man sitting to my left. On how I'd seen him last night.

I closed my eyes and exhaled.

On how much I wished I could've been the man he'd left with and—

Kurva. Jarek. Get a fucking grip.

"Mish. Yars. Dima." Coach barked. "You're up."

Already? Apparently so—Mayweather's line had put Chicago on their heels, and they were starting to peel away for a line change. Hunter went in for Mayweather, and Dima went over the boards just before Williams came through the door. Cole was a little slower to come off—he was tied up in a puck battle near the net—but he finally got the puck to Hunter and skated toward the bench. I swung my legs over the boards, waited until he was within a couple of feet, and then took off to join Hunter and Dima.

Mayweather's line had set us up perfectly. Chicago's forwards and defensemen were deep in their own defensive zone, backs almost literally against the wall, and they didn't stand a chance against the three of us. Especially when Hunter and Dima started passing the puck back and forth so fast, none of them could keep up. Both of their defensemen were, unsurprisingly, closing in on Hunter. Dima faked like he was going to pass to him, then sent it to me instead. I rushed toward the goal, which pulled the defensive attention on to me. I ran them around a little, giving my teammates time to set up.

When I made my move, it happened in seconds. The puck zipped from my stick to Hunter's and then on to Dima's as if it were drawn by a magnet, and Dima one-timed it from the blue line.

For the third time tonight, the red light came on and the

goal horn sounded. The fans roared to their feet, and this time it was Dima getting crushed in hugs.

I smacked his helmet. "Finally broke the streak!"

"About fucking time," he said, and we headed for the bench for more fist bumps. I was relieved, too. I didn't even care about racking up another assist; I was just glad Dima had scored. He'd been a little snakebitten lately, and his frustration had been impossible to miss.

I hoped this wasn't a fluke, and that he'd get back to his usual form of averaging a point a game.

By the end of the second period, the score was four-nothing. Chicago came out swinging in the third, determined to grab the lead. If that wasn't possible, tie it up and go into overtime. At the very least, keep Dolls from getting another shutout.

They managed to snatch the shutout out of his grasp— two goals in the first half of the period. That was admittedly Pittsburgh's fault. We got a little cocky and took our foot off the gas. After those two goals, though, we got our shit together and held the line.

Mayweather scored, bringing us to five. When my line hit the ice again, I managed three shots on goal in a row, mostly because their exhausted goalie had zero rebound control and their defensemen were too busy fending off Hunter and Dima. The netminder eventually managed to freeze the puck, though, and a ref blew the whistle.

On the way to the faceoff dot, Hunter grinned at me. "You want that hatty, don't you?"

I want you.

My face had to be the color of the goal light and I almost tripped over my own skates, but I cleared my throat. "Hell, yeah. Let's do this."

He nodded. Then he swept his gaze around Chicago's on-ice players, and—covering his mouth with his glove so no one could lip read—indicated a set play.

I returned the nod, and we separated to let Dima and our defensemen know which play we were using. With everyone on the same page, Hunter skated up to the dot for the faceoff.

It didn't go quite as planned.

Hunter was spectacular on faceoffs, but no one won every time. The other center snatched the puck away, and he and his teammates made for the neutral zone.

Ferns, however, was there to intercept a badly judged pass. He and Sawyer sent it back and forth, keeping Chicago busy while Hunter, Dima, and I set up for the play we'd planned. Once everyone was in position—which took all of a handful of seconds—Ferns sent the puck to Dima, who was closest to the goal. The goalie lunged toward him, ready for the tip-in, but instead, Dima hit it to the boards, sending it sailing around behind the goal and almost to the blue line where Hunter was waiting. Chicago's defense had wisely put someone on Hunter, but Hunter danced around him and passed the puck back to Dima. Again, the goalie anticipated a tip-in and dropped into a butterfly... leaving his other side wide open for *me* to tip in the puck after Dima passed it to me.

The crowd roared, and I'd barely had a chance to pump my fist before hats started flying out onto the ice. My sixth career hat trick. Fourth with the Pittsburgh Hornets.

First with the man who'd just hugged me so hard, we'd both almost toppled onto the ice.

"Fuck yeah!" Hunter beamed, giving my shoulder a smack as he let me go. "Way to go!"

"Thanks!" I grinned, hoping no one could see anything except pride and excitement in my expression. "When're you gonna get one?"

Hunter rolled his eyes. "I got four assists tonight! Cut me some slack!"

"Pfft." I gave him a shove. "And I got one on top of—"I gestured at the hats still coming down all around us. "So what?"

He muttered something I didn't catch, but he was chuckling, and we headed for the bench.

As the ice crew rounded up the hats, the announcer bellowed over the roaring crowd, "The Pittsburgh goal, his twelfth of the season and third of the night—a hat trick goal scored by number twenty-three, Jaromir Badura!" More cheers. Still more hats. Then, "Assisted by number eleven, Dmitry Meknikov. And number forty-one, Hunter Michaud."

I didn't think it was the roar of the crowd that made my heart pound even harder. I didn't quite know what it was. The hat trick. The fact that Hunter had played a role in getting me all three of those goals. That he'd come to the faceoff intending to get the puck to me so I could score. It wasn't unusual for teams to do that; if someone was on hatty watch, the opposing team would be wise to guard the hell out of him because odds were, his teammates were going to try to help him get that coveted third goal.

But Hunter Michaud, the generational talent and star player who could've focused on his own stats and just scoring for the team... had made sure I got my third goal.

I wished he wasn't like that. I wished he was a selfish player who racked up countless goals but few assists. I wished he and I didn't play this well together. I hated how much I loved playing alongside him. How easily we jelled. How playing with Hunter Michaud was just as incredible and rewarding as I'd imagined it would be back in the day.

I hated it because it was what might have been, but also because it felt like I was betraying myself.

And it meant I couldn't justify suggesting to the coaches that maybe I'd work better on a different line. They'd laugh me out of the locker room if I suggested breaking up Pittsburgh's current top scoring line. As it was, they were probably all praying to several gods and performing sacrifices so that Hunter, Dima, and I didn't get hurt.

I didn't want any of us to get hurt. Truth be told, I didn't want our line broken up either. I *liked* the hockey player I was when I was playing hockey with Hunter Michaud.

But that fucked with my head, too. It hurt. It brought things to the surface I wanted to forget. Things I'd almost succeeded in moving past, right up until he'd signed with my team.

And there wasn't a soul in the world I could tell.

There were teams I didn't like playing against for various reasons. Seattle was exceptionally good at drawing bullshit penalties. I was pretty sure Houston had dirt on every ref in the League, because those fuckers almost never took penalties even when they richly deserved it. Ottawa was... I just hated playing against Ottawa. I couldn't even put my finger on why.

But there was only one team I truly dreaded, especially when we played on their ice.

Toronto.

God, I hated this place.

That wasn't true. I liked the city. For the handful of years I'd lived here, it had been home. I'd thought it would stay that way. The people were great. I loved the fans. The winters—well, I'd already been living in Canada for a number of years by the time I'd come here, so they weren't much of a shock. I'd made friends. I'd settled in. I liked it.

But the Toronto Shamrocks locker room had been hell.

I'd been more or less okay with my older teammates being dicks to me. I'd been the new guy, the barely nineteen-year-old kid skating in on a ninth overall draft pick, with analysts and team staff alike acting like I was the team's new Messiah. With me on their roster, their rebuild was complete. They could be an actual Cup contender now instead of a League punchline.

Except they hadn't rebuilt at all. They'd just waited for someone with enough talent to singlehandedly elevate the team.

That had, everyone had convinced themselves, been me. And they weren't going to build the team around me. No, I was going to take it from there and pull them all to the top while they continued doing what they'd been doing.

Not much different from what they'd done to Hunter, honestly. I wondered how it was for him, coming back to this place. I wouldn't have even blamed him if he suddenly "came down with something" or had some old injury flare up that he "needed to rest." If I'd had more of a spine the first time I'd come back here in another sweater, I would've done that, and the fans hadn't hated me *nearly* as much as they hated him.

Even now, I was tempted. I could ignore the fans well enough, and I could tune out the venomous chirping from my former teammates. The few who were still playing for Toronto, anyway.

What I couldn't cope with was Coach Robertson.

I hated even being near Toronto's bench. The Plexiglas divider between theirs and ours wasn't enough to muffle that voice. And whenever I skated near their bench and he shouted something at one of his players, my heart would skip and my stomach would somersault. When he got pissed and screamed at the refs over a bullshit call, my skin would crawl beneath my gear and I'd pray like hell the officials would eject him.

They never did.

I mean, he'd been ejected more times than any other active coach in the League—just never while the Shamrocks were playing whatever team I was on at a given time.

God, I hated him. Every damn season, I hoped he'd get fired for something. Or maybe retire. Go be a commentator —at least then I could mute the TV so I wouldn't have to hear that voice.

Or, as one of his ex-wives had suggested in an interview, he could just walk into the ocean and never come back.

Not much I could do about him, and I'd have to be in the same building as him tomorrow. For now, I busied myself settling into the room just to give myself something to do. Even that didn't help much; we always stayed in the same hotel when we came to town, too. The Hornets, but also my previous teams. Everything about this place—the view, the lobby, the aesthetics, the smell—put me on edge, because it meant we were *here*. In *this* city.

Near *that* coach.

I abandoned my open suitcase and paced the room beside the king-size bed, rubbing the back of my neck as I did. I hated it here. Fucking hated it. There'd been a time when I'd hoped I'd be a Toronto Shamrock for my entire career, but that had ended *long* ago. Now I was grateful any time our team's charter jet got the fuck out of here. A few seasons ago, I'd been day-to-day with an injury; I'd still come to Toronto with the team and still joined them for the morning skate, but I'd been a gametime decision, and they'd decided to keep me scratched. I didn't think I'd ever been more grateful to take my ass up to the press box. Sure, I still hadn't wanted to be there at all, and I'd still seen his face on the Jumbotron from time to time, but at least I hadn't been able to hear him.

Because even now, all these years later, I could still hear that voice, and not from far away. Not from the safety of the opposing team's bench.

"Did we waste a first round pick on you, Badura?" he hissed, standing way too close to me. *"Do you know how much we traded to get that pick? Huh? Do you understand how much this club is investing in you and counting on you?"*

Back pressed against his office door, I nodded, and my own young, shaky voice echoed in my ears: *"I know. I know. I'm sorry. I'm trying. I—"*

"I'm sorry, I'm trying," he mocked, then flailed his arms just inches from my face.

I flinched as if I thought he might put hands on me. He hadn't yet, but there was always a first time, and I was always terrified *this* would be it.

Coach Robertson pushed out a harsh breath through his flaring nostrils. *"Do you want us to trade you? Admit to the whole League we made a fucking mistake? Maybe put your worthless ass on waivers so you can be someone else's problem?"* He laughed humorlessly, making me shrink back even more. *"As if anyone would claim you now that you've proven how utterly overrated you were.*" He stabbed a finger at my chest. "*You want to go down to the minors? Is that it? Go from ninth overall to sucking your thumb on the farm team because you can't hack it above juniors? Is that it?*"

"No," I gritted out. I wanted to insist I wasn't overrated. That I was *one* player—one barely out of major juniors—and I couldn't be expected to carry an entire team of experienced professionals. Especially not when those experienced professionals either resented me for what all the analysts said about me, or were bound and determined to put me in my place and show me that I was nothing more than a stupid child who was in way, way over his head.

"*Kid, this is how it's gonna be.*" Coach Robertson faced me, and even though I was taller, it still felt like he was glaring down at me. "*Turn it around this season. Do what we brought you here to do, or you're done. You will never see another League paycheck again. Am I fucking clear?*"

Stomach roiling, I nodded. What else could I do? "*Yeah, Coach.*"

"*I mean it,*" he snarled. "*We miss the playoffs?*" He laughed and clapped my shoulder hard enough to throw off my balance. "*You better be packed and ready to go to whatever team will take you.*" Narrowing his eyes, he added, "*Good thing you're already fluent in Russian, eh?*"

I gritted my teeth. No, I didn't speak Russian—not much, anyway—but that wasn't what had me ready to break. It was the underlying threat. He'd "jokingly" dangled it over my head from day one—mentioning how a Russian locker room probably wouldn't be so welcoming to an openly queer kid. It wasn't like he or the GM had the power to send me to another League, but the threat still hit the nerves he was looking for.

And besides, I'd come to North America because I

wanted to play *here*. This was my dream. Not the Russian League. Not the other European Leagues. I wanted to be *here*, and I was not going to be chased out by a man who wanted me to perform actual miracles for a team that didn't want me.

I didn't know how I was going to do it, but in that moment, I'd vowed I was staying in North America. Because fuck him.

In the present, I sank onto the end of the bed and kneaded my neck, wondering when I'd started sweating. I fucking hated that asshole. Just like I did every time I stayed in this hotel, I reminded myself that it was only temporary. I was just here for a game, and then I'd move on with my team. With the teammates and coaching staff who liked and respected me.

No matter how much it sometimes felt like it, Coach Robertson *hadn't* succeeded in destroying my career.

And I should've felt a surge of triumph every time I skated out onto the ice, still wearing a sweater for a team in this League. Still holding on to the career he'd threatened to ruin so many times.

But I didn't. Yeah, I'd held on to my place in the League, but at what cost?

I sighed and chafed my arms as the memories crawled over me. Sometimes, even now while my life was pretty good, I wondered if I should've just let him fuck me over. If playing in Russia or Sweden or Czechia would've really been that bad. A blow to my pride, yes. But maybe I'd sleep better.

Maybe I wouldn't have lost so much time

Maybe I'd still have everything I'd lost.

Because sometimes I wondered if while Robertson

hadn't succeeded in destroying my career, he'd destroyed parts of me and my life that I would never get back.

Was it worth it? I'd asked myself millions of times over the past several years. *Was it really?*

To this day, as I sat here a Toronto hotel, I still didn't have an answer.

CHAPTER 12

HUNTER

It was weird to be back in Toronto. Uncomfortable as hell, too. Just flying in late last night had had my stomach tied up in knots; the familiar skyline wasn't as welcoming as it had been for seven years.

Now I was alone in the hotel bar. Most of my teammates had left in search of dinner—and I'd given a few recommendations for some excellent restaurants in town—but I hadn't joined them. I had other plans for this evening.

As I waited for my ride, I thumbed through emails and texts, resolutely ignoring the view outside. Too much familiarity. Too much of my past colliding with my present. And I was irrationally—maybe?—afraid someone might recognize me and give me a piece of their mind. I was well aware of all the stereotypes about us Canadians being polite and friendly to a fault, but we took this sport very seriously and a lot of people in this city had taken my departure *very* personally.

The thing was, the fans were amazing. Always had been. This town loved hockey, and they loved their hockey team. But the instant I'd signed with Pittsburgh, they'd turned on me.

Truth be told, I couldn't even blame them. My former team's front office had fed most of the hostility. The customary response to a departing player was to wish them the best even when they didn't leave on good terms. Animosity was to remain behind closed doors.

Coach Robertson, along with Wilcox, the GM, hadn't kept *anything* behind closed doors. Phrases like "pulling the rug out from under us" and "turning his back on a team and city who adored him" and "paycheck over people" were made into sound bites and played ad nauseum. I left "without warning," "rejected Toronto's more than generous offer" and "didn't even give us a chance to counteroffer when Pittsburgh put in their bid." They told fans point blank that I didn't give a damn about them and "would rather take the easy road with a team that's already built instead of putting in the work to create something here."

Small wonder Toronto collectively hated me. The version of me my old club had painted of me? I'd have hated him too.

Exhaling, I put down my phone and rubbed my fore-head. Tomorrow night's game was going to be surreal, and not just because I'd be in the visitors' locker room for the first time. It would be like sitting down at an ex's table for Christmas dinner or something—surrounded by people who weren't thrilled to have you back, but everyone would grit their teeth and be polite until it was time to leave.

Well, that was how it would probably be with my old teammates. The fans... yeah, I'd see how polite they were. Wasn't like I hadn't noticed all those videos of fans burn-ing, shredding, or otherwise destroying their Michaud jerseys. I suspected there'd be booing tomorrow night.

Signs. Maybe even an object or two tossed onto the ice if someone didn't mind getting banned from the arena. From the way fans had responded to me "abandoning" them, it wouldn't have surprised me if at least one or two thought a lifetime ban would be worth it to throw something at me.

Sighing, I stared down at my dormant phone, which was faceup on the table beside my empty glass. Yeah, fans hadn't been happy, that was for sure. I'd been sent dozens of photos of crying kids in Michaud jerseys, grown adults burning my sweater and photos, and there were countless memes at my expense.

I was just musing about whether the guy who'd jammed his lawnmower with my jersey had ever managed to get it fixed when my phone lit up.

Outside.

Grabbing my phone, I got up and nodded at the bartender. I'd already closed my tab, so I headed outside. One lane over from the valet lane, a familiar silver Land Rover idled. I pulled open the door and slid into the passenger seat.

"Hey, man." Potts—Casey Potter to the rest of the hockey world—offered me a fist bump, then quickly pulled away from the hotel. Probably a good idea. Fans sometimes hung out where visiting teams stayed, and I doubted he wanted to be seen driving off with Toronto's public enemy number one.

"How've you been?" I asked as I put on my seat belt.

"Good." He glanced at me. "You? How's Pittsburgh treating you?" There was a subtle crease between his eyebrows, as if he wasn't just making small talk but genuinely asking how the city was treating me.

I pressed my elbow under the window and shrugged.

"Pretty good. They're happy with the season so far, and every fan I've met seems excited. So... yeah. Good."

Potts smiled. "That's great. They're lucky to have you. And"—he whistled—"you're *killing* it out there with Meknikov and Badura! Especially Badura. Goddamn."

I laughed quietly, not wanting to get into the bizarre office dynamic I had with my left winger. "He's a hell of a player. I'm still trying to figure out how he five-holed Balabanov the other night. I've watched the replay like six times, and I just..." I shook my head. "It was an incredible shot."

"Damn," Potts said with a laugh. "I might have to watch that one later. I don't know why anyone bothers trying to get one through Balabanov's five. It's impossible."

"Except for Badura."

"Except for Badura," he grudgingly acknowledged.

We caught up and shot the shit about games and players as he drove us out to Leaside where our buddy Gonzo lived. To my surprise, though, Potts didn't park on the street or in the driveway. Instead, Gonzo's Mercedes GLC was outside, and Potts pulled into the empty bay of the open garage.

I cocked a brow as the door came down behind us. "You win a bet and take over his garage or something?"

Potts laughed uncomfortably. "Not... Not really. But Taylor and Wex live out here."

It took a second for the wires to connect. When they did, my shoulders dipped. "You guys don't want them to see me here."

He grimaced. "Sorry, man. It's nothing personal. I mean, it's—"

"Nah, I get it." I shook my head and clapped his arm. "I don't blame you. Just... didn't realize they'd be quite so heated about things."

Another grimace. He started to speak, but right then,

the door opened, and Gonzo's kids came thundering in with their dad on their heels.

Despite the cannonball in my stomach, I smiled and got out. "Hey, guys!" I crouched to let the three tackle hug me. "Wow, you're all getting so big!" They really were. The oldest was six, the other two four, and I'd joked during my last season that every time I turned around, they'd each gained an inch. This time that wasn't such an exaggeration.

Man, I missed these kids. I missed a lot of the families here in Toronto. I'd kept in touch with some of my team-mates, but this was my first time moving teams, and I hadn't thought about how much I'd miss the people I was used to seeing all the time.

After the kids were duly greeted, their dad gently instructed them to go inside and wash up for dinner. They took off, and Gonzo faced me.

"Hey, Mish." He offered a hug, which I accepted. "It's been too long."

"Yeah, it has." I slapped his back. Agapito Gonzalez and I had played in juniors together, and I'd been thrilled when he'd been traded to Toronto during our second year as pros. He'd been one of the toughest to leave behind.

I went inside with the guys, and I said hello to his wife, Liezel. Then Potts and I took seats at the island in the kitchen, and we all chatted and caught up while Gonzo and Liezel went about cooking what promised to be a huge meal. My mouth watered—these two had introduced me to Filipino cooking, and that was yet another thing I'd been missing since I'd left. I could live on nothing but Liezel's lumpia for the rest of my life and die a happy man.

That cannonball got even colder. I'd been so focused on settling into Pittsburgh and finding my groove with my new team, I hadn't spent a lot of time thinking about everyone and everything I'd left behind. I'd been aware of it, and I'd been sad about it, but it hadn't hit me like it did right now.

Leaving Toronto had been necessary. My sanity had depended on it.

But it had definitely come at a cost.

───────

After an amazing dinner, Liezel herded the kids upstairs for their baths and bedtime. Gonzo handled bedtime whenever he was in town and didn't have a game, but for tonight, Liezel took over. He was scrupulous about spending as much time as possible with his kids, not to mention sharing the load with his wife, so I suspected they'd made a deal for this evening.

Which was why I didn't feel too bad trooping down to the rec room with him and Potts to chill for a while.

We dropped into the recliners in front of Gonzo's giant TV, and he picked up the remote. During the regular season, there was pretty much always at least one hockey game on a given night. Tonight, we tuned in just in time to catch puck drop in the Seattle-Anaheim game, and it turned out both teams were... not having a good night. Seattle was a solid contender for a top three spot in the Pacific division, and Anaheim was holding strong in the wild card, so it wasn't like either team was struggling this season. But every team had bad games, even during their most spectacular seasons, and this was a bad game for *both* of them.

So, the three of us spent the next couple of hours doing what we did best off the ice—playing armchair coaches and GMs.

"What the fuck is he doing?" I scoffed after one of

Anaheim's defensemen turned over the puck for like the eighty-seventh time. "Which team does he play for?"

A few minutes later, Potts scoffed and rolled his eyes after Seattle's goalie let in a soft, *soft* goal. "Trade him. Gone. Done. Launch him into the sun."

"Oh come on!" Gonzo threw up his hands. "How is that *not* a double minor? Does the ref think he just spontaneously got a nosebleed?"

"Totally," I said with a shrug. "He started bleeding, then took a high stick to the face."

Potts nodded sagely. "Happens all the time."

"Absolutely," Gonzo muttered. "All the fucking time."

Between both teams sucking balls and the refs doing what refs did (which is to say, ignoring the egregious offenses and calling the bullshit soft penalties), it was a shitshow from start to finish. They ended up tied five-five. Overtime should've been brief after a Seattle player foolishly slashed someone—a penalty in OT is almost a guarantee that you're fucked. But since Anaheim couldn't make heads or tails of hockey tonight either, they not only couldn't convert, they took a penalty themselves, which Seattle in turn couldn't convert.

"Well, this should be interesting," Potts mused after the buzzer sounded. "A shootout between two goalies having an off night and shooters who can't control the puck."

He wasn't wrong. No one scored until the fifth shooter from Seattle, and the disaster was finally over.

"Jesus Christ." Gonzo sat back, shaking his head as he brought up his drink. "Coach would have us all sent down to the farm team after a game like that."

"Right?" Potts muttered. "Or traded and banished from Toronto for life."

The last part of his comment gave me pause. Gonzo, too. Potts caught on a second later, and he winced.

"Sorry, man." He nudged my leg with his foot. "You know that's not what—"

"I know. I know." It wasn't like I'd been traded. Quite the opposite. But still, if Coach Robertson had anything to say about it, I probably *would* be banished from Toronto for life, if not from Canada.

Gonzo and Potts exchanged uneasy glances, and I had to fight back a sigh. So much for the chill vibe with my former teammates.

It was Gonzo who spoke. "Listen, man." He put his empty glass aside and sat back, studying me with worried eyes. "We gotta be straight with you. Tomorrow night—it's gonna be rough."

I swallowed. "Yeah. I know." Scratching the back of my neck, I let go of that sigh. "The fans fucking hate me."

"It's, um..." Potts cleared his throat. "It's not just the fans."

"I figured as much." I motioned in the general direction of Gonzo's garage. "If you guys don't want the boys seeing me here."

"It's not that we don't want to be seen with you." Gonzo spoke slowly, as if he were carefully choosing his words. "If they've got a problem with us still being friends, they can get fucked."

I watched him, a chill working its way down my back.

Potts and Gonzo looked at each other again.

Potts faced me. "It might be nothing. Honestly. Guys can..." He laughed dryly. "Guys can talk a big game, you know?"

That chill turned even colder. "Okay, what kind of game are they talking?"

They exchanged another glance. Exhaling, Potts ran a hand through his dark hair. "I can't give you any specifics. I don't know any."

"Neither do I," Gonzo said solemnly.

"But the guys..." Potts shook his head, looking exhausted. "They took it hard, you know? You leaving without warning?"

Chewing my lip, I nodded. "I wanted to tell them. But..."

"But you couldn't until something was finalized," Gonzo said.

"Yeah." They both knew. They'd been the only two who'd known anything was in the works. At the time, there'd been no guarantee someone would sign me. My agent and I had been optimistic—a dozen teams had started courting me during my last season before free agency—but nothing was ever done until the last dotted line was signed. My worst fear had been all those possible deals falling through, at which time I'd have to return to the locker room full of men who knew I'd been trying my level best to bail on them.

I studied my two friends. "So, what? Are they planning on taking it out on me on the ice?"

From the way they both avoided my gaze, I wasn't far off the mark.

My stomach curdled, and I sat back with a whispered, "Fuck." They wouldn't do anything egregious. No one was going to drop gloves and beat the shit out of me. But hockey players had ways of letting each other know that something wasn't cool. Like if a ref let a penalty slide—another player would happily make sure the offender knew in no uncertain terms that he'd fucked up.

I hadn't crashed a goal or slashed someone. I hadn't

high-sticked the rookie or speared the captain. But in their minds, I was due some on-ice retribution. It didn't matter that trades and free agency were a thing. Every player understood that, and we regularly hung out with former teammates the way I was hanging out with Potts and Gonzo tonight. But when someone left like I had—bailing by choice on a team that had been counting on him—people took it personally.

And when hockey players took things personally—well, good thing we wore a lot of protective gear.

Plus, the fans would eat it all up. My ears already rang with the preemptive roar of thousands of fans getting drunk on tomorrow night's schadenfreude.

"Well." I laughed nervously. "This is gonna suck."

Potts and Gonzo both grimaced.

And neither disagreed.

Fuck my life.

CHAPTER 13

JAREK

Hunter was in a weird mood on game day in Toronto.

He hadn't joined us at the bar last night, and someone had said he was hanging out with some local friends. Made sense. I did the same whenever I was back in Denver or Edmonton, and I hadn't been in either of those cities as long as he'd been in Toronto.

This morning, though, he was someplace else. Physically here, suiting up for our morning skate, but on another planet. Rattled, maybe.

Great. That would help us win tonight.

Not that I could blame him. Coming back to Toronto for the first time had been weird for me, too; I could only imagine how much worse it would've been if they'd hated me like they did Hunter.

The best thing he could do was focus on hockey, not on anything else. Easier said than done, of course, but it was better than letting them into his head.

Fortunately, in the short time we'd been playing together, I'd learned what could hold his focus more than other things. One hushed conversation with the faceoff coach and our captain, not to mention a promise to buy them beers later, and Hunter and Mayweather were on either side of a faceoff dot. Our third and fourth line centers joined them, and even after the rest of us had finished cooling down and were heading for the locker room, the centers were still working on faceoffs.

I was already back from my shower when they came into the locker room, chirping and laughing.

"I did not cheat," Mayweather was insisting. "Not my fault you're too slow."

"Yeah, so how about we video it next time?" Hunter said over his shoulder. "Let's see what the camera says."

"Eat a dick, Mish," Mayweather muttered. "Just because you'll never be as fast on the dot as I am, you're—"

"Bet your wife wishes you were that fast on the dot," Carlson, the third line center, snarked from behind Hunter.

Hunter barked a laugh, Mayweather shot Carlson a glare. The kid put up his hands and feigned innocence, not the least bit intimidated by our captain, who rolled his eyes, shook his head, and headed for his locker, chuckling to himself.

Everyone continued getting out of their gear, heading in and out of the showers, and meandering out to find food. I dragged my feet a little so I could try to get a bead on Hunter.

Whatever distraction that extra faceoff practice had offered, it hadn't lasted long. By the time he came back from the showers and was pulling on a set of team sweats, he was as distant as he'd been all morning.

Shit. That didn't bode well for tonight.

I wasn't the only one who'd noticed, either.

"Hey. Mish." Dima nudged him. "You still here?"

Hunter laughed uneasily. "Yeah. I'm... Yeah, I'm here." He shook himself. "Sorry. Just, uh..." He hesitated, as if scrambling for an answer. "Weird to be back here, you know?" His laugh sounded even more forced. "First time I've set foot in this building since before I signed with Pittsburgh."

Okay, I could buy that. I could relate, too, and my tenure in Toronto had been shorter than his.

Still, I was sure there was more to it.

"Is that all it is?" I asked. "Just... being back here?"

Hunter winced, though he tried to hide it by turning toward his locker and moving some gear around. As he faced us again, he shrugged but didn't meet either of our gazes. "I didn't leave here on the greatest of terms, you know?"

"It's hockey." Dima waved a dismissive hand. "Players come and go."

"They do," Hunter said with a faint grimace. "But people have been pretty pissed about me leaving. And I, uh, don't just mean the fans."

I studied him, trying to read between the lines.

Hunter gnawed his lip and shifted his weight. Then he pushed out a breath. "Listen. I'm not asking anyone to protect me out there tonight." He glanced back and forth between me and Dima. "I can take whatever they dish out. Just... It's going to be a rough one. I can almost guarantee it. So... you guys be careful."

Dima and I exchanged puzzled looks.

Hunter went on, "Let's just say I have it on pretty good authority that my old team still isn't happy about me leaving, and I wouldn't put it past anyone to take that out on one of you. Anyone on the team, really, but *especially* my linemates."

The warning didn't chill my blood, but the fear in his eyes did. I couldn't imagine his old teammates would actually do something to hurt him or any of us, but he knew these guys better than I had. Better than anyone in our locker room.

"What the fuck do you think they're going to do?" I asked. "Cut the brake lines on the bus?"

That got an actual laugh out of him, even if it was a bit halfhearted. "Nah. But you know how it is when players let their emotions run hot and they lose control." He gave a tight half-shrug. "Bad shit can happen. I just don't want any of you getting fucked up because my old locker room has a vendetta against me."

"They can try." Dima clapped Hunter's shoulder. "They'll wish they hadn't."

Hunter laughed. "Just don't get yourself fucked up out there, eh? I really don't want Chloé to be mad at me when her man's got a black eye or something."

I snorted. "Wouldn't be the first time." Smacking Dima's arm, I added, "And hey, at least it would be for a good reason this time."

That earned me a huff of annoyance and some cursing from Dima, but also an odd look from Hunter. One I couldn't quite parse and really didn't want to think too much about.

I cleared my throat. "We'll be careful out there tonight. But if they know what's good for them, they won't fuck with one of us." I gestured around the room.

Hunter actually smiled, and I refused to read into the weird warm feeling that ignited in my chest. Or the surge of protectiveness.

Go ahead and fuck with him, some part of me wanted to tell Toronto. *I fucking dare you.*

Yeah, we didn't need any of that. Not my weird mix of feelings about Hunter, and definitely not anyone fighting, getting suspended, or getting hurt in Toronto.

But Dima and I would absolutely have our teammate's back tonight.

Hunter was right about one thing—Toronto fucking *hated* him.

A lot of fans booed when the opposing team came out for warmups. It was just one of those things we learned to ignore.

But when Hunter stepped out onto the ice tonight, the arena *shook* with boos. The glass wobbled with pounding fists. Angry faces and obnoxious signs, all directed at Hunter, ringed our end of the ice.

There was usually a crowd of away team fans at any game, especially when we weren't far from home, and they'd gather by the ice during warmups to show support. If there were any black and gold jerseys here now, they were swallowed up in a sea of orange and green. There were probably Pittsburgh fans in the building—Toronto was only like a five-hour drive away—but they were nowhere near the glass tonight.

Hunter kept his head up enough to skate and shoot properly, but he pointedly didn't look at the glass or the fans beyond it. When he stopped by the boards to stretch, he ignored the people banging so hard on the glass that it flexed above him. The ushers even stepped in and told them to knock it off, but that didn't last long.

"Gavno," Dima muttered to me as we set up for line rushes. "He wasn't joking about them hating him."

"No, he wasn't." I glanced at the other end of the sheet, catching a glimpse of some players shooting daggers out their eyes at someone on our side. As if I had to guess who. I met Dima's gaze. "The fans are just noise. The Shamrocks..."

Dima scowled and nodded.

We didn't have time to keep talking—line rushes were getting started. Of course, when our line took our turn, there was more booing, and I was almost certain that random puck that went sailing between Hunter's skates hadn't come from a Pittsburgh player.

This game was going to be interesting, that was for sure.

After the puck dropped, both teams were off and running. No slow starts for either side—this was a division game, and we were in the most competitive division in the League. Every point was critical.

Whenever my line was on the ice, Toronto cranked up the heat. The crowd would boo furiously every time Hunter had the puck, and the checks on all of us were harder and more frequent. They were so focused on ramming us into the boards and taking potshots at Hunter, they seemed to forget what they were *supposed* to be doing.

Toronto iced the puck—again—which meant another faceoff in their zone. On the way to the dot with our second defensive pair, Hunter, Dima, and I exchanged glances and gestures with each other and the defensemen. A set play off the faceoff.

The centers set up for the faceoff. Hunter's eyes locked on the puck in the ref's hand, but the other center—Daniels —said something to him. Something snide, if his expression and the snarl of his lips were any indication. Hunter didn't react.

The ref, however, straightened up, and he booted the other guy out of the circle.

"What the hell?" Daniels put up his gloved hands. "What did I—"

"Out, unless you want to go to the box for unsportsman-like conduct." The ref gestured again for him to switch with one of the other forwards. I couldn't hear what else was said —not over the fresh thunder of boos rattling the ice beneath my skates. Hunter watched the interplay, his expression neutral except for the way he was playing with his mouth-guard. The movements of his jaw spoke of barely contained irritation.

Keep it together, Michaud, I silently begged. His old team (not to mention the fans) wanted under his skin so they could take advantage, and I just hoped he wouldn't take the bait. So far, he'd been solid despite his obvious nerves about facing his pissed-off ex-teammates.

Right then and there, I decided we were winning this game. Full stop. In regulation. Then Hunter could have the last laugh on people who treated him like shit.

The issue was finally settled between the ref and the center, and the left winger replaced the center at the dot. The faceoff was a brief battle, but Hunter won, and he passed the puck to Ferns, who passed it to me. I faked like I was about to pass to Hunter, then sent it along the boards to Dima, who was waiting, completely unprotected, by the other circle. No one in a Toronto sweater—least of all the netminder—was ready for his shot, and the puck sailed over the goalie's shoulder.

The crowd was *not* pleased. Neither were Toronto's players.

Fuck 'em. Maybe if they focused more on hockey and less on Hunter, they wouldn't get scored on.

Our shift ended after that, and as we caught our breath on the bench, Hunter muttered, "Does it count as a hostile work environment if I'm not on the team anymore?"

I laughed. "If we keep playing the way we are, they'll be bitching about the score during intermission instead of you."

He turned to me, eyebrows up. "I like that idea."

Grinning, I held up my gloved hand. "Let's do it."

He returned the grin as he bumped my fist.

We watched while we waited for our next shift. A pair of bullshit icing calls kept our top line out for almost two minutes, and they couldn't get the puck out of our end or themselves off the ice. Ferns managed to force one of their guys over the blue line and into the neutral zone, and the Toronto player stupidly tried to go back across the line while his teammates were still in our zone. Offside. A much-needed whistle and a line change.

Hunter narrowly lost the faceoff, but Ferns wrestled the puck away from their center. He passed it to Hunter, but another Toronto player got in the way. Hunter battled it out with him against the boards, eventually getting the puck free and sending it to Dima, who made a run for the offensive zone.

Hunter and I both sprinted after him in a three-on-two rush. Dima was headed off before he could take a shot, but he sent the puck around the boards to Hunter. Hunter had to race for it, and he leaned forward to get some more reach with his stick. It worked. He *just* managed to get his stick on the puck, gain control, and pass it—

Before another defenseman came out of nowhere and *slammed* him headfirst into the boards from behind.

Hunter didn't just go down—he crumpled.

And my temper snapped.

I had no idea where the puck had gone or what any of my teammates were doing, only that Hunter was down, that defenseman was grinning, and there hadn't been a whistle.

The defenseman saw me coming, and he grinned as I threw off my gloves. He dropped his, too, and in a flash, the fists were flying. He caught me a few times, but I grabbed a handful of his jersey landed a solid punch to his jaw. One that drove a grunt out of him that even the crowd's blood-thirsty roar couldn't drown out.

I followed that hit with more, and we tumbled to the ice in a pile of flailing limbs and half-removed jerseys, and someone was grabbing at me, trying to pull me off. Fuck that. I yanked my arm free and threw my fist into the asshole's face. There was blood on his nose and mouth. *Good.*

Someone got a solid grip on me and hauled me off him. I rose on shaking legs, barely able to stand on my skates as fury and adrenaline vibrated through my body. There was blood on my face, running hot from my nose and down my chin. My white away jersey looked like a crime scene.

Whatever. It was worth it.

A linesman had me by the arm, and he guided me toward the penalty box as I spat blood and curses at the defenseman, who was being led to the other box. Once the Plexiglas doors had been shut on our cages, I grabbed a towel and started mopping up my face. He kept screaming at me through the glass.

But I forgot all about him.

Because Hunter was still down.

My heart went into my throat. One of the trainers was beside him. Dima and Sawyer were standing over them while the linesmen broke up another fight.

Hunter was moving, at least. Not quickly, and with that restless and miserable writhe of someone who *wished* he was unconscious. Hurting but moving. His hands. His skates. Every time he flexed and straightened a leg, dragging his skate boot an inch or two across the ice, cool relief ran through me. He could still move his limbs. He might've been concussed and miserable, but I'd seen someone get boarded in juniors and sustain a serious neck injury. One he recovered from, though it had been scary there for a while. After a hit like the one Hunter had taken, movement of limbs ruled out a lot of worst-case scenarios.

At some point, the second fight had been broken up, and Ferns joined me in the box while another player joined my still shouting opponent in the other.

The arena was unnervingly silent. Didn't matter how much the fans hated Hunter for leaving—no one wanted anyone to *actually* get hurt. A little blood here and there, maybe a black eye? Fine. A tooth or three on the ice? Cool. Fans loved fights, not to mention nights when we all joked it was prison rules because the refs were letting everything slide.

But sometimes people got hurt for real, and no one enjoyed that.

And Hunter was *still* down.

One official hovered over him before breaking away to join the other three. As someone stepped out onto the ice with a cervical collar in hand, the officials conferred at center ice with the captains from both teams. There were grim looks and nods in between glances toward Hunter. The EMTs who were now joining the trainer at Hunter's side would make the decision about him, but the captains and officials had to deal with me and the asshole I'd roughed up, plus Ferns and the other guy.

As everyone waited for something to happen, Hunter's pregame words echoed in my ringing ears.

"Listen," he'd said. *"I'm not asking anyone to protect me out there. I can take whatever they dish out. Just... it's going to be a rough one."*

Now he was down after a dirty hit.

Christ, had they threatened him? Or did he just know his teammates well enough to expect that kind of attack?

Maybe getting traded out of Toronto after they drafted him wasn't such a bad thing.

I shuddered.

A linesman came up to the door. To Ferns, he sharply said, "You sit there and wait until we decide what to do with you." No shock there. Turning to me, he jerked his thumb over his shoulder. *"You're* done."

I nodded and didn't argue. I'd expected as much. A match penalty, too, if I had to guess. A hearing. A fine. Maybe a suspension.

With my teammate—my *linemate,* damn it—still flat on the ice, surrounded by medical staff, I'd take everything they gave me.

I was just glad I'd had the chance to beat the fuck out of that defenseman. I hoped like hell he'd be getting ejected, suspended, and fined for boarding Hunter, but if nothing else, I'd let him know that his bullshit did not fly with the Pittsburgh Hornets.

Fuck you, asshole.

Still jittery with adrenaline, I left the box and glided across the ice toward the bench. My teammates tapped their sticks against the boards and called out encouragement, which was swallowed up by the wave of boos. Then the booing intensified, and I looked back to see the man I'd roughed up coming out of the box, too. Then the crowd started chanting, a mix of "Evans sucks" and "fuck you, Evans."

The broadcasters must've been apoplectic by now, scrambling to mask the profanity.

I was fine with it. Fans were more pissed at their own player than they were me. Good. They could hate Hunter to hell and back, but there were lines. I wasn't at all surprised this crowd didn't tolerate their players pulling shit like that.

As I crossed the ice, I watched the trainers and EMTs with Hunter, hoping for some kind of sign that he was all right. Maybe just stunned? Wind knocked out of him?

Or not, I realized with a sinking feeling as someone with a backboard carefully jogged ahead of another EMT pushing a stretcher.

Fuck. That wasn't good.

I stepped through the door from the ice to the bench, and paused. To Dima, I asked, "Is he okay?"

Dima turned a worried look on me. "Don't know. He's awake, but someone said his neck hurts."

Sakra. Not good.

Someone barked at me to get off the ice, and I didn't argue. Legs still shaking and heart still pounding, I retreated to the visitors' locker room and started stripping off my bloody sweater and the rest of my gear. I was trembling all over from adrenaline. Sick with horror, worry, anger, fear. I barely felt the throbbing in my face. I was vaguely aware that my knee was sore; even with pads on, it still didn't feel great to hit the ice. All that was distant, though. Hidden beneath a layer of fear and anger.

I was almost down to my base layer when one of the equipment managers, Jackie, came into the locker room to get something.

"Hey," I called out to her. "Any word on Michaud?"

Jackie gestured toward the ice. "They're taking him to the ER just to make sure he didn't injure his neck. Sounds like it's precautionary, though. He's in a ton of pain, but he's lucid with full movement and sensation."

Exhaling, I sat back. "Thanks."

She nodded, picked up a roll of tape, and jogged back out.

Well, that was good. Hunter would be hating life for a while—even the mildest neck injuries were fucking miserable—but it sounded like he wasn't seriously hurt. Being in a lot of pain after that kind of injury was the best-case scenario; another teammate of mine in juniors hadn't been so lucky. He'd regained the ability to walk, but he'd permanently lost some fine motor control.

Nobody in this sport took neck injuries lightly.

Except, apparently, Evans. God help me if I ever met that man somewhere we weren't governed by League rules. I wasn't a violent person by nature, but I didn't buy that he'd accidentally hit Hunter like that. Not after Hunter had been rattled before the game and worried that one of his former teammates might go after him or someone else on our team.

Evans had known *exactly* what he was doing. The thought of how badly he could have hurt Hunter in the process had renewed anger simmering beneath my skin. I ground my teeth, which hurt, so he must've caught me in the jaw at some point. Fine. He was lucky I hadn't grabbed him by the hair and slammed his face into the ice.

You don't. Injure. Another player.

The vehemence of my own thoughts didn't surprise me any more than my reaction on the ice had.

The way I started choking up? That was... weird.

Because that asshole could've paralyzed my teammate. Or worse.

They could've ended his career. Or worse.

That was all it was. I'd have felt this way about any teammate who'd taken such a dirty, dangerous hit.

I supposed it was just weird because everything I felt when it came to Hunter Michaud was weird. I was fiercely protective of him. I'd have done the same for Dima.

But... no. There was something off about my reaction to Hunter. Something I was too rattled and shaky to make sense of. I'd resented his existence and his presence and the effect he'd unknowingly had on my career and my life, but at the same time, I didn't want anything to happen to him. Nothing that could hamper his career or cut it short. Nothing that could fuck up his body or his brain. It was as if the only thing that could possibly make me feel like everything in the past was worth it was if Hunter had the long and full career he deserved, retiring a healthy legend with an armload of Cups and a space in the Hall of Fame.

For him to make it this far and then have it all yanked away from him would be horrible in its own right, but it would also be my fault. Because my career wasn't the only one whose trajectory had been affected by what I'd done back then. Anything that happened to him now was part of the butterfly effect, and it was, at least in part... my fault.

He wouldn't be here if it wasn't for me.

Which meant he wouldn't be on his way to the hospital right now.

He wouldn't be hurt.

His health and his career wouldn't be on the line.

I leaned forward, elbows on my knees, and rubbed my temples. Okay, I was crashing now that the adrenaline was draining away. I was irrational and emotional. Maybe *I* needed to go on concussion protocol.

Or maybe I just needed to get some sleep. Ideally after someone told me, definitively, that Hunter was all right.

Footsteps came up the tunnel. Shoes, not skates. And from the sound of it, the period was still in full swing. It felt like I'd been back here for hours, but maybe not. Though we'd only been like twelve minutes into the game when everything had blown up, and the game had obviously been delayed while they scraped Hunter off the ice. The ice crew had probably needed some time to clean up the blood, too; Evans and I had both been bleeding, and I was pretty sure Ferns had sprung a leak.

I looked up as Leo, one of the athletic trainers, came into the locker room. "All right." He offered me a sympathetic look. "I need to check you out." He cocked a brow. "That eye's going to need some ice."

Yeah, he had a point. Now that I paid attention, my eye was swollen enough I could barely see out of it.

He took me into the one of the rooms off the locker room so we could go through everything in relative privacy. Concussion protocol, of course—all the neurological and cognitive tests to determine if I'd had my bell rung. I wasn't giving any signs of a concussion, thank God. I was a bit woozy, but we both agreed that was part of the comedown from the adrenaline.

"Okay, so your head is good," Leo declared. "How's that hand?"

My hand? What was wrong with my hand?

I looked down, and... oh.

I gingerly bent and straightened my scraped fingers. My knuckles were puffy and raw, and there was a hell of a cut on one of them. Grinning, I held it up for him to see. "Think I knocked his tooth out?"

He huffed a laugh. "Let's hope." He reached into his kit. "But that also means I need to *really* clean out that cut."

I muttered a few choice words. This wasn't the first time I'd cut myself on someone's tooth. I knew the drill. It just fucking *stung*. "Dickhead should've worn his mouthguard," I muttered.

"That's supposed to be for *his* protection, not yours."

"Eh." I waved that away with my uninjured hand.

Leo chuckled and got to work. By the time he'd finished cleaning up my hand—ow—the first intermission was over. I grabbed a shower, carefully keeping the bandage on my hand dry, and dressed, and not long after that, the buzzer sounded again.

A moment later, my teammates filed in. I got a lot of fist bumps (on my uninjured hand, of course) and shoulder slaps from my teammates. Everyone was still fired up about what had happened to Hunter, and several of the guys voiced their determination to win this game no matter what. In regulation, too.

"They don't get *any* points after they did that to one of our boys," Mayweather declared. "No overtime. Not a fucking chance."

"Hear, hear!" Cole said.

"They got three of our players," Dima growled. "They're not getting any points. Fuck them."

"Wait, *three* players?" I sat up. "What did I miss?"

"Eh, Freeman wasn't their fault," Dolls grumbled. "He blocked a puck with the back of his wrist."

I sucked in a breath as I rubbed my own wrist in sympathy. I'd taken pucks there before, too. Not hard enough to do damage, but sakra, it *hurt*. "Is he all right?"

"He's good," Dima said. "Done for tonight, but he's good."

Well, that was encouraging.

Coach did his usual encouraging intermission speech, reiterating Mayweather's declaration that Toronto deserved to lose in spectacular fashion. "No team who plays like this deserves a win. I want them losing in regulation, boys. No points. *None*."

Nods and murmurs of agreement all around.

As everyone continued with their intermission routines, Coach pulled me aside. "Leo says you'll make it. No concussion?"

I shook my head and gestured at my face. "Nah. Looks worse than it is."

"Good, because it looks like hell."

I laughed. "Thanks."

He grunted. "Listen, just a heads up—you're probably looking at a fine and suspension after this. The refs would've left it as a ten-minute major, but after you kept whaling on him after he went down, they're calling it intent-to-injure."

I rolled my eyes. "I suppose they didn't see him still punching at me, too."

Coach shrugged. "It is what it is, kid. Personally?" He nodded sharply. "I'd have done the same thing after what he did to Mish." He squeezed my arm. "You did good out there. Nobody targets a Hornet like that without retribution."

That said a lot coming from him; he didn't like us fighting because it meant injuries and suspensions, both of which could be costly for the team. But he'd been a hockey player at one time too. He knew that there was a time and a place for fighting. I was glad he agreed that tonight in this arena had been one of those time and places. The refs prob-ably agreed—I suspected the match penalty and the likely fine and suspension were just a pound of flesh to appease angry fans and players.

Whatever. After what that son of a bitch did to Hunter? I'd kick his ass again in a heartbeat.

CHAPTER 14

HUNTER

Oh, God. This sucks.

I lay there on the hotel bed for the longest time, eyes closed as I tried not to move. I also tried not to tense up, since that only made the pain worse. The muscle relaxers they'd given me at the ER had helped enough to let me sleep, but they weren't a magic cure-all. The stiffness in my neck and shoulders was back in full force, and I had no idea how much of that I could help by staying still versus moving around. That was the shitty thing about sore muscles—sometimes it was best to keep them still. Sometimes it was best to move them until the stiffness unwound itself.

And boy, if you picked the wrong option...

I indulged in a pathetic groan and reached up to rub my eyes, which my shoulder wasn't thrilled about. Even though it was the *other* shoulder.

Eh. Could've been worse. I'd broken my collarbone in U16. I was pretty sure that was worse. In fact, I had vivid memories of being in horrible pain for ages. Ditto when I broke a couple of ribs my third season as a pro and that time I broke my jaw.

But right now, this seemed like the worst thing ever. Sort of like how a stubbed toe or a foot cramp always feels in the moment like the most terrible pain to occur to anyone ever on earth. Not because it *was* the worst, but because it was happening *right now*.

This was happening right now, and it sucked, and I didn't care if I was pathetic about it.

My phone cheerfully announced an incoming text. I felt around for it, knocking over what sounded like a bottle of pills in the process, and picked it up. None of the muscles in my neck and shoulder appreciated *any* of that, and I had to hold my breath for a moment as the pain ebbed.

Once it had returned to a dull roar, I exhaled. Then I blinked my eyes into focus, held my phone up over my face, and read the text, which came from Pat, the athletic trainer who'd gone with me to the hospital last night.

Breakfast is over at 11. Do you want me to order something to your room?

That was when I realized the time at the top of the screen: 10:32.

What time had we even come back from the ER? I swore the sun had already been up as I'd come shuffling into the lobby with Pat on my heels so I didn't collapse and split my head open or something. That felt like a lifetime ago. But it also kind of felt like I'd just landed in bed.

Either way, I was hungry. And I doubted I was going to get any real restful sleep until my neck stopped hurting. Or at least felt less like a Great White had used me as a chew toy.

It took some work, but I managed to type out, *Room service is good. Can barely move.*

He replied, *Check the menu and LMK what you want.*

He was adorably optimistic about my ability to function

well enough to find the menu, never mind read words and make a decision about them.

But then he must've remembered what a wreck I was, because he added, *There's a western omelet that comes with toast and coffee. Will that work?*

If only because it meant a hell of a lot less effort on my part... yes. It would work. He got back to me and said room service would be there in about half an hour, so I dragged my ass into the bathroom for a shower. The hot water felt good. Better than anything had felt in... In I didn't know how long. Time had stopped making a whole lot of sense at some point last night, and it wasn't in any hurry to get back on track.

After my shower, I checked my phone again and found some more texts. Among others, Gonzo and Potts had both messaged me to see how I was doing.

I'm good, I told them. *Sore, but docs think I'll be back on the ice soon.*

That much I remembered. No amount of drugs or pain could cloud out the part where the doctor had reassured me I hadn't done any serious damage, and that there was nothing to indicate this was any worse than some moderate whiplash and muscle strain. I'd been incredibly lucky, all things considered. The pain had been awful in the moment and it was no picnic now, but my spine and spinal cord were fine, and I'd even managed to escape a concussion, probably from sheer dumb luck. As miserable as I was right now, this was the best-case scenario after a hit like that.

I chatted with them for a few minutes, and then room service arrived. As they were leaving, Pat showed up.

With the food situated on the table by the window, I settled into one of the chairs, wincing all the way, he took the other and watched me. "How are you feeling?"

I answered with a pathetic groan.

Pat chuckled. "Yeah, I bet."

I uncovered the plates, and though my stomach wasn't thrilled about anything, the food looked and smelled surprisingly appetizing. As I cut into the omelet, I said, "Shame I couldn't have gotten fucked up at home. I swear the worst part of injuries on the road is the trip afterward. And it's way more fun to be miserable in your own bed."

"I know it is. But you've got some time before you have to travel—we're not leaving until tomorrow."

Well, that was a relief. "The rest of the team's already gone, I'm sure."

He nodded. "Already in Montreal." He paused. "Well, except for Badura."

I straightened hard enough to instantly regret it. Wincing and rubbing my neck, I gritted out, "What happened to him?"

"He's got a hearing this afternoon, but he'll most likely be suspended."

"Sus—huh? For what?"

Pat grinned. "For beating the ever-loving fuck out of Evans after he boarded you."

I blinked. "I... Wait, are you sure I don't need to be on concussion protocol? Because I swear I just heard you say Jaromir Badura is suspended for beating the hell out of someone on *my* behalf." I chuckled dryly. "Was he pissed that the guy beat him to it or something?"

Pat laughed and shrugged. "You'd have to ask him. But it was a pretty impressive fight! Especially from someone who doesn't throw gloves very often."

That was an understatement. Jarek's mouth could get people fired up, but that usually resulted in the other guy taking a penalty for slashing him or trying to fight him.

Once in a blue moon, he'd throw gloves, but for as prickly and snarly as he could be, this was not a guy who lived up to the stereotype of hockey players who liked to fight all the time. If anyone had answered the bell last night and fought the asshole who'd boarded me, I'd have guessed Sawyer, Ferns, or even Dima, since they were both spicier than Jarek.

"Did he win?" I asked.

Pat chuckled. "He put Evans on the ice, and his face looked a whole lot better after, so... I'd say yes."

I whistled. "Wow. Wonder how long it'll be before Evans hears the end of it." For a notorious shit talker like Evans to lose a fight to Jarek Badura... no, that would not earn him any points from the guys. He'd probably have pictures of Jarek randomly appearing in his locker, his luggage, and his phone for the rest of the season.

Serves you right, dickhole.

"Anyway." Pat got up. "I'll leave you to your breakfast."

"Great. Thanks. When, uh—I assume we're going to back to Pittsburgh at some point." Ugh, even a first class seat sounded miserable right now. "Tomorrow, right? I didn't hallucinate you saying that?"

He laughed. "No, you didn't hallucinate it. We've got a charter to Pittsburgh tomorrow morning. There was availability today, but everyone figured you'd want a day or so to relax before you had to get on a plane."

I could live with that. "Okay. Sure. Sounds great. Just let me know when I need to be ready to roll."

Another nod, and he left the room.

I ate a little bit, but my mind was mostly occupied with what he'd told me about last night. Jarek. Fighting Evans. For boarding me.

Seriously?

I couldn't resist, and I opened one of my social media apps. Big shock—our names were both trending. As was Evans's.

I tapped one at random, and it didn't take long to find a video. The title: *No Joke—Badura makes Evans pay for BOARDING Michaud.*

I kind of hoped the video would start with the fight and skip the part that set it off, but no such luck. I winced and looked away for a second as a commentator said, "Oh! And Evans just checked Michaud into the boards from behind. That's a dangerous hit. Dangerous. Ought to be a penalty, Jim, but—oh, it looks like Badura has taken exception to that!"

I returned my attention to the screen just in time to see Jarek sprinting toward Evans, leaving his stick and gloves in his wake before the two of them came together. Both men were shouting at each other, but there weren't any hot mics nearby. The message was clear enough, though, especially as they came together in a flurry of flying fists. Evans put up a hell of a fight—he was pretty notorious for it—but Jarek, despite being smaller, absolutely *whaled* on him.

In seconds, they were down, Jarek landing on top of Evans and continuing to pummel him until they were dragged apart by officials. Even as he was hauled off Evans, Jarek kept running off his mouth, shouting at Evans as blood trickled from his nose and mouth and stained his jersey.

The video switched to the trainers and now EMTs hovering over me, and the commentators were saying... something. Something about how I was still down, and it had been a scary hit, and gee, guys, you don't fucking say.

The video changed again, this time showing the penalty boxes. Evans was ranting and raving through the divider, but Jarek didn't even seem to notice. He was focused on something outside the box. Even as he dabbed blood off his face and neck, he was fixated on something else.

There was no anger in his expression now, either. None of the fury that had contorted his features during that fight.

He looked...

Was he...

Was that *fear?*

A moment later, the penalty box door opened, and an official gestured for Jarek to come out. He pointed at the bench—quite obviously telling him he was being ejected.

Jarek acknowledged him with a nod but didn't even look at him. Usually, when someone was ejected after something like that, their temper was still flaring and they'd either try to rile up the crowd or they'd fly across the ice before stomping down the tunnel.

Jarek skated toward the bench while his gaze was fixed elsewhere. As the camera zoomed out, I realized...

He was watching me.

I'd still been down at that point, oblivious to anything except how much my neck and shoulder hurt. But there he was, watching me worriedly on his way across the ice.

He stepped through the door and paused by the bench, blood still running down his face, and though I wasn't the greatest at reading lips, his words to Dima were clear as day:

"Is he okay?"

Dima looked just as worried, and he shrugged, saying something I couldn't make out. Jarek glanced my way one more time, then scowled and reluctantly headed down the tunnel.

I paused the video and lowered my phone. Sitting back, I rubbed my neck as I replayed everything I'd just watched.

Yes, things had been less tense between Jarek and me than they'd been during training camp, but he was still hard to read. He still had walls up, and he clearly wasn't comfortable around me. Not even when he was obviously trying to pretend he was. What any of that meant, I had no idea.

And I was even more confused after watching this video. Not just the fight, but his expression afterward. His obvious worry.

What is going on in that head of yours, Badura?

Would it hurt to feel him out a little? At least let him know I appreciated him going to bat for me?

Guess I'd find out.

I picked up my phone, thumbed through my contacts from the team, and hesitated when I reached Jarek's. After three or four false starts, I managed to type out and send: *Looked like a hell of a fight last night.*

I'd just put my phone down and picked up my fork again when my text app pinged.

He deserved it. How is your neck?

I indulged in believing he wasn't just making small talk and that he was actually concerned.

The video flickered through my mind, and my heart jumped.

Maybe he *was* concerned. That, or he'd just been worried because, like me or not, I was his teammate, and I'd been down with a potentially catastrophic injury. Whatever his obviously mixed feelings about me, I didn't imagine even in his surliest moments that he wanted me or anyone else to get hurt for real.

Except maybe Evans. Who he'd beaten the fuck out of. For boarding me.

My mouth had gone dry, and I took a swallow of coffee before I wrote back, *Sore. Could've been worse.*

He started typing right away. *Leo said it wasn't as*

serious as it could've been. Lucky for Evans. He followed that with a knife emoji, and I laughed.

LOL Nah we don't want to lose you for more games. Trust me, he's getting enough shit in the locker room.

I bet he is.

I almost said, *Dude, you have no idea*, but then I remembered Jarek had played for Toronto. Most of the roster had changed since then—seven seasons was a long time—but they still had the same GM and some of the coaches. Including the head coach. Between Jarek's tenure there and mine, the culture hadn't changed much. There was a meaner vibe to the chirping than on other teams, and fuck-ups were not soon forgotten.

Maybe that was the real reason he'd lost his shit on Evans. Maybe it was some longstanding bitterness that had been waiting for an outlet all this time. After all, Evans was one of the few remaining players from Jarek's time in Toronto. So it was possible he'd just flipped out because he'd had it up to here with that jackass, and watching him board a teammate had been enough to set him off.

Which totally explained the bone-deep worry on Jarek's face while Evans had continued talking shit from the other penalty box.

I stared at the texts we'd exchanged.

Why do I feel like the more cards you show, the less I really know about you?

Jarek looked like shit. Could've been a lot worse, given who he'd been fighting, but he'd skated away with a shiner, some bruising on and around his nose, and a wicked bruise on his cheekbone. There was no swelling to indicate he was down any teeth, and he could talk well enough—clearly and without any signs that his mouth hurt or he was concussed. His hand was bandaged and obviously sore. Stitched, maybe? Couldn't tell for sure.

If he took his shirt off—which I absolutely did *not* want him to do, shut up—there would probably be some more scrapes and bruises. All came with the territory of fighting.

Sitting across from him at the table in my room, I felt a lot better now that I saw for myself that he hadn't been hurt. Roughed up, sure, but that was to be expected.

Technically, he wasn't supposed to have any contact with teammates or even team staff while he was suspended. After today's hearing, he was suspended for one game, and since that game wasn't until the day after tomorrow, he was *supposed* to be sequestered from all of us for the next forty-eight-plus hours.

Technically.

In practice, we were stuck at this hotel for tonight with Pat, and we'd be on the plane together tomorrow. I doubted anyone on the team was worried about Jarek and me doing much interacting, and even if they did catch us all hanging out in my room for dinner... oh fucking well.

"As far as anyone knows," Pat said from the armchair as he cut into his room service steak, "I'm keeping an eye on both of you, which means you both have to be in the same room." He half-shrugged. "They can deal with it."

There'd been a time not so long ago when Jarek would've made a face and clearly been unhappy about the idea. This time, he just chuckled as he picked up his burger. "If they want to keep me isolated, they should've left a second babysitter."

"Hey." I jabbed my fork into my poutine. "I do not need a babysitter."

Pat barked a laugh. "Uh-huh. Let's see how that goes after you take another one of those muscle relaxers."

I cocked a brow and glanced at the prescription bottle on the nightstand. "Ooh, they gave me the good stuff?"

"With the way you were weaving on the way back in last night?" Pat snorted. "Yeah. They gave you the good stuff."

"Nice." After I'd eaten some of the poutine—which I had seriously missed since moving to the States—I said, "Oh, hey. I just realized—I never did ask who fucking won last night."

Jarek huffed a laugh. "Jesus. How good *is* that stuff?"

"Good enough to make him think he can sing," Pat muttered

Jarek's eyebrows shot up. I eyed our trainer.

He shrugged. "And as long as you don't make my life difficult on this trip, that video will never see the light of day."

"The... video?" I gulped. "You're joking, right?"

Another shrug.

"Ugh. Fuck you." I picked up another fry. "So who won?"

Jarek scoffed. "We did. Of course."

"Barely," Pat muttered.

"Hey." Jarek tried to kick him, but missed. "Toronto was down a defenseman. *We* were down two forwards *and* a defenseman before the end of the second period. 'Barely', my ass."

"Wait, two forwards and a defenseman?" I eyed Jarek. "Which defenseman did we lose?"

"Freeman." Jarek sighed as he dipped a fry in some ketchup. "Took a puck to the back of his wrist."

I winced, shaking out my hand to ward off that phantom pain. "Is he down, then? He went with the team, so..."

"He's day-to-day," Pat said. "Sounds like he'll be able to play the Montreal game, but they're bringing up one of the kids from the farm team just in case." He paused. "Since they're already bringing up two for..." He gestured at us.

Jarek's expression turned a little sheepish. "Well, they'll get some experience, I guess."

"It'll be good for them," Pat agreed. "And the next couple of games aren't division games, so..." He shrugged.

He had a point. There was never really a good time to lose two of the top six, but better to have that happen when we were playing out of our division.

Toronto was in our division, so the *last* thing we needed to do was give them points.

"So what was the score last night?" I asked.

Jarek reached for his drink. "Three-two."

"Not bad," I said with a nod. "Bet the fans were thrilled."

From the way Jarek and Pat laughed... yeah, probably not.

I chuckled. "Good." It felt weird to revel in my old fans having a bad night. I'd loved them when I was in Toronto. They'd lined up around the block every time I'd done a signing, and whenever I'd run into someone in public, they'd been polite and friendly. But they'd taken it hard when I'd left, mostly thanks to the lies spun by the Shamrocks' front office. I didn't blame the fans for hating me.

It still stung, though. After the boos and the signs last night, their collective opinion of me had been crystal clear. Not that there'd been much doubt after the videos of people burning, tearing, lawnmowing, or otherwise destroying Michaud jerseys.

So... no, I didn't feel bad about them walking away from last night's game disappointed.

"The fans were pretty pissed about what happened to you," Pat said.

I turned to him. "They were?"

"Didn't you hear them booing?" Jarek asked incredulously.

"I thought they were booing you."

"They were," Pat said. "But when Evans left the ice... Well, let's just say I'm pretty sure the broadcasters censored what they were chanting."

"No shit?"

"No shit," Jarek said. "I thought they were booing me, too, but it was more 'fuck Evans' than anything." He made a face as he picked up his burger again. "And I'm glad they did it."

The venom in his voice caught me off-guard. "You are?"

He looked at me like I was a complete dumbass. "Yes?" He shrugged. "Fighting and shit is one thing. You don't *injure* another player."

Ah, okay. Now it made sense. He didn't give a shit that it was me who'd gone down. He'd have done the same in defense of anyone in a Hornets sweater.

That actually made me feel better about the situation. There weren't any weird lines to read between, but also, at the end of the day, Jarek saw me as a teammate. I was one of the Hornets, and regardless of what he thought of me (or why the fuck he thought it), he'd go to blows in my defense just like he would Dima or Dolls or anyone else.

Whatever the inexplicable bullshit between us, he saw me as a teammate.

I could live with that.

CHAPTER 15

JAREK

I'd once played with a defenseman who was no stranger to suspensions. He deserved it, too—he did some dirty shit, and he could be reckless in ways that caused injuries. Even being a personable guy off the ice could never quite erase the fact that this was someone who reporters accurately described as "a man who set records by leaving a trail of broken bodies in his wake."

I didn't like the guy, but I'd been too much of a coward back then—too afraid of another punitive trade or stint in the minors—to give him so much as a cold shoulder, let alone a piece of my mind. So I'd been... maybe "friendly" was generous, but I'd hung around with him and our teammates enough to hear some of his thoughts on things.

And one of those thoughts had made me roll my eyes, because dude, you kinda brought it on yourself: that the worst part about a suspension wasn't the forfeited pay or the finger-wagging from reporters. It was the isolation.

I didn't have a lot of sympathy for him, but his words thumped against some nerves today.

Because, yeah, the isolation of a suspension *sucked*.

Especially when there was a full day between the announcement of my suspension and the game I'd have to sit. I was, for all intents and purposes, suspended for over forty-eight hours.

During that time, I couldn't even be around the team. That was easy enough, considering I'd come back to Pittsburgh while they continued on to Montreal. But they were forbidden from communicating with me.

That didn't stop some of the guys from sneaking a few texts my way in between the morning skate and warmups. I appreciated the contact, but somehow it made me feel even more isolated when I could imagine them trying to discreetly text me without anyone looking over their shoulders. I could tell when they were back in their rooms versus out and about with our teammates, because they'd write more than a few words and exchange more than one or two messages with me.

I didn't blame them. Nobody liked getting tangled up in the League's disciplinary gears, and I didn't want anyone getting in trouble just for talking to me. It just sucked because it was a constant reminder that I was supposed to be cut off from the majority of my social circle for two full days.

I also didn't regret it. That son of a bitch Evans had deserved every last blow for boarding Hunter, and I only wished I'd managed to get in two or three more before the officials had pried me off him.

In a moment of boredom, I'd made the mistake of scrolling some sports news sites. That was where I'd stumbled across an "article" speculating that there was bad blood between Evans and me from our time as teammates in Toronto. Even after I'd closed that browser window, I'd been fuming.

No, I didn't like Evans. No, I hadn't liked him back when we'd played together. But that hadn't even crossed my mind during the other night's game.

Evans hit Hunter. Hunter went down. And I saw red.

It was that simple.

Eh, let 'em speculate, I reminded myself. Because God knew there was plenty of that out there about me. Plenty of unflattering nicknames and cringe-inducing theories about everything I ever did.

At least they don't know the worst parts.

I shuddered. God help me if *that* ever got out. Just being the butt of jokes or the center of wild speculation was enough to make my skin crawl. The vitriol from fans and players alike was miserable, especially when they had no idea what was really happening behind the scenes. Didn't I know it.

I wondered how Hunter was handling everything now. The mental aftermath of something like that was rough. Plus we'd face Toronto three more times this season. More, if both teams made the playoffs.

I snickered at that. *Good luck getting to the playoffs without Hunter Michaud, assholes.*

The Hornets would rally around him when we did face Toronto. Anyone so much as buddy-bumped him, they were getting pummeled into the ice, match penalty be damned.

Assuming, of course, Hunter played the next time we faced them. His current status was day-to-day, and everyone seemed optimistic he'd only miss maybe two or three games. But I was curious how that was playing out in practice.

Despite the League rules and wanting to protect my own sanity, not to mention all the contradictory thoughts that swirled in my head every time I thought about engaging with Hunter, I texted him. *How is your neck?*

He responded with an unhappy emoji, followed by, *Neck injuries are bullshit.*

I breathed a quiet, sympathetic laugh into the stillness of my condo. *They are. Any idea about your recovery timeline?*

Right now it feels like I'm never going to turn my head again. But the staff thinks I'll be able to skate in a day or two. A grimacing emoji followed that.

As soon as you can move again, you'll be itching to skate.

Probably. I already miss it. Just fucking feels like I'll never be able to stand comfortably. Skating... Another grimace emoji.

I chuckled to myself. Yeah, I knew that feeling well. Every pain seemed like it was going to last forever, and there was something about neck pain that was exceptionally eternal. Then, somehow, it would be gone, and things like breathing, sleeping, walking, and even skating were as comfortable as they'd been before.

I was about to write out a text to that effect, but then I realized Hunter was typing, so I waited.

After a moment, his message appeared: *BTW, I know you're the one who got me and the other guys doing extra faceoff practice the day of the Toronto game.*

I stared at the screen. Oh. Fuck. Had Mayweather told him? Maybe. I had no idea what to say to that, but I went with, *Just didn't want you beating me to the showers and using all the hot water.*

LOL Whatever you say, man. Then he was typing. Not typing. Typing again. After a solid minute, he said, *It got my mind off my old team's bullshit. Can't really complain.*

My mouth had gone dry. I hadn't breathed a word to anyone—not Mayweather, not the coaches—about why I'd thought some faceoff practice would be a good idea right then. Maybe they'd put two and two together. Or maybe Hunter thought it was an unintended consequence.

I eventually wrote back the only thing I could think of: *I know how it feels. When your old team doesn't like you. Been there. So... glad I could help.*

He started and stopped typing several times before he sent, *At least I know this team doesn't hate me.*

Fresh guilt knotted in my gut. No one in Pittsburgh had given him any reason to believe he was anything but welcome here.

No one but me.

Heart thumping, I wrote back, *Nah. We're lucky to have you.*

Hunter didn't respond.

I was kind of glad.

"Wow, you look like shit."

I rolled my eyes as I stepped into Eliška's house. "Thanks."

"Did you get checked for a concussion?" She shut the door behind us. "You should've at least had a head CT and—"

"Eliška." I sighed and took off my shoes. "Just be my sister today. Not Dr. Badurová. All right?"

She pressed her lips together and gave me an unhappy look.

"I mean it. The medical staff on the team is thorough." With a humorless laugh, I added, "They pay us way too much money to ignore our injuries."

Her scowl deepened.

"Let it go," I pleaded. "Please?"

Then, mercifully, she sighed. "Fine. But if I think you're showing signs of—"

"*Eliška.*"

She muttered something that would've infuriated our mother, then gestured for me to follow her into the kitchen.

I understood. We'd had plenty of conversations about potential hockey injuries, and they'd only intensified as she'd gone through pre-med and into medical school. I kind of dreaded her emergency room rotation, because she'd probably try to physically restrain me from playing hockey.

"*I don't care if it's how you're paying for my university and my house,*" she'd told me one night. "*I don't want anything happening to my brother.*"

As it was, she'd read too many case studies and shadowed too many doctors seeing athletes, from youth all the way up to professional. She'd read about and seen for herself the horrific injuries that could happen, and she'd told me more than once she lived in fear of me getting one of those injuries that seemed like no big deal, then suddenly *became* a big deal. Head injuries were especially prone to that.

But I'd been checked out in Toronto and again after I'd come back to Pittsburgh. The bruises on my face were getting that sickly yellow-green halo while the worst parts stayed purple, like around my eye. My knuckles were still bruised all to hell, plus they'd been thoroughly bloodied, including that impressive cut from Evans's tooth.

Not exactly a picture I'd be putting on a Tinder profile, and not one my physician-in-training sister was going to let slide.

Eliška did drop the subject for the moment, though. She got us both some coffee, and then we moved into the living room. This room looked much different than it had before the season began. She still wanted to redo the walls—whoever had picked out that puke-green wallpaper must've been huffing paint thinner—but that was a project for next summer. She'd arranged furniture and put up a few pictures to make it look as nice as possible in the meantime.

I took a seat on her couch, and she sat in the armchair, pulling her bare feet up under her. Then some heavy thumps on the stairs signaled that her cats were joining us, and a second later, they trotted into the room—Alena, the abnormally fluffy black cat, and Boleslav, the hefty orange shorthair.

Boleslav deposited himself in my lap, purring loudly as I scratched under his chin and he kneaded my leg. Alena took the empty cushion beside me and started licking her ass. Typical.

Eliška watched her cats and tsked, shaking her head. "I feed them and house them, and they..." She gestured at them and rolled her eyes. "Traitors."

I chuckled. I'd gone with her to the shelter where she'd found them, and they'd both made a big show of falling in love with her. Ever since we'd brought them home, though, I'd been the favorite. And I didn't feel too bad about it. They really did like her—they just fell all over me whenever I came to the house. Since this was as close as I could get to having pets while I traveled constantly? Eliška could live with it.

As Boleslav settled in my lap and started to go sleep, Eliška watched me over her coffee cup. "So—the team. They suspended you? Because of the fight?"

I nodded. "Well, the League did. But yes. And I'm not surprised. I did beat the shit out of him."

My sister made an irritated noise as she sipped her coffee. "What about Michaud? Is he all right?"

I didn't understand the sudden heat in my face, and I had no idea why I suddenly couldn't look at her. Staring down at Boleslav, I focused on petting him, tracing my thumb over one of the darker stripes along his side. "Michaud's fine. It could've been..." I swallowed bile. "I keep seeing that hit over and over in my head. That fucker could've ended Michaud's career. Or worse."

"I know," Eliška whispered. She was quiet for a moment, and I braced for the well-meaning dead-horse beating about what this sport was doing to my body, how that could've been *me* getting boarded and all the ways that could've ended my career or upended my life. I wasn't ready for the soft, "I don't think I've ever seen you so angry."

I turned to her. "Huh?"

"When you fought the man who hurt him. That's..." She shook her head. "Where did that come from?"

"He could have crippled my teammate." I watched myself petting Boleslav. "He's lucky I was the only one who got hands on him."

I could feel her gaze on me, but I couldn't meet it.

"He's out too, yes? Michaud?"

"What?" My head snapped toward her. "What does that have to do with anything?"

Her eyebrow rose, as did one corner of her mouth. "Do I look stupid to you?" I was about to ask if that was a rhetorical question, but she jabbed me in the arm. "Don't you dare."

I laughed, rubbing the spot she'd poked. "You asked!"

My sister groaned and rolled her eyes. "Don't change the subject."

I sobered and reached for my coffee. "Then answer my question—what does him being out have to do with anything?"

To my surprise, all the teasing had gone out of her voice when she said, "Because outside the family, there's only one other person on the planet I can imagine you ever protecting so..." She hesitated as if she couldn't find the word, and finally settled on, "Viciously."

The swallow of coffee I took didn't want to go down. Neither did the truth. Especially because she didn't have to tell me who she knew I'd have gone to blows to protect or defend.

Marc-Yves.

The man I'd loved more fiercely than any other.

I managed to get the coffee down, and as I put the mug aside, my voice came out raw. "Michaud is a *teammate*. Nothing more."

Her silence was so full of skepticism, it left my ears ringing more than Evans's punches had.

I turned to her, jaw tight. "*Nothing* more."

That damn eyebrow again.

I exhaled and shifted on the couch as much as I could with the cat sprawled across my lap. "We barely know each other. And even if I wanted him—*which I do not*—I've been..." I snapped my teeth together, shame twisting in my stomach.

Eliška tilted her head. "You've been... what?"

I swallowed hard. "I was an ass to him when he first came to Pittsburgh."

"Why?"

I waved my hand. "It was just in the beginning. I'm—"

"But *why?*"

God. I knew that tone. That was my stubborn little sister letting me know we were discussing this whether I liked it or not.

Except I couldn't tell her any more than I could tell Dima or anyone else. Including Hunter.

I shook my head. "There's... It's complicated, and it has nothing to do with either of us being gay or him being attractive." I shot her a look. "Not a thing."

She wasn't buying an ounce of what I was selling. "Okay, but you were an asshole to him. Your teammate. Because...?" She inclined her head.

"I thought he was going to take my place on the second line." It was a lie, but I knew my sister, and a diversion tactic like this was the only way to get this pit bull to let go of a bone. The only way besides the truth, and the CIA and KGB together couldn't pry that out of me. They especially weren't getting to the part where I'd felt personally responsible for anything that happened to Hunter. I'd had a bigger hand in his career than he would ever know, and it had been, on some level I couldn't explain to anyone, my fault he'd been there that night. In Toronto. In a Pittsburgh jersey. Targeted by an angry former teammate.

That hit he'd taken? The guilt went right to my core because had I done things differently—had I been less of a goddamned coward—he wouldn't have been there at all in that moment. He'd have been someplace else in the League, living his best life and racking up Cups like he'd always been destined to do.

My throat was starting to get tight, and I didn't want to let my sister see the way I was breaking apart inside. No one could know, least of all her, since she still looked up to me for some reason.

Focusing on petting Boleslav, I pushed back the lump in my throat and took a deep breath. "It was... I know, it was stupid. I finally got back to a good place on a team. Then they got him. A fucking generational talent." I met her gaze. "I thought I was going to get bumped down again."

Okay, it wasn't entirely a lie. That fear had crossed my mind. It hadn't occurred to me I'd wind up as Hunter Michaud's winger, or that we'd be so damn good together, or that he'd be so—

Nope, not letting *that* train of thought leave the station.

"Jarek." She nudged my knee with a sock-covered foot. "You're blushing."

I rolled my eyes. "*Anyway*. He confronted me. And so did Dima. And they were right—I was being a dick. So... I stopped."

Eliška nodded. "That sounds like you."

This time I knew I was blushing—the heat made the bruise under my eye throb. I wanted to wring my hands, but the one still hurt. Then I debated reaching for my coffee cup again just so I had something to do with my hands and to wet my suddenly dry mouth. "The point is, yeah, we're good now. I guess? We're..." I shrugged and started thumbing Boleslav's toes, which made him purr louder. To my sister, I said, "Michaud and I—we play well together. But if I had any shot with him..." I laughed bitterly. "Pretty sure that ship sailed before training camp was over."

"But you *want* a shot with him."

"No, Eliška." I let the sarcasm drip as I rolled my eyes again. "The most incredible hockey player of our generation is on my team, and he also happens to be the hottest man I've ever laid eyes on, and I definitely *don't* want a shot with him." I huffed a dry laugh. "Of course I do. But he's..." I trailed off and stared at the cat in my lap.

He's got every reason to think I'm a dick.

He's out of my league.

He's a reminder of the lowest moments of my life.

"Jarek." She nudged my knee again. "I'm sure you've convinced yourself he's not interested in you, but I'm pretty sure you put yourself on his radar the other night."

I eyed her.

She smirked. "Oh, come on. You beat the ever-loving hell out of someone in his defense. You got yourself"—she gestured at her face—"and got suspended... to defend him."

"Because that's what hockey players do," I retorted. "I wasn't going to let someone get away with that shit."

"No, but I'm pretty sure you wouldn't have beaten him down quite so hard if he'd done that to one of your other teammates." The smirk turned into a grin. "If he's not watching that replay with hearts in his eyes, then he needs to turn in his gay card immediately."

I almost choked on a laugh. "He's not a damsel in distress. He'd have answered the bell for me if the roles had been reversed."

"Mmhmm. I'll bet he would have."

"For fuck's sake." Had the cats not been here, I'd have grabbed a throw pillow and tossed it at her head. "Stop."

"What?" She giggled. "You don't think that brought you up a few notches in his mind? It was probably almost enough to negate you being a dick to him at the start of the season."

"Yeah, right." I chuckled, but as I sobered, I kept running my thumb along Boleslav's soft paw. "He's a teammate, though. And he's... I mean, he's Hunter fucking Michaud. I've literally seen him in action at a club—he can have any man he wants."

Both eyebrows came up this time. "You perved on him at a club?"

"Perved on—" I exhaled sharply and kicked her shin

even as renewed heat rose in my cheeks. "*No*. But we were both there, and he's, um, not exactly easy to ignore."

"I'll bet he isn't." She met my gaze again, and she sobered too. "Look, in all seriousness, I know you. And I know when you're into someone."

I flinched away. God, she wasn't going to let this go, was she?

Apparently not, because she kept going: "I also know you haven't let yourself be happy since Marc-Yves."

Sakra. Ouch.

Softly, she said, "Am I wrong?"

I pressed my elbow in the armrest and wiped a hand over my face, regretting that instantly since I'd somehow forgotten I was bruised all to shit. Wincing away from my own touch, I said nothing. I couldn't admit out loud that she was right. No, I hadn't been happy—genuinely, deeply happy—since the years with Marc-Yves. She'd tried for a long time to understand what had happened back then, but when it came to that subject, even my sister was kept at arm's length. Explaining all of it to her would mean explaining why I'd started spiraling in the first place, and how that had been why Marc-Yves had eventually left.

And there was no explaining to her why it didn't matter how attractive Hunter was, or how much I wished there was some way to convince him I was worth dating. Because every time I looked at him, I remembered everything that had driven me to my lowest point—personally and professionally. I remembered everything that had driven away the man I'd once thought was the love of my life.

There was no reality in which Hunter and I could have a relationship while all those things existed.

To my sister, I said, "It doesn't matter. I can't be with him."

She opened her mouth to speak, but I collected Boleslav into the crook of my elbow, pushed myself to my feet, and grabbed my coffee cup.

"We should get to work." I gestured at the stairs. "You still wanted to rip out the bathroom tile today, right?"

She peered at me, lips pursed as if she were weighing whether to argue.

Let it go, Eliška, I wanted to beg. *Please, please, just this once—let it go.*

After a moment, she exhaled and got up. "Okay. Let me put these in the dishwasher, and we can get started."

She took my coffee cup, picked up her own, and went into the kitchen.

I indulged in a sigh of relief as I trailed after her. She meant well. I knew she did. And God knew I needed someone to smack me over the oblivious head with the truth sometimes. I could be stubbornly clueless about a lot of things, and my sister was always happy to annoy me into seeing the light.

But not this time.

Because no matter how attracted I was to Hunter...

He and I just weren't in the cards.

CHAPTER 16

HUNTER

A week after I was boarded, I felt fine. Not quite a hundred percent, but enough that I was sure I could play through it. Dr. Erickson was a little less optimistic—damn medical professionals, protecting us from ourselves and not letting us play through injuries. Jerks. At least he'd cleared me to do on-ice conditioning after the first day, and that had helped me loosen up the pissy muscles.

After the second week, I was cleared to practice with the team, though Dr. Erickson insisted on keeping me no-contact for another day or two. He also kept me listed week-to-week.

Ugh. Fine. I'd played this game before. He wanted to see how I performed at practice intensity, and once he did, he'd probably upgrade me to day-to-day.

On my first day back with the team, I started the same way I'd been for the last few: working out on-ice with Belov and Nilsson, who were recovering from a concussion and a shoulder injury, respectively. We did some drills and worked with the skills coaches, plus some conditioning. It was intense, because hockey was always intense, but dialed back from the normal level to give us all a chance to rehab.

Afterward, I put on a gray no-contact jersey and came out to practice with the team.

God, it felt good to skate out with them after a break and not have a stomach full of dread. I'd had some lengthy periods of inactivity throughout my career, like when I broke my jaw and after a particularly nasty concussion, and coming back meant more than just getting my body used to the abuse. There had always been the mental bullshit from my old coach and GM. That never quite let up while I was out with an injury, but the second I was reactivated—or even day-to-day but practicing with the team—the pressure came down on me tenfold. Not only was there the usual pressure to carry the entire team, but now I had to single-handedly make up for lost time, since Toronto's record invariably went to shit whenever I was out. I'd felt like one of those goalies who was so good, he made the rest of the team look unstoppable, but the second he went down, everyone saw the truth: the team sucked, and they were just leaning hard on him to make up for their inability to defend.

Those days were behind me, thank God, and when I skated out onto the sheet this morning, I was greeted with shoulder smacks and chirping. Lots of "good to have you back" and playful "about fucking time, freeloader." It was like being back on my major junior team. I *loved* it.

And to my surprise... even Jarek seemed genuinely happy to have me back.

"How's your neck?" he asked as we warmed up.

"Still bitches at me if I don't baby it after skating," I replied. "But it's a lot better."

"Good." He nodded sharply. "Glad it wasn't worse."

"Tell me about it."

I was caught off guard by him talking to me and being glad to see me. The more I thought about it, though, the more the cynicism kicked in. Of course he wanted me back —our line was leading the team and most of our division in points. It wasn't me he wanted. He just wanted his winning line back.

Eh. I'd take it.

Coach Henley skated up and touched my back. "Doc says you're gonna make it. You feeling all right?"

I nodded, trying to hide the profound relief and persistent surprise at a coach who cared about my well-being. "I thought I could come back a few days ago, but you know him." I rolled my eyes. "Gotta heal before I play."

Henley tsked. "Won't let my boys play through concussions. Won't let them play through stress fractures." He gestured with his stick. "What next? Not letting them play while there's blood gushing from their mouths?"

I snorted. "I know, right? What a baby."

He chuckled, gave my back a pat, and then skated toward center ice. I smiled to myself as I watched him go. Holy hell, I was glad I'd signed with this team.

Practice started shortly after that. We did some skills work and special teams. That was great—nothing helped me stay sharp like practicing against our penalty kill unit. They'd been, well, killing it all season, and going up against them in practice was making the power play sharper, too. These were usually full-contact drills, too, but Coach wanted my power play unit to get back in our groove as soon as possible, so he was playing us low- and no-contact just to get our timing back.

I was pretty sure it was working, too. I slid right back into my role, and the passes between all of us were crisp and unhesitant. I even managed to score on Dolls, which earned me high fives from the whole unit... including Jarek.

It was fucking good to be back.

My neck did get a little cranky when I was bent over during the faceoffs. Not painful, just tight. The position combined with the tension that came with being poised for a quick puck battle didn't go well with healing neck muscles. I'd put some heat on it after practice, and my physical therapist could eat a giant "cold not heat" dick.

Coach wanted to practice the special teams full-contact, too, so I leaned against the boards and watched. Apparently Carlson had been filling my role on the second power play unit, and he took my place to practice. He was good; I could see why Coach had picked him to step in. He played on the third line, and he was a strong center. Good on the faceoff, which could make or break a power play. Some more aggression would serve him well, though. He wasn't timid, per se, but there were moments when he'd have benefitted from holding onto the puck and hip-checking someone out of his way instead of passing to take the heat off himself.

It was something he could work on. I might mention it to one of the coaches, or maybe even work with him myself.

Hanging back and watching the special teams practice didn't just give me a chance to suss out some things my teammates could work on. It also turned out to be a rare opportunity to stand off to the side and watch Jarek skate.

And oh, hell, I watched.

God, the way he moved. He was tall, but he had the speed and agility some of the smaller guys were known for. He could dance away from defensemen, and if he got the puck on his stick and a clear path, he could cross the ice so fast I was amazed flames didn't shoot out of his skates. If he didn't have a clear path? Well, between his skating and his stick handling, he still flew, protecting the puck all the way, and he'd happily use his shoulder or a well-placed hip check to clear that path. Damn. Maybe Carlson needed some lessons from *Jarek*, not me.

Well, whatever. For right now, I indulged in just... enjoying watching him. Hockey prowess aside, the man was even sexier in person than he'd been on-camera. There were still moments when he didn't seem to want me anywhere near him. Then there were moments when I seemed to be like all our other teammates—just one of the guys who he'd banter with and practice with.

And then there were moments—

I pulled my gaze away from Jarek and pretended to be interested in the tape on my stick. Because out here, geared up and surrounded by my teammates, was not the time to be thinking about those times when I swore Jarek looked at me like he *wanted* something. Times like that night at the club.

God, if he gave me *one* clear signal—*one* green light that he was attracted to me and wanted to act on it—I'd rock his world.

But Jarek was not a man of clear signals, so the best I could do was get along with him when he was feeling friendly, and try not to implode from sheer frustration when he was either inexplicably irritated with me or unmistakably horny for me.

Or when he beat the ever-loving fuck out of someone bigger than both of us in my defense. Like all hockey players did. For any of their teammates. All the time. Even players who rarely dropped gloves at all. Like Jarek.

Christ. Could he just draw me a picture or *tell* me what he was thinking? Because his mind was *impossible* to read.

Dr. Erickson was pleased with my progress. He'd watched practice from the GM's office, which overlooked the rink, and after asking me a battery of questions and running me through some more tests, he decided there was no reason to keep me on the bench.

"We'll put you in a full-contact jersey tomorrow. I'll have you upgraded to day-to-day, and if you're feeling all right tomorrow, you'll be a gametime decision tomorrow night."

I exhaled. "Thank you."

"But if I think you're too stiff or in too much pain," he warned, "that gametime decision will be a no."

I nodded. I'd known that drill since my youth days. "Got it. Guess I shouldn't go bungee jumping tonight."

His don't-you-fucking-dare-even-joke-about-that glare mixed with the why-do-you-boys-do-this-to-me? fatigue had me chuckling all the way downstairs to the players' lounge. Most of my teammates had already come down here to eat; I'd grabbed a bite on my way up, but I was starving, so I filled a plate and joined some of the guys.

"So." Dima smacked my arm as I sat down. "What did the doctor say? How much longer are you on vacation?"

"Vacation. Yeah, right." I rolled my eyes. "Day-to-day. Full-contact. And tomorrow night?" I held up crossed fingers. "Gametime decision."

My teammates all chimed in with things like, "All right!" and "Nice!"

Except one.

Why was I even surprised?

Things had been smoother between Jarek and me lately, but oh, big shock, he just scowled and focused on his food.

What the hell, man?

I barely kept myself from rolling my eyes again. I didn't know how much more of this hot and cold and wildly mixed messages I could take before I went insane. Even the non-stop hostility had been better than this shit.

Either hate me or don't.

But just make up your damn mind, will you?

CHAPTER 17

JAREK

Hunter was a gametime decision, and I had mixed feelings about that. We needed him—good God, we needed him—but after a few practices and games without him beside me, I was suddenly off-balance around him again. I didn't know if I wanted him to be available for tonight's game, or if I was secretly hoping the team doc would go extra cautious and bench him for a little longer.

Not that it mattered, because Dr. Erickson's decision didn't take my opinion into consideration.

"Hey, hey, there he is!" Ferns gave Hunter a punch to the shoulder. "Comeback goal tonight? Hmm?"

Hunter laughed and shrugged. "Maybe if you do your job and keep their boys out of our end?"

That prompted a chorus of, "Oooh" and "yep, he's back" from our teammates, and Hunter just chuckled as he continued toward his locker.

At my own locker, I focused on putting on my gear. Hunter was back. That was a *good* thing. He could've been out for weeks or months after a hit like that. Hockey could've been over for him forever. He was back, which meant he was okay, and of course I was relieved because he was my teammate and my linemate, and even if he wasn't, he was a hockey player. None of us wanted anyone to get hurt, regardless of any bad blood or less than charitable feelings.

Except there's no bad blood between us. Just my stupid brain and my stupid past and my stupid—

"You coming, Yars?" Dima smacked my back with a glove. "It's almost warmups."

Fuck. It was, wasn't it?

"I was just waiting for you." I grabbed my stick and tapped it against his shin. "When are you going to be ready?"

He tsked and rolled his eyes, muttering something that was lost in the sound of skates clomping out of the locker room. I snickered and followed our teammates toward the ice.

The fans sure noticed when Hunter stepped out onto the ice. Even through all the bullshit constantly tumbling through my brain where Hunter was concerned, I knew he deserved the roar from the crowd. Toronto may have hated him, but Pittsburgh loved him, and they weren't going to let him forget it. They knew they were lucky to have him. So did we, his teammates.

Now if I could just get my head out of my ass...

That was easier said than done. I still couldn't quite find my balance around him, though I was getting used to that. I didn't want to admit it out loud, but it felt right having him there in our warmup routine. Whenever someone missing—either because they were newly traded or out with an injury—it threw me off, and having them back was always a relief. It put everything right.

Having Hunter back...

That made things so right it threw me off all over again.

I pulled my gaze away from him for the tenth time and focused on my own warmup routine. Find a puck, shoot it at the net. Not difficult, Jaromir.

I did, and it wasn't difficult... mostly. I made it through warmups, though, and retreated to the locker room with my teammates to grab some water before the first period.

Shortly after that, I was on the bench. I'd gone through the pre-game routine a million times, and quite a few times with Hunter, but his brief absence had reset my ability to breathe around him. I was still getting used to that. I barely heard the announcer reciting our top line and defensive pair's names for the starting lineup, and almost zoned out enough to forget to stand for the anthem. Never a good look for a player, especially a foreign one.

But I caught myself, stood, and took off my helmet...

And didn't hear a single lyric of the song I'd heard hundreds of times.

The whole time, my recent conversation with my sister tumbled through my head. I didn't think I'd ever been more tempted to show the cards I'd held tightly to my vest all this time. With him so close by, so fucking unavoidable, the need to tell someone the truth was almost painful.

I couldn't, and I knew I couldn't, but now with him back on the ice...

With the lingering remnants of that fear and guilt I'd had the night Hunter had been injured...

With how relieved I was to again be standing next to the healthy, recovered man who had no idea why I was such a mess over him...

Pull it together, Jaromir. Kurva.

I would. I wasn't sure how, but I would.

Or... I'd try. Because one minute, my brain wanted to

fixate on everything his presence dredged up from my past. The next, I almost faceplanted on the ice because, sakra, there wasn't a sexier man anywhere in the League.

I wasn't usually in the running for any of the big year-end trophies, but I swore somebody should put me in for something if I made it through this season without my head exploding over Hunter.

———

We lost that first game after Hunter was reactivated, and I was livid afterward.

Not at anyone in particular, except maybe myself. And the officials, who wouldn't know goaltender interference if it crashed the net like a wrecking ball, and who changed their minds from minute to minute about what counted as offside.

I was pissed at our performance. At the bad puck luck. At the hockey gods, who were being total dicks tonight. At that Philadelphia forward who'd come up to me after I'd missed a shot and snidely suggested that, "Maybe you'd have better luck scoring in your own net."

Oh, I hadn't needed that particular nerve stomped on tonight, and I'd had to call on all the restraint I'd ever possessed to keep from cross-checking him in the smug fucking face. He'd wanted me to do it, too—from his challenging grin, he'd been hoping to goad me into a reaction and draw a penalty.

Not today, Satan.

Yeah, he'd still managed to get under my skin, and yeah, it still fucked with my hockey, but that wasn't why we'd lost tonight. It was just one of those nights. Every team lost some games. But it always stung when we had a crap night, and to add insult to injury. Atlanta had won their game, and as a result, they'd bumped us down a spot in the standings. It didn't matter that we were still in a solid playoff spot with months to go before the postseason; dropping to third sucked.

I hated that Hunter's first game back had been a shit-show. I hated that Philly had won tonight, closing the gap between our teams by two precious points. I hated that I felt responsible for not only getting this team to the playoffs, but getting *Hunter's* team to the playoffs.

All of which just made the resentment burn even hotter whenever I looked at him.

None of this is his fault, I reminded myself. *Stop being stupid.*

But telling myself not to feel something was like ordering myself to eat oysters without gagging—no amount of stubbornness and willpower could override that visceral response. I could no more talk myself out of resenting Hunter than I could talk myself out of being attracted to him, and that second thing wasn't helping any of this at all.

"Hey. Yars." Dolls tapped my shoe under the table. "You still here?"

I shook myself and glanced around the table at him, Ferns, and Dima, all of whom were watching me like I was a space alien. Oh. Fuck. How long had I been zoning out? Long enough for them to notice, anyway?

"Are you good?" Ferns tilted his head. "You've been on another planet all night."

"Of course he is." Dima smirked, though there was still a hint of concern in his eyes. "Mish is back."

"Oh, fuck you." I gave him a shove and hoped my face wasn't as red as it felt.

"He's got a point, though." Dolls peered at me. "You've been... I don't know. Weird ever since Toronto."

"I'm fine." I reached for my drink. "Seeing a teammate get hurt like that sucks. You were all shaken up by it, too."

"Not like you were," Dolls said. "And shit's been weird between you and Mish since he got here. What is up with that?"

"Yeah," Dima said. "Because I thought you two settled everything, but now..."

"I know, I know." I sighed. "We did. I... It's..." I waved a hand. "I'm just an idiot."

"You don't have to tell us that."

Rolling my eyes, I laughed. "Kiss my ass."

He punched my arm. "Would you just fuck him and get it over with?"

It was just as well I'd had so much practice lately at hiding my anger. That practice stopped a sudden surge of fury that Dima didn't deserve. Neither did the man who was the reason why I had to put so much energy into managing my anger these days. Instead of lashing out like I'd almost done, I rolled my eyes and punched him back. "Shut up, or I'll tell Chloé I saw you drinking Michelob."

Beside me, Ferns choked on his food. Dolls made an attempt to stifle his laughter. Not a very good one, but an attempt.

Dima narrowed his eyes. "Don't. You. Dare."

I inclined my head. "Then are you going to stop it with the jokes about me doing Michaud?"

He pursed his lips. "Probably not."

I shrugged and took my phone out of my pocket. "Fine."

"Damn it, you fucker!" He snatched my phone away. "You're going to get me in trouble!"

"No shit. That's the idea."

"Don't worry, Yars." Ferns was typing something into his own phone. "I've got you."

"What?" Dima squeaked. "What are you—hey!"

I took advantage of his distraction and grabbed my phone back. Dima swore, then tried to get Ferns's phone while Dolls ran interference.

"How do you even spell Michelob?" Ferns was asking as he kept his phone out of reach. "M-I-C—goddammit, auto-correct!"

Right then, a clearing throat stilled all of us, and we turned to see Coach Henley and Rachel, our head of media relations, who'd been walking by the open door. We stared at them. They stared at us, probably seeing an accidental Renaissance painting of four hockey players in hoodies and sweats, fighting over a couple of cell phones while we almost knocked our food off the table.

"Uh." Dolls cleared his throat. "Hey, Coach. Rachel."

Coach and Rachel glanced at each other.

"Do you want to know?" he asked.

"Nope," she responded, and they continued down the hall.

"For fuck's sake," Dima muttered.

Dolls just snickered.

"And... sent." Ferns held up his phone triumphantly. "You better get home and do some damage control, Dima!"

A string of profanity tumbled out of Dima's mouth. He kicked Ferns under the table hard enough to make him yelp, which had Dolls and me laughing. We both got the finger from Dima and Ferns.

Chloé wouldn't be mad. She was just more of a beer snob than Dima was, which said something, and she'd tease him for ages about slumming it with such a pedestrian brand of beer. She, after all, never drank any brands that could be found in the supermarket. And she'd never in a million years believe him when he insisted he hadn't touched the stuff... especially since Dolls, Ferns, and I would swear on our lives we'd not only watched him drink it, but had to listen to him wax poetic for hours about how spectacular it was.

At least the chirping and bickering about getting him in trouble with his wife derailed the conversation from whether I should fuck Hunter and get it over with.

Didn't derail my train of thought about it, though.

Truthfully, I just didn't know what to do when it came to Hunter. Those times when we were on the same wavelength—when I forgot what he meant to my life, and he was just my gorgeous and talented teammate—were fucking gold. And then those near-green hazel eyes would lock on mine, and he'd smile just right, or he'd give me a conspiratorial grin, and something in me would... melt.

And then I'd remember. And the walls would go back up. And I knew damn well he could see it and he could feel it, and he'd break eye contact and skate away, probably wondering what the fuck my damn problem was.

I didn't *want* to be hostile toward him. I didn't *want* to resent him. I was just afraid of what might happen in those moments when I forgot what the name Hunter Michaud meant in my world.

Dima had joked that Hunter and I should just fuck and be done with it.

In another lifetime, maybe. If things had happened differently, sure. If I hadn't given Hunter a fuckload of reasons to want nothing to do with me, okay.

But this was the timeline I was living in, and something told me I didn't want to find out what it would feel like to wake up beside Hunter Michaud.

CHAPTER 18

HUNTER

I was done. Just a hundred percent done.

Jarek and I were tearing it up on the ice, but I couldn't handle how unpredictable he was in the locker room. One minute he cold-shouldered me. The next, he looked at me like he wanted to eat me alive in a very good way. It was exhausting.

Our teammates noticed. Everybody noticed. But I just kept telling people it was okay, that everything was fine, that *"Look how great we are on the ice—it's all good!"*

It wasn't all good. I hadn't escaped all the stress in Toronto to sign up for this bullshit.

And I was completely. Fucking. *Done.*

We needed to hash this out before we ended up dropping gloves over it. I wasn't about to make a scene in front of our teammates, though, so I waited for the right opportunity to catch Jarek alone.

That opportunity came after a long flight out to Colorado. Everyone should've been jetlagged and ready to pass out, but we were hockey players with too much energy. Despite the flight and the time change, we were too wide awake to go to bed at a reasonable local time, so naturally, we were all in the bar until after midnight. The staff and anyone who'd been playing for any length of time warned the new guys to go easy on the booze; the altitude in Denver could really fuck with your alcohol tolerance.

That didn't stop anyone from drinking like normal, but at least they couldn't say they were warned. Good thing we only had a practice tomorrow. The game wasn't until the next night.

I didn't drink this time. I kept an eye on Jarek, who was on his third, and waited for him to call it a night. He was notorious for turning in before the rest of the crowd, so it was a safe bet I could catch him alone on his way to his room.

At a little after one-thirty, he paid his portion of the bill and left. I'd closed my tab ages ago, so all I had to do was wait a couple of beats, then slip out after him.

I didn't miss the side-eye as I stepped into the elevator with him. Didn't miss the faint sigh, either.

Yeah, yeah, I know. You hate having me around.

Lucky for you, this elevator ride is only the beginning.

We got out on the seventh floor. He headed left. My room was to the right, but I planted my feet.

"Hey." I called after him, though not too loud since we were in a hotel hallway in the middle of the night. "Hold up a second."

Jarek halted, and I could tell from the drop of his shoulders and the way his head fell back that he was irritated. I was probably the last person he wanted to deal with, especially when he was trying to enjoy what seemed like a solid buzz.

Too bad, fucker. We're doing this now.

Matching his energy, I adopted a tone laced with annoyance. "You got a minute?"

The sharp exhalation suggested he wasn't interested in giving me that minute, but he turned around and faced me anyway, his expression echoing that sentiment. A subtle upward flick of his eyebrows prodded me to get on with it.

I tried my level best not to look as confrontational as I felt. "Man, I gotta know. What's the deal?" I gestured at myself. "Do you have a problem with me?"

Okay, maybe a little confrontational.

He gave a humorless laugh that only slightly hinted at how much he'd had to drink. "Are we supposed to be best friends because we're linemates?"

That kind of stung. No, not *all* teammates were close, not even linemates. But it helped if they could at least be cordial.

"We don't have to be best friends," I said evenly. "But you've clearly disliked me from day one. And even after I said something—and someone else must've said something, since you flipped the switch—it's still fucking obvious. Like, it's so obvious I'm getting grilled about it by reporters, and I have no idea what to tell them." Fuck not being confrontational—I crossed my arms and glared hard at him. "So, you tell me. What should I say when they ask about it? Should I just make up some beef between us? Because hell if I know why I've apparently been persona non grata with you since training camp."

Jarek's temper was legendary throughout the League. Light his fuse on the ice, and he'd go off. He didn't go to blows very often, but he'd shout and argue, and on the rare occasion his mouth wrote a big enough check, he'd happily do five for fighting. I was playing with fire by talking to him like this even if he didn't already dislike me, especially when he'd been drinking. Still, I stood my ground and just braced for him to tell me exactly why he couldn't stand me. Maybe even take a swing because I'd stomped on his last nerve... and because part of me still expected any off-ice confrontation to end with me getting punched.

He didn't do any of that.

He cut his eyes away, but not before something shifted in his expression. A crack in the irritation and terseness. His jaw worked, and my heart jumped into my throat. Apparently I *had* stomped on a nerve, but not one that was connected to that famously fiery temper.

I watched him silently, because I had no idea what to say. Or what I'd said to throw him like this.

After a moment, Jarek swallowed hard. When he met my gaze again, all the irritation and anger were gone from his eyes, replaced by... fatigue? Resignation? Pain? Nothing that I expected to see after I'd decided to get in his face.

He took a deep breath, and his voice was startlingly quiet and unsteady when he said, "If you knew how much I lost so you could have the career that you do, you'd understand."

Then he turned on his heel and stalked down the hall, leaving me there with my jaw on the floor and question marks floating above my head. Before I could convince enough synapses to fire so I could demand to know what the fuck that even meant, Jarek's door had already closed.

I stood there stupidly for a moment, staring down the empty hallway as I tried to figure out what the ever-loving hell had just happened. What in God's name had he lost for my career? We'd never even played on the same team until now. He'd been gone from Toronto before I'd—

Something turned to ice in my spine.

Echoes of all the abuse I took from our coach and GM—

the same men who'd held those positions while Jarek had played for Toronto—made my stomach lurch.

Had he...

"If you knew how much I lost so you could have the career that you do, you'd understand."

My whole body was as cold as if I'd walked out onto the ice barefoot. Sick to my stomach and a breath away from shivering all over, I returned to my own room. My mind was going a million miles an hour, and some very ugly pieces were trying to come together. I fought them because I didn't want them to fit. They couldn't. It wasn't true.

Was it?

But I'd kept a finger on Jarek's career for too long not to know by heart the trajectory he'd taken. I'd even felt bad when my own career had hit the ground running and soared at the same time one of my idols had seemingly fallen apart.

It had just never occurred to me that the timing had been anything but a coincidence. His last year in Toronto— the one before I was drafted—had been his worst by far, but that happened sometimes. Players had bad seasons. They had slumps. And then he'd been traded multiple times after that, and it had taken until the last two or three seasons for him to get back to who he'd been early on.

The timing—him falling from grace and me being drafted—had been a coincidence.

Hadn't it? It had to be.

But...

What if it wasn't?

As much as I needed to get some sleep so I'd be fresh for tomorrow's practice, I wasn't going to be able to until I'd tugged this thread. With a sigh, I sat up against the headboard and propped my laptop on my knee.

Then I Googled *"Jaromir Badura, Toronto Shamrocks."*

And oh, boy—there were a lot of results. A lot of the headlines were variations of the same theme. I'd seen them before but dismissed it all as a wild conspiracy theory, since there were a lot of those out there. This time, though, it landed differently, sending cold water trickling down my spine:

Did Badura Throw Season to Secure #1 Pick for Toronto?

My mouth went dry.

He hadn't. No one in their right mind would torpedo his own stats and make his team take a dive. His club sure as shit wouldn't put up with it.

Curiosity wanted me to keep pulling that thread, though, so I clicked on an article at random.

Toronto superstar center Jaromir Badura, 21, noticeably plummeted in stats across the board this past season. At the same time, Toronto Shamrocks head coach Hal Robertson refused to bench him, allowing the faltering number one center to rack up record-breaking minutes night after night despite numerous costly blunders.

Badura played at his usual consistent level in October and November, prompting analysts to predict he was on-track for his third hundred-point season in a row. His team didn't fare nearly as well; at the same time Badura was shining, Toronto saw any hope of playoff contention all but dashed after abysmal performances.

Beginning in December, after Badura returned from missing several games due to a lower body injury, his play shifted dramatically. Instead of another hundred points, he closed out the regular season with a dubious honor: most own goals by a non-goalie since Ottawa's Cork Murphy in the 1964-65 season.

The forward's penalty minutes also skyrocketed, with the

*usually well-disciplined player soaring from an average of
12 PIM per season to 114 this season. This would be less
than ideal under any circumstances, but with Toronto's
penalty kill ranking in the bottom three for the League all
season long, Badura's increased PIM was nothing short of
disastrous.*

The writer went on to speculate that Jarek intentionally
tanked his team in order to tilt the odds in favor of Toronto
landing the number one overall draft pick. After all, having
a shitshow of a season was worthwhile if it led to a club
obtaining a talented prospect, especially in a season where
there was one standout player who *everyone* wanted.

I leaned back against the headboard and exhaled.

I remembered that year's draft very well. There was still
a framed newspaper article in my parents' house with the
headline, *Who Will Win the Hunter Michaud Sweepstakes?*
As an eighteen-year-old, that had been exhilarating, even if
it meant a ton more pressure. I'd busted my ass to get to that
level, and it still blew my mind sometimes to imagine how
badly every team in the League had coveted the number
one pick that year. How badly they'd coveted *me*.

But if I was reading between the lines correctly…

If I was putting the pieces together correctly between
Jarek's cryptic comment, this article, and the stats he'd put
up that season…

Had my draft catastrophically derailed someone else's
career?

Holy shit.

But… no, that couldn't be it. This article was just speculation. And Jarek was probably projecting because I was a
convenient target for his frustration with himself.

Right?

With my heart in my throat, I switched to another tab. I

searched for videos, using only his last name and no other prompts. The results?

Compilation: 10 Minutes of Joke Badura Own Goals

Badura Forgetting How to Win Faceoffs for 9 Minutes Straight

Joke Badura's Most Boneheaded Penalties This Season

I clicked on one at random, switched to full-screen mode, and watched.

It was one thing to see a highlight here and there, especially at full speed. Or to hear one of the commentators rip apart a particular mistake; one of those could make someone believe a player had no idea what he was doing, even if the reality was that hockey moved at breakneck speed and we all made dumb mistakes. Put one of those errors in context with the things a player did right, and the whole picture wasn't so bad.

Compilations like these could have that same effect—making the viewer believe this person had no idea how to play hockey. There was one out there somewhere of my worst turnovers. Anyone who watched it would probably walk away thinking I couldn't control the puck to save my life, even though my stats made it clear that wasn't the case.

I knew Jarek could play hockey. He was a damn good player, and these videos wouldn't convince me otherwise.

No, what I wanted to see was exactly *how* those errors played out.

And holy shit...

After six or seven videos, my eyes were heavy with fatigue, but my mind was whirring. This couldn't be real. No way.

Yeah, I'd seen all this before, but looking at them through this lens was jaw-dropping.

One of the own goals looked like a bad case of unlucky

bounces and the hockey gods being dicks. An opposing player shot at Toronto's goal. Jarek was part of the screen, and the puck bounced off his stick and into the net. Frustrating as all hell, but it happened.

The person who'd compiled the video had slowed the clip down dramatically, though, and in slow motion, zoomed way in... that puck did *not* bounce off Jarek's stick. He *tipped it in*.

It was subtle. Could've even passed for a reflex or a failed deflection. But that minute shift of Jarek's stick unmistakably directed the puck into the net.

Which, again, could've been accidental. The frustrated, disgusted look on his face after the lamp lit up definitely sold it.

But in the next clip, another blink-and-you'll-miss-it movement slowed down and zoomed in showed a puck hitting his skate blade at an angle that should've sent it safely out of the crease. The slightest turn of Jarek's foot, however, changed the trajectory, and the puck slipped right through the five-hole. The goalie even tried to claim it was a kicking motion, so it shouldn't count. After all, goals from opposing teams didn't count if they were kicked in. Why should own goals? But the refs determined it was not a kick, so it counted, and Toronto lost three-two.

At one point in the video, a caption demanded, *Why hasn't Robertson benched this idiot?* Another declared, *This Joke is getting paid $1.3 million per season to make mistakes that would get a kid cut from the peewees.*

The most telling was during a clip of an own goal *in fucking overtime* when bright red letters screamed, *Badura is better than this. What the fuck happened?*

I swallowed hard. I'd wondered that for a long, long

time. Even as he'd pulled himself back up and started playing at his usual level in recent years, I'd wondered.

After what he'd said in the hallway, and after these articles and compilations, the truth was almost impossible to avoid.

I was what the fuck happened.

CHAPTER 19

JAREK

I really, really wished I'd had more to drink last night.

Yeah, I'd be feeling like shit right now, and yeah, I'd probably want to die all through practice and even the game. But at least I wouldn't be losing my damned mind over that conversation with Hunter. Maybe I would've been too drunk to engage with him. Or I'd have slurred something that would get me a stern talking-to from Coach or a fist in the mouth from Hunter.

Anything but what I'd actually said.

I sat on the edge of my hotel bed and rubbed my face. God, I couldn't believe I'd done that. I hadn't even been that drunk. What was wrong with me?

Maybe it was the alcohol and the jetlag and the altitude and... Fuck, just being face to face with the reminder of my biggest mistakes. All of it had come together in the same moment he'd decided to confront me, and I'd let the cracks show and the words just came tumbling out.

Oh, fuck me. I'd been so careful, kept this so close to the vest for so long, and then... Jesus.

Facing Hunter was always fun, and it was going to be a

real treat today, because I had no idea what he thought of what I'd said. The best I could hope for was that he took it as some half-drunk bullshit and me being an asshole. The worst...

Well, thinking about the worst-case scenario didn't do good things to my stomach, so I let that go for now. I could dwell on it once my hangover had cleared up and I could—

A sharp knock made me jump, which didn't help my head *or* stomach.

Grimacing against the pain and nausea, I eyed the door. Was it too much to ask for housekeeping to be showing up early?

Yeah, probably.

Another knock, harder this time. A teammate who'd forgotten about this thing called texting?

I indulged in some pitiful grumbling before I shuffled to the door and peered through the peephole.

And stiffened.

What the hell?

When I pulled open the door, Hunter brushed past me into my room. "We need to talk."

I wanted to roll my eyes, but between my throbbing head and my churning stomach, I didn't dare. And honestly I wasn't even all that annoyed that he'd waltzed into my room without being invited; at least he didn't want to do this out in the hall where someone might see or hear.

Fine. We could talk, I guess. Hooray.

I winced as I shut the door, then turned around. I wasn't sure what I expected when I faced him, but I was definitely surprised to see him pacing, crossing and uncrossing his arms as he refused to look at me.

I'd never seen him this agitated, not even the first time he'd confronted me outside of training camp, and I didn't know what to make of it. What did *he* have to be this spun up about? I was the one who'd let it slip that I'd royally fucked myself all those years ago, not him.

I took a breath, ready to ask, when he suddenly spun and faced me. His wide eyes, bloodshot and framed by heavy circles, were pleading and worried in ways I didn't understand. His words came out quiet and strained, as if he were fighting the urge to shout at me because he didn't want anyone else to overhear.

"Tell me the truth," he half-begged, half-demanded. "Did you throw a season so Toronto could draft me?"

The question hit like an accusation, and the heat in my face was nauseatingly similar to the burn of too many reporters' lights blazing over me while they grilled me. And fuck my life, but searing right through all of that was sympathy I didn't deserve. Not from this man. Not for what I'd done.

Goddammit. Couldn't he have just told the staff or our teammates so everyone could hate me? Maybe told the press so people would know who I was? Then maybe I could stop getting swallowed whole by the guilt that came with knowing everyone around me thought I was someone I wasn't.

Something must have registered in my face or my posture, because Hunter spoke before I could: "You did, didn't you?"

I flinched, avoiding his gaze. What could I fucking say? He'd obviously figured it out. Even if he was just speculating, it wasn't like I could look him in the eye and tell him he was wrong because I *hated myself* for how right he was.

When one of us finally spoke, it was Hunter again, and what came was a single breathless syllable: "Why?"

Shame roiled inside my already iffy stomach. There were so many answers I could give, and most of them came down to fear. Fear of failure. Fear of letting my team down. Fear of... something far less abstract. My spine prickled at the memory of being backed against the wall of Coach Robertson's office, blood pounding in my ears as he screamed at me and threatened me and screamed at me some more. Even after all this time, I could still smell the coffee on his breath as vividly as I could still feel that cold wall behind my shoulders and the queasy certainty that the next time he wound his fist back, he was going to let it fly. The man had never laid a hand on me, but my God, he'd had me *terrified* he was going to.

My voice came out as a croak as I admitted, for the first time in my life, "I was afraid of them. Coach and Wilcox." Sighing, I sank onto the edge of the bed and rubbed my neck with both hands, refusing to look at Hunter. "And I thought doing this would mean... I guess I thought I wouldn't have to be so fucking terrified of them if they got what they wanted." Closing my eyes, I said, "And they told me over and over that with you and me on the team, Toronto would be unstoppable."

The exhalation was harsh and ragged, and when I chanced an upward glance, Hunter's wince was hard to take. And hard to understand.

I dropped my gaze again and continued. I'd already let the cat out of the bag. Might as well just get it all out. "They drafted me during their rebuild. Said they planned to build the team around me. But I wasn't..." Trailing off, I closed my eyes and shook my head.

"You couldn't carry an entire team on your back."

"I tried," I whispered. "I played my ass off. Did everything I—"

"No one can say you didn't. You were a hundred-point player for three straight seasons."

I looked up at him again, startled that he knew my stats.

It was his turn for a blush, though it wasn't as pronounced as mine had probably been. Avoiding my gaze, he admitted, "I watched you play. Studied the way you played, actually."

My lips parted. "You... You did?"

Still not looking at me, he nodded. "You were good. Right from the start." He finally turned to me. "I was under a ton of pressure. From the time I was in 12U, everyone knew I was going to go pro. I studied the players I wanted to play like." He half-shrugged, his voice barely audible as he said, "You were one of them."

I didn't know what to say to that.

Hunter swallowed, shifting his weight. "So they said they were going to build a team around you and me...?" He raised his eyebrows.

Exhaling, I leaned back on my hands and tilted my head from side to side, working out some tension. "They basically told me I hadn't done as much for the team as they'd expected. I was a failure and a disappointment. A wasted investment. Since I couldn't do what they'd signed me to do, I owed it to them to help with Plan B."

Hunter stared at me.

I went on, "Coming in dead last in the League wouldn't guarantee us the top pick, but it would mean seriously good odds. Wilcox—he was..." I waved a hand. "I don't know. He was going to wheel and deal with some of the other teams. Do everything he could to land that top pick. But at the end of the day, our best bet was still for us to finish last." I swallowed against the acid in my throat. "They literally told me to my face that because I was the best player on the roster, all they needed to guarantee last place was for *me* to throw the games. The rest of the team…" I closed my eyes, shame and guilt and all kinds of emotions I couldn't define churning in the pit of my stomach.

Hunter was quiet for a long moment. When he spoke again, he sounded dazed. "So since they didn't think you were good enough to make the team win, they told you to take a dive so they could find someone better."

The sting in my eyes caught me by surprise. I thought I'd made peace with it—as much peace as anyone could— but putting these cards out in front of someone, especially Hunter, cut me to the bone. I hated myself for agreeing to it instead of demanding a trade or going to the media or… or *something*. God knew what twenty-one year-old me would've had the spine or wherewithal to do if I'd found more courage than I'd had in that meeting. It didn't matter, though, because I hadn't found anything.

"*So, just make sure we lose?*" young me had timidly asked my coach and GM. "*That's it?*"

"*That's it.*" The GM had met me with a sharky smile. "*We'll take it from there.*"

In the present, I cleared my throat. "I shouldn't have done it. But I did. I convinced myself it would be worth it. But it…" I wiped a hand over my face and sighed. "It wasn't."

There was some movement, and I looked up to see Hunter pulling out one of the chairs at the table and easing himself down into it. I gnawed the inside of my cheek, waiting for him to say something, wondering if maybe I was the one who needed to keep talking. What else was there to say? I'd never admitted this out loud to anyone. I had no idea what was going through his mind, or what might excuse… Hell, anything. What I'd done. How much of a dick I'd been to him since he'd come to Pittsburgh even after I'd tried—really tried—to treat him better. How I could still look at myself in the mirror.

Hunter shifted, making the chair squeak. "Question."

I lifted my gaze to meet his.

He chewed his lip for a moment. Then, softly, he asked, "Is this why you requested a trade out of Toronto after that season?"

"Requested—" I flew to my feet, rage instantly replacing every other emotion. "Are you fucking kidding me? Is that what they said?"

Hunter drew back against his chair, eyes wide. "I... Yeah? They said—"

Every curse I knew—Czech, English, the Russian and Swedish I'd picked up from my teammates—tumbled out of my mouth as I paced across the room. I didn't even give a shit at this point if someone heard us through the walls. Too pissed. Too far beyond caring about anything.

"Hey. Hey." Hunter was suddenly in front of me, palms up and eyes locked on mine. "Dude. Take a breath."

I did. It didn't help much, but it did stop the tirade. So did the obvious concern in the face of a teammate who I'd given every reason to hate me. Another breath brought my heart rate down a little. Gritting my teeth, not sure if I was fighting harder to hold back fury or tears, I said, "I *never* requested the trade."

Hunter's lips parted and his eyes went huge. "What? But they—are you serious?"

I nodded, rubbing the back of my neck as I shuffled back toward the bed. I dropped onto its edge. "Turns out they were never going to build a team around the two of us. They were going to build it around *you*." I laughed bitterly. "After they used me to *get* you."

"Jesus H. Christ." Hunter sank into the chair again. "So they used you, then chewed you up and spat you out. God, no wonder you've got a chip on your shoulder."

"Wouldn't you?"

"Absolutely."

Our eyes locked, and my stomach somersaulted. I'd been an asshole to him ever since training camp. Even now the resentment burned whenever I laid eyes on him, though it was dampened by the shame and guilt sliding over me like a wet blanket.

I cleared my throat, and when I spoke, my voice was unsteady, dangerously close to breaking. "I know none of this is on you. I *know* that. But you've got to understand that every time I look at you, I'm looking at everything I was supposed to be, and the biggest mistake I ever made."

Hunter stared me, looking so dumbstruck for a moment, I wondered if I'd spoken in Czech without thinking. Then he shook himself. "I... Holy shit. I had no idea."

"You weren't supposed to." I swallowed. "No one was."

"No one—" His brow furrowed. "How many people *do* know?"

I shook my head. "No one. Just me, Robertson, and Wilcox." I shrugged. "They might've had others involved. I don't know. But I've never told anyone. Not until now."

Hunter breathed a string of curses.

"I *can't* tell anyone. Ever." I met his eyes. "Yeah, I'd love to see Wilcox and Robertson go down in flames over it, but they wouldn't be the only ones who'd burn, and neither would I."

Hunter cocked his head. "What do you mean?"

"I wasn't the only one who had a shit season that year. Not just in Toronto, either. If this comes out, everyone who didn't play normally is going to be under a microscope."

"But it isn't like there's any evidence against them. It's all speculation."

I swallowed. "There's no evidence against me, either. I can't prove Wilcox and Robertson put me up to it. I can't prove they didn't put anyone else up to it. Tate Collins played worse than I did that season. Yeah, it came out later that he had a knee injury that was hurting his play, and he did a lot better after surgery. But who's to say that wasn't just a smokescreen?" Grimacing, I shook my head. "Even if nothing ever happens to him or anyone else professionally, it'll stick to them for the rest of their careers. Every error they make, every bad season their teams have—they'll never be able to get away from it."

Hunter swore but didn't add anything else.

Silence hung between us, and I rewound this conversation and everything that had led to it. In particular, our confrontation in the hallway last night. Not what I'd said—the things *he'd* said.

"Do you have a problem with me?"

"I'm getting grilled about it by reporters, and I have no idea what to tell them."

"So, you tell me. What should I say when they ask about it? Should I just make up some beef between us? Because hell if I know why I've apparently been persona non grata with you since training camp."

Fresh shame wound itself around that ball of lead in my stomach. Rubbing my eyes, I sighed, exhausted by... Fuck. By *everything*. Hunter was right to be pissed at me, and he'd been right to call me out.

"We're a good pair," I whispered unsteadily. "On the ice, we're..." I waved my hand before letting it drop heavily into my lap. "We've got chemistry."

"We do," he said.

I swallowed hard, and it was a struggle to look him in the eyes. "But it's hard, too. Because every time we do a shift together, it just makes me think that it was supposed to be this way a long time ago. I was only supposed to lose one season. And then this"—I gestured at him and myself—"was going to make it worth it."

"But it never happened," he said almost soundlessly. "Until now."

I nodded, lowering my gaze. "I don't think it would've been worth it if it had worked out the way they promised." I let my shoulders sag under an invisible weight. "But the way things *did* play out…"

He paced a little, seeming to digest that. Then he sat in the chair again, leaning forward on his elbows and looking right at me. "Listen. There's nothing I can say that's going to unfuck all of that. It's…" He shook his head. "They shouldn't have done that to you. Any of it. And for what it's worth, I'm sorry it happened. I know it's not my fault—I didn't do anything—but I get it, you know? Now that you've told me all this, I get why you have a hard time being around me."

I couldn't hold his gaze, and I was barely holding on to my composure. All this time, I hadn't realized how much I'd needed to tell *someone* what I did all those years ago, and why. More than that, I hadn't realized how desperately I needed someone to tell me Wilcox and Robertson had been wrong to put me in that position.

It was more freeing than I'd anticipated. I didn't know if it was because the person saying it was Hunter Michaud, but I'd take it.

He wasn't finished yet, either. "They didn't do me dirty like they did you, but they tried to put the whole team on my back. Same as they did your first few seasons."

A bitter laugh escaped my parched throat. "I'm not surprised."

"Right? But the thing is... we're out from under their bullshit now. Free and clear."

I lifted my gaze to meet his, and the simultaneously cautious and devilish grin on his lips jolted my heart back into motion.

"We're here," he said again, "and we're linemates. Surrounded by exactly what we both needed in Toronto—a team and a club that expects us all to pull our weight. I mean, fuck—that's *why* I came here."

"It is?"

"Are you kidding?" He scoffed, sitting back in the chair. "When the GM in Pittsburgh told me I'd have to be a team player and couldn't expect to get extra leeway or special treatment just because I'm Hunter Michaud?" He chuckled. "I basically said, 'Copy that. Where do I sign?'"

"Really?"

He laughed. "Uh, yeah? I want to be on a *team*. Pittsburgh is a team. Toronto..." He scowled and shook his head. "It isn't. And it wasn't going to be any time soon. So I bailed as soon as I was a free agent and came someplace where everyone pulled their weight."

I rubbed the back of my neck. "And you ended up linemates with me."

Hunter acknowledged that with a neutral grunt.

Fresh shame piled on my shoulders, and I stared at the floor. "I'm sorry. I... I know I've been a dick to you from day one."

I braced for, *"Yeah, you have, you asshole. What the fuck?"*

What I got instead was more silence. An expression that

told me nothing. Maybe I needed to offer more before I deserved a response.

"I don't *want* to resent you," I said, barely whispering. "I never did. None of this is your fault, and I've always known that." I swallowed hard. "But every time I look at you..."

Hunter's shoulders sank. "You can't look at me without thinking about..." He circled his hand in the air as if to encompass our whole situation.

I nodded. "I know I shouldn't. It's not..."

"I don't blame you, honestly. If someone did me that dirty, I don't think I'd be able to look at anyone who was involved. Even if it wasn't direct."

My throat tightened and my eyes stung, but I didn't want him to notice that, so I just gave a non-committal shrug.

He studied me. "And you really haven't told anyone else? Ever?"

"I wish I could. But I can't." Sudden panic surged in my chest, as if he were about to bolt for the door and out me to the entire team. "I *need* you to keep it between us. Please, Hunter."

Hunter pursed his lips.

"Please," I whispered.

"I will," he said. "I... It's not my secret to tell. But Jesus Christ, how long are you going to carry this?"

With a heavy shrug, I said, "I'll take it to the grave. I have to."

"No, you don't. You can—"

"I do." I wrung my hands in front of me. "It would fuck over too many people if it came out."

"People who fucking deserve it for gaming the system and hanging you out to dry!" The vehemence surprised me. Maybe it shouldn't have.

"Yes, them," I admitted. "But also, like I said before, people who don't deserve to be pulled in. Like Tate Collins." I blew out a breath. "God, if anyone even suspects what I did, they'll go after him for sure. I mean, he barely made it through each game, even when Coach had him playing fourth line minutes. He could barely fucking walk." I wiped a hand over my face and sighed. "And the way he bounced back the next season after he was done recovering... If I blow the whistle..."

Hunter swore, raking a hand through his hair as he pushed himself to his feet. Restlessness came off him in waves as he started pacing across the room. "Fuck. There has to be something. They can't just... For Christ's sake, they can't fucking get away with that bullshit. They can't!"

"But if they go down," I whispered unsteadily, "they'll take me with them. And too many other people who had nothing to do with it." I paused. "It would probably stain you, too."

"How? I didn't do anything."

"No, but no one will be able to talk about you or the trajectory of your career without mentioning this." I shook my head. "It's one thing when people speculate and make shit up. It's another thing entirely when they have facts they can spin into lies."

His eyes lost focus. Then he swore and rubbed his eyes, his shoulders sinking with what I could only assume was resignation.

Guilt and shame piled onto the already queasy feeling in my stomach. If there was one person on this planet who should've been able to stay blissfully ignorant of what I'd done, it was Hunter Michaud. And he would've, if I'd just been able to keep a poker face and not be a dick to him until he'd cornered me up while I was drunk and demanded the truth.

God, I'm so sorry.

Lowering his hand, Hunter met my gaze. "Why did you agree to it?"

I dropped my own gaze to my lap. "I was a kid. They—Wilcox and Robertson, they made it sound like it was what we all needed." I shrugged, which took work. "I wanted to help my team. That was all. We weren't doing so hot and we desperately needed to rebuild. They picked me ninth overall, but I'd failed to live up to what they expected."

Hunter swore under his breath, shaking his head.

I went on even as my voice threatened to crack again, "I didn't live up to what they put on me. Everyone was convinced you were the answer to that. And I was..." Heat flooded my face as acid tried to crawl up my throat.

"Tell me."

I couldn't look at him, and I struggled to speak through the nausea, but I managed to croak, "I really was afraid of them. Wilcox and Robertson." That acid very nearly chased the words up my throat. I'd never admitted that out loud before today. Not to anyone. "In every way. Not just professionally. I was a kid, and I was..." My eyes stung, and I pushed out a ragged breath before I whispered, "I was scared of them."

And I wasn't ready when Hunter said, "So was I."

My head snapped up. "What?"

"Are you kidding? I was terrified of them." He chafed his arms. "I still don't know how I made it through seven seasons without Robertson laying me out. Maybe he was just that intimidating."

My mouth had gone dry. I wasn't the only one? Someone else had seen that?

Before I could comment on that, though, Hunter spoke, and his voice was gentle. Not judgy or confrontational, I thought, and with more compassion than I probably deserved. "You really were the best they had. You were their star." What little laughter there was faded. "And when you couldn't work literal miracles, they made you tank the team so I could come in and carry them instead." He shuddered. "God help whoever they draft in the first round now that we're both gone."

I swallowed bile and swore in Czech. "It... I mean, they came up with this after I had been out for an injury. The team dropped way down in the rankings while I was out, so maybe they saw..." I shook my head and sighed. "I don't know. And maybe there were others. I have no idea. All I know is that everything I was trying to do to make the team better—it wasn't working. They told me it was my fault, so it was on me to fix it. If I couldn't get us to the top, then I owed it to the team to do whatever it took to bring in someone who could." I laughed bitterly as I cautiously met his gaze, and again my voice cracked as I said, "They told me they'd make us linemates. You and me."

Hunter blinked. "They did?"

"Yeah. I don't know if they saw something. Since, I mean, we're obviously good together. Or if it was just bullshit. They just told me that if I kept us from winning enough to land last in the League, and we managed to draft you, that they'd put us on the same line. Make it look like I just had a bad year—blame it on some bullshit injury or something—but then made a huge comeback."

Hunter swallowed. "But... you played center back then."

The comment caught me off guard. "You knew what position I played?"

A blush I couldn't quite understand bloomed in his cheeks. "I told you—I followed your career."

For some reason, that didn't seem like the whole story, but I let it go.

"I played wing in juniors," I explained. "I only played center in Toronto because we were short on forwards who were worth a damn on faceoffs. When we hatched this stupid plan, they said a few seasons on your wing would make everyone forget about my one bad season."

"Jesus." Hunter dropped into the chair again and rubbed his forehead as if this were all giving him a headache. Maybe it was. "I feel so guilty about this."

"Guilty? Why? You didn't do anything."

He met my gaze, one eyebrow up. "Didn't stop you from resenting me. Why should it stop me from feeling bad about what you went through?"

Oh. Huh. Well, he had me there.

Before I could figure out some way to respond, he exhaled and sat back in the chair. "I had no idea. I... Christ, I didn't think anyone was out there sacrificing their career for..." He closed his eyes and swallowed, and he grimaced as he said, "And in the end, I didn't even make anything out of the opportunity with the team, so—"

"That's not on you. You know it wasn't."

"It..." He sighed, avoiding my gaze. After a moment, he met it again. "I *wanted* to do what everyone expected me to. Not just because of the pressure, but... I mean, I wanted to be on a winning team, you know? And I thought if we made it from rock bottom to winning the Cup, it would be incredible."

"But you couldn't do it by yourself."

Wincing, he shook his head. "No. I couldn't."

"And you shouldn't have to. They shouldn't have asked you to carry them all to the top."

Hunter looked right in my eyes. "They shouldn't have asked you to drag them to the bottom."

"No," I said hollowly. "They shouldn't have."

We sat in weird silence for a long moment, as if neither of us knew quite what to say. This was the most we'd ever said to each other at one time, and we were both laying a lot of heavy cards on the table. The resentment had evaporated, and I wondered if that—along with telling him things I'd never told anyone before—was part of why I felt so raw and brittle.

After a while, I swallowed. "*Promise me* none of this leaves this room."

"It's not my secret to tell," he said again. "I won't breathe a word to anyone. I promise."

Nodding, I murmured, "Thank you."

Silence hung between us again, but then, to my surprise, Hunter grinned. "You know there's only one thing left to do, right?"

My heart jumped into my throat, and my mind went in some irrational directions involving that club where I'd watched him with another guy. Clearly not what he meant, but that was where my mind went. "Uh..."

Mercifully oblivious to my ridiculous thoughts, Hunter narrowed his eyes and grinned even bigger. "Let's be what Toronto promised you we would be."

Renewed fire kindled in my soul, melting the edges of ice that had been there for far too long, and I couldn't help smiling. "I think we already are, aren't we?"

"I think so." He shrugged, still grinning. "But maybe with the air cleared..."

Hell. Maybe? If we could be as good as we'd been lately

while things were weird, it could only get better now that we'd come to an understanding.

"I guess we can start tomorrow night?" I said. "Denver is on a winning streak." I held up my fist. "Help me break it?"

Hunter's smile did things to me it had *no* right to, and as he fist-bumped me, he said, "Fuck yeah. Let's do it."

CHAPTER 20

HUNTER

If the conversation with Jarek had been surreal, the aftermath blew my mind.

I kind of expected him to still be frosty toward me, or at least guarded, until he was sure I could be trusted to keep his secret. Or he might be walking on eggshells around me, afraid that if he so much as looked at me the wrong way, I'd say, *"You know what? Fuck it. Where's the team reporter?"*

But no. It wasn't like that at all.

One conversation—one jaw-dropping conversation full of confessions he'd never made to anyone else—and the wall of resentment between us was just... gone. I couldn't say all the tension between us was gone—*something* was still simmering beneath the surface that I did *not* need to think about—but the hostility and the resentment? They were so gone, it felt like I'd imagined them all along. I knew I hadn't, but the sudden shift was unreal. No cold shoulder. No dirty looks. No feeling like Jarek wanted me to drop dead.

When we were at the same table at breakfast or a post-game meal, he didn't find an excuse to leave or try his level best to talk to me *just* enough to make it seem like everything was fine. Sawyer, Dolls, and I needed another player for a card game on a flight to Washington, and Jarek joined in. On the next flight, I took Dima's place at their table so he could grab a nap and they could have four people for a game of Hearts. No awkwardness. No discomfort.

During practice, we interacted the same way as our other teammates. Games, too. And holy shit, did that elevate our play as a line. I meant what I'd said to Jarek about us being what Toronto had never let us be, and apparently he was still onboard too. Jarek, Dima, and I had been compatible from the start despite everything Jarek had been carrying. Now that we'd cleared the air, it was like someone had punched in a cheat code or something. By the third week after our conversation, we were four points ahead of Mayweather's line, the Hornets were firmly back in second place, and Dima and I both had hat tricks.

Tonight, we were in Minneapolis for a game, and I was supposed to be catching a nap before we headed to the arena. I couldn't, though. Not after a long lunch with several of my teammates—including Jarek—at a restaurant Dolls had insisted we all needed to try. The food had been amazing. So had the camaraderie. I had the bond with my teammates that I'd taken for granted in juniors and craved in Toronto.

All because Jarek had finally broken his silence.

That conversation had loomed large in my head for the past three weeks, and today, I couldn't relax enough to sleep. My mind was whirring in too many directions, trying to reconcile the man who'd hugged me so tight I couldn't breathe after assisting on my game-winning OT goal two nights ago with the kid who'd been on the verge of tears as he'd confessed how our paths had first crossed. After weeks of walking on eggshells to avoid pissing him off, I'd suddenly been staring slack-jawed while he apologized for being an ass and begged me to keep his secret between us.

Even after some time had gone by, I couldn't process everything we'd talked about. The change in him was jarring and mind-blowing. What he'd told me, though? It just... What the actual fuck? I knew Wilcox and Robertson were dicks, and I knew they weren't above threatening players or doing whatever it took to get what they wanted, but strong-arming someone into taking a dive? That was... Jesus. I couldn't get my head around it.

And did those asshats have any idea how lucky they were that Jarek had been rational enough to see what a disaster it would be to blow the whole thing open? Maybe they'd (correctly) banked on him being too scared and humiliated to speak up. Because I couldn't say for sure that young me would've kept my mouth shut in that situation. Didn't matter how much of my life had been spent getting media-trained—I'd had a hothead streak at that age, and I could absolutely see myself going in front of a camera and diming them out.

Then again, hadn't I kept it to myself how my former coach and GM had treated me? Hadn't I cowered against office walls before going back to my condo or my hotel room to puke? Wasn't I *still* keeping all that a secret out of... what, fear? Shame? Some feeling I couldn't name or define but also couldn't escape?

So yeah, maybe I would've kept my mouth shut. Especially since those assholes had been seriously good at manipulating me into believing anything and everything was my fault, and I vividly remembered the shame in Jarek's eyes as he'd told me his story. Not just the anger and resentment—the *shame*. The guilt. As if the weight of what he'd done landed solely on his shoulders, even though he'd just been a naïve kid being manipulated by powerful, abusive people.

And like, what if Toronto *hadn't* drafted me? What if Jarek had taken that dive and thrown his whole career into chaos, only to have another team snag that coveted top overall pick? What would've happened to him then?

There was no telling, of course. Though I didn't imagine the outcome would've been much better for him. Toronto would've had what appeared to be an absolute trash fire of a forward who'd clearly dragged his team to the bottom of the rankings, and they'd want to shed that albatross one way or another. To the minors. To another team. Maybe put him on waivers and hope he was claimed so he could be someone else's problem.

I couldn't imagine, and I couldn't process everything. We'd talked three weeks ago, and just thinking about it left me as dazed as I'd been during and immediately after that conversation. I hadn't been all that surprised to find out the assholes in charge had lied about Jarek demanding a trade. Truth was, the longer I'd been in Toronto, the more I'd understood why he'd—I thought—demanded to leave. Learning that he'd *wanted* to stay, and that he'd been promised things would get better once he took a dive for the good of the team, hit me hard, because who the hell did that to someone? Least of all a kid who was bending over backwards for a team that didn't appreciate him?

And yet once I'd thought about it, I wasn't as surprised as he probably thought. I knew Wilcox and Robertson, and something like this was, while extreme, a hundred percent on-brand for those ruthlessly toxic assholes. That they were both still in their positions after all these years—far longer than much better head coaches and GMs often held those jobs—didn't sow a lot of faith in the club or the League doing anything about them.

At least Jarek had finally been able to tell someone. There wasn't fuck all I could do about it, but hopefully it had done him some good to get the words out.

And now that he had...

I exhaled and wiped a hand over my face, then stared up at the ceiling in my hotel. Who knew it would be *harder* to coexist with Jarek now that we were coexisting peacefully?

Because... Jesus. He'd been attractive already. Even back when I was a teenager who couldn't talk without my voice cracking, Jaromir Badura had been hot. Time had refined his features, sharpened them, and maybe it was a side effect of him scowling and glaring at me for a while, but that smile... God, it did things to me. Especially when he *really* smiled. Like when he was celebrating a goal. Or when Ferns and Dima were talking trash and he couldn't stop laughing.

Or clear back in the beginning when we'd been at Dima's barbecue, and Jarek had offered to hold the baby for a moment while Chloé stepped inside; he'd been drinking, but he hadn't been drunk, and he'd taken a seat by the firepit and held Ilya in his lap and...

I swallowed. It was just as well Jarek and I had still been on weird ground back then. If we'd been getting along like this that night, I might have literally melted at the sight of him smiling at Dima and Chloé's baby like that.

Against my better judgment, I felt around on the night-stand for my phone. When I found it, I pulled up a photo album that included some pictures I'd saved from the team's group chat. It only took a few swipes to find the one I was looking for.

And I just... stared.

It was a shot of Dima, Ferns, Dolls, and Jarek. Of course it was—the four of them were inseparable. Someone had taken it in the locker room during an intermission, and the guys were relaxing on a bench. Ferns had his helmet and jersey off, dark hair sweaty and askew. Dolls had taken off his mask, but he still had on all his pads, which made his head look comically small. Like Ferns, Jarek had stripped off his jersey, though he still had on his chest protector, and he was squirting Dima with a water bottle. Dima was trying to shield himself and retaliate at the same time. Ferns and Dolls were laughing hysterically.

Jarek...

My God.

He was laughing, too, using a glove to fend off Dima's water attack. In that moment, I didn't imagine he gave a damn about anything. Not the past. Not the future. Maybe not even the game that wasn't over yet. He was just taking a breather and horsing around with his friends, and he didn't look like he had a single care in the world except squirting Dima in the face and not getting hit himself.

Because I was apparently determined not to get any sleep this afternoon, I swiped to another photo. This one had come from our media team. Like a lot of hockey teams, the Hornets often featured young players, who would skate out and join us at the blue line for the anthems. One night— I want to say it was when Long Island came to Pittsburgh?— the kid had been from a local U8 team, and she couldn't have been more than six or seven. She'd frozen at the Zamboni gate, either too scared to move or unsure where to go.

Our line had been the starters that night, and Jarek had skated across to the gate, given her tiny stick a gentle tap, and coaxed her out onto the ice. Her little smile lit up the whole arena, and the crowd cheered as she skated with him back to the blue line. They stopped there, and he leaned down to say something to her. No one but them knew what he said, but she was beaming as they shared a gloved fist bump.

That was the instant this photo was taken. It caught the two of them in profile—little blond curls sticking out of her helmet and face cage as she bumped her glove against Jarek's. Even through the face cage, the stadium lights picked out the tears still clinging to her lashes from her now forgotten moment of panic. She was so cute, and I could guess who her favorite player would be until the end of the time.

And Jarek's smile just...

God, he *liquefied* me.

It would've made me swoon before. Something about being on better ground with him now—about having seen him raw and vulnerable—made his smile and his sweetness completely throw me off-balance. Seeing his softer side with kids, and his playful side, and his fun and relaxed side...

I was going to lose my mind in Pittsburgh, wasn't I? For entirely different reasons than I'd been losing it in Toronto.

Exhaling, I turned off the screen and put my phone facedown on my chest. Not that it helped—even as I stared up at the ceiling again, his carefree laugh and his gentle, sweet smile were burned into my mind.

You're already beautiful, asshole.

Do you have *to be such a good guy, too?*

I wasn't the only one who noticed the changed dynamic between Jarek and me.

Sawyer stopped me on the way to the locker room that evening. "Hey, did you and Yars kiss and make up or something?"

I almost dropped my coffee, and I laughed a little too loudly, the sound echoing in the concrete hallway. "Kiss and make up? What are you talking about?"

He shot me a pointed look. "So I've just been imagining the way you two have been cool lately? Or that you were one dirty look away from throwing gloves before that?"

"I, uh..." Okay. Fine. He was right. And I wasn't surprised he'd noticed. Others probably had, too. Clearing my throat, I started walking again, and as he fell into step beside me, I said, "You know how it is sometimes. Guys don't always get along right at the start."

"Uh-huh. But that's not 'not getting along.' And the way things are now—"

"We're racking up points and don't want to kill each other." I elbowed him. "That's a good thing, right?"

He eyed me as if he were contemplating whether to push. Then he put up his hands. "All right, all right." He gave my shoulder a squeeze. "For the record, I don't care if you boys are blowing each other as long as—"

"Shut up before you're down a third tooth."

He laughed and we continued into the locker room.

Of course, I zeroed right in on Jarek, who was helping Ferns tape something to Dolls's paddle while Dima kept watch. I chuckled to myself even as my heart did that weird fluttery shit it had started doing every time I looked at Jarek.

I quickly *didn't* look at Jarek, and I concentrated on getting into my gear. No point in drawing anyone else's attention to the changed dynamic between us.

I was just pulling on my shin guards when a Swedish-accented, "Goddammit!" broke through the noise of the room.

Everyone turned. Of course it was Dolls, having discovered the mess Ferns and Jarek had made of his gear.

"Are you fuckers serious?" He pointed at his gear, which had been fastened together in a heap with stick tape, and he glared at the three of them. "This was you guys, wasn't it?"

Instantly, all three of them were talking over each other, declaring their innocence and demanding to know where he found the audacity to make such ridiculous accusations.

Dolls just rolled his eyes and flipped them off.

They started cackling, and the rest of the room joined in, myself included.

As Dolls got to work breaking apart his gear so he could get ready, Jarek high-fived Ferns and Dima. So much for innocence. Then Jarek turned to head for his locker, and as he did, his gaze snagged on me.

And for a second...

Just a beat or two...

Our eyes locked.

His laughter seemed to freeze in his throat. Faltered a little. And then...

Oh, sweet Jesus. That smile wasn't a laugh. It wasn't a reaction to Dolls or their prank.

It was for me.

I didn't know what the fuck it meant, or what the fuck I should do, but my pulse soared and my knees went weak, and—

Thank God, he broke away and continued toward his locker, letting me breathe again.

What the hell was that all about? And what the hell was my reaction all about?

Right. As if I didn't know why I'd reacted that way.

But I still didn't know what to make of that smile. I had no idea what was going on in his head these days, never mind this minute. Just that he was driving me out of my mind.

I made myself focus on getting myself put together for the game. Not that it helped much. My heart was racing behind my chest protector, and my knees weren't quite sure about staying up on my skates.

I hadn't imagined that exchange, had I? I had no idea what I'd been seeing, or if he thought he saw something, or —I didn't know. But something zinged between us in that half a heartbeat of eye contact.

And Sawyer had noticed that things had changed between us. Our stats reflected something wildly different from before. This dynamic—it was objectively better than what we'd had in the beginning. I just wasn't so sure my brain or my heart could handle it.

If we kept getting along, and if we kept playing like we'd been the past three weeks, we would absolutely be what Toronto could've had.

But that assumed I survived whatever the fuck was crackling between us.

CHAPTER 21

JAREK

I severely underestimated how much harder it would be to coexist with Hunter after that conversation in my hotel room.

I couldn't hide behind my resentment anymore. Without the walls, there was nothing to shield me from the simple truth that I wanted this man. And without that occasional shift to bitter resentment, there was nothing to temper that attraction, either.

Because oh, God, Hunter was hot. I'd known that. I just hadn't bargained for how much hotter he'd be after I'd seen how kind and compassionate he was. Especially to someone who didn't exactly deserve it.

That conversation had made him even more attractive. Because he could still look at me? Because he hadn't echoed my own brain and told me I was a shitty, spineless, worthless player for throwing that season? Because his first instinct was to say Wilcox and Robertson had been wrong for using me that way?

Whatever. All I knew was that I couldn't keep my

thoughts straight and my skates under me when I was around him now.

Which was kind of a problem because right now we had this thing called a hockey game to win, and I needed both my thoughts and my skates to be in working order.

"You good, Yars?" Dima skated up to me during a stoppage.

"Of course I am." I laughed. "Why wouldn't I be?"

He shot me a pointed look. "You tell me."

"I'm good." I gave him a playful punch to the arm. "Just trying to cope with the trauma of watching you skate."

"Oh, fuck you." He laughed and rolled his eyes, but some concern lingered as we set up for a faceoff.

At the dot, Hunter looked over his shoulder, probably making sure we were all where we needed to be. His gaze snagged on me for a heartbeat, and something like panic flickered across his face before he jerked his attention back to the faceoff.

I wasn't sure I wanted to know what that was about.

The ref held the puck between the two centers. We all tensed, poised to jump into action as soon as the puck dropped.

The ref's hand twitched, and Hunter jumped the gun. That prompted a warning from the ref that I didn't hear, but could guess. God knew I'd had my share of faceoff violations when I'd been a center.

Especially on nights when my concentration was trash.

I eyed Hunter's back. Was *his* concentration trash? Shit. Had everything I told him screwed up his game? Because in his skates, I would've been a little messed up after hearing something like that.

A whistle pulled my focus back to the dot, and I looked

up to see the ref gesturing sharply. Hunter stood and skated off, some red in his face and frustration in his eyes.

Oh. Shit. He'd gotten himself kicked out of the faceoff.

I skated in to take his place, since I was the only other Hornet on the ice right now who could do faceoffs well. As we passed each other, we made brief eye contact.

And I had to wonder if maybe Dima should take this faceoff. He would be the first to admit he sucked at them, but in that moment, he had a better shot at winning it than I did.

I wasn't about to explain that to him or Coach, though, so with my heart in my throat, I joined the other center in the faceoff.

Sheer dumb luck or a lapse in concentration from my opponent were the only possible explanations for me winning that faceoff. It sure as shit wasn't my skill. Not this time.

But I didn't argue with it, and the game was on. It was in these moments that my focus came easier. Hockey moved too fast to think about anything else, and my mind zeroed in on the puck, the other players, and the goal. When Hunter registered, it was as my teammate and linemate, and for the most part, we had our shit together.

Right up until the whistle blew again.

And I glanced at him again.

And my brain started blinking 12:00 again.

I was losing my fucking mind. I'd told someone that awful secret, and the relief had left me off-balance. The fact that that someone had been my incredibly attractive team-mate just screwed with my head even more.

I needed to reset my stupid brain. Just... do something to snap myself out of this and fucking focus again.

A good lay would probably help. Usually did. How long had it been anyway?

Too long. *Way* too long.

During the next intermission, I took out my phone and checked the team's schedule. Oh, look at that—we had tomorrow night off.

Maybe it was time to visit Lanterns again.

CHAPTER 22

HUNTER

Fuck it. I needed to get laid.

This... *thing* with Jarek was about to drive me insane. Who knew it would be harder to be around him when he *wasn't* blowing hot and cold? Like it was great to have that hostility out of the way and come to a real understanding, and thank God I didn't have to walk on eggshells around him anymore. Clearing the air had gone a long, long way.

Being on more comfortable ground with him did absolutely fuck all for my concentration, especially since I'd previously been able to reclaim my focus just by remembering what a jackass he was. Nothing could down-boy my dick quite like, "*Oh, right, he's a jerk who needs to go fuck himself.*"

Now he *wasn't* being a jerk, and my stupid brain was hung up on how hot it would be for him to fuck *me*...

Yeah, to hell with it. Time to go get laid. It wouldn't fix whatever the hell was thrumming between me and my no-longer-mercurial teammate, but an orgasm courtesy of someone who wasn't my hand would clear my head.

Right, I thought as I strolled into Lanterns, *because I*

absolutely won't be thinking about Jarek all the way to that
orgasm.

I was legitimately losing my mind.

Once I had a drink in hand, I stepped away from the bar so someone else could order, and I gave the room a slow scan. Plenty of hot men here tonight, including some who didn't seem to be attached to anyone else. Yet. What I was looking for—oh, yeah, I'd find it here. A set of talented hands, an eager mouth, hips that could move just right to send me into the stratosphere—none of that was too much to ask, was it?

No, it wasn't. After a swig of liquid courage, I left my empty glass on a table and wove my way into the crowd. As I slid into the mass of people on the dancefloor, I made eye contact with different men. Danced with one. Then another. Oh, fuck, yes, this was what I needed. Body heat. Hands on my own body. Rhythm. Conversations with nothing more than eyes and closeness.

One guy got in close enough to kiss me, and oh, it was tempting. Even here, where discretion was as guaranteed as it could ever be. Still had to be careful, though, and we kept our mouths apart enough for plausible deniability. No camera was going to make it through the lights, shadows, and bodies to catch the hand in my back pocket or the way his belt buckle clicked against mine.

It wasn't a done deal. Not with the way his gaze kept flicking away, clearly still scanning the room to keep his options open. I could live with that. In fact, I could do the same, and after an exchange of grins with this guy, I gave the crowd around us a slow sweep.

And—

Really?

Fucking *really?*

He had to come into this club again? Tonight?

Goddammit.

I lost my concentration, and with it, my rhythm. My partner gave me a quizzical look. I tried to shake it off and keep dancing, but... no. That wasn't happening. I mean, I could still dance, and I was still close to him, but my neck prickled under the weight of Jarek's gaze. I didn't even know for sure if he was watching me—my senses had just decided he was.

And that shouldn't have been this hot.

I wanted to dance closer. To grind against this stranger. Feel more than just the occasional brush of his hard-on. Push the envelope and maybe steal a kiss out here where we could be seen after all.

Where Jarek would see us.

Where he would see *me*.

Fuck. It was one thing to resign myself to fantasizing about him when I landed in someone's bed tonight. It was another to be locked into his presence and getting more out of Jarek watching me than this man touching me.

I gave up and backed off. After a few beats, my dance partner had vanished like a mirage, slipping into the crowd in search of someone else.

I couldn't make myself look Jarek's way. But the more I danced alone, hyperaware of him as if everyone else in this room had turned into faceless, featureless shadows, the less I could pretend I was going home with a stranger tonight.

But that didn't mean I had to go home alone, did it?

Because I'd seen the way Jarek looked at me when he didn't think I'd notice. We'd looked all the hostility in the eye, so maybe we needed to do the same thing to this mutual attraction we were both failing to ignore. Wouldn't make anything worse, would it?

Only one way to find out.

Heart beating like this was sudden death overtime in a playoff elimination game, I left the dancefloor. When I could finally stop and look around, I was almost immediately overcome with the panicked certainty that I'd missed my chance. Jarek was gone. Blood pounding in my ears, disappointment weighing heavy in my stomach, I searched the crowd, but that set of sharp features and mesmerizing gray eyes were nowhere to be found.

Goddammit. Had I imagined him?

He might've left. With someone or alone, I had no idea. All I knew was that he wasn't here.

And I suddenly didn't want to be either.

With a sigh, I headed toward the bar to close my tab. I was almost there and had zeroed in on an empty space at the bar when—

Oh, God. Those eyes I'd seen through sweat-dotted hockey visors under stadium lights. And under the bright LEDs in the locker room. And in the sun in a teammate's backyard.

And on one particular night, across the console of my car, lit only by the headlamps and the soft glow of the dashboard lights.

I swallowed. He didn't seem surprised to see me. Had he come looking for me?

For a split second, I was afraid he was going to give me shit for encroaching on his territory; what could I say? I still expected him to be an ass at every turn.

The way he was looking at me, though—I couldn't begin to read him. No surprise, no hostility, but maybe some nerves? A little fear? As if his heart were doing the same overtime things mine was doing right then, and he had no idea what to do next.

Something smoldered in his eyes. Something I couldn't have misread if I'd wanted to.

Especially not when he dropped his gaze and raked it all the way up my body to my face again.

Had someone turned off the air conditioner? Because holy hell, it was getting hot in here.

There was a speaker right over us, so we had zero hope of hearing each other. I went for the next best thing— nodding toward the dancefloor, then raising my eyebrows.

Jarek's lips parted. He mirrored my nod, and his own upraised eyebrows asked if he was reading me right.

I shrugged. *Why not?*

He glanced toward the dancefloor again, chewing the inside of his cheek. He shifted a little, as if he couldn't get comfortable.

Damn. Maybe this *was* the wrong move. Maybe I had misread everything about his presence and his eyes and the way he'd looked me up and down. Dancing probably would make things weird, wouldn't it? After I asked him to dance and he rejected me, maybe we—

Jarek's nod caught me off guard.

I blinked.

And then we were in motion. Making our way through the crowd. I was ahead of him, but I knew without looking that he was behind me. I could *feel* him.

Fuck, I wanted to feel even more of him. *All* of him. I wanted—

Oh.

God.

Jarek's hands were on my waist. His chest was against my back. His undeniably hard dick was against my ass. I didn't even hear the music anymore over the whisper of his breath beside my ear, so I had no idea if we were dancing with the beat or doing our own thing entirely. I didn't care. We fell into sync just like we did on the ice—moving together, reading each other, my senses zeroed in on him even when I couldn't see him.

I *wanted* to see him, though, and the odd glance in the mirrored wall wasn't nearly enough.

Without opening more space between us than was absolutely necessary, I turned around. Now we were face-to-face, my arms on his shoulders and his hands curving unabashedly over my ass. Those eyes—Jesus Christ, if they'd been beautiful before, they were beyond sexy now, pupils blown as he gazed at me with pure hunger. Knowing how he'd looked at me before—ashamed, disgusted, angry— made the knee-shaking desire in his gaze right now even sexier. This wasn't someone who'd picked me out of a crowd and decided he wanted a piece of me tonight. I was at the core of something Jarek had been wrestling with for years. The flesh-and-blood reminder of something he regretted and couldn't even talk about.

And somehow...

He was looking at me like *that*.

God, I wanted to put my hands on him. I mean, my hands *were* on him, but I wanted to *really* put them on him. No clothes. No inhibitions. I wanted to feel him in ways we didn't dare in a place like this, regardless of Lanterns' no-camera policy.

Fuck. I wanted him. I'd *been* wanting him.

And tonight...

This close to him...

If his lips flicked to my mouth one more goddamned time...

Well, hell. Why were we holding back? Because we were teammates? Because hooking up could somehow plunge us into the deepest depths of awkwardness, as if we hadn't spent months thoroughly exploring the Mariana Trench of Awkwardness?

Fuck it.

I gestured for him to lean in close, making it clear I wanted to say something into his ear. He dipped his head, and thank God for the thumping bass to drown out my pounding heart.

"Do you kiss hookups on the mouth?"

The shiver that went through him. The way his fingers twitched on my side. Holy hell.

He turned his head just a little, and the warm tickle of his breath had my own breath stuttering so bad I almost didn't hear the words he shouted over the music:

"Doesn't matter what I do with hookups."

I drew back and met his eyes, confused.

His grin made me forget all about balance and rhythm. I didn't hear a word he said over the music, but I was too fixated on his lips not to read every syllable:

"I want to kiss you on the mouth."

Oh. *Fuck.*

I jerked my chin toward the bar. "Maybe we should close our tabs."

Jarek nodded. "Let's go."

In a matter of minutes, we'd both closed our small tabs, and we were working our way through the crowd toward the exit. I was almost there when his hand materialized on the small of my back, dangerously close to sliding down over my belt, and thank God for the push bar on the door. It gave me something to catch myself on so I didn't fall and look like an idiot. I recovered, got the door open, and stepped out in the brisk night, Jarek walking close beside me with his palm still resting just above my ass.

I fumbled with my phone. "I can get as an Uber. We'll—"

"I'm parked around the corner."

I looked up at him. "You drove?"

Jarek shrugged. "I don't drink much when I want to get laid." Then, with a wicked look, he added, "And if I'm leaving with someone, I prefer not to have an audience."

The filthy promise in those words sent a shiver up my already melting spine.

Oh hell. We should've done this *months* ago.

We followed the sidewalk around the corner, and he led me into a parking garage. I was tempted to suggest taking advantage of one of the stairwells or even a shadow in a camera's blind spot, but... no. It would be just our luck we'd get busted, and this was not how I wanted the team to find out I was sleeping with Jarek.

Fuck. I was about to sleep with Jarek?

God, yes, I was.

The sight of his familiar deep red Jaguar sent a rush of heat through me. I walked a little faster. Jarek didn't comment—he'd done the same damn thing. As if he wanted this as much as I did.

I almost lost my mind when we got into the car. Not just because we were a step closer to getting out of here, but because of the not-so-subtle way he paused to adjust himself as he settled into the driver side.

Jarek wanted me. Badly.

Fuck. Fuck, fuck, fuck.

It took all the restraint I possessed not to lunge across the console and kiss him. I wanted this man so damn bad. Wanted his body. His hands. His mouth.

But we needed to get someplace private first. There were too many cameras. Too many potential eyes to bust us, especially now that we were in a car that was anything but discreet.

Neither of us spoke as he left the garage. A mile or so up the freeway, he asked, "At the risk of sounding like a cliché —your place or mine?"

A nervous laugh rushed out of me. "Maybe yours. This thing"—I gestured around us to indicate the car—"might be a little conspicuous in my parking lot."

His eyes widened with a flicker of surprise, and he gulped. He'd probably forgotten—same as I had until just now—that two of our teammates and one of the trainers lived in my complex. I wondered if he was reconsidering what we were doing.

Or not, judging by the way he accelerated.

Silence held steady between us for the twenty-five solid minutes it took to get from downtown to Cranberry. It wasn't awkward, though. Uncomfortable, yes, but in an impatient, are-we-there-yet kind of way. My hands itched with the need to be on him. My mouth watered at the prospect of tasting him. We both had to shift around a few times and adjust ourselves; tight pants were sexy as hell, but they weren't the greatest for insistent hard-ons on long drives.

My heart was thundering as he eased off the freeway. A ramp and a turn later, we were on a dark side street. There was a faint glow of civilization up ahead, but this was one of those shadowy stretches with no streetlights or even stoplights.

Up ahead, a stop sign came into view, and my pulse jumped again. As Jarek slowed down, I moistened my lips. "Set the E-brake."

He glanced at me as he came to a gentle stop. "What?"

"The E-brake." I held his gaze in the low light and unbuckled my seat belt. "Set it."

He studied me. But then came the creak of the emergency brake setting.

And I finally did what I'd wanted to do in the parking garage—I lunged over the console, grabbed the back of his neck, and kissed him. *Hard.*

The little whimper that escaped his throat wasn't the sound of a startled man. The way his hand slid up into my hair and his fingers twitched in my scalp sent goose bumps prickling down the length of my spine.

Holy hell, he was a *masterful* kisser. Assertive. Explorative. Downright fucking decadent. If not for the console biting into my side and my zipper pressed obnoxiously against my dick, I could've stayed right here all night and just made out with him.

Jarek was the one to break the kiss, and his voice came out as a hoarse whisper, his accent thick as he breathed, "Christ, I want you."

The words made me dizzier than his kiss. "How far is your place from here?"

He let his head fall back, and he glanced around as if he'd forgotten where he were. Then he looked up at me with fire in his eyes. "Five minutes." Beat. "Three minutes."

I grinned. "You're not going to get a ticket, are you?"

"Only if I get caught."

"Hmm." I brushed a kiss across his swollen lips before returning to the passenger seat. "How about not getting caught, eh?"

He didn't answer. He just released the brake, and the engine roared as he peeled through the deserted intersection. I pulled on my seat belt and tried not to lose my damn mind for the five—three—minutes it took to get to his condo.

He pulled into the garage, and as the door shut behind us, we somehow held on to our dignity all the way up the steps, into his kitchen, and—

"Finally," I growled, and pushed him up against the door he'd just deadbolted behind us. I kissed him even deeper and harder than I had in the car, and Jarek didn't miss a beat. He kneaded my ass, pulling me in tighter as our hard-ons rubbed together between us. I moaned and rutted against him, driving a helpless sound from him.

I drew my hips back a little and slid a hand between us, cupping his erection hard enough to feel exactly what he had on offer. His helpless, shuddering moan almost undid me, and when I ran my thumb over the head of his cock, he broke the kiss just enough to curse in at least two languages.

I stroked him through his pants. "Would you think less of me if I said I wanted this in my ass?"

Oh, that strangled moan. That full-body shiver. Jarek kissed me again, and one of his hands left my ass and went to the back of my neck, gripping hard as he explored my mouth and pushed his cock into my hand. Holy fuck, he had me trembling all over. And *he* was trembling all over, too. I was no virgin, but I couldn't remember ever feeling this wanted. This *craved*. Like the man I was with might actually lose his mind if we didn't fuck in the next few minutes.

That this man was Jaromir Badura was not lost on me.

He was panting when he grabbed my wrist, stopping my hand, and touched his forehead to mine. "Bedroom." He tugged my hand away from his crotch. "You're going to make me come in my pants, and I'd much rather come in you"

It was my turn for a shiver. I drew back a little to give

him some space, and then I let him lead me into his bedroom.

Getting out of pants this tight wasn't a sexy or glamorous process, but I had it down to a science, and apparently so did Jarek. We both made short work of it, and...

Oh. Wow. What a view.

Naked men were not a novelty in our line of work. Naked *Jarek* wasn't a novelty.

But seeing Jarek naked, hard, and gazing at me like he wanted to eat me alive? Oh, fuck yeah, that was new.

His body felt even better than it looked. I'd been with hockey players before—I was familiar with the lean, powerful physique that was all sculpted muscle and mouthwatering planes and contours—but not *this* hockey player. Everything I did to him and everything he did to me—every caress, every grope, every kiss, every bite—felt like a victory. Like we were knocking down the last remaining walls and giving in to something we'd been resisting for too long.

He nudged me back toward the bed, but I countered and pressed him up against the wall. He gasped, likely from the cool surface against his skin, and I didn't give him a chance to recover before I went to my knees.

One slide of his dick between my lips, and Jarek was mumbling all kinds of things I didn't understand. Czech, probably. Curses, hopefully. All good, if his moans and the way he rocked his hips were any indication.

In English, he murmured, "You are so... God, you are so good at that."

I hummed around his cock and took him deep, earning me a low groan and a shiver. When I moved down to tease his balls with my tongue, his narrow hips bucked in my hands.

"Oh. *Sakra*. I..." He shuddered. "Get... Come up here

before you make me come."

Just the thought of Jarek blowing his load in my mouth almost sent me over the edge, but I was also desperate to be fucked. Especially now that I knew what he was packing.

So I did as I was told and stood. He dragged me into a hungry, breathless kiss, gripping my hair and rubbing his cock against my thigh.

"Your mouth," he murmured against my lips. "Fuck."

I laughed. "Probably should've mentioned," I panted, "but I fucking love sucking dick."

"You don't say." He kissed me again, carding his fingers through my hair. "What else do you like?"

"Depends." I tugged him with me toward the bed, and then hauled him down on top of me. "What makes you scream?"

Jarek bit his lip, looming over me as his hips settled between my thighs. "A lot of things. We don't have to fuck, but you said you wanted my dick in your ass..."

Oh, hell yeah.

"I did." I slid my hands up his chest. "And I absolutely do."

"Jesus," he whispered between kisses. "You can go more than once, right? In a night?"

I licked my lips. "You better believe it."

"Good." He arched against me. "Because this is probably going to be a quickie."

The words and the hunger gave me goose bumps. Seeing and feeling and hearing Jarek this turned on was heady as hell. He made a sound somewhere between a whimper and a moan, and then he was kissing my neck, driving me wild with the scrape of his stubble, the soft skate of his lips, and the warm whisper of his breath.

"Jesus, Jarek. Oh my God."

He growled something I didn't understand, and we were moving together, touching and rocking and kissing with all the same intuition we did on the dancefloor and on the ice. As if we both just knew where the other would be, what the other would do, what the other would want. The feedback loop was dangerously effective on the ice. Sexy as hell on the dancefloor.

And arousing beyond words in bed.

"Fuck me," I whined. "Goddammit, I want your dick."

Jarek shivered. Pushing himself up over me, he grinned. "I will. Believe me, I will." He bent to brush a kiss across my collarbone. "But first... you're not the only one who loves sucking dick."

He wasn't kidding, either. Jarek went down on me like there was nothing in the world he wanted more than to lick and suck me into oblivion. Every now and then, he'd flick his gaze up to meet mine, eyes smoldering with desire, and it was a genuine miracle I didn't lose my mind every time we locked eyes. When he pushed a couple of spit-slicked fingers into me, I thought fucking me might be a moot point —he was going to make me come so hard like this, I wouldn't be able to take any more. As much as I wanted him to ride me into the mattress, I'd have been perfectly okay with that, because *goddamn*.

"Jarek." I licked my lips and struggled to find breath and words and thoughts and everything that was required to speak, which was a challenge when the wet heat of this man's mouth and the amazing things he did with his fingers had me so close to the edge. Somehow, I managed, "Please. Fuck me."

I didn't speak a single word of Czech, but whatever it was he said right then, I'd have bet my life it translated to, *"You're damn right I'm going to fuck you."*

Then he was getting a condom and some lube, and he ordered me to my hands and knees.

I shivered and let my head fall forward, trying not to collapse. It wasn't like I was new to being dicked down, but I couldn't remember the last time I'd been as turned on as I was tonight, and that was before Jarek pushed his cock into me. Now that he was in me, I was so far out of my mind, this may as well have been my first time.

For all we were both trembling with need, he still took his time, easing in until I was taking him without even a hint of resistance. After a few strokes, Jarek pushed all the way in. Hands on my hips, he rocked in and out a few times, as if making sure we really were moving together fluidly.

We were. Oh, God, we were. Holy fuck.

Then he leaned over me and murmured... something. Words. My brain must've registered on some level what he wanted, because I started lowering myself to the mattress, and he followed. As I settled on my stomach, he slid his arms under me, hooking his hands over my shoulders.

For leverage.

Oh fuck.

With a groan, he picked up speed, using that leverage to thrust in hard and deep, every stroke pushing my own cock against the sheets and driving me a little farther into bliss.

"Fuck," I managed to grit out. "God, Jarek. Fuck..."

"This good?" he panted in my ear.

"Uh-huh. It's... more. Gimme more."

There was a huff of what I thought was amusement, and then, sweet Jesus, he gave me more, fucking into me until I forgot where I was and who I was—anything but who was riding me and how amazing it felt.

Jarek grunted. His rhythm faltered a little, and as he recovered—sort of—he muttered something I didn't understand. It took me a second to realize it hadn't been my scrambled brain that had made his words unintelligible. He must've figured it out in the same instant, because he murmured in breathless English this time, "I'm gonna come."

My head spun. "Please."

He muttered something else I didn't understand, and his iron grip on my shoulders was almost painful, and he held me still as he thrust as deep as I could take him, groaning from low in his throat as he fell apart on top of me. He shuddered hard and swore before stilling, dick still buried inside me as he trembled and gasped for breath.

I closed my eyes and exhaled, disbelieving this was even real.

Jaromir Badura just fucked me.

He just rode my ass, and came in me, and now he's kissing my neck like... oh, God...

"You didn't come yet, did you?" he growled in my ear, his accent thick and his words slurred.

By some miracle, I hadn't. "N-no."

His lips curved against my skin. "Good." Oh, that one word was full of so much dirty promise, I almost came after all. But then he whispered, "Don't move," and carefully pulled out. The lack of his heat and weight over me was almost more jarring than his cock slipping free.

The kiss he dropped on my shoulder was surprisingly soft. "I'll be right back."

I just nodded.

He wasn't gone long. Or maybe he was—my head was still swimming, and time had ceased to be a thing. All I knew was it felt like a minute or so at most before the mattress dipped beside me and his hand ran up my back.

Then his voice, soft but somehow still commanding: "Turn over."

I did as I was told, fully expecting him to go down on me to finish me off. Instead, he lay beside me, and he claimed a kiss that stole my breath. *Fuuuck.* My body was still electrified with need, and then his fingers closed around my dick, and I arched off the bed. When he'd put the lube on his hand, I had no fucking idea, but oh, wow, his strokes were *magic.*

I broke the kiss with a breathless, "Holy *fuck.*"

His laugh was a warm rush across my cheek. "One of these nights," he murmured, "I'll blow you until you come down my throat." He paused for a deep kiss, and his lips left mine just long enough to add, "But I love when a man comes while I'm kissing him."

Then he had my mouth again, and he was pumping me hard, his slick strokes driving me right to the brink. I could barely get enough air like this, but I didn't care. I didn't hold back, either. I was too keyed up, too desperate for release, so I just grabbed his shoulder and thrust up into his hand, whimpering into his kiss as we made out and he stroked me and—

My orgasm was sudden and perfect, turning everything to white light, and Jarek's low groan thrummed against my mouth as if he were coming right along with me.

As I settled back to earth, the room still spun. My body still trembled. Jarek's warm, strong arms wrapped around me as he murmured something that must've been in Czech. Or maybe my brain was just too fried to make sense of anything.

All I knew was that I was naked and satisfied in Jarek Badura's bed. In his arms.

And this was perfect.

CHAPTER 23

JAREK

I couldn't quite get my head around how we'd landed here, sweaty and satisfied in my bed.

At the same time, it seemed like the most inevitable thing in the world. Like we'd always been heading in this direction, always on this collision course even if we hadn't realized it, and *of course* we'd ended up here.

I couldn't explain what had drawn me across the club to head Hunter off at the bar. Why I'd had a surge of determination and hadn't been able to talk myself out of it, and why the second I'd met his gaze, I'd forgotten I ever wanted to talk myself out of anything. It might've been courage or hubris that had shoved me into his path, or maybe the semi-panicked and irrational certainty that this had been my one and only chance to make this connection.

All I knew for sure was that I'd done it, and then we'd danced, and now...

I trailed my fingertips over the tattoos on his right arm.

Hunter's eyelids fluttered open, and he turned his head toward me as a sleepy grin curled his lips. "I didn't fall asleep on you, did I?"

"You might've." I slid closer and draped my arm over him. "I probably did, too."

"Yeah?" His eyes closed again, though the grin stayed in place. "Then I wore you out. Nice."

I laughed, pressing a kiss to his shoulder. "I don't know about that. I meant what I said about going more than once."

He looked at me again, amusement and interest both sparking in his eyes. "Oh, yeah?"

"Mmhmm." I shifted a little so I was on my side and partway over him. "I've got more if you do."

"Ooh, bring it." He curved a hand behind my neck, drew me down, and claimed a languid kiss that almost had me instantly ready for that second round. Jesus, he was an amazing kisser.

Who was I kidding? Everything he did to me was amazing. The way our bodies had moved together in the club had made my head lighter than sex with other men had. That moment when he'd ordered me to set the E-brake because he couldn't wait a second longer to kiss me—fuck, that had turned me on like nothing else. And then the clothes had come off and, well... It was a wonder we hadn't burned down my condo.

Now there were no clothes to push out of the way. There was nothing but hot skin beneath my hands as I slid them all over his body, memorizing him and savoring him like this was a dream I was determined to remember as vividly as possible. When Hunter pushed me onto my back and straddled me, I was overwhelmed by everything—his scent, his heat, his weight over the top of me. The thick erection beside mine had my head spinning even faster, and we both rutted against each other for some friction, moaning into a long, breathless kiss.

After a while, Hunter broke the kiss, and he gazed down at me, breathing hard and trembling. "I feel like this is the part where we're supposed to talk about how stupid this is and how we should keep it a secret."

I laughed almost soundlessly and licked my lips. "Probably. I don't care how stupid it is, though." I ran my fingers through his disheveled hair. "This the best I've felt in a long time."

Since I found out you signed with Pittsburgh, I didn't say.

Since long, long before that, I kept to myself.

Hunter studied me, and my stomach clenched. Damn it. We were about to talk about how stupid this was and how we should keep it a secret, weren't we? Worse than that—how it was so stupid and reckless, we needed to stop before we started. All this heat between us was about to cool as we spelled out the reasons why the most incredible thing I'd ever experienced had to be done and over with before I'd even had a chance to savor it.

But then he came down to me, slid his hands up into my hair, and met my lips with a kiss that didn't say a damn thing about putting out this fire.

"God, I want you," I growled between kisses.

That moan from deep in his throat—Jesus Christ. "We probably will get in trouble." He didn't sound at all like that was a deterrent. Quite the opposite, in fact.

"Then I guess we don't let anyone know." I ran my hands up his sides and nipped his lower lip. "Our little secret."

"Mmm, so if I wanted you to fuck me in a hotel?" His lips grazed mine. "With our teammates staying all around us?"

Ooh, I liked this rebellious side of him.

"I'll fuck you anywhere you want me to," I purred. "Long as you keep kissing me like this."

He hummed, and then he kept kissing me just like that. Christ, turned on as I was right then, I swore I'd blow him on Coach's desk if he asked me to.

"We should..." I dragged my nails across his shoulders, reveling in the way that made him shudder. "This really has to be our secret."

"I know." His lips curved against mine, and he rubbed his dick alongside mine. "Sounds kind of hot—sneaking around and banging every chance we get."

Something about him acknowledging he wanted more than just tonight made my head light. "Name the time and place."

He just kissed me again.

After a moment, though, he spoke. "There is nothing I can say to justify doing this when it will probably get us in trouble," he murmured. "I can't explain any—I can't explain a goddamned thing about why. I just..." He lifted his head and met my gaze, beautiful eyes full of fire and emotion. "I want this. That's all I know. If we have to keep it a secret?" He shrugged. "Fine. But I don't want to stop."

"I don't either." I ran my hands up his chest. "We can... Later, we can figure out if we'll tell other people."

He nodded. "But for now..."

"Just us."

"Deal."

"Good. And what I want right now is for you to do something about this." I pressed my dick against his hip.

Hunter whimpered, and then he kissed me like he had every intention of doing something about my hard-on. And even if he didn't, I could've made out like this all damn night; I'd been with plenty of men who loved kissing, but not like Hunter did. His kiss was sexy and consuming—utterly perfect, and almost scarily good at making everything outside this room cease to exist. Nothing mattered in that moment except how much I wanted Hunter. Consequences didn't matter. Just heat and want.

Arms wrapped around him, I rolled him onto his back again, and the press of his thighs against my hips almost did me in. So did the way he arched under me as I kissed up and down his neck.

"Fuck, Jarek..." He dragged his nails up my back. "Oh God..."

I nipped his shoulder. Not hard, but it was enough to be rewarded with another helpless whimper, so I did it again.

His voice was ragged as he whispered, "You have more condoms, right?"

I shivered, which pressed my body against his. "Uh-huh." I kissed under his jaw, along the edge of his beard. "Plenty."

"Mmm, maybe..." He gasped and squirmed. "Maybe get one?"

A shudder arched my back and curled my toes,

Pushing myself up so I could look in his eyes, I licked my lips. "You're not too sensitive to bottom twice?"

That grin made my whole body hot with need. "You didn't fuck me *that* hard."

I cocked a brow. "That a challenge?"

"Don't know. You up for it?"

I considered it. Then I returned his grin. "All right—how about you ride my dick and show me how hard you like it."

The fire in his eyes—oh my God. "Game on."

I stole another kiss before I rolled onto my back. Hunter knelt beside me, stroking himself slowly as I put on the condom, because I needed that goddamned distraction. How was I supposed to maneuver a rubber into place with him sitting there like that, hard and ready?

Fucker.

As he started to climb on, I stopped him with a hand on his hip. Before he had a chance to ask why, I pushed myself up on my elbow and took his cock between my lips. With my free hand, I cupped his ass; so what if there was some lube on my hand? We'd probably be showering before long, so... fuck it.

"God, Jarek..." He rocked his hips, sliding in and out of my mouth as he raked his fingers through my hair. "Your fucking mouth..."

I groaned around him, which made him curse again.

Abruptly, he tightened his fingers in my hair, the sudden sting making my whole body break out in goose bumps.

"No more," he panted as he withdrew from my mouth. "I don't want to come until I'm on your dick."

I bit my lip. "Then get on."

Oh, he did. Some guys could be a little sensitive, even tender, the second time around, but if Hunter was, he sure didn't let it show. He took me quickly, curses rolling off his tongue as he found a hard, steady rhythm. When I pressed my heels into the bed and thrust up into him, he threw his head back and cried out with what could only be pleasure.

Holy hell. Sakra.

This man was so hot. So sexy.

So damn beautiful.

He's Hunter Michaud, a stunned voice in my head reminded me. *And he's... fuck, he's...*

He was. God, he really was.

The last thing I wanted to think about right now was

why Hunter had been significant to my life before he'd come to Pittsburgh, but I couldn't chase away those thoughts.

I couldn't chase away the rush of emotions as I gazed up at this sexy, responsive man. As I met those fiery, hungry eyes. As we moved together. As I watched bliss taking over his expression.

Hunter... *knew*.

He knew what I'd done, and how much it had eaten at me for years, and how it explained—but didn't excuse—me being an absolute dick to him... and he was still in my bed. Naked. Breathless. Riding me like there was nothing in the world he wanted more. Looking at me like that through heavy-lidded eyes that saw what no one else in the world did.

He *knew*.

Holy shit.

Hunter slowed, and he gazed down at me, concern breaking through the arousal. "Hey." He touched my face with a shaky hand. "You all right?"

I swallowed hard and nodded. Covering his hand with mine, I kissed his palm. "Make yourself come like this." I grinned, hopefully masking all the thoughts that had tried to cloud my mind. "Let me feel it."

Hunter bit his lip. Concern held on, but when I rocked my hips, he gasped and closed his eyes. "Oh, God..."

"Ride me," I ordered. "C'mon, baby. Come all over me."

The way he shivered and groaned, I thought for a split second he was going to come right then and there. But no, he stayed in control, and when he gazed down at me again, the fire had returned full force. He planted his hands on the bed beside my shoulders, and when I say he rode me...

Oh, fuck, he *rode* me.

"Jerk me off," he demanded through his teeth. "God, you've got me right—*ooh*, yeah." His rhythm faltered as I started pumping him. "Fuck, Jarek..."

I stared up at him. Stroked him. Completely lost myself in the pleasure of feeling him and seeing him and hearing him, all the while knowing...

He knows.

And he still wants me.

Oblivion closed in fast, and I swore in both English and Czech as I thrust harder into him. Hunter cried out, the sound strangled and throaty, and the second his dick stiffened in my hand and his hole clenched around me I knew he was there—right there—and that was too heady to take. When he shouted again, his voice almost a sob, I lost it, coming inside him before the first drop of his cum landed on my stomach.

Simultaneous orgasms were something out of pornos and romance novels, but with Hunter... What could I say? His orgasm turned me on so much, I couldn't hold back. Once he went over that edge, he hauled me over it with him, shaking and cursing all the way to bliss.

We came together, and we came down together, both trembling and breathing hard as he slumped over me on shaking arms. I had cum all over one hand, but I curved the other behind his neck, brought him down to me, and held him against me. He sighed as if he were relieved he didn't have to hold himself up anymore. I was just relieved for this moment to catch my breath and maybe collect all the emotions that had tried to surface.

Eyes closed, I stroked Hunter's hair and just listened to him breathing and my own heart pounding.

I had no idea if this was going to last beyond tonight, or

if that had just been the kind of fantasizing two people did when they wanted to wind each other up.

All I knew was that Hunter knew how our pasts intertwined. He knew what I'd done.

And if only for tonight...

He'd wanted me.

———

After two orgasms apiece and a long shower together, it was a genuine miracle we didn't both pass out the second we landed in my bed.

Somehow, though, we didn't. We were wide awake, kissing lazily, and Hunter wasn't making any noise about getting out of here.

Please stay, I tried to tell him as we made out beneath the sheet. *Even if this is over tomorrow.*

Truthfully, I'd have been okay with this being a one-night thing. If we kept screwing in secret like we'd talked about—great! But if we didn't, I could live with it. I was just relieved we'd had tonight despite everything Hunter knew.

When he broke the kiss and drew back to look at me, though...

I'm okay with this being a one-night stand, huh?

Yeah. About that...

Hunter must've seen something in my expression, because he caressed my cheek and whispered, "What's on your mind?"

I avoided his gaze, which wasn't easy when we were this close. Where to even start?

"Hey." He tipped up my chin, twin creases forming between his eyes as he gazed at me with deep concern. "Talk to me."

I wasn't so sure I could. Then again, I'd bared my soul to him once before, and somehow he was here, skin warm against mine, lips swollen from kissing. But would I scare him off if I got all emotional and sappy after one roll in— okay, *two* rolls in the hay? Because this wasn't like me at all.

"Jarek?"

"I, um…" I struggled to keep my voice even, but I more or less managed. "Just… it hit me, I guess. That you're the only person in the world who knows about…" I winced.

"The past?"

I nodded. "Yeah. You're the last person I thought would even like me, and you do, even after I was an ass to you, and after told you what I did. It's… I mean, fuck. You were miserable in Toronto. They were awful to you. And you were there because of *me*."

"No, I wasn't." He said it firmly, but not sharply.

Still, the words made me jump, and I met his gaze.

"I was there because Wilcox and Robertson figured out how to game the system" he said. "And they manipulated you into gaming it for them, and then discarded you after they got what they wanted." He shook his head. "It wasn't your fault I ended up in that toxic mess. You were a victim of the same mess."

I swallowed hard. It was impossible to explain how profoundly liberating it still was to hear that, and how much deeper that relief went because it was coming from him. I couldn't find the words, and I wasn't sure I could've spoken them anyway.

Hunter leaned in and brushed his lips across mine. When he drew back and looked in my eyes again, his expression was serious but soft. "I know it doesn't seem like it from where you're standing, but you didn't commit some heinous crime or sin." He ran his thumb along my cheekbone. "No one should've asked you to do what you did. And with the position they put you in?" He half-shrugged. "Jarek, you were a kid. I know how much pressure they piled on your shoulders because they also piled it on mine. And I know how toxic and abusive they were to you because they also were to me."

My heart did an unpleasant thump against my ribs. "Fuck. I'm sorry."

He shrugged dismissively. "So am I. But I mean, I'm honestly not surprised they told you to do it."

My spine straightened. "Really?"

Hunter nodded. "Yeah. It was a shock to hear it, but then I realized, oh, right, this is Wilcox and Robertson we're talking about. Makes perfect fucking sense."

That... was something I'd needed to hear a lot more than I'd realized. As I tried to stay composed, I closed my eyes and pushed out a ragged breath.

"There's nothing I can say that'll convince you to stop beating yourself up over what you did," he whispered "But would it help if I told you that I get it, because I've been there? And even if I hadn't, I can't in a million years imagine blaming you for being threatened and manipulated?"

I looked up at him.

His smile was as gentle and sweet as his words. So was the kiss that followed.

I wrapped my arms around him and let the warmth of his embrace mingle with relief. I didn't think the guilt would ever completely disappear, but knowing Hunter didn't blame me—it helped. A lot.

As much as I didn't want to push my luck with him, I also had a chance to get things off my chest. A chance, and for the first time in my life, the courage.

Running my fingers through his hair, I murmured, "Can I confess something?"

Hunter drew back and met me with a playful look. "Is it something I might have to lie about to law enforcement?"

The laugh that poured out of me was almost as freeing as this whole conversation. "I don't think the cops will ever be interested."

"Good. So..." He sobered. "Tell me."

I swallowed. "The night you were boarded—when I beat the crap out of Evans."

His eyebrows rose, and he nodded.

I took a deep breath. "It wasn't just because he'd hurt a teammate. And it wasn't just because..." Some warmth rushed into my face, and I avoided his gaze as I quietly said, "It wasn't *just* because I was attracted to you. Which I was."

I wasn't looking at his face, but the subtle tension in his body told me I'd caught him by surprise.

Before he could tug at that particular thread, I barreled on: "Ever since you were drafted, I've felt..." I searched for the words, and the fact that this was my second language wasn't even the problem. I just didn't know how to put explain this. "You know what the butterfly effect is, right?"

Hunter tilted his head a little. "Yeah?"

"Okay. Well." I cleared my throat and made myself meet his gaze. "It felt a little like that. Like anything that happened after you were drafted..."

"It was your fault?" He sounded incredulous. Horrified, even.

I nodded. "You, um... You said you've followed my career a bit, right?"

"Mmhmm."

"Do you remember about when I was playing in Denver, and everyone said I was snakebitten?" I laughed despite myself. "When I couldn't find the back of the net to save my life for a while?"

Chewing his lip, Hunter nodded. "I remember."

Once again, I couldn't look at him. "Do you remember what was going on in your career at that point?"

He was silent, and when I chanced a peek, his eyes had lost focus and his brow was furrowed. "I... not really. I mean, I remember watching a couple of games while I was —" His head suddenly snapped toward me and his gaze locked on mine. "It was right after I broke my jaw."

Shame roiled in the pit of my stomach as I nodded.

"Jarek..." He cupped my cheek and stared at me, his expression pained. "You blamed yourself for... God, that was *years* after I was drafted."

"I know. And I tried to tell myself that. But I just... I don't know. I felt responsible. Like anything that happened when you were on that team was my fault. Every time you got hurt... Every time you guys missed the playoffs..." I rubbed a hand over my face. "And I think that night in Toronto, something in me just fucking snapped. That guy could've seriously injured one of my teammates, but there was also a part of me that felt responsible for you being at that game and on Toronto's shit list in the first place."

"Jesus," he breathed, and I had a split second to expect him to shove away from me in disgust before I was wrapped up in his arms. Closing my eyes, I gritted my teeth and tried to hold on to my composure as he stroked my hair.

"None of this was on you," Hunter murmured. "None of it. Baby, it's... You were caught up in the gears as much as I was."

"I had a choice." My voice came out thick. "You didn't."

"Did you, though?" He loosened his embrace and met my eyes again. "What would've happened if you'd said no?"

I opened my mouth to respond, but I came up short. *"No"* hadn't been an option back then. Not one I'd been brave enough to consider.

"We both know they would've made your life hell," Hunter whispered. "They might've even found a way to end your career." He exhaled. "Look at what they did after you *did* do what you were told. You think that would've played out any better if you'd told them no?"

Sakra. He made a good point.

"I, um…" I cleared my throat. "I never really gave myself a chance to think about it. I just knew I was too scared to say no."

"Of course you were. They had half the team walking on eggshells."

That gave me pause, and I studied him. "They did?"

Hunter huffed a dry, humorless laugh. "Are you kidding? One of the guys I played with told me one night he was scared to show up to practice sometimes."

I straightened. "Seriously?"

"Oh, yeah. Coach was always threatening him or berating him over stupid shit. He's a fucking bully and hides behind being 'old school'. Says we're all too soft and…" He waved a hand and rolled his eyes. "Nobody talks about it because they don't want to be seen as the guy whining that a coach was too hard on him. But it was bad." He shuddered, gaze turning a little distant. "*Really* bad."

My heart jumped into my throat. "He did it to you, too."

Hunter nodded, discomfort tightening his jaw. "He was fucking awful." He shuddered. "God, I swear I will never forget what it was like getting screamed at in his office…"

My stomach lurched.

He pushed a hand through his mussed hair. "I can't tell you how many times I thought the first time I lost a tooth in my hockey career, it would be because my fucking *coach* had decked me."

A flood of nauseating memories crashed through my mind. It had been bad enough knowing Robertson had done that to me. He'd done it to *Hunter*, too?

"Shit." I closed my eyes as acid climbed the back of my throat. If I hadn't done what they'd told me to, I could've saved Hunter from—

"Jarek." He touched my face. "Don't you dare go there."

I stared at him. "What?"

"I know you're blaming yourself." He ran the pad of his thumb along my cheekbone. "If you hadn't thrown the season, I never would've been subjected to that locker room."

I swallowed hard. "You're good at this."

"No. Just... kind of the logical conclusion after everything you said." He shifted a little, pushing himself up on his elbow, and cradled my face in his warm hand. "I mean it. None of this was on you."

Squeezing my eyes shut, I exhaled. "But I could've—"

Soft lips stopped the protest short, and he let the kiss linger until all the muscles in my neck and shoulder started to relax. I hadn't even realized I'd been tensing up all over, though that happened whenever I talked about Wilcox and Robertson. Sighing, I slid closer to him and basked in the gentle affection I still didn't believe I deserved.

The steel tightness in my neck was a distant memory when Hunter touched his forehead to mine, and he was out of breath as he whispered, "You were as much a victim in this as any of us."

His words pushed all the air out of my lungs, and I was genuinely shocked I didn't break down crying. That was still a possibility, though, and I wrapped my arms around him, pulling him in while I pulled myself together.

Hunter didn't object at all. Here was this man who had every reason to resent me, and somehow he was the one to come along and say the words I didn't know I needed to hear for all these long, miserable years.

You were as much a victim in this as any of us.

When I spoke, my voice sounded as raw as I felt: "Thank you."

He held me tighter and kissed the side of my neck. Then he sniffed, and I straightened. Drawing back from him, I didn't even care if he saw that my eyes had welled up, because I was startled to realize that *his* had.

"You okay?"

"Yeah." His laugh came out a little watery as he swiped at his eyes. "Guess it all still fucks with my head, too."

I blinked. "It does?"

"Well, yeah." He sniffed again. "After seven years of putting up with that shit? Hell, when we played in Toronto, I almost jumped out of my skin when Coach Robertson yelled at one of the refs."

"Me too," I said, still stunned to hear my own words coming out of his mouth.

"We're not the only ones." He took my hand again and looked in my eyes. "And we're away from him now, you know? Yeah, he did damage. And it fucking sucks. It pisses me off just to think about it. But he ruled enough of my life." He brought up our hands and kissed the heel of mine. "This isn't his. This is ours."

I swallowed. "So you... You really want to do this?"

Hunter laughed softly. "I'm sorry—were you not there when I was coming so hard I almost passed out?"

"Okay, but there's sex, and there's..." I trailed off, not

wanting to give him a reason to second guess anything, but also not wanting to get my hopes up that this was more than a hookup.

He smiled and slid closer, pressing his warm body up against mine. "It took a lot for us to get to this. We had to get past a lot of bullshit."

"Some of that from me," I admitted.

Hunter shrugged dismissively. "We got here despite all of our stubborn best efforts not to." Another shrug, this time accompanied with a sly grin. "So maybe let's give it a chance to be something, eh?"

The relief flooding through me was weird but good. Cool and dizzying. "Okay. Yeah. Let's..." I touched his face. "There's gotta be something here if my personality didn't scare you away."

The laugh that broke through was just...

Christ, he was beautiful.

"Don't sell yourself short." He lifted his chin and kissed me softly. "We had a lot of decks stacked against us, but we got here." This kiss was longer and more intense, and I was out of breath when he murmured, "If you didn't scare me off before, you're not going to now."

I laughed myself, dizzy with relief, and wrapped my arms around him. "So I won't have to talk you into staying here tonight?"

Hunter snorted. "Do you think I could walk out to the car?"

Chuckling, I leaned down to kiss his neck. "Hmm, that worked out better than I thought."

Neither of us had a third round in us tonight, but that was okay.

Hunter in my arms and shaking with delirious laughter was everything I could ask for.

CHAPTER 24

HUNTER

Ever since I was a teenager and throughout my professional
career, guys came and went. My focus was on hockey and
on living up to the pressure that had been piling on my
shoulders starting with that news story someone did about
me being a hockey prodigy when I was nine.

Once I made it to the big Leagues, guys either wanted
my ass and my money, or they wanted a boyfriend but
didn't give a damn about hockey or care why the sheets I
spent most of my time on were made of ice. Nobody stuck
around for long. I had some fuck buddies who lasted a
couple of months—three was the record, I thought, and that
ended when the offseason did—but that was pretty rare.
And I didn't meet too many guys who spared much
sympathy for a rich professional athlete who broke out in a
sweat at the prospect of going to practice.

*"You get paid millions of dollars to play hockey. What
the fuck do you have to be stressed about?"*

My mentally abusive coach, but okay.

In the end, that meant that as my teammates got
married and had kids, I'd still never had anything I'd call an

actual relationship. It got kind of lonely sometimes, especially whenever I went to a friend's wedding or when I noticed a teammate smiling to himself as he typed out a text, but I'd always been mostly okay with it.

A week and a half into this thing with Jarek, I couldn't believe I'd made it this far in life without a stronger connection to someone than sex or friendship. I'd never experienced that little rush of excitement when my text tone pinged. I'd never had someone to exchange secretive glances with when no one else was looking. For the first time, I understood for real why some of my teammates took off as soon as they could after practice or a game.

The fact that Jaromir Badura was the person on the other end of all this giddy excitement kind of blew my mind, but honestly? Once we'd hooked up for the first time, all the animosity seemed like a distant memory. Like something between me and a teammate whose name I'd since forgotten from a team I'd played for a lifetime ago.

Now I had a toothbrush in Jarek's bathroom, his favorite coffee was in my kitchen, and it felt like we'd been heading in this direction all along.

We hadn't been quite brave enough to sneak into one of our hotel rooms on a road trip, but to be fair, we'd only had two away games since we'd started hooking up. Both had been short trips, so there hadn't been a lot of time or energy for sex anyway. A longer road trip could get interesting, especially now while we were keeping this between us; we'd play that part by ear.

In the meantime, whenever we were in town and not working out, practicing, playing, or—in my case—going to physical therapy for my stupid neck, we were at his place or mine. Last night, we'd come to my apartment after the game. I'd picked him up at his condo so his not-exactly-subtle car wasn't parked conspicuously outside my building, and later this morning, I'd drop him off so we could arrive separately to practice.

For now, though, we had a couple of hours to just be lazy.

Coffee cup in hand, I eased onto the couch beside Jarek, who had no business looking that sexy in a pair of faded Hornets' sweatpants. "Think anyone on the team is catching on?"

He shrugged as he draped his bare arm across my equally bare shoulders. "Dolls, Ferns, and Dima are probably suspicious."

I shot him a look. "What? Why?"

Jarek rolled his eyes, bringing up his coffee for a sip. "Because they've been telling me to sleep with you since training camp."

"They *what?*"

He laughed and kissed my cheek. "Chirping. Trying to rile me up."

I cocked a brow. "By suggesting you sleep with me."

He made a *what-can-you-do?* gesture with his coffee cup.

Chuckling, I rolled my eyes and settled against him, leaning my head back on his arm. "As much as I don't like golf, I almost want to go out on the green with you guys just to listen to the shit-talking."

Jarek laughed. "What makes you think we talk shit while we golf?"

I eyed him.

He snickered. "Okay, point taken."

"Uh-huh."

He absently ran his fingertips up and down my arm. "If they do start chirping about us getting along, and say we must be together or something..." He shook his head. "It's just chirping. I promise. They have no idea."

"Suuure, they don't."

It was his turn to shoot me a look. "Unless you've told them something."

"I haven't told them a thing." I elbowed him playfully. "But those three can read you like a book. Especially Dima. So if they figure it out, I'm blaming you."

Jarek tsked and brought up his coffee again. "God, they're going to be insufferable when they find out."

That gave me pause. "*When* they find out?"

He stilled, but after a second, he shrugged and turned to me. "I mean, if we keep doing this, sooner or later..." He trailed off into another shrug.

"Oh. Okay, true." I stared into my coffee for a moment. "How do you think that'll go over? The two of us... dating, I guess?"

Jarek seemed to think about it for a moment. "Don't know, to be honest. Ever since players started coming out, people have been saying it's only a matter of time before two teammates ended up together."

I nodded. "Yeah, and they don't all seem too happy about it."

"Sure, if you listen to the old school guys who also think we've all gone soft because their generation didn't need so much safety gear." He pressed a kiss to my temple. "Ignore the old men yelling at clouds."

I chuckled. "I guess it is mostly those guys, isn't it?"

"Mmhmm. They're the same assholes who thought Colby Larsen should be kicked out of the League when he came out." Jarek swore under his breath and rolled his eyes. "Good thing there were rational people in charge then."

He had a point. I vividly remembered when Colby

made headlines as the first openly gay player in the League. The controversy had been all anyone would talk about for that entire season, and there'd been rumors about talks to release him from his contract over it.

Most of that stopped when he led his team to the second of their back-to-back Cup wins, and people remembered that he was being paid to play hockey, not be straight. After that, the League changed the rules to explicitly state that players of all sexualities were eligible and welcome, and that players who objected to playing alongside us could be released from their own contracts without penalty.

The message had been clear: *if you aren't willing to play hockey with someone who's gay, you're welcome to not play hockey at all.*

To my knowledge, no one had taken the League up on that offer.

I shifted a little, draping my legs over Jarek's thighs and leaning back against the armrest. "You know, I was thirteen when Larsen came out."

He met my gaze as he slid a hand between my knees, and he balanced his coffee cup on my leg. "Yeah?"

"Mmhmm. He, um..." I laughed, shaking my head. "He couldn't have timed it better, honestly."

Jarek's eyebrows rose.

I thumbed the handle on my own coffee cup. "Everyone was already making noise about me making it big. They had been since I was nine."

Jarek whistled. "Shit. That must have been a lot of pressure."

Blowing out a breath, I nodded. "Still is sometimes. But some of the major junior teams were already sniffing around for me, and my coaches said there were some League scouts paying attention to me, too."

"At thirteen?"

I nodded. "Yeah. And the thing is, I'd known since I was eleven or twelve that I was gay. But all that pressure for the future—it still seemed kind of abstract, you know? When I was thirteen, it was getting more serious, and people were talking about where I might actually end up. Talking about what my career in the League might look like." I laughed. "Someone even had a countdown to when I was eligible for the major junior and League drafts, even though they were still a few years away."

Jarek studied me, and the hand on my knee squeezed gently. "So at thirteen, you were already thinking about a career in the majors. As a gay man."

"Or about someone finding out I was gay and deciding I couldn't play hockey," I whispered. "I think that scared me more than anything—losing hockey because people found out about me."

He grimaced, patting my leg. "Yeah. I know that feeling."

"You do?"

"Well, yeah." Jarek half-shrugged. "I was sixteen when he came out. Sixteen. In my first year of major juniors. With a, um…" His eyes lost focus, and he softly added, "With a boyfriend."

"Oh. Shit."

"Mmhmm. So, I get it." He met my gaze again. "When Larsen came out, I felt like everyone was going to know. My boyfriend and I—we kept things on the downlow. The whole rest of that season, I still don't know how I managed to play. I think I convinced myself if I played my absolute best, then that would keep anyone from figuring out I was…" He laughed and rolled his eyes. "It… made sense to a scared kid."

"Yeah, I know what you mean." I slid my hand over his on my knee. "When everything quieted down and people realized it was possible to be gay *and* a good hockey player... Fuck, what a relief. Because I wanted to be out. And I wanted to do it on my terms—not get outed."

"Me too. That's why I came out my second season of juniors. That way everyone knew, and no one would care anymore by the time the draft came around."

"Must've worked." I smiled. "Ninth overall—can't argue with that."

"Highest ever pick for an openly gay player." He poked my leg. "At least until *someone* came along."

I snorted. "People stopped bitching about gay players after us." I paused. "And, um... I heard about you coming out, too."

Jarek's eyes went wide. "You did?"

"I followed a lot of the major junior teams. And any time a player came out in either League, it was big news, you know?" I stared down at our hands as some warmth rose in my face. "You were the first major junior player I knew of who'd come out. And that was..." I took a deep breath and looked in his eyes. "You were why I came out when I did."

His eyes got even bigger. "I... Really?"

"Yeah. Someone else paved the way in juniors. I didn't have to be the first."

He stared at me in surprise for a moment. Then his smile came back to life. He gently nudged my legs off his lap and put both our coffees on the table. Then he turned toward me and gathered me in those amazingly strong arms that had become so deliciously familiar.

"I'm glad I helped you come out," he murmured. "Maybe, down the line, other players will come out as couples because of us."

I grinned as I pulled him closer. "So are you saying we're..." I waggled my eyebrows. "Relationship goals?"

Jarek laughed, rolling his eyes. "Oh my God."

"What?" I chuckled. "Are you saying we're not?"

He didn't say anything. He kissed me instead, and my humor melted away. It was hard to believe this man who'd put up such icy walls between us at the beginning could make me warm all over like this, but he did. Every time.

Did we *have* to leave in an hour for practice? Couldn't we just stay here and let the morning take us to the very intriguing places his soft, playful kiss promised?

Though... an hour was still a fair amount of time.

And we could save even more time by showering together.

I wrapped my arms around him and pulled him down onto the couch with me.

Turned out we had plenty of time.

"Come on, Mish!" Ferns steered me toward the hotel bar. "After a game like that, you'd better be partying with us!"

"But... I..." Laughing, I let myself be herded across the lobby. The guys had been insistent all the way back from the arena that they *were* buying me drinks and that was final. And what was I supposed to say? *No, because I need to get Badura naked?*

So... fine.

At least Jarek was coming in with us, and when eight Pittsburgh Hornets took over a large corner booth, I ended up right next to him.

Okay. I could live with that. Especially since we had to pack in pretty tight in order to fit eight hockey asses on this bench, which meant we were touching from hip to knee. I was touching Ferns the same way, but that contact barely registered. Every nerve ending was focused on Jarek's body heat mingling with mine through our clothes.

God, this was torture. As much as I loved celebrating a hard-won victory with my team, I was itching to call it a night and drag my left winger upstairs. We were on game three of a five-game road trip, and we hadn't had a moment alone together since we'd left Pittsburgh. The one night we would've had some time had been after the second game, but that game had been a grind to end all grinds, and we'd lost in overtime. Between sleeping on one of the flights and taking a hard hit in that game, my neck had been sore, and Jarek had been exhausted, so we'd settled on a few suggestive texts.

Next time we've got some downtime, he'd promised me. *You're all mine.*

You better believe it, I'd responded while I'd iced my neck three doors down the hall.

From the looks we'd both been exchanging in the locker room tonight, we were very much on the same page about when that downtime would be occurring, and could our bus driver have maybe driven a *little* faster back to the hotel?

But now we were waylaid because our jubilant teammates wanted to celebrate.

I could hardly follow the conversation at the table, which consisted of everyone rehashing tonight's game. To be fair, it *had* been a pretty wild fucking game, and it had looked grim there until the very end. Calgary held us to two-nothing for fifty-one minutes before Mayweather *finally* got us on the board. Then Jarek scored four minutes later, only to have it successfully challenged for goaltender interference. That was a steaming mountain of bullshit because their goalie had been fully out of the blue paint when Sawyer collided with him, and he'd have had plenty of time to recover and return to his crease if he hadn't wasted precious seconds cursing out Sawyer. Instead, he'd left his net wide open, and Jarek had taken full advantage.

Goaltender interference, my ass.

That hadn't been great for our morale. Mayweather's goal had given us hope we could turn this game around, but losing that second one—the one that would've tied the game—had us frustrated, pissed off, and demoralized. We weren't winning this one, that was for sure.

With twenty-three seconds left in regulation, though, I'd fired a one-timer off a pass from Dima, and it whizzed right past the goalie's glove hand.

From the way we'd all celebrated, we may as well have just won the Cup.

And we'd *still* very nearly lost in regulation. Dolls was getting his drinks paid for tonight just like I was, because he'd made an absolutely miraculous save on a shot that, against a lesser goalie, would've been a buzzer beater for sure.

Overtime was a grind, and neither team scored.

Shootout, then. My favorite. Ugh.

"I can't believe you faked him out." Dima pushed a beer toward me on the table. "We spend whole game trying to get into his head, and you do it, by yourself, during shootout."

"To be fair," Jarek said, "the guy had played three periods plus overtime by that point." He picked up his own beer. "He was probably exhausted."

"Hey!" I elbowed him hard enough to make him sputter his beer. "So it wasn't a perfectly glorious masterpiece of a shot? The goalie was just tired?" I rolled my eyes. "Eat a dick, Yars."

That had the whole table roaring with laughter, and I just hoped nobody noticed the wicked look he shot me before he joined in.

God, it took all I had not to slide a hand over his thigh or lean over and kiss him. Good thing I was used to keeping PDAs to a minimum since cameras had been in my face most of my life.

Can't I just drag him behind closed doors right the hell now and go to town on him?

Somehow, I kept myself from squirming at the thought. One beer. I'd just have one beer, and then I'd go upstairs and see how much Jarek and I both had left after that monster game. Just needed to—

"There's the men of the hour." Coach Henley appeared and clapped Dolls on the shoulder as he gave me a sharp nod. "Well done, boys. All of you. How about a round on me?"

Everyone cheered their approval of that, which fortunately drowned out any sounds of frustration that might've escaped Jarek or me. We glanced at each other, and my own impatience was written all over his face. I schooled my expression. So did he. We feigned enthusiasm and accepted our drinks, and Jarek rubbed his leg against mine under the table. Fuck, I couldn't *breathe* when he did that.

Could we break away now? Please?

Guys, I appreciate the enthusiasm and the drinks, but there's a man in this table who needs to put his dick in me.

Jarek was the first to escape. With a glance at his watch, he said apologetically, "Guys, I'm beat. I've got to call it a night." He nudged Dolls, who was sitting to his left.

As Dolls got up, Ferns huffed. "What? Come on, old man. You can party with—"

Jarek's middle finger shut him up. "I also have to log on and pay my sister's tuition. So unless you all want to tell her why she's getting kicked out of medical school..." He looked around the table, eyebrows raised.

Everyone shook their heads.

"Have a good night, Yars," Mayweather said. "Tell your sister she better be getting straight As."

Jarek snorted. "Trust me. She is."

The guys all said their goodbyes to him, and he left without a backward glance at me. That was fine. We had to be discreet. And it also meant I got a spectacular view of that ass on his way out. I really needed to write a thank-you card to his tailor, because goddamn.

More than that, though, I had to find a way to bow out of this party without anyone catching on.

About a minute after Jarek left, my phone vibrated with a text.

Room 1322.

I exhaled and shoved my phone back into my inside pocket. He'd probably be waiting for me. Naked. Hard. Impatient in that way he got when he was too horny to sit still. I almost wanted to make him wait a little longer just to drive him wild.

But that would mean making *myself* wait longer.

And I needed Jarek.

Now.

CHAPTER 25

JAREK

I could live to be a hundred, and I'd never know how Hunter and I managed to slip away from our team and into my room without being busted.

I could live to be *two* hundred and still not care.

"Jesus fucking Christ," Hunter panted between kisses as I shoved him up against the door. "One more... One more minute out there, and *everyone* was going to know about us."

"Uh-huh." I claimed his mouth again, rutting against him as he dragged his fingers through my hair. He was probably right—with the smoldering looks we'd been exchanging all night, it had only been a matter of time before something went up in flames.

"We should..." He whimpered, arching off the door as I went for his neck. "Maybe the bed? So nobody walks by and hears us?"

There was that. Two bodies squirming and thumping against a door wouldn't exactly be subtle to anyone strolling past, and the rest of the team was staying on this floor.

I slid my hands into his front pockets and hauled him

away from the door. He stumbled a little, but his arms around my neck kept him upright. We staggered and tripped, but between the two of us, navigated across the room and onto the bed. Without needing to worry about gravity or balance anymore, we focused on the important things—getting each other hard, breathless, and naked.

Those first two were easy. I'd been rock-hard and out of breath before Hunter had even touched me tonight. Got the impression he was in the same state.

Clothes, though, were kind of a pain. Every time one of us moved to take off some clothes, that meant using our hands, and our hands were quite well-occupied at the moment. No matter how much I wanted his hot, bare skin against my body, I just couldn't make myself pull a hand away long enough to deal with it.

Eventually, we succeeded, and we touched each other all over as we made out breathlessly on the hotel bed. I wanted to suck his dick and drive him wild, but I couldn't stop kissing him. He didn't seem to mind.

Then Hunter pushed me onto my back and straddled me, his dick right alongside mine as we made out, and my palms and fingers drifted over exposed, hot, perfect skin.

Hunter lifted himself up on those gorgeous, powerful arms of his, and he met me with gleaming, lust-filled eyes. "*Please* tell me you brought condoms with you," he growled.

"Mmhmm." I curved my hands over his ass. "Let me text the equipment managers to bring some up."

Hunter snorted. "Fuck you."

I laughed and pulled him down to me. "I seem to recall you prefer if it *I* fuck *you*."

He bit his lip. "Is that you saying you want to fuck me?"

I arched an eyebrow. "Do you want me to fuck you?"

"Hmm. Maybe you should text the equipment managers."

"Yeah?" I dragged my nails up his back, reveling in the moan that drew out of him. "Why's that?"

Hunter whimpered, rubbing his dick against my hip. "You know exactly why."

"Uh-huh." I lifted my head to kiss his neck. "But it's so fun to hear you say—"

"Goddammit, Jarek," he gritted out. "Get a condom on and fuck me. Right now."

I groaned softly, arching beneath him. "Oh my God..."

"Am I to assume that's a yes?"

"Something like that." Without warning, I grabbed him, threw him on his back, and kissed him deep and hard. He raked his nails up my sides as he squirmed and moaned under me, returning my kiss as if he needed it like air.

I pushed myself up. "How about I get that condom?"

"Yes." He licked his lips. "*Now.*"

One more kiss, and then I got up. At home, I had condoms and lube within arm's reach, but at a hotel—well, I hadn't completely unpacked, let's put it that way. Good thing I knew which pocket of my shaving kit had the essentials, and I returned in short order.

The second I had the condom in place, Hunter took over. He got on top, and once I'd lubed us both up, he sank down onto me with a throaty, "Fuuuck."

Christ, he was sexy. As he moved slowly, his abs tensed, deepening the contours of that mouthwatering six-pack. When I started stroking him, he closed his eyes and swore, tightening around me as he picked up speed.

"Jesus, Jarek," he mumbled. "You have... the perfect cock."

"Mmm, yeah?" I added a subtle twist to my strokes. "Yours isn't so bad either."

I was pleased that if he'd meant to come back with something witty, he either forgot it or decided it was less important than what our bodies were doing.

"Do you like it like this?" I asked. "Or faster?"

His eyes were full of lust and fire as he gazed down at me. "Do *you* like it fast?"

I licked my lips. "I like it any way makes you"—I thrust up into him, *hard*—"moan."

I'd knocked him off-balance, and he caught himself on one arm, moaning exactly as I'd hoped. "Oh God..."

I grinned up at him, still stroking him because I knew that fucked with his ability to speak. "Like that?"

Hunter's eyebrow flicked up. Without a word, he stopped my hand. Then he took my wrist and pinned my arm to the bed. A second later, the other. And then...

Oh, holy fuck...

Pinning my arms, he rode me like his life depended on it. If we'd been anywhere other than a hotel full of our team-mates, I'd have been shouting in English, Czech, and probably a couple of languages I didn't even know, because oh, Jesus, he felt amazing. He was so damn tight, and the way he moved his hips was *magic*, especially this fast and hard. As much as I wanted to touch him—his powerful thighs, his broad shoulders, his sculpted arms—the way he held me down was so fucking sexy. His grip was painful and unrelenting, keeping me still so there was nothing for me to do except lie here and enjoy what he did to my dick, not to mention the view of this absolute god of a man driving himself out of his mind.

Well... almost nothing.

He must've felt it when I moved my legs a little, because

he shivered, and he grinned down at me, and that first upward thrust drove a delirious whimper from his parted lips. We fell into sync with each other, fucking hard and fast, the bed frame shrieking from the abuse, and in that moment, I didn't care if our teammates *did* hear us. I wasn't sure I could hold back anyway. Not when I was this turned on.

Then Hunter leaned down, and his mouth against mine made our combined rhythm falter, but only for a second. We were slower now—kind of came with the territory of not wanting teeth clacking together—but it was still hot, still amazing, still driving me right to that precipice. From Hunter's sharp, erratic breathing and his painfully tight grip on my arms, he was almost there too.

"Come," I pleaded against his lips. "Just... Just like this."

"Yeah?" He nipped my lower lip. "While I'm on top?"

"While you're kissing me."

His throaty groan was fucking amazing, and so was the way he kissed me as he kept riding me toward his peak. Some guys thought my whole thing about kissing a man when he came was weird. Hunter—I swore he got off on it as much as I did.

He shivered hard, throwing off his rhythm again. I managed to get my hands free, and I grabbed his hips. Digging my heels even more firmly into the mattress, I thrust up as hard as I could, desperate to be as deep as he could take me, and I swallowed his moans and whimpers as he started to fall apart. God, I couldn't get enough of him.

Then he tensed all over and sucked in a breath through his nose. His body jerked, and he clenched around my dick. He grunted as his hot cum landed on my stomach, and then after a few more desperate thrusts, I was releasing inside him, arching off the mattress and trembling from my spinning head all the way down to my curling toes.

With a shuddering moan, Hunter slumped over me. I wrapped my arms around his hot, shaking body, and I closed my eyes as we both caught our breath.

"You really get off on that, don't you?" he murmured. "Kissing me while I come?"

"Can't explain why." I stroked his hair with an unsteady hand. "It's just hot."

His sexy, sleepy laugh made my head light. "You don't have to explain it. If you like it..." He half-shrugged. "You like it."

"Do you?"

Hunter laughed again, almost soundlessly this time. "I love kissing you, and I love coming. Doing both at the same time?" He gave me a thumbs up.

I chuckled and pulled him in closer, pressing a kiss to his forehead.

And I prayed to anyone who would listen that this time...

Just this *one* time...

Something good didn't blow up in my face.

Between an orgasm and a shower, I wasn't at all surprised that Hunter fell asleep not long after we'd climbed into bed. He usually did, and truthfully, this was one of my favorite things with him—just lying here with his head on my shoulder while I stroked his damp hair and let my mind wander. The warmth of his body next to mine, the strong arm draped over my stomach, that lingering bliss from some good sex—it didn't get any better than this.

It was different, too. Everything about this thing with Hunter—the sex, the affection, the way we touched and talked—it was all new and different, as if I'd never been close to a man in my life. It had been that way from the start, but I still couldn't quite put my finger on *how*.

It was hot and intense, of course. He was incredible in bed, and he clearly enjoyed getting his partner off.

But plenty of guys I'd fucked had been like that.

And I didn't think we were *just* fucking. We'd sort of danced around the subject of what this was. Not just sex, maybe some future potential, but no talk beyond that so far. That was fine—I was happy to let things happen organically and see how they shook out on their own before we started putting names on them. It wasn't a one night stand, though, that was for sure.

There was something *else*, though. Some feeling or undercurrent I couldn't chalk up to us sort-of-dating rather than this being a one night stand. It was too different.

And also too familiar.

Stroking Hunter's hair, I closed my eyes. As much as I didn't want to think about my ex while I was in bed with Hunter, the memories of Marc-Yves weren't going to be ignored. Not tonight.

So... I gave in.

Though his name was ashes on my tongue these days, there'd been a time when we'd loved each other. We'd done more than just float the idea of getting married. There'd been talk of children. A home. A future.

But there'd been distance between us that we could never quite bridge. Marc-Yves probably still claimed to this day that I kept him at arm's length. Shut him out. Refused to give as much of myself as he gave of his. As much as it

shamed me to admit it, he was right to say that, and it ulti-
mately, that was why he'd left.

I didn't feel that distance between me and Hunter.
Which was weird. I'd been with Marc-Yves for seven years.
I'd been closer to him than anyone else on the planet.
Hunter, I'd only known for a handful of months, and I'd
spent most of that time being an asshole to him because I
resented him for—

I stiffened. My fingers stilled on Hunter's arm.

Hunter *knew*.

The deep, dark, humiliating secret I'd been paying for
in silence—I'd told him.

And he was here. Beside me. Naked. Satisfied. Asleep.

God. That was it, wasn't it? Hunter knew who I was.
He'd known it since before he'd ever put an affectionate
hand on me.

I would never know how different my relationship with
Marc-Yves would've been if I'd come clean. There was no
telling how he would've taken it. I wanted to believe he'd
have been the compassionate and understanding man I'd
loved. But there'd always been that doubt. Always that fear.
The relentless knowledge that once I told him, there was no
going back.

That had kept me silent, and my silence had driven him
away.

I swallowed an unexpected lump in my throat. I was
over him. Had been for a long time. The sudden flood of
emotions wasn't because I longed to return to that time—it
was just a wave of grief over something else I'd lost to that
one fateful hockey season. It had taken until now—lying
honestly and openly in Hunter's arms—to truly realize the
toll that secret had taken on my relationship with Marc-
Yves.

I regretted that. I didn't want to go back, and I didn't want to trade the present with Hunter for the past with Marc-Yves, but it shouldn't have ended the way it did. The regret was a hot coal in the center of my chest as that old grief reignited. I shouldn't have had to keep a secret like that from him until it finally drove us apart.

Hunter... knew. What I'd done. What I hadn't been able to tell Marc-Yves.

Did that mean there was hope for us instead of this thing being destined to fail from day one?

Or was I just deluding myself, believing someone like him might—

"Jarek?" Hunter's sleepy voice pulled me out of my thoughts, and I looked down to see him gazing back at me. He pushed himself up on his arm. "You okay?"

"Yeah, I'm..." Was I? How had he even caught on?

"Hey. You got all tense." He touched my face, concern creasing his. "You all right?"

"I'm good," I whispered. "Just... thinking."

The concern deepened. "Not about anything good, I'm guessing."

My first impulse was to insist it was nothing, but hadn't I *just* been realizing how few secrets and barriers there were between us? Did I really want to create one?

Hunter already knew my worst secret. He deserved my honesty.

I shifted onto my side and slid a hand over his waist. "Did you know I almost got married once?"

He blinked, clearly caught off guard. "I... No, I don't think so." His brow furrowed. "Was that what you were... About your ex, or...?"

"Sort of comparing that to... Well, to this." I paused,

then quickly added, "Not that we're getting married or— that's not what I mean. Just..."

"Comparing then to now." He nodded. "I get it."

Maybe he did. It was an alien feeling, someone under-standing me. Someone *wanting* to.

And for the first time in I didn't know how long, I wanted to tell someone about that part of my past.

I chewed my lip. "Do you remember when you took me home from Dima's barbecue?"

He nodded, brow furrowing. "Yes?"

"Okay, well, you said something about him and Chloé being like high school sweethearts. The way a lot of players are with the partners they meet in major juniors."

Another nod. Then, voice soft, "You had someone in juniors."

I winced. "Yeah. I had someone." And oh, yeah, the memory hurt. I took a deep breath and focused on fiddling with a wrinkle in the sheet. "His name was Marc-Yves. I met him when I was sixteen. He was a little younger—couple of months, nothing major. And he was..." All the emotions trying to come pouring out were painful, but I kept going. "We started dating around the same time Chloé and Dima did." A laugh broke through, which felt good even though it was tender around the edges. "The four of us—we were inseparable."

Hunter put a hand on my arm and ran his thumb along-side my wrist. "How long were you with him?"

It was harder than it should've been to speak, and I had to swallow a couple of times. It didn't help as much as I'd hoped, and the emotion came through when I whispered, "Seven years."

Hunter blinked. "Really?"

I nodded, lowering my gaze again to the wrinkle in the

sheet. "We were each other's first everything. *Everything.* Talked about getting married, families—all of it." I managed a quiet, choked laugh. "We talked about our kids being trilingual."

Silence hung between us for a moment. Hunter must've crunched the numbers, because he said, "You were in... Denver, right? When it ended?"

The question caught me by surprise. Sometimes I still forgot that other people knew my career trajectory. Releasing a long breath, I nodded. "I don't know if that was a blessing or a curse, honestly. He went with me when I was traded to Edmonton, but he couldn't come to the States with me. Not unless we got married. And we were..." I chewed the inside of my cheek as I tried to find the right way to phrase it. "We'd talked about getting married, but by the time I went to Denver, we just weren't in a good place for it. Not where either of us wanted to be when we got married. But we couldn't get him a visa unless..." I waved a hand. "And we were in an even worse place to be living apart."

"Damn," Hunter said. "That sucks. I'm sorry."

I nodded to acknowledge it. I wasn't sure I could speak without my voice breaking.

"Did he know?" Hunter asked. "About..."

I flinched, and my eyes welled up as I shook my head. Was it the topic? Or maybe trying to talk about it right after we'd had sex? Sex made people emotional, didn't it? Fine. I'd go with that. I swiped at my eyes. "No one knew. It was driving me insane, and I think..."

"It drove you guys apart," he whispered.

"Yeah. He knew something was up with..." I tapped my temple. "But I couldn't tell him. And the more it ate at me, and the less he knew..." I made a heavy, frustrated gesture.

"You can't keep a relationship going when there's a secret like that, you know?"

"I can imagine."

"It was awful." I chewed my lip. "You're the first person —the only person in my life who knows what happened. What I did."

Hunter caressed my cheek. "You make it sound like you committed a murder or something. You were a *kid* who was manipulated into—"

"I know," I whispered. "But... I still did it. And I hated myself for it. I was so ashamed and humiliated, I never told anyone." I trailed my fingertips along his arm. "You're the only one who knows. My ex..." I shook my head. "I couldn't tell him. The secrecy... It pretty much killed our relationship."

"Jesus. I'm sorry."

I studied him, and an icy ball of dread swelled in my stomach. "I don't want to go back to him. Just so we're clear. I have a lot of regrets about what happened, but that part of my life is over." I intertwined our fingers between us. "This is where I want to be right now."

Hunter's smile almost chased away all the lingering hurt from my past. He kissed my knuckles, then my mouth. "I know. You can move forward and have unfinished business at the same time. I get it."

"I know. But just... Don't think I want to go back." I kissed him softly and gripped his hand tighter. "This—what we're doing—I want that."

Hunter's smile was gentle. "I get it. We all have regrets, even if we don't actually want to change the way things are now."

I exhaled, relieved he understood. "Honestly, I don't know if we'd have made it or not. We were young and stupid, and we didn't have any experience except with each other. So who knows?" I sighed, shoulders sinking. "But the only thing I regret more than what I did for Toronto is how I let it destroy my relationship with Marc-Yves. Because it just... It wasn't fair to him."

"It wasn't fair to you, either."

I stared at him incredulously.

"You shouldn't have had to carry that secret," he said. "Someone else put that burden on your shoulders, and look what it cost you? How is any of that fair to you?"

I shrugged. "But I... Fair to me? I'm the one who threw a goddamned season and—"

"Because you were threatened and manipulated."

"I was." I brought my hand back down and watched it run along Hunter's tattooed arm. "But there were things I did that I shouldn't have. I pushed Marc-Yves away. I was... Sakra. Back then, I was a wreck about it. I was angry and ashamed. I pushed a lot of people away." The memories made my chest hurt. "And I guess it took longer for me to get my head together than Marc-Yves was willing to wait. Can't really blame him, I guess."

Hunter smoothed my hair. "Jesus. It's no wonder you didn't like me when I first came to Pittsburgh. All this shit you had on your mind..."

I flinched. "I didn't even know you. You were just—"

"A reminder of everything you lost so someone else could win Cups."

I closed my eyes and released a breath. "I still shouldn't have been an ass to you. I'm sorry."

"I know you are. Have you, um... Have you ever thought of reaching out to him? Your ex?"

I shook my head. "God, no. He wouldn't want to hear from me."

"But maybe *you* need him to hear from you."

The thought made my stomach shrivel. "I can't imagine he has anything good to say to me."

"You never know."

Again, I shook my head. "No. I can't. Especially since I still can't tell him why." I paused, then met Hunter's eyes. "I haven't had anyone I could be completely honest with in all this time." I drew my thumb along his cheekbone. "Not until you."

Hunter took my hand and pressed a kiss to my palm. "I'm glad you could finally talk to someone." He leaned in closer and brushed his lips across mine. "And… I'm glad that someone was me."

My heart fluttered. "Me, too." I looked in his eyes. "I don't know what this is. What we're doing—I don't know what to call it. I'm not ready to tell anyone about it. But… I like it." I caressed his cheek. "A lot. And I don't want to fuck it up."

Hunter's smile was the sweetest thing I'd ever seen. "I like it, too." He lifted his chin for a soft kiss, but as he settled onto the pillow again, he sobered. "The rest of it—same. I don't want to rush anything or go public. So let's just keep it between us for now. Until we have a better handle on what we're doing."

I nodded. "I can do that."

He flashed me a wicked grin. "I assume you won't object to the part where you keep fucking me into the mattress at every available opportunity?"

I laughed as a rush of heat crackled through me. Pulling him closer, I murmured, "Not a chance."

"Will we still be able to skate tomorrow?"

Chuckling, I slid a hand down his back. "You're the one

who rode me that hard, so if you can't skate..." I half-shrugged.

"Hmm, okay. Fine." He pressed his hips to mine, letting me feel his hard-on coming back to life. "But I don't think an enthusiastic blowjob will hurt my skating."

Oh, my own dick was definitely interested in where this was going.

"Yeah?" I nudged him onto his back and straddled him. "So this enthusiastic blowjob that won't hurt your skating—are you giving or receiving?"

He licked his lips. "Yes."

Well, then.

Game on.

Mayweather: *Anyone up for something this afternoon? Golf got rained out.*

Dolls: *Rained out? WTF does that even mean?*

Cole: *Uh, it means it's raining? So we're not golfing?*

Sawyer: *C'mon, Dolls. You golf. You know what it means.*

Dolls: *No, because I don't golf with a bunch of wimps who can't handle getting a little wet.*

Mayweather: *The course won't let us out there with our spikes when it's wet, dumbass.*

Ferns: *We don't wear our spikes when it rains! We're not animals.*

Cole: *So you golf... without your spikes?*

Dolls: *Obviously. They would tear up the grass.*

Dima: *Oh shut up both of you. You do too wear your spikes or you'd fall on your asses.*

Mayweather: *Uh-huh. Pictures or it didn't happen.*

Dima: *I've got pictures!*

Dima has sent four images.

Cole: *Jesus Christ. WTF.*

Jarek: *Rain on the golf course separates the men from the boys.*

Mayweather: *LOL*

Cole: *Yeah no.*

Dima: *Hey, there's Yars!*

Dolls: *Where TF have you been?*

Jarek: *You saw me at practice this morning, numb nuts. Or were you too busy coloring?*

Dolls: *(middle finger emoji)*

Mayweather: *They're right, man. We never see you outside of hockey anymore. You got a boyfriend you haven't told us about?*

Dolls: *YES DO YOU?*

Sawyer: *Wait Yars has a boyfriend?*

Ferns: *Who? Dude is that why you didn't want to go ax throwing with us?*

Jarek: *Ferns, I wouldn't go ax-throwing with you and Dolls if my life depended on it.*

Cole: *That's not exactly a no on the boyfriend thing.*

Norris: *Hold up, Yars has a boyfriend?*

Freeman: *Like a blowup doll? Or an actual dude?*

Jarek: *I hate you guys.*

Mayweather: *We know, but tell us about the guy you obviously don't hate.*

Jarek groaned and put his phone facedown on the armrest of his couch. "Jesus Christ. This team."

"What?" I asked through my laughter. "It's funny! And it's cute!"

He shot me a glare that didn't help me compose myself at all.

"It is!" I insisted. "Come on, admit it. It's cute."

He rolled his eyes, but the blush gave him away. As did the little twitch at the corner of his mouth.

"And do you guys actually golf in the rain?" I cocked a brow. "That's... not actually a thing, is it?"

A chuckle finally broke through. "Oh, yeah. As long as there's no lightning. It gets cold as balls, but it can be fun."

"Eww. No." I pursed my lips. "No lightning, eh?"

"Well, no. You really don't want to be the only thing standing in the middle of an open space, especially not while holding a piece of metal."

"Okay, well, at least you take some safety into consideration."

"Not us." He shrugged. "The courses shut down. Won't let us play." He huffed with annoyance and deadpanned, "Liability bullshit, I guess."

I snorted and nudged him with my foot. "I'm sure that's just what they need—a lawsuit after a couple of hockey players get fried on their green." I paused. "Fried green players?"

The eyeroll and facepalm had me cackling.

Still laughing, he reached for his phone. "Let's see how out of hand the group chat has gotten."

I was curious, too, and... Yep, our teammates had definitely kept it rolling.

Cole: *You guys are letting us down. How do YOU not know who Yars is dating?*

Dima: *Because he hasn't told us either!*

Cole: *And?*

Mayweather: *Come on. How are we supposed to razz him for it if you guys are falling down on the job?*

Norris: *Hey Dolls, what's his Grindr profile again?*

Jarek: *WTF? Dolls, what did I tell you about using my Grindr to pick up men?*

Michaud: *Ok, NOW it makes sense.*

Jarek shot me a look. I batted my eyelashes. On the screen, our teammates went nuts.

Mayweather: *Wait what? You found Yars on Grindr?*

Michaud: *I mean I thought I did, but then I was like, that tattoo looks suspiciously like the one on Dolls's shoulder.*

Dolls: *OMG fuck you both*

Jarek: *Did he use the butt tattoo pic this time? Seems like it got him a lot of tail last time.*

Dolls: *Yars your such a dick*

Ferns: *LOLOLOL I am so telling Leia about this*

Dolls: *FERNS DON'T YOU DARE*

Dima: *hahaha omg*

Mayweather: *Ferns he knows where you live*

Ferns: *oops too late*

Dolls: *GODDAMMIT*

"Oh my God," I laughed. "Do you think he actually told his wife?"

"Don't know." Jarek was typing. "But I am."

I almost choked. "You guys are such dicks to each other."

"Eh." Jarek shrugged unrepentantly.

I slid my foot up his thigh, stopping just below his groin. "Now I kind of want to see your Grindr profile."

He laughed. "Not much to see. I haven't been on Grindr in a while."

"Really?"

"Nothing bad." He curved a hand over my shin. "Just didn't get the results I wanted. Hookup apps are…" He seemed to think about it. "I don't know. I just prefer to meet people in person."

I grinned, sliding my foot a little higher and letting my toe tease him through his sweats, making him gasp. "I have no complaints about you preferring to meet people in person."

Jarek squirmed, moving his hand down to my ankle. "To be fair, we didn't meet at the club."

"Didn't meet on Grindr, either."

"Point taken." He gently lifted my foot off his lap, then crawled toward me and settled on top of me. "Lanterns was way better than Grindr. Ten out of ten."

I wrapped my arms around his neck. "We should send them a fruit basket."

Jarek laughed and lowered his head to kiss me. I held him to me and let that kiss linger for a moment. Neither of us probably had the energy to go another round any time soon—we'd exchanged a couple of blowjobs after practice this morning—but this was fine with me. I loved kissing this man, and there was almost nothing better than being under him, bracketed between those strong arms as his weight settled on top of me.

On the coffee table, both our phones pinged.

We glanced toward them, then at each other.

"Oh, God." He touched his forehead to my shoulder. "I don't even want to know."

"Right?" I kept one arm around him and felt around on the table for my phone. When I found it, I peered at the screen.

Rachel: *Hey guys, emailed schedules to you for photo shoots. Let me know if you have any conflicts.*

"Oh." I exhaled as I tossed my phone back on the table. "Just Rachel pinging everyone about those photo shoots." The team's magazine was running an article about several of us soon, and they needed shots of all of us. No surprise.

From the way Jarek relaxed, he'd also been uneasy about the simultaneous texts.

"I swear to God," I said, wrapping both arms around his neck, "I thought it was one of the guys saying he'd figured us out."

Nodding, Jarek exhaled. "Me, too. Bullet dodged, right?"

"Right." But his worry unsettled me. "Are you good with all this? The guys sniffing around for a boyfriend?"

"It's fine," he murmured. "I think it's kind of fun, letting them guess."

"Yeah?"

"Well, yeah." His grin was adorable. "Keeps them busy, and they end up ripping on each other half the time anyway. It's entertaining."

"I'll give you that. It's definitely entertaining." I stroked his hair. "Just... I don't want this causing you stress, you know?"

"It's okay." He brushed his lips across mine. "It comes with the secrecy. When we come out later, we can relax a bit." Resting his weight on one arm, he touched my face. "But it's not enough to make me want to stop doing this."

"Me neither. But I don't want you stressed about—"

Jarek's kiss silenced me. He cupped my face in one hand as his tongue teased my lips apart, and I whimpered as I pulled him closer. I might've forgotten I'd been speaking at all if he hadn't mentioned it, whispering, "If the choice is a little secrecy and the guys chirping at me nonstop, or not doing this..." He shook his head. Then he kissed me again, and he didn't relent this time.

I didn't know if this would lead to sex, or if we were just going to lazily make out on the couch. Either way, I was perfectly happy. His kiss, his body, his warm skin, his thickening erection against my hip—I had nothing to complain about. Lying here and kissing for ages? Sounded perfect to me.

Jarek pushed himself up on his forearms and gazed down at me, breathing hard. "I'm not sure if you've noticed this, but my bed is a lot more comfortable than my couch."

"Hmm, is it?" I curved my hands over his ass and pulled him against me. "Don't know. Might need to do some more research on that subject."

He rolled his eyes and then rolled to his feet. Offering his arm, he said with a grin, "Come on, you."

Grinning, I clasped my hand around his arm and let him help me upright. Then I followed him into the bedroom.

Yeah, I could've spent half the day kissing on his couch.

But this?

Ooh, fuck yeah. This was even better.

CHAPTER 27

JAREK

Ever since the night I'd told Hunter about Marc-Yves, that part of my past had *itched* to be dealt with. I could never go back, and I didn't want to, but it felt unresolved. After Hunter had suggested reaching out and burying the hatchet, the itch was almost unbearable. It pestered me awake at night whether I was lying alone or had Hunter sleeping beside me.

Enough already.

I had no idea where he was now, but Marc-Yves and I did have some mutual friends. I reached out to one and asked if they would pass a message along to him—my email, my phone number, and that I'd understand if he didn't want to contact me.

When a week had passed and I hadn't heard from him or our mutual friend...

Well. I had my answer, didn't I?

But then I got a text on my way to our morning skate in Los Angeles.

If you want to talk, call me.

There was no mistaking who it had come from, either. My cell provider didn't just show phone numbers—it included names, even if they weren't in my contacts.

And there it was:

Marc-Yves Beaulieu.

My throat tightened around my breath as my eyes flicked between his name and his short message. Hands unsteady, I managed to type out, *Heading to morning skate. Can I call this afternoon? On west coast right now. 2pm okay?*

I was in the locker room, halfway into my gear, when he responded, *2pm is fine.*

It was a genuine miracle I made it through practice without faceplanting. My mind was completely focused on the man I hadn't spoken to in years and what we might say to each other today. Because we were going to talk. *Today.*

Finally—and somehow too soon—I was alone and as ready as I'd ever be to call him. All my teammates had gone back to their rooms for pregame naps or to otherwise relax before we had to return to the arena. This was when Hunter and I would often sneak into my room—sometimes for an afternoon quickie, always to curl up together for an hour or so to recharge before the game.

"I need to call my ex," I'd told him. *"Do you mind if we, uh..."*

Hunter's smile had lightened the weight on my shoulders and the ball of lead in my stomach. *"Text me to let me know how it goes, eh? If I don't reply, I'm asleep."*

Why did I wish he was here with me? I didn't want him to see me fall apart or lash out or beg forgiveness—whatever I ended up doing once I heard my ex's voice. But I still wanted Hunter here. Maybe because I always wanted him close by. Maybe because I was tired of facing every goddamned thing alone.

Well, I was doing this on my own, and if I didn't do it now, I'd never again find the courage. Marc-Yves would probably block my number, too—I had a feeling this was my one and only shot at connecting with him before he lost whatever sliver of patience he had left for me.

I stared at the phone for a long moment, waiting for my stomach to settle and my pulse to slow down. They didn't. I doubted they would.

So, fuck it. Heart still pounding, stomach still roiling, I sent the call.

It rang twice before a voice I hadn't heard in ages came down the line, soft and maybe even a little startled.

"Jarek."

I swallowed. "Hey. Hi." Silence hung on for a few seconds, punctuated only by my thumping heart. "Do you have a few minutes?"

"I do."

I swallowed nervously. I wanted to take a moment to catch up. Ask him how he was. *Where* he was. What he was doing.

But Marc-Yves's tolerance for small talk wasn't much higher than his tolerance for hockey, and I didn't imagine I had much leeway before he'd end the call and be done with me.

Sitting up a little straighter as if that might help me somehow I said, "I, uh..." Fuck. Where to start? Fortunately, my mouth worked faster than my brain, and the words tumbled out: "I wanted to tell you I'm sorry."

Silence.

Sakra. We should've done this on FaceTime. Then I

could at least see the reactions that didn't make it through the phone.

"It was all a long time ago," he said softly.

"I know. And it's been eating at me all this time." I pinched the bridge of my nose and exhaled hard. "I just... I just wanted you to know I'm sorry. The way things ended—it shouldn't..."

Marc-Yves sighed heavily. "We were kids, Jarek. Maybe we would have worked out, maybe we wouldn't have. We'll never know."

"I know," I whispered. "And I'm not asking to go back."

"You're not?" He sounded surprised but also relieved.

"No. It's... We're over. I know we are. There's no going back." I cleared my throat. "I'm with someone now, and I—"

"So now that you've met someone, you'll apologize to me," he growled.

"No! No. It's nothing like that." Closing my eyes, I leaned forward, elbow on my knee as I rested my forehead in my free hand. "Being with him just... It made me look at things differently. The way I should have a long time ago."

"How so?" The hostility had ebbed, but his guard was still up.

I fought back tears even though there was no one around to see them. I didn't want him to hear them. In that moment, I was beyond tempted to just tell him the truth, same as I'd told Hunter. No matter what bitterness there was between us, I trusted Marc-Yves. He wasn't the vindictive type who'd throw a piece of gossip out into the public eye so he could watch my world burn. And knowing him, even if he would have been the kind to get back at me like that, he'd understand the implications this would have about other people. Marc-Yves didn't do collateral damage any more than I did.

And for that matter, he'd *been* collateral damage in this himself. I'd hurt him. Shoved him away. Turned his life on its head by ruining our relationship. He didn't need to carry this burden, too.

"It's hard to explain," I said. "When Toronto traded me —I didn't take it well. I know I didn't." I winced, hating myself for lying by omission, even though I wanted to protect him from the truth. "I just didn't understand until recently how much that had bled into everything in my life. How much I'd hurt you."

The only reason I knew he was still on the line was the almost inaudible sound of him breathing. For long seconds, he said nothing, and with every passing heartbeat, the truth threatened to explode out of me. This was probably my one and only chance to settle things with Marc-Yves, so why not just put it out there and tell him the whole truth? Tell him the real reason I'd been so wracked with guilt and shame that I'd made us both miserable until I'd driven him away?

The words had reached the very tip of my tongue when he finally spoke.

"I'm glad you finally understand." He sounded tired. "I worried about you. All this time. Even now, you seem fine in interviews, but sometimes... Sometimes I can tell."

I squeezed my eyes shut, letting a few hot tears slide free. "You watch those? The interviews?"

"Yes. Sometimes."

"You hate hockey."

"But I don't hate you." He exhaled. "Not even when I wanted to."

I covered my eyes with my free hand and tried like hell to pull myself together. Of all the things I'd hoped for when I'd reached out to him, it turned out what I'd needed the most was to hear those four words.

I don't hate you.

"Jarek?"

I didn't realize how long I'd been trying to compose myself until his voice gently prodded me. I cleared my throat a couple of times. "I'm here. I thought you did hate me."

"I might have for a while," he admitted, sounding absolutely drained. "I wanted to. But I know you. Knew you. Whatever was happening in your head, I..." He blew out a breath. "I couldn't reach you. I wish I'd known more then. How to get past... whatever was going on." He paused. "Maybe if we hadn't been so young, I'd have figured something out, but..."

"Maybe. But I wouldn't *let* you in."

The sigh on the other end sounded like one of profound relief. As if he'd needed to hear that as much as I'd needed to hear him say he didn't hate me. His voice was startlingly thick and raw as he said, "I could have done more."

I closed my eyes again. "We can't change it. But... I'm sorry."

"Me too," he whispered. "Even if we wouldn't have made it in the long run..."

The words kicked up a flurry of mixed emotions in my chest. Among them, relief—as if we'd both acknowledged that time and maturity might have spelled an eventual end for us anyway. Hockey players were notorious for marrying young, especially those who met their partners in juniors or in college, but those relationships didn't always make it in the long run. Anything could have happened. Neither of us had to make some catastrophic mistake or drive an icy wedge between us for our relationship to eventually end.

"I just... I wish we didn't go out like that." I swallowed

hard, and fresh tears made it into my voice: "I wish I didn't push you away."

There was silence again. It felt like ages but probably wasn't more than ten or fifteen seconds.

"It's in the past. But it's good to hear from you."

"Yeah." I rubbed my stiffening neck. "Thanks for, uh... For taking my call."

"I figured it must be important if you were reaching out after all this time."

"Still. Thanks."

"Thanks for reaching out. It's, uh... It's good to put the past to rest."

"It is." I swallowed. "If you're ever in Pittsburgh, let me know. We could get a drink."

"Maybe," he said. "If, um... I'm in Victoria now. Next time you play in Vancouver, if you have time..."

I was curious about that. What in the world had driven him to British Columbia after swearing up and down Quebec would be his home forever? Then again, he'd said he would come with me if hockey ever took me out of Canada, and he nearly had. So maybe there was someone else.

I hoped there was. I hoped Marc-Yves was happy out west.

Despite my curiosity, though, I said, "I'll let you know. It would be good to see you again."

"You too, Jarek."

We ended the call not long after that, and it felt both weird and right to end it without exchanging "Je t'aime" and "Miluju tě." If nothing else, it was an improvement over a tear-choked, "Go fuck yourself," followed by a slamming door.

In the silence of my hotel room, I lay back on the bed as I let the emotions roll over me. I couldn't remember the last time I'd felt this raw. The last time I couldn't stop the tears. It was bittersweet—a lot of relief, but also some fresh guilt and hurt over what had happened to Marc-Yves and me. What I'd done to us.

For a long time, I'd been angry at him for not fighting for us more than he had. After talking to him, though, most of that anger abated. Yeah, there was a part of me that still thought he'd jumped ship too soon, but it was hard to blame him now. I'd shut him out, and we'd also been so, so young. We'd been together since we were both barely sixteen. We were each other's firsts for everything—kiss, love, sex, heartache. Could I really hold it against him if he didn't know any more than I did how to fix what had gone wrong between us? Especially since he hadn't even known why it had all gone to shit?

We were kids. At least now we'd finally said things we hadn't known how to say back then. The bitterness wasn't so intense now, which let the hurt crack through. Let me truly and completely miss the boy I'd fallen in love with and the man I'd lost.

I supposed tears were inevitable.

I thumbed the edge of my phone, which was still warm from me gripping it while we'd talked. It was done. And even while I cried, I felt better. We probably wouldn't be friends going forward. Not close ones. A drink if we were in the same city. A text around the holidays or on a birthday. We'd have the type of relationship where we'd stop and say hello if we ran into each other somehow, but little more than that.

I decided that was enough. Marc-Yves had a life now, one I hoped was everything he needed and wanted. I had one, too. He might've had someone there with him who made him happy.

And maybe...

Just maybe...

I had someone like that, too.

I was too emotionally wrung out to figure all that out right now, and things were too new with Hunter anyway, but the thought gave me a spark of hope I hadn't had in a long, long time. I'd made peace with Marc-Yves, and I had someone now who saw the ugly side of me—who'd seen that side of me *first*, before I'd shown him any other—and he somehow still looked at me like I was the only man in the world.

Time would tell if there was something here besides sex and honesty.

In the meantime, I was exhausted, and I needed to grab a nap before tonight's game.

First things first, though, I texted Hunter.

Call went well. Going to sleep for a bit.

Before I'd even turned off the screen, he was typing, as if he'd been staring at his phone and waiting for me to respond.

A second later, *Glad to hear it. Me too. See you on the bus.*

He followed that with an image. On it was what looked like ten hockey players all dogpiling each other in front of and *in* the net, as if they'd all crashed the goal at once. Below it was a caption that read, *Upon review of the play, there is no goaltender interference.*

I snorted, and the laugh made me dizzy. After that heavy conversation with Marc-Yves, it felt amazing to laugh.

And realizing Hunter had probably been waiting with that meme, not just knowing I'd need it but giving a damn, did things to my heart that I was too wrung out to think too hard about.

I just responded with a laughing emoji.

Then I put my phone aside, my face still damp from tears and my lips still curved into a smile from Hunter's meme.

In minutes, I was sound asleep.

CHAPTER 28

HUNTER

I managed to get a little bit of sleep after Jarek texted, but I was still restless. I needed to see him and be sure everything was all right.

When it was time to head for the buses, he texted me to let me know he'd meet me in the lobby shortly; Dima needed help with something. Probably tying his tie—he was good at it, but he'd hurt his hand two nights ago in a collision with another player. Though he could still play just fine, a couple of fingers were just sore enough to make some two-handed tasks difficult.

So, I went downstairs to wait. Our teammates were milling around and meandering toward the bus, coffee cups and snacks in hand. I tried not to look fidgety. I talked to the guys. Browsed the shop for something to drink before settling on a bottle of water. Pretended to be interested in something on my phone.

Finally, Jarek strode into the lobby next to Dima, looking like an absolute god in that pinstriped charcoal suit. Especially with the matching waistcoat that may as well have been painted onto his perfect body.

Dima was saying something to him, gesticulating wildly, and Jarek was laughing, lighting up the entire lobby with that beautiful, relaxed smile.

God, what a relief. Even if he still had some feelings about that call with his ex, I knew more than a lot of people how terrible he was at hiding his emotions. If he could laugh that freely with Dima, then he was okay.

When he met my eyes, the smile got even brighter, but he quickly schooled it. We were, after all, surrounded by our teammates, including at least one who would give us no end of shit if he caught on. There was still a sparkle in Jarek's eyes, though. A promise of more later when we were alone.

Goddamn. That call must've gone well if he was in this good a mood.

Curiosity was killing me, and when I finally got him alone for a moment—he needed something from the shop—I asked, "So, it went okay?"

His smile fell a little, letting some fatigue show through, and he nodded. "Yeah. It was…" He exhaled, rolling his shoulders under that gorgeous jacket. "It was a lot. But I feel better now. About a lot of things."

"Good. That's great."

He nodded again, and the smile that came to life this time was too sweet for words. "You were right. About calling him. It… I should've done it years ago."

"Better late than never, right?"

"Definitely." He gestured around the shop. "Do you want anything?"

I held up my water bottle. "I'm good."

He got some Gatorade and a pack of M&Ms, and we headed out to join the rest of the guys. I decided I wouldn't ask what he and his ex said to each other. Not even when we were alone. If he wanted me to know, he'd tell me.

But it was plain to see how much weight that conversation had taken off his shoulders. He was quicker to laugh as we bantered with our teammates en route to the arena. He was chattier with staff and reporters in the locker room. During warmups, he was skating more easily than I'd seen him before.

And when the game started, Jarek was on *fire*. Focused. Moving fast and loose. Any time he got the puck on his stick in the defensive zone, he was barreling toward the other end of the ice at full tilt, the rest of us on his heels.

That wasn't to say he scored half a dozen goals and singlehandedly won us the game. We still had to work for it, and for all Chicago's offense left a lot to be desired, they were fucking incredible defensively. Their goalie was already in the conversation for the year-end award, and he deserved it.

We played our hearts out, but so did they, and in the end, the game was theirs. Two-one in regulation. Disappointing, but no one was disappointed in how we played. Their goalie stood on his head and deserved that win. Dolls had stood on his, too, but we couldn't win them all.

Still, Jarek's mood on the way out was as light as if we'd pulled off an easy win. He laughed and joked with our teammates. Answered reporters' questions without so much as a scowl.

Man. I'd known before today that his ex was weighing heavily on him, and I'd had some idea how heavily, but nothing drove it home like seeing him without that weight for the first time.

As we headed out to the bus, I thought that on some level, I should feel weird about seeing him like this after talking to his ex. Like jealousy should be flaring in my chest at the sight of my... boyfriend, I guess? We hadn't really landed on a name for what we were doing. But either way, the sight of him being in such a good mood after talking to his ex seemed like it should've made me jealous.

It didn't, though, and I felt stupid for even thinking about it. Jarek didn't have that look on his face like someone would get when they were flirting with someone. No hearts in his eyes or swirling around his head. If anything, he looked like he was basking in the relief of cutting away an anchor he'd been dragging around for too long. Same as after we'd talked about the season he'd thrown. He wasn't in a good mood like someone who'd just spent the afternoon flirting—he was just visibly relieved to the core.

Christ, he must've been miserable all this time. It must've been absolute hell, silently blaming himself, convinced he'd committed some unforgivable sin he couldn't confess to anyone. Not even the man he loved. The man he'd lost, and he'd blamed himself for that, too.

The more I thought about that, the more I thought that maybe that place where I'd thought jealousy wanted to swell wasn't home to jealousy after all. Maybe...

Maybe it was guilt.

Because ever since the night Jarek confessed his past, even as we'd gotten closer to each other, I hadn't been able to shake off this guilt. Tonight, watching him enjoy the relief of closure, I didn't know how to process knowing Jarek had lost someone he loved because of me. It didn't matter if it was directly or indirectly, or if I'd even known what was happening at the time. It sucked, and the guilt was sharp and acidic.

"Hey." Sitting beside me on the bus, Jarek bumped his

dress shoe against mine. "Where are you?" He tapped his temple.

I shook my head. "Just... You know. Replaying the game. Hard not to after a loss, right?" A little white lie, but I didn't want to ruin his good mood.

Jarek smiled, giving my foot another nudge. "Eh, it's not so bad. We need the losses as much as the wins."

An interesting take. "How do you figure?"

"Too many wins in a row..." He half-shrugged. "They can make us lazy. Like winning is a given. Or the other way around—they can make us get up in our own heads and freak out that we need to keep the streak going. A few losses keep us grounded."

I blinked. Someone was feeling optimistic tonight. "I hadn't thought of it that way."

Jarek chuckled. "Spend enough time around Dima, and he'll make you see things that way."

"Now that makes sense."

"What?" Jarek eyed me. "You don't think I can be optimistic and philosophical?"

"No, I think you can. I just know you well enough to be surprised when you are."

His bark of laughter made my whole body warm, and he elbowed me. "Pako."

I narrowed my eyes. "Should I be offended by that?"

He shot me the least convincing innocent look I'd ever seen, accompanied by an absolutely bullshit *"who, me?"* shrug.

I snorted and gave him a shove. "Fuck you."

His wink gave me goose bumps. So did the *"Later"* he mouthed at me.

Christ, I was a wreck for this man.

As the bus pulled away from the arena, Jarek's phone

pinged, and he took it out of his pocket. I didn't read over his shoulder, but the smile on his face was a serene one. Then he laughed, and he showed me the screen.

On it was a photo of a girl who must've been nine or ten. She was wearing a Vancouver T-shirt, I thought, and she had an incredibly skeptical look on her face.

Below it, the message read, *My stepdaughter's face when I told her I dated Jaromir Badura. She doesn't believe me.*

"Is that..." I looked at Jarek. "Is that from your ex?"

He laughed, that relief still coming off him in waves. "Yeah. I guess he's got stepkids now."

"Wow." I gestured at the screen. "You going to prove him right?"

Jarek grinned wickedly. "Should I? I kinda want to write back, *new phone, who's this?*"

I laughed. "You're such an ass."

He shrugged without an ounce of repentance. Then, "Can I borrow your phone's notepad?"

"Sure. Yeah." I took it out, unlocked it, and handed it to him with the notepad app open.

On it, Jarek wrote out, *He's not lying!*

Then he held up my phone, used his to take a selfie, and gave mine back to me.

When his phone pinged again a moment later, he took one look at the screen and burst out laughing. He showed it to me, and it was the same little girl, but her eyes were huge and her jaw was slack. Below the picture, *I think she believes me now, LOL.*

"Wow," I said. "That, um... That conversation must've gone really well. If he's..." I nodded toward his phone.

Jarek seemed to think about that for a moment. Then, slowly, he released a breath and nodded. "Yeah, I guess it did." He wiped a hand over his face and sighed. "Maybe I can finally put this all behind me." He turned to me. "Thank you. For suggesting I talk to him. I don't think I'd have..." He trailed off, shaking his head.

It took all the restraint I possessed not to wrap my arms around him right here on the bus, surrounded by our teammates. Instead, I just whispered, "I'm glad it helped."

"It did." He turned to me again, and...

Oh. Hell. He hadn't had that flirty, lovey-dovey look in his eyes when he'd been enjoying the post-call relief, but the way he was looking at me right now?

Holy fuck. Was that the look of a man who wanted to celebrate knocking the weight of the world off his shoulders? Because if it was... oh God.

Using the relative darkness on the bus to my advantage, I slid my hand over his thigh. "Any chance you want some company tonight?"

Jarek licked his lips. "Is that company interested in skipping the bar?" Oh fuck. The hunger burning in his eyes promised one hell of an evening behind closed doors.

"That company couldn't care less about going to the bar."

His grin made my spine tingle.

And when we made it to the hotel, he absolutely made good on that promise in his eyes.

"All right, Yars." Dolls pointed at me with a golf club. "Something's different about you lately. What's going on?"

I put up my hands. "What? There's nothing going on."

"No, no." Ferns peered at me. "That's a lie. You *do* have a boyfriend, don't you?"

"No! I don't!"

Dima, who'd been teeing up, twisted around to give me an incredulous look. "Do we look stupid to you?"

I smirked. "Is that a rhetorical question?"

Dolls poked me with his club. "Don't change the subject. Something is up."

"Yeah, don't bullshit us, Yars." Ferns shot me a pointed look. "We know you, and this"—he flailed a hand at me—"is not you."

"What?" I said. "You guys don't want me to be happy?"

"Of course we do." Dima cuffed me upside the head, knocking my hat off. "But you are never *this* happy. It's not normal and it's freaking me out. So what's going on?"

I glared at him as I fixed my hat. "Fuck off."

He returned my glare, but then he shook his head and

returned to teeing up. "He's not going to tell us." He paused to take his swing, and as his ball sailed down the green, he added, "We're just going to have to beat it out of him."

"Sounds good to me," Dolls said.

"Yep." Ferns nodded sagely. "Blood's good for the grass, so..."

I laughed. "You're all idiots."

They chuckled, but they stopped pushing. For now, anyway. I'd known them all—especially Dima—way too long to think this was anywhere close to over. But at least for a minute or two, the focus went back to golf. They'd wait until I let my guard down, so I promised myself I wouldn't.

I should've known that wouldn't last long.

Halfway to the third hole, my phone vibrated in my back pocket. I was itching to read the message, since I was pretty sure I knew where it came from, but I waited until the guys were distracted.

My opportunity came before too long, while Dima and Dolls were chirping at Ferns for his shit technique. Perfect.

I slipped the phone out of my pocket and checked the message.

This new PT is mean.

I suppressed a laugh and quickly wrote back, *Isn't PT supposed to hurt? That's how you know it's working.*

You're supposed to be sympathetic and tell me how mean she is.

I could refer you to my PT.

Is he better?

No. Way, way meaner. But after a session with him, you'll appreciate this one.

He responded with a middle finger emoji, followed by, *You suck.*

I started to respond but realized the chirping and Swedish cursing had stopped.

I looked up to find three sets of suspicious eyes watching me. Pocketing my phone, I said, "What?"

"There's no phones on the golf course." Ferns sounded affronted but curious.

Dolls pointed with the club again. "Who are you talking to?"

"Was just Coach," I said. "Shouldn't—"

"Bullshit." Dima cocked a brow. "You don't chat with Coach with that"—he gestured at his mouth—"on your stupid face."

That was when I realized I was still grinning.

Kurva.

"Would you just tell us about your new boyfriend already?" Dolls huffed. "What's with all the secrecy?"

I almost winced. Secrecy. Yeah. I wasn't a fan of that. But it was temporary and necessary. Hunter and I would come out to the team sooner or later. Just... not yet. This wasn't a deep, dark, dirty secret. It was nothing shameful. We just weren't ready to have anyone else in on our business.

Somehow I kept my poker face firm. "I don't have a boyfriend!"

"Bullshit, you don't." Ferns tucked his club under his arm and started ticking off points on his fingers. "You're almost never around. You barely have time to golf. You—"

"You do know I'm helping my sister renovate her house, yes?" I shrugged. "She's trying to get it done before—"

"Bull. Shit." Dima shook his head sharply. "Because renovating your sister's house doesn't make you..." He gestured at his face. "Smile like fool."

"You never know," I said. "Those polyurethane fumes can get you pretty fucking high."

Dolls groaned and rolled his eyes. "You're no fun, Yars. How are we supposed to tease you about your new boyfriend if we don't know anything about him?"

"And therein lies the challenge, doesn't it?" I tapped his shoe with my club as I walked past him to tee up my own shot. "You have to figure it out."

"So there *is* a boyfriend!" Ferns exclaimed. "You just admitted it!"

"No, I didn't." I flashed a toothy grin. "You're just seeing what you want to see."

That prompted some Swedish cursing, and I laughed.

I wished I *could* tell them. For the first time since juniors, I had a close knit group of friends on a hockey team. And for the first time in half a decade, I had a man I wanted to talk about like a lovesick teenager. I *wanted* to hear the good-natured teasing about the man I was seeing, just like the whole team had given Cole when he'd met his now-fiancée two seasons ago.

We had our reasons for keeping this quiet, and none of them had to do with shame or fear of homophobic backlash.

I just hoped we eventually did come out as a couple.

And I couldn't wait to hear Dolls, Ferns, and Dima give me shit for it.

Ferns and Dolls went into the clubhouse to get us a table for lunch, and Dima and I took the golf carts back.

It had been a good game. The weather was chilly but dry and not too windy, and we'd all played pretty well. Okay, not Ferns, but he never played well. That was quite literally par for the course. There'd been chirping and shit-talking all the way through all eighteen holes, and it had been a much-needed break from the frenetic pace of travel and hockey.

On the way into the clubhouse, Dima stopped me with a hand on my shoulder. "Hey. You got a minute?"

I eyed him. "For...?"

He studied me, and I knew what was coming. After eighteen holes worth of snark, it didn't take a psychic to know what he was going to ask about.

"Listen, jokes are fun," he said, "but... really—what's going on with you?"

The truth wanted to jump out of me so bad it was painful. Both because I didn't like lying to my best friend, and because I wanted to tell someone—*anyone*—about this amazing thing I had with Hunter.

I could tell him *some* truth, though. Because there was more going on than just my relationship with Hunter.

"I, um..." I shrugged. "I talked to my ex."

My friend stilled, and his sunglasses didn't hide the way his eyes widened. "You... talked to Marc-Yves?"

It felt good not to flinch at that name, and I managed a smile as I nodded. "Yeah. Put a few things to bed." I blew out a breath. "Should've done it years ago."

"So you settled things? Are you guys friends now, or...?"

"I don't know about that." I chanced a small chuckle. "He sent me a picture of his stepdaughter's reaction after she found out he used to date me, so that's probably a good sign. Right?"

Surprise registered across his face, followed quickly by profound relief. "That's great! I'm glad to hear it. You two were such... I always hoped you could be friends, you know?"

"Yeah. Me too. Guess we'll see how things play out."

"Guess so." He paused then nudged my foot with his. "That's still not whole story. I know you."

I chuckled and offered up another shrug. "Well, then you know me well enough to know you're not getting the whole story out of me, don't you?"

He pursed his lips, and from the crinkles on either side of his sunglasses, he was narrowing his eyes at me.

"Come on." I clapped his shoulder. "Let's go eat lunch."

"This isn't over," he informed me.

"Yeah, we'll see about that."

CHAPTER 30

HUNTER

Keeping our relationship a secret was fine, but it didn't take long for us both to get restless behind closed doors.

Sure, there was a ton we could do at our respective places. Each other, obviously. We also cooked together. Worked out together. Watched movies or hockey games together.

But the walls were starting to close in. We were itching to go out, and not just as a couple of teammates grabbing dinner, which didn't make anyone bat an eye. We wanted to go out as a couple. If we were dating, then we wanted to... like... *date*.

Our options were limited if we wanted to keep doing this on the downlow, so we went back to Lanterns, the club where we'd first connected. It was a safe, discreet place. Somewhere we could find our footing as a couple out in public without being outed to the world.

It was nice and crowded tonight, too. More people to potentially recognize us, sure, but also more faces to obscure us. We could disappear into a dense crowd much more easily than we could a handful of scattered people.

There were also two bachelorette parties occupying some of the larger booths. Great. I hoped they were as well-behaved as many of them were. I was admittedly a little pessimistic about those groups, simply because I'd encountered a few too many who seemed to forget whose house they were in.

As Jarek and I made our way to the crowded dancefloor, I sent up a silent prayer that the two parties here this evening were good houseguests.

A few beats later, though, I'd all but forgotten they were even here.

There was always something intensely sexy about dancing with someone I'd slept with. Something about having intimate knowledge of everything hidden beneath a man's clothes. Or maybe we just danced closer and touched with more confidence. Whatever the case, I loved the way Jarek's body felt against mine. How we moved and it reminded me of the way we moved in bed. How his hands were sure and hungry—navigating every contour of my body with familiarity and an unmistakable desire for more.

I'd often wished I could do like other guys on these dancefloors and get carried away. Make out. Slide a daring hand over a groin. Get each other hot enough to be tempted by the backseat of a car, the alley behind a club, or even the men's room. I wanted to do all those things I didn't dare get *caught* doing.

And with Jarek...

Fuck. It was probably just as well we didn't make out when we danced. A teasing kiss on the neck now and then, especially when my back was pressed to his chest, but nothing more risqué than that.

Because Jarek wasn't just some guy I'd hooked up with before. He was my boyfriend. He was the man who was worth all the stress and secrecy of this relationship. He was the man who was looking at me like he simultaneously wanted to bend me over the nearest table and rail me until I couldn't skate tomorrow, and like he just wanted to gaze at me all night to be sure I was real. There was both heat and warmth. Sex and so, so much more.

Yeah, if he kissed me now, I'd one hundred percent forget where I was and all the reasons why we didn't want to get outed like that. I mean, we didn't want to get outed at all, but least of all with something sordid like a video of us practically fucking on a dancefloor. Could a camera pick up the way he was looking at me right now? Because holy shit, if a photo leaked of Jarek's smoldering eyes locked on mine, with that lip bite and all that romantic *and* pornographic desire written all over his face, we'd be having a very awkward conversation with the team's front office.

The thought sobered me a little, and though I kept my hands on Jarek's hips, I opened up a sliver more space between us. Not trying to get away from him—just some breathing room.

He laughed, though the sound was swallowed by the music, and I shrugged apologetically. What could we do? He rolled his eyes. So did I. Yeah, such was the fun reality of being public figures who weren't out as a couple. We'd get there.

For tonight, we could just dance and be thankful this club was vigilant about people with cameras.

They *were* vigilant, too, because like two songs later, the music suddenly stopped and the deejay barked, "Hey! No cameras!"

A spotlight landed on the patron in question, and a second later, he was being escorted out by a bouncer who probably could've taken on our top defensive pair with a giant arm tied behind his back. People applauded as the guy with the camera did the walk of shame, drowning out his protests and his insistence that he would never come back to this place again. Don't threaten us with a good time, buddy.

Then the spotlight was gone, the music kicked back on, and the camera was forgotten. Jarek had me close to him again, though still with a little daylight between us so we didn't do something the tabloids would enjoy.

We kept dancing, moving together and sharing wicked grins. Though neither of us was in any hurry to get out of here, we both knew where this night would end. Part of me wanted to haul him someplace private and go to town on him.

Part of me, though?

Hell, this was exhilarating. We were out in public. Not fully "out," but we were dipping our toes into what it was like to be a couple somewhere other than condos and hotel rooms. It was like how some of my teammates along the way had described that first time getting called up from the minors—even if you knew it would be a while before you were there for good, that taste of the real thing was spectacular. It made the hunger for the real thing—for the permanent place in the spotlight—almost unbearably intense.

I couldn't wait to be out publicly. For real. Openly, unashamedly, out to the world as Jaromir Badura's boyfriend. We weren't ready for that yet, and that was okay. The only thing I wanted more than coming out was for us to let this thing progress on its own time. I was terrified to rush it. To do anything that might spook him or me or just throw off this perfect chemistry.

We'll get there, I wanted to say. *But right now? This is perfect.*

The song changed, and a few bars into it, the crowd

suddenly seemed to get denser. A shoulder hit my back. Then someone bumped into Jarek. When I glanced around, it made sense.

So much for being good houseguests.

The song was apparently a favorite of one of the two brides, and she and her entourage had surged onto the dancefloor, drinks in hand, laughing drunkenly as they windmill-danced and almost took out a few bystanders' eyes with their nails.

Jarek scowled.

I rolled my eyes and nodded past him toward some unoccupied tables. "Might as well take a breather."

He shot the interlopers a glare, then muttered something I didn't catch and headed off the dancefloor. We made our way through the crowd, which had also become denser —most of the guys on the floor had moved aside and were watching with a mix of annoyance, amusement, incredulity, and impatience. They were probably hoping this would only last a song or two, which in my experience... well, one could hope.

Others had the same idea we did and were retreating from the dancefloor in search of tables. By a stroke of luck, we managed to snag the last empty table near the far side of the room, where the music wasn't quite so loud. That worked for me—maybe we could even have an actual conversation over here.

I took a seat, but Jarek hesitated. Nodding toward the bar, he asked, "Should I get us some drinks?"

"You don't mind?"

He shook his head, gracing me with one of those smiles that made my knees go weak. Jesus, when had I turned into a complete romantic sap? About the time I'd started to like Jaromir Badura, I guess.

"I'm driving," he said. "What are you drinking?"

I considered it. "How about a beer? I'm not picky."

He flashed me another smile, and for a split second, I thought he might steal a kiss right here in the club. Instead, he brushed his hand over mine, then disappeared into the crowd.

I sat back and exhaled. I loved this. It was something I'd never been able to do. Too many cameras knew my face. Coming out fully sounded better and better, because how could I *not* want people to know I was with this beautiful man?

Well, we'd get there. Maybe? This felt less and less like some casual, temporary thing. The chemistry we had on the ice was spectacular, and it had nothing on this connection we had away from hockey.

That was real, right? I wasn't imagining it? Because it sure felt real.

Jarek returned a few minutes later with our drinks, and the smile he flashed me made me think, yeah, this *was* real. Or was it just because he'd done such a one-eighty from when I'd first come to Pittsburgh? That was bound to make anything good between us seem amazing.

Except... no. I didn't think that was what this was. Most of the time, I forgot he'd ever been snarly with me in the first place. The adversarial dynamic was a distant memory when we were like this.

Jarek tilted his head, studying me over the small table. "What?"

"Nothing. Nothing." I picked up my drink. "Just, uh..." Right. Because I could think when I was this close to him. Especially about something *other* than how much I was thinking *about* him.

So. Hell. Why not just own up to it?

Beneath the table, I slid my hand over his thigh as I gazed into those beautiful gray eyes. "You know, I gotta admit—I didn't think this would be so... easy."

Jarek furrowed his brow. "What do you mean?"

"I mean... This. Us." I ran my thumb along the seam of his pants. "It's easy."

He studied me for a moment, and I thought he might still be confused. If something was lost in the translation—he was fluent in English, but it was still his second language—or if he just didn't quite follow. But then he smiled, and he reached for my face, and oh, fuck... He kissed me. Right there in the club.

His kiss was soft. Gentle. Nothing inappropriate in public, even if we hadn't been in a place where guys did a hell of a lot more than share a long, chaste kiss.

But my God, with the way my pulse surged, he may as well have been pinning me to a wall or a bed and devouring my mouth. Except... no. That wasn't what this was. A rush, yeah. A high, definitely. But for all we would absolutely be making each other scream later, this was nothing like when we were tearing up the sheets together.

He drew back enough to meet my gaze, and I swore the fingers he trailed along my beard were trembling. "It *is* easy. It's..." He dropped his gaze and laughed, the sound swallowed by the noise and music around us, though the lights couldn't quite hide the extra color in his cheeks.

I ducked my head to try to catch his gaze. "What?"

Jarek chewed his lip. When he took his hand off my face, I was afraid I'd done something wrong and he was pulling away, but he laced our fingers together instead. He brought our hands up and kissed my knuckles, and his voice just carried over the noise. "I still can't believe I was such a dick to you."

I shook my head. "Don't. I know why you were, and I know it had nothing to do with me."

"But I still—"

I cut him off with a soft kiss. "Maybe it was a good thing."

Jarek's brow furrowed, and he watched me, searching my eyes with an expression that pleaded with me to elaborate.

Gripping his hand tight, I slid a little closer to him. "If I'd never confronted you, would you have ever told me about the past?"

He shook his head without hesitation.

"Right. And if you hadn't gotten that off your chest, we wouldn't have..." I gestured at the two of us.

He glanced back and forth between us, then stared at our hands.

"When you think about it," I said, "a lot of really shitty things happened to get us here. If we'd ended up in Toronto together, who knows? I was nineteen and thought I was hot shit. You were dealing with... well. Everything that happened your last season in Toronto. Do you think we'd have even coexisted as teammates, never mind ended up..." I nodded toward our joined hands.

Jarek stared at our hands for a moment before he released a breath and slowly started to relax. "I guess? I just wish we could've gotten here without all the..." He waved his other hand.

I chuckled. "Me, too. I think—" I bit back a comment that the end justified the means; that wasn't for me to decide when he was the one who'd sacrificed so much and had even more taken away from him. Instead, I went with, "The past is what it is. But I like where we are now."

Jarek smiled, and he leaned in. I met him halfway, and we were again lost in one of those perfect, gentle kisses.

As he drew back, he grinned. "I like where we are now, too." Then he peered at his glass. "Except for the part where my drink is gone." He sighed theatrically, which made me laugh and roll my eyes.

"Do you want me to go get you another drink, baby?"

"I can get it." He started to get up, but I stopped him.

"You got the last round." I nudged him back into his chair and silenced his protests with a kiss. "More of the same?"

He narrowed his eyes as if he were thinking of arguing, but chuckled and nodded at his glass. "Just make it a double this time, yeah?"

I snorted. "A double ice water. Got it."

He just chuckled.

"All right—I'll be right back." I slid my hand over his arm, and we exchanged one more glance. When I turned to go, his smile carried me all the way through the crowd to the bar. I didn't mind shouldering my way through throngs of people, and I didn't even care anymore than we'd been elbowed off the dancefloor earlier—as fun as it was to dance with him, I wasn't going to say no to the quieter moments.

While I waited for our drinks, someone appeared beside me at the bar, wedging into the narrow space between me and another person. I stepped away, thinking this was someone who needed to order a drink, but she looked right in my eyes, smiling a smile I recognized all too well.

"I'm sorry to bug you," she shout-talked over the music. "But are you Hunter Michaud?"

I returned the smile as enthusiastically as I could fake it. "Uh, yeah. I am. You must be a hockey fan?"

"Uh-huh." She was *beaming* now, and I realized she was

clutching her phone to her chest between both hands. "My friends and I were so excited with you signed with Pittsburgh!"

"Me too!" I didn't have to fake that, though I did try to telepathically urge the bartender to hurry up. This wasn't a place I came to be recognized or draw attention to myself.

Thank God, the bartender appeared right then, plunking down an ice water for Jarek and a beer for me. I tipped him an extra twenty just for unknowingly rescuing me from this situation.

As I collected the drinks, I said to the fan, "Well, it was great meeting you. Go Hornets!"

She giggled. Then she gestured with her phone. "Would you mind doing a selfie?"

I froze. Full-on deer-in-headlights paralyzed.

Only for a second, though, thank God. As gently and apologetically as possible, I said, "Any other time or place, I'd say yes, but here..." I grimaced as I gestured around us with one of the drinks.

Her face fell and her shoulders sank. "Oh. Yeah, I suppose some people don't want..." She held my gaze as if she were hoping I'd change my mind. When I didn't, she brightened again, though the smile was obviously forced this time. "Well, it was nice meeting you."

"You, too." I gave her another smile, then slipped into the crowd, my stomach a mix of relief and guilt. I always tried to be friendly with fans, but there were times when I needed to say no. In a club with a strict no-camera policy? When I was here with my secret boyfriend *because* of that no-camera policy? Yeah, that was exactly the time to say no.

As I approached the table, Jarek peered up at me. "What's wrong?"

"Nothing." I put his glass down in front of him. "Just

couldn't remember if I actually got you the double ice water."

He rolled his eyes, muttering something in Czech, but he was smiling.

I laughed, relieved to be back at our private little table with him. As I slid onto my seat, though, he eyed me.

"Are you sure you're all right? Something's..." He gestured at his face as he furrowed his brow at me.

Why did I still try to get anything past him?

Sighing, I trailed a fingertip up and down the side of my glass. "I ran into a fan at the bar."

He tensed so slightly I wondered if I'd imagined it. "Oh. Here? Really?"

"Hey, hockey fans come to..." I motioned around us.

"Yes, they do, but they're usually more, uh, discreet? In places like..." He mirrored my gesture.

"Hmm, yeah. True." I sipped my drink. "I think she was with one of the bachelorette parties."

The tension wasn't so slight this time, and he swept an uneasy look around the club. "Those groups always make me nervous."

"I know. I think they mean well, but a lot of them don't really get..." I trailed off. I probably didn't need to elaborate to him. Most of the straight women I met at gay clubs were great, clearly enjoying a place where they didn't have to worry about predators. There just those obnoxious few who forgot that this was *our* safe place *first*, and they could at best annoy us, at worst, take away from the safety we all came here to find.

But aside from taking over the dancefloor and politely approaching me for a selfie, the ladies here tonight didn't seem to be out of line. Drunk and loud, sure, but that described half the people in this building, and it wasn't even ten o'clock yet.

And now that I thought about it, the group that had descended on the dancefloor was no longer there. They might've been taking a breather, or doing shots, or moving on to another club, but there was space on the floor now. Jarek and I could finish our drinks and rejoin the crowd.

But... we didn't.

By halfway through the song that was playing when I sat down, we were lost in talking about tomorrow night's game. Sometime after that, we were laughing over his antics with Dima, Ferns, and Dolls on the golf course. When I pushed my long since empty glass out of the way so I'd quit checking to see if there was anything left, Jarek was listening intently to a story about Gonzo, Potts, and me engaging in our own shenanigans on the green the one time they dragged me out to play golf.

"He didn't actually try to hit it out of the water hazard, did he?" Jarek was chuckling as he spoke. "That's against the rules! And didn't he bend his club?"

"No," I said. "He bent *Gonzo's* club, because Gonzo didn't see him steal one for the express purpose of trying to hit the ball out of almost half a meter of water."

Jarek almost choked on a laugh. "I'd have killed him. With the bent club."

"Gonzo almost did." I reached for my glass, having again forgotten it was empty, then set it down again. "I mean, Potts replaced it and all. He was just trolling him. And he was also pissed because Gonzo said he was going to hit it *into* the water, so as far as he was concerned, Gonzo deserved to help him hit it *out* of the water."

Jarek shook his head as he laughed. "That sounds like something Dima would've done." He paused. "No. Dolls.

Dolls would've done it, absolutely."

"Of course he would've. He's a goalie."

"Mmhmm." Jarek picked up his glass, apparently realized his was also empty, and set it back down. "But sometimes I think he's crazy even for a goalie."

I whistled. "Okay, I'm not a fan of the game, but I *definitely* need to golf with you guys one of these days."

Jarek's eyebrows flew up, and I realized what I'd said.

Heat rushing into my face, I cleared my throat. "Down the line, I mean. When we're... You know..."

"We're all teammates." He shrugged, offering up a sweet, almost shy smile. "Nothing says we can't golf with our other teammates."

"You... Really? You want me to come golfing with you guys?"

"Why not?" The smile gained some confidence. "You can chirp like the best of them, so you'd fit in just fine."

"Hmm, I may have to take you up on that." I again reached for my drink, and then rolled my eyes. "For fuck's sake. I should go get us some refills."

"No, no. Stay." He got up, sliding his hand over my arm. "I'll get one." Tilting his head toward my empty glass, he asked, "More of the same?"

I considered it but shook my head. "Nah. Just water or Coke or something." I grinned up at him. "I don't want to be trashed when we get out of these clothes."

He wasn't even moving, and I swear to God he stumbled. Then he cleared his throat and nodded toward the bar. "Two Cokes. Be right back."

We exchanged grins, and he disappeared into the crowd.

I sat back in the chair and smiled to myself.

Tonight was just... perfect. Everything about it. The

two of us. The long, ridiculous conversation about whatever. The lingering looks. I didn't care anymore that we'd been crowded off the dancefloor if this was where we'd ended up.

I searched the crowd and found him at the bar. Though I'd been right earlier that it was easy to disappear into a sea of faces, I could've found Jarek in the crowd of a sold-out hockey game in two seconds flat. I just knew where he was. I felt it. And as soon as I found him, my heart sped up. Every single time.

What in the world are you doing to me?

And how do I tell you I never want you to stop?

It was still way, way too soon to know where this was headed. Way too new for words like "love" to come into the equation. For all I knew, this was just the high that came with incredible chemistry, and time would prove that we weren't good for each other.

I was happy either way. My entire life had been about the future. Other people's futures as much as my own. From my youth teams on up through my time in Toronto, I had been something to invest in for someone else's future glory and immortal sports dynasties. My prep school used my name to entice the next generation of hockey players to attend. My major junior team had my number hanging in the rafters and my face all over every piece of promo literature in existence. Even my U10 team boasted about being the place where Hunter Michaud was either made or discovered, depending on who you asked.

This thing Jarek and I were doing—this wasn't about glory or fame or investing in anything. It was about now. About us.

We'd deal with the future when we got there.

The heat between us in the club didn't abate when we got home. Not when Jarek had me up against his condo door. Not when we stopped halfway down the hall to peel off shirts and make out before stumbling onward. Not when we landed naked on his bed, his perfect body hot and heavy over mine as he stole my breath and drove me higher.

Hands all over each other. Hips moving together. Lips brushing lips and skating across skin. Had sex before Jarek been good? I was pretty sure I'd enjoyed it before him. All I knew was that sex *with* him was electrifying. Nothing turned me on more than finding just the right touch to make his breath catch or his back arch. The breathy curses, the purred promises—it was all too hot for words.

And tonight...

Tonight felt different somehow. As if being outside these walls as a couple had made us both a little bolder, a little braver; we were a step closer to being out, and the thrill of it had us both trembling with need. I didn't even care if we fucked—sometimes we did, sometimes we didn't —as long as Jarek kept holding me this close and his hot breath kept gusting across my skin or between our lips.

We did fuck, though. At some point, we separated long enough for him to get a condom and lube, and then I was on my stomach and Jarek was moving inside me, chest to my back and lips against my neck as he rocked in and out.

"If I could've gotten away with it," he murmured breathlessly in my ear, "I'd have done this at the club."

I bit my lip. "God, Jarek..."

He moaned, burying his face in my neck as a full body shudder pushed him all the way into me. "I know we can't... in public... but..." He brushed his lips over my shoulder. "I have fantasized so many times... about finding a dark corner..." He shuddered hard. *"Fuuuck."*

I closed my eyes, arching against him as the pleasure almost overtook me. Jarek fantasizing about us in the first place... The thought of us finding that dark corner... How much it turned him on... All on top of the delicious sensation of his dick sliding in and out of me... I could barely fucking stand it, and I didn't want him to stop.

"We'd have to find a louder club," I slurred, clawing at the sheets as I rolled my hips and tried to both keep myself in control and drive him out of his mind. "Or else we'd get caught for sure."

His lips curved against my shoulder. "Yeah?" He thrust a little harder. "Why's that?"

My vision blurred and my mind did the same, but I managed, "Because everyone in the building would hear me come."

He growled deep in his throat as he kissed up the side of my neck toward my ear. "Let 'em hear you." We both gasped as he picked up some more speed. His voice was a breathy whisper as he said, "Let everyone hear how much you love this."

"Oh my God," I moaned, and I was gripping handfuls of sheets now, dizzy from his words and from everything he did to me. Every thrust pushed my dick against the sheets, and the friction was mind-blowing, especially alongside his slick, powerful strokes. "Jarek... Oh, fuck..."

"That's it," he purred. "Come for me. Take..." His rhythm faltered, and as he recovered, he ground out, "Take me there with you."

That was all I needed. The plea, the realization he was on the edge too—I fell apart, crying out so loud the people back at Lanterns might've heard me after all. He fucked me for all he was worth as I came, and then he was shuddering too, holding me tight in his strong arms as his hips bucked and he tried to get as deep as humanly possible.

Then we both relaxed, trembling and panting as we came down from our orgasms. Jarek still held on, though, and the soft kiss he pressed to my shoulder almost shook me apart. I loved the tenderness from him. Those little touches were right up there with the secretive smiles we'd shared when no one was looking.

Perfect. Just perfect.

"It's a good thing we left the club when we did," he murmured.

I turned my head slightly. "Yeah? Why's that?"

He chuckled, sounding a little drunk, and kissed my shoulder again. "Because after that, we'd probably both be going to jail."

Laughing, I buried my face against the pillow. Still holding me, still inside me, Jarek shook with laughter too.

"It'd be worth it," I said. "For an orgasm like that."

This time his chuckle sounded smug. He paused to pull out, making us both gasp, and then he added, "I think Rachel would have our heads."

I grimaced. Yeah. Probably. She had her work cut out for her, running the team's PR. "I mean, it can't be the worst thing she's had to deal with, right?"

Jarek sat up. "What would be a bigger headache than, 'hey, what do you have to say about two Hornets being caught fucking in public?'"

I sat up too, moving a little slower than he was, because goddamn, he'd fucked me good. "Eh, I could think of a few things."

He pursed his lips, then shrugged. "Yeah. Me too." He leaned in closer and kissed me softly. "She'd still hate us."

"Mmhmm." I ran my fingers through his hair. "So, how about we keep the sex behind closed doors and not make her job any harder, eh?"

Jarek's laugh made me warm all over.

We managed to stumble into the bathroom and share a shower—with a lot of kissing and touching, of course—before we landed in his bed.

Jarek was a little distant as he rested his head on my chest, though.

"Hey." I smoothed his damp hair. "What's up?"

He pushed himself up so he could meet my gaze. "I was just thinking about everything with Rachel. With us coming out. All of that." He chewed his lip. "I meant what I said—I really do want us to... eventually. Be out, I mean. Just, um..."

"Not yet?"

He nodded. "I don't want to keep you a big secret. I'm just..."

"You're not ready for us to go public." I caressed his cheek. "I get it. I'm on the same page, trust me."

"Yeah?"

I nodded. "Just going out to Lanterns felt ballsy as hell, even though I know they're really protective of people's privacy. It's a risk, you know?"

"It is. And I don't mind doing that much." He paused, and a sly grin came to life. "Minus finding a place in the club to fuck. It's fun to imagine, but..." He shook his head.

I chuckled. "I get it. Trust me. But if you want to tell me all your pervy fantasies while you're riding my ass, by all means, be my guest."

Jarek's laugh was so beautiful. God, this man...

"Okay," he said. "But it's just that—fantasies." He sobered. "Coming out—we'll get there." He slid his hand into mine and held my gaze. "Once we're out, the whole world will know. And people will have opinions."

Nodding, I said, "Once the cat is out of the bag..."

"Exactly." He squeezed my hand. "I want this to be ours for a little while. Because once people know, it won't be just ours anymore."

The thought made my chest hurt. I hated that part of this life—that we were considered public property to some extent. Privacy was hard to come by, and a lot of people in this realm learned quickly to hold on to whatever privacy they could find.

"We'll keep it between us," I whispered. "Same as we've been doing. When we're both ready, we can let people in. Family. Friends. Team. Then down the line, we can make it public." I brought our hands up and kissed his knuckles. "We'll get there. But I do like it just being us for now."

"Okay, good." He released my hand and trailed his fingertips down my cheek. "I want to see what we can do without the world breathing down our necks, you know?"

Oh God. He wants this to really go somewhere.

"Yeah, I know exactly what you mean."

Jarek smiled, and then he brushed his lips across mine. "We should get some sleep. We have to skate in the morning."

I whined theatrically. "Oh, man. Couldn't you have reminded me before you topped me?"

He laughed, rolling onto his back and pulling me with him. "Would you have told me no?"

"Hmm. Okay. You've got me there." I reached past him to switch off the light, then settled against him, an arm draped over his abs and my foot nestled between his calves. "I'm still going to blame you if I'm sore tomorrow."

He just chuckled and kissed the top of my head. "Good night, Hunter."

I lifted my chin to kiss under his jaw. "G'night."

It was way too early to put any names or long term predictions on this. Much too soon to let anyone but us know what was going on. We could touch in the safety of a club that prioritized discretion, but the rest...

No, we weren't ready for that.

Yet.

Lying here in Jarek's arms, satisfied and aching from the best sex of my life, I hoped this was only the beginning. I hoped I got so used to falling asleep beside him that it felt weird to sleep alone.

And I hoped I fell in love with this man.

CHAPTER 31

JAREK

The obnoxious trill of my cell phone annoyed me out of a sound sleep. Recognition of the ringtone hauled me from vaguely conscious to fully awake.

But the warmth of Hunter's body beside mine made our PR rep's call a hell of a lot less important.

Instead of rolling toward the nightstand, I rolled toward Hunter, and he murmured sleepily as he tucked his head under my chin. Arms around him, I closed my eyes again, basking in this lazy closeness and all the lingering aches and twinges that had nothing to do with hockey.

"Gonna get that?" Hunter mumbled.

"No," I murmured into his hair.

He laughed softly and curled in closer to me.

After another twenty seconds or so, the sound died away. We were left in silence apart from a polite chirp to let me know she'd left a voicemail.

Whatever that was about, it could wait.

I kissed the top of Hunter's head, his disheveled hair tickling my nose. Mornings like this were too good to rush.

As I held him, some of the emotions from last night

simmered beneath the surface. Everything he'd said at the club. Everything we'd done in my bed. The way he'd looked at me. The way he'd touched me.

It's so easy, he'd told me.

It was. It really was. With all the walls and resentment out of the way, we'd collided so perfectly, and somehow we'd landed here. Making love at night. Cuddling in the morning. Talking in between like two people with nothing to hide and nowhere to be but together. It was all still new, and maybe we'd do this long enough that we'd figure out how to annoy each other the way partners did. I hoped so. I liked this, and I liked him. With enough time to let this thing happen at its own pace, we could be something.

Eventually. In the meantime, I was more than happy to enjoy every second of this delicious honeymoon phase. So, yeah. A morning like this was too good to waste on—

Another ringtone broke the silence and scattered my thoughts.

I'd been so blissed out and relaxed, I was confused for a couple of seconds before Hunter grumbled, "That's not a good sign." He pushed himself up a little. "Can you hand me my phone?"

I reached for the nightstand, fumbled around, and found his beside mine. As I handed it over, I caught a glimpse of the name on the screen, and something cold twisted behind my ribs.

Why was PR calling both of us this early in the morning?

Hunter rolled onto his back, accepted the call, and rubbed his free hand over his scruffy face as he put the phone to his ear. "Hey, Rachel. What's—"

I couldn't hear what she was saying, but she was talking fast, and not in the way she did when she was excited. That something in my chest was solid ice now, and it only got colder as Hunter tensed all over, and his expression morphed from vaguely awake to caught off guard to wide-eyed and speechless.

"Seriously? Oh, fuck." There was a pause, then, "Yeah. Yeah, I can..." He glanced at me. "I'll let him know. We'll be there as soon as possible."

Oh, *that* sounded good.

When he ended the call, he didn't even give me a chance to ask what was going on. Already swinging his legs over the side of the bed, he said, "Someone outed us."

That ball of ice plummeted into my stomach. "Sakra," I hissed as I started getting up too. "I assume she wants to see us for damage control."

Hunter nodded. "She's already getting hammered with questions from the media."

I whistled. "Gossip travels fast these days, doesn't it?"

He grunted in agreement.

Neither of us said anything as we showered and dressed. There was plenty to say, but my mind was racing too fast in too many different directions. From the dazed, distant expression on his face, his wasn't any better.

Goddammit. Everything we'd talked about last night felt like it had gone up in smoke.

This was supposed to be ours for a while. Something that could develop on its own without the camera flashes and intrusive questions and all that pressure and scrutiny that could drive us apart. For fuck's sake, we'd both watched teammates' relationships crumble because their partners couldn't handle the media exposure. Sure, we had the advantage in that we were both used to life in the public eye, but we were also two of the *very* few queer players in the League, which would mean *a lot* of extra attention.

We'd had something that was intimate and private, not ready for other people's consumption. We'd had a plan to let it happen on its own time and come out on our own terms, and that had been yanked away from us.

The world fucking knew.

Our families. Friends. Teammates. Coaches. Fans. Haters. Probably even people who didn't follow hockey but caught the scent of gossip and scandal, because God knew this would get labeled a scandal even though we hadn't done a damn thing wrong.

That whole train of thought made me want to break down and sob. I was sure this thing we had—this fledgling relationship that was still fragile and precarious—was going to fall apart now. That one way or another, when this was over...

I wouldn't have Hunter.

I actually had to force back a lump in my throat.

Maybe I was jumping the gun. We'd been outed, and it was violating and humiliating to have our private lives splashed all over the place in exchange for someone else's internet clout, and I was admittedly less than rational right now.

But I couldn't shake that bone-deep fear that Hunter and I weren't ready to weather something like this.

A hand on my arm made me jump, and I turned to meet his worried eyes.

"Hey." His brow pinched. "You okay?"

I swallowed. "Not really."

His shoulders dropped. "Me neither."

My stomach roiled. "Are we making this bigger than it is?"

Hunter chewed his lip, eyes unfocused. "I don't know. I..." He sighed and looked up at me again. "I'm used to my personal shit being made public, but this..." He wiped a hand over his face. "Fuck."

My heart sank. I was miserable enough. Seeing my own misery on Hunter's face and hearing it in his voice—that wrecked me. Was it really last night that we'd been tangled up in each other and pure bliss? That seemed like a million years ago now.

I touched his waist. "I guess all we can do is go in and see what's going on. Then..." I shook my head. "Go from there?"

Chewing his lip, Hunter nodded. "Not much else we can do."

In silence, we headed out. We didn't even have the luxury of doing this at the training center, because there was a game tonight and a skate this morning. No, we had to go all the way into Pittsburgh, driving in uncomfortable silence as I imagined all the ways this was going to go to shit.

All the way into the city, I was a mess of nerves and fear. In silence, I pulled into the parking garage. A few of our teammates' cars were already here; they probably either wanted to visit with friends from the away team, or they were getting in light workouts before the morning skate. Either way, Hunter and I avoided the locker room and went straight upstairs to where several staff members had offices, including Rachel.

When we walked into her office, that cold ball in my stomach got impossibly heavier and colder.

Coach Henley. Andrew, the general manager. Bruce, the president of hockey operations. All of them loomed behind Rachel, who was seated at her desk.

Holy shit. That wasn't good—not that I'd expected it to be. Though we were both out as gay, this was a more serious situation because we were teammates. In fact, it occurred to me in that moment—just a *wee* bit too late—that I didn't actually know if there was a rule against teammates getting involved with each other. One of my previous teams had expressly forbidden it. Another hadn't said anything one way or the other.

But maybe I should've looked into Pittsburgh's policy sometime between screwing Hunter and awkwardly facing down the entire front office.

"Hunter, do you mind closing the door?" Rachel said evenly.

Oh, *that* sounded promising.

Hunter shut the door, and we both took the chairs in front of Rachel's desk. He was the first to break the silence. "So… someone outed us."

My stomach lurched. The other men in the room shifted uncomfortably. Rachel was tense, too, and she nodded. "A video went up late last night. Early this morning, actually. By the time any of us were aware of it, it was already going viral and had a ton of attention."

I winced. The PR team did their level best to stay on top of things like this, but they had to sleep sometime.

Hunter cleared his throat. "Uh. What…" He folded his arms and shifted in his chair. "What video? What exactly did they say about us?"

For about half a nanosecond, I held out hope that Rachel would just give us the rundown.

No such luck—she picked up her phone and tapped the screen a few times. Then she handed it to Hunter, and though I wanted to look anywhere but at that video, I leaned in to watch.

On the screen, a young woman who was very, *very* drunk was talking in front of a background I immediately recognized. It was one of those videos where the person would explain what was going on, then move out of the way to reveal the dramatic image or whatever they'd been blocking.

From the dim, purple-tinged lighting, I knew where she'd been. And in fact, I was pretty sure I'd seen her.

Last night.

At the club.

In one of the bachelorette parties.

I gritted my teeth.

"So we were at Lanterns tonight," she slurred. "It's this gay bar in downtown Pittsburgh, right? Best drinks in town. Anyway..." Her eyes got huge and she gave a big grin. "You'll never guess who we saw on a da-ate!" She singsonged the last word, then got out of the way of the background video.

And there we were.

Not dancing. Not subtly feeling each other up. Not leaving together.

No, she'd caught us at the table, Hunter's hand on my knee as we smiled at each other and shared a conversation that the music drowned out. Even if he hadn't been touching me, it was plainly obvious we were a couple. The way he'd looked at me—Jesus.

Then the video ended, and there were some stills that were slightly clearer... including one when I'd worked up the courage to steal a brief kiss.

There was no mistaking who we were or who were to each other. Sakra, I should've known better than to go out in public. But Lanterns was safe. It always had been. I'd seen celebrities there with their boyfriends or hookups, and the internet was never the wiser.

It was *safe*, damn it.

Right up until it wasn't.

The photos and video made my stomach turn. My fucking skin crawled. It was violating to be outed at all, especially when we'd been in a place where patrons were supposed to adhere to a certain code of silence. Maybe it was naïve to think that was a realistic expectation in an era of camera phones and social media, but if you couldn't trust other queer people to understand the need for discretion, who could you trust with anything?

But the worst part was knowing exactly when those images had been taken. Remembering exactly what Hunter and I had been saying in that moment.

What right did someone have to turn such a beautiful, intimate moment into a cheap attempt at internet clout?

Beside me, Hunter sat back and swore. Wiping a hand over his face, he pushed out a breath. Then he dropped his hand and gazed at the powers that be. When he spoke, he sounded resigned and defeated. "All right. Well. I mean I guess that's it. We're out." He shrugged, shifting a little as if his skin was crawling like mine was. "Now what?"

It took all I had not to reach for his hand. We wouldn't be revealing anything by doing that, but I couldn't read Hunter right then. I didn't know if he'd want my touch, reassuring or otherwise.

"Listen." Bruce folded his arms. "What you boys do in your private life is your business. But you *are* teammates. This can affect the dynamic of the entire team."

Well, that wasn't a *you're-both-getting-released-from-your-contracts-for-screwing-teammates*—yet—so I called it a good sign.

"If we'd known," he went on pointedly, "then Rachel and the club could've had something in place in case this happened."

All four of them peered at us, and I could feel the unspoken question: *Why the secrecy?*

"We weren't hiding it," I said. "It was just..." I considered my words, which sucked when I was under pressure. I could speak English on the fly, but make me nervous enough and it wasn't so easy. And I was nervous as fuck right now.

Hunter mercifully picked up where my second language had failed me. "It was new. We didn't even really know what it was yet." He glanced at me then shrugged as he returned his gaze to the others. "We wanted to figure it out before we told anyone."

I nodded. "Exactly." I swallowed. "Even our friends and families didn't know."

Coach peered at me. "So if I ask Dima, Ferns, and Dolls..."

I managed a laugh. "They've, uh... They've had their suspicions. But they didn't *know*."

"Why did they have their suspicions?" Bruce asked flatly.

Coach snorted. Bruce and Andrew eyed him. Chuckling, Coach made a *what-can-you do?* gesture. "Those four —they know each other." He motioned toward me. "If they didn't have a reason to suspect, they would've made it up just to entertain themselves."

I couldn't even argue with that. Coach knew us almost as well as we knew each other. Well enough I was kind of surprised he hadn't caught on that something was going on between Hunter and me, but I wasn't looking that gift horse in the mouth.

"So you weren't out, then," Bruce said. "But the images were taken in public." His eyebrow arched, reminding me of the look Eliška always gave me when she saw through my bullshit.

"Actually," Rachel spoke up, "the owner of the club issued a statement this morning, too." She twisted around to look up at Bruce. "It sounds like the establishment is advertised as a discreet place where patrons' privacy is respected."

"That's true," I said. "They have a no-camera policy that they strictly enforce." I sighed, some heat rising in my cheeks as I glanced at Hunter. "We knew it was a risk, but... a small one."

Bruce quirked his lips. To Rachel, he said, "I'd like to see that statement."

I wanted to see it too, and Hunter had already pulled it up on Instagram. As Rachel showed her screen to Bruce and Coach, Hunter showed me his.

Against a faint rainbow background was some black text:

Lanterns is meant to be a venue for dancing and fun, but it's also meant to be a safe space for LGBTQ+ people in a time when their safety cannot be guaranteed elsewhere. Part of that safety includes not being photographed, videoed, or otherwise recorded and outed without their consent.

We have tried to make this a welcoming and inclusive place for everyone, including straight people. We have trusted our patrons of all orientations to be respectful of our rules and of the consent and privacy of other guests.

That trust was broken last night.

Effective immediately, bachelorette events will no longer be permitted inside Lanterns. The group who released the video is permanently banned, and should they return to our establishment, they will be removed by police for trespassing.

Our deepest apologies to our two patrons whose privacy

was violated, and whose relationship was made public without their consent. If there is anything we can do to rebuild your trust and make up for what happened at our club, please don't hesitate to reach out.

Sincerely,

Lanterns ownership & management

Hunter sighed as he pocketed his phone. "It's not their fault."

I nodded. "Now I know why the bachelorette parties always made me nervous."

"Same," he muttered.

That got us some odd looks from the others, but they didn't press.

Hunter drummed his nails on the armrest of his chair. "So... what now? You know we're seeing each other." He half-shrugged. "Where do we go from here?"

At least one of us was capable of being direct instead of beating around the bush.

Coach, Andrew, and Bruce exchanged looks.

Then Bruce took a breath. "Well, you're not in violation of any club policies. As long as this relationship isn't causing any disruption to the team..." He glanced at Coach.

Coach shook his head. "No. I couldn't even tell you how long it's been going on. They kept it pretty quiet."

"Right." Bruce folded his arms loosely. Not like he was being confrontational—more like this whole conversation made him uncomfortable and he didn't know what to do with his hands. I could relate, though probably not for the same reasons. He cleared his throat. "If it becomes a problem for the team, then we'll need to have another discussion. But at this stage..." He shrugged. "It isn't like we can tell you to stop."

He kept his cards pretty close to his vest. I couldn't tell

if he *wanted* to tell us to stop, if he was disgusted by the idea of two players screwing, or if he didn't care either way. I wasn't sure I wanted to know.

Beside him, Coach nodded, sliding his hands into his pockets. "Can I trust you boys to keep this off the ice?"

"Yes, Coach," we both said.

"We really weren't hiding it," I said. "Not... I mean, we were, but we just... wanted to figure it out first."

He nodded again, looking more tired than anything. I hoped he wasn't angry with us. Somewhere in my mind, I had visions of him getting us alone—either both of us or one at a time—and backing us against walls and shouting threats at us until his voice gave out.

But that wasn't Coach Henley. I knew it wasn't. That was Coach Robertson, and he wasn't here now.

Thank God for that, I thought with a nauseated shudder.

"All right, then," Coach said. "I'm sure there's gonna be some talk about this at practice, but I expect that once the whistle blows..." He inclined his head.

"Yes, Coach," we repeated.

And that... That was it. I supposed I didn't expect much more than that from the club. They'd brought us both onboard knowing we were openly gay, and we weren't the only queer men who'd played for Pittsburgh. It had to have crossed someone's mind at some point that there was potential for teammates to hook up, but no one had thought anything of it, at least not enough to create any policy forbidding it. Or maybe they were afraid of a discrimination lawsuit or something. I didn't know. I was just glad this was all the heat we were going to get from our coach, GM, or president of hockey operations.

Rachel tapped her nails on her phone case. "There is

going to be a press conference, because I'd rather have the two of you get in front of cameras and nip all the rumors in the bud than have everyone speculating leading up to tonight's game."

Hunter and I nodded.

"So, I'm going to go make sure everyone is where they need to be." She rose. "We'll leave the two of you to discuss what you want to say, and come up with any questions you'd prefer to be off limits."

I scowled. "I suppose I can't say any questions about our relationship are off limits?"

She grimaced apologetically. "Sorry, hon."

"It was worth a shot," Hunter said.

Everyone left Rachel's office except him and me. With a sick feeling in my stomach, I took out my phone to see how far and wide this had gone.

With a sinking heart, I realized it was trending all over social media. I was, however, pleasantly surprised to see a lot of people criticizing the woman who'd outed us, saying it wasn't cool to out a couple (regardless of sexuality) who hadn't gone public themselves.

Others...

Well. There was the usual homophobic shit that came up whenever Hunter's name or mine were mentioned at all, and this time it was even louder because our sexuality was actually relevant. Others speculated about where I'd be traded, since there was no way Pittsburgh was letting go of Hunter without a fight.

Beside me, Hunter grumbled, "Fucking hell." He wiped a hand over his face. "We're already a *meme?*"

Acid rose in my throat. "Seriously?"

He offered his phone. As much as I didn't want to know, I took it.

On the screen was one of the images from the viral post. It was the one where we'd either just kissed or were just about to, and Hunter was grinning, his lips a breath away from mine.

And below it, someone had written: *Guess we know why 41 ditched Toronto.*

"For fuck's sake," I muttered, giving him back his phone. I wished I could say that meme was an isolated one, but the *"Michaud deserted Toronto for Badura"* conspiracy theory spread like wildfire. Other photos and videos of us were dredged up, with people speculating about what every look and touch meant. Every image of us exchanging even the most fleeting eye contact was filtered through what people knew about us now.

A photo of me laughing at something he'd said on the bench was us flirting.

A post-goal hug, both of us smiling broadly, looked just like any other moment of two players celebrating like we all did during every game. But man, snap the photo at just the right moment, and it was easy to turn it into proof that we'd been flirting in plain sight all season long.

There was a shot of him appearing to snarl something at me while I was scowling, and it was interpreted as us taking a lover's quarrel out onto the ice with us. I couldn't remember that exact moment, but the camera had most likely just caught him at an awkward instant while he was speaking, and my expression was one of intense concentration. If I had to guess, he'd been indicating a set play, and I'd probably nodded right after the camera had frozen us in time.

Christ. It was bad enough someone had turned that moment in the club into a punchline. With all these memes and comments, they'd managed to turn *us* into one.

"Fucking Christ." Hunter tossed his phone on the desk and leaned over his knees, rubbing his temples.

Alarm straightened my spine. "What?"

He swore under his breath. Then, "Guy I hooked up with a while ago. He's..." Hunter glanced at his phone, shook his head, and made a disgusted sound. "He thinks he's gonna blackmail me."

"Blackmail—*what?*" Fury surged through me, even hotter and sharper than my anger over this whole situation, and sent me to my feet. "What the fuck?"

Laughing humorlessly, Hunter leaned back in the chair and gazed up at me, a mix of bitter amusement and bone-deep exhaustion in his eyes. "He thinks he's going to out me as a cheater. Says he's got footage of us on his Ring camera that's date-stamped and everything." He snorted and rolled his eyes. "Go ahead, fucker. Just..." He waved a hand, and whatever amusement he'd managed faded, leaving behind nothing but fatigue.

My chest burned with rage. The guy didn't have a damn thing on Hunter, but if he went public anyway, it would still wind up adding to Hunter's humiliation. Some people would buy that he'd cheated. Others would judge him for having a one night stand, as if hookups were taboo anymore. Even those who didn't care one way or another would *know*. It was none of anyone's fucking business, but people would know something private and personal.

One more facet of Hunter's life exposed to the public without his consent. One less reason for him to trust anyone with his privacy.

"I'm sorry," I whispered shakily.

Hunter rose and faced me. "For what?"

"For..." I gestured with my phone. "He wouldn't have any reason to threaten you if it wasn't for—"

"Baby." He touched my arm. "Look at me."

It took some effort, but I did.

Hunter's expression was as earnest as it was sweet. "I know you've spent the last several years blaming yourself for anything that happens to me. But this isn't on you. *You* didn't out us. *You* didn't pull me into this relationship against my will." He squeezed my arm. "Don't pile it all on your shoulders. You haven't done anything wrong."

I nodded in acknowledgment, but I was restless, and I got up and started to pace across Rachel's office. "This is... Sakra. I fucking hate it."

"Me too." Hunter leaned against Rachel's desk as he watched me pace. "At least we're not getting kicked off the team."

I grunted but said nothing.

"Jarek." Hunter stepped in front of me, halting my nervous strides, and put his hands on my shoulders. "Take a breath, okay?"

I stubbornly wanted to shake him off, but I took a breath. Not sure how much it helped, though.

He looked right in my eyes. "We'll be okay. We're not losing our contracts."

I swallowed. "But what about us?"

His brow furrowed. "What *about* us? We're—" He stiffened. "Wait, do you mean is this going to... like drive us apart?"

"What if it does?" Damn it. I sounded pathetic.

"It won't," he insisted. "Jesus, it isn't like we did anything wrong. Neither of us cheated or anything." He touched my face. "We're fine."

"For now?" I let my shoulders slump under his hands as I exhaled. "I've played with at least three guys whose marriages have fallen apart because their wives couldn't cope with the media attention on top of everything else. They just... They couldn't handle it."

"I know," he whispered. "But that doesn't mean I'm going to bail." He laughed dryly. "I've been under the media microscope since I was a kid."

"Yeah. You have." I swallowed. "But now they're breathing down your neck about us. And I mean, those guys whose wives left? They'd been together for a while, you know? At least long enough to get married and even have a couple of kids." I hated how unsteady my voice was getting. "We've... We just started dating."

Hunter stared at me, but then understanding seemed to dawn. His shoulders fell with the same resignation that crept into his voice. "So you're worried this is too new to weather the stress."

"Isn't that why we were keeping it on the DL?" I hated the way my throat tightened and my eyes burned now that we'd both said the words out loud. "If we'd had more time first..."

"I know," he whispered. "But we've been dealt worse hands before, right?"

"Not as a couple."

"No, but all the bullshit we've been through before—we had to do that alone. We're doing this together." He cupped my face and touched his forehead to mine. "I'm not going anywhere, Jarek. Let people talk—I want this. I want *you*." He brushed a kiss across my lips, and when he spoke, his voice was unsteady, but still full of that fierce determination I adored so much. "We'll get through this together."

God, I wanted to believe him so badly.

I didn't trust myself to speak. Instead, I wrapped my arms around him, and for a long time, we just stood there, a million miles and lifetimes removed from the lazy, warm embrace in my bed just an hour ago.

Being outed as a couple wasn't a disaster, per se. We weren't being kicked off the team. In fact, we had the support of the front office. We hadn't done anything wrong.

The whole thing was just violating and disgusting. It cheapened and ruined that moment in the club last night, and deep down, I was terrified it was going to do the same to our entire fledgling relationship. We'd been outed without our consent, and now we had to do damage control by going in front of a room full of reporters and answering questions that were none of anyone's business.

I wasn't worried about this hurting my career. I'd come back from far worse.

No, what I was worried about was what it would do to us.

What if this *was* too much for Hunter? For both of us? What if this brand new relationship was still weeks or months away from the kind of solid ground that could weather something like this?

What if, in the end, this really did cost me Hunter?

CHAPTER 32

HUNTER

Rachel returned to her office about half an hour after she'd left us to figure out what we wanted to say.

"Are you boys ready?"

"No," I told her honestly. "But we can do it. I think?" I turned to Jarek for confirmation.

His response was a non-committal shrug.

She sighed. "I'm sorry, guys. I really am. You shouldn't have to address something like this publicly, but unfortunately, it's really the least awful option in the long run. We're better off nipping all the rumors in the bud now."

We both nodded.

"Yeah," I said. "It just sucks."

Jarek exhaled. "Do we at least have time to talk to our teammates first?"

Grimacing, Rachel shook her head. "Practice isn't until noon, and the press conference is at ten."

He muttered something that was probably both Czech and obscene. Whatever it was... I concurred.

Rachel left us again, likely to wrangle the media or deal with any of the million plates she had to keep spinning.

After she'd closed the door, Jarek turned to me and took out his phone. "There's always the group chat."

"True." I took out my own cell. We both muted the group chat when we were sleeping, and I realized I hadn't gotten around to unmuting it since I'd been a little preoccupied this morning.

As soon as I did...

"Holy shit," Jarek said with an actual laugh.

Yeah. Holy shit was right.

The group chat was on *fire*.

Ferns: *Yars, you fucking liar. You said you didn't have crush on Mish!*

Sawyer: *Wait, why didn't anyone tell me we can date teammates?*

Dolls: *Because none of us want to date you.*

Sawyer: *oh fuck you Dolls. Your married anyway.*

Dolls: *And I wouldn't date you if I was single.*

Dima: *Same.*

Ferns: *Same.*

Cole: *Same.*

Mayweather: *Same.*

Sawyer: *omg you guys suck. (middle finger emoji)*

I glanced at Jarek. "You told Ferns you didn't have a crush on me?"

He rolled his eyes. "I *didn't* have one." He glanced at me, a somewhat sheepish expression on his lips as color rose in his cheeks. "Not at the time."

"But why did they think you did?"

He made a non-committal noise and accompanied it with a dismissive wave.

"Wait, is that why they kept telling you to sleep with me?"

The blush deepened, and Jarek rolled his eyes again.

I just chuckled, grateful for a moment of levity.

I returned my attention to the chat, which was still going ninety miles an hour.

Norris: *Is this why Yars doesn't hang out at the bar anymore?*

Ferns: *No, it's because you won't stop doing karaoke.*

Norris (*middle finger emoji*)

Mayweather: *Hey we totally called it—Yars has a boyfriend!*

Cole: *Can't believe it was Mish all along. Right in front of our faces.*

Ferns: *I thought he had better taste in men.*

Mayweather: *Which one? Mish or Yars?*

Ferns: *Yes*

Dolls: *Hey has anyone heard from either of them today?*

Dima: *Not me. Texted Yars. No answer.*

Cole: *The front office isn't fucking with them, are they? If someone tries to kick them off the team I will cut a bitch.* (*knife emoji*)

I didn't even realize Jarek was typing until a message appeared on the screen.

. . .

Jarek: *They're not fucking with us. Briefed us + setting up a press con. All good. Thanks, guys.*

Dolls: *Oh thank God. I haven't had enough coffee to yell at anyone.*

Norris: *What Dolls said.*

Williams: *idgaf if you guys are doing each other as long as your getting along*

Carlson: *this has to be why they play so well together*

Maxwell: *Carlson, do NOT get any ideas. You want us to play better? Practice more. We're NOT screwing.*

Dolls: *it couldn't hurt to try*

Ferns: *With the way they're playing? Really couldn't hurt.*

Maxwell: *I hate you guys*

I chuckled, glancing at Jarek. "Guess they're taking it well."

He was smiling as he read the screen. "Figured they would." His cheeks colored a little as he added, "I think they really are just glad we get along now."

"Ah, so that's the secret." I grinned. "Show them what happens if we don't like each other, and then they'll be totally onboard when we start dating."

"Exactly." He grinned, somehow looking both sheepish and devilish. "It was all part of my evil plan from the start."

We held each other's gazes and both chuckled, if a little halfheartedly. This was definitely a relief, and I was glad to see we had our team in our corner.

But this wasn't over yet, because the Hornets' group chat wasn't the only corner of cyberspace that was blowing up, and not everyone was taking it quite so gracefully.

The homophobic comments—well, I'd expected those,

and they kept on coming. They were there like clockwork with every Pride game and every player who came out. I didn't like them, but they didn't really faze me anymore.

No, it was the more personal shit that burrowed its way under my skin. Because Toronto fans were having a damn field day with this. Some were mocking me for it. Others hated me even more than they had yesterday.

Oh, now it makes sense why Michaud hightailed it to Pittsburgh.

Look at that—two players who screwed over Toronto, and now they're screwing each other. Nice. (middle finger emoji)

LOL And they told us he signed with the Hornets because he was an unrestricted free agent. Bullshit—he went to Pitt because he's Joke Badura's little bitch.

My stomach roiled. They'd already hated me for leaving, but I was a damn punchline now.

One of my former teammates had posted, *I'm not surprised. Michaud was only in Toronto for himself. He went to Pittsburgh because there was something there he wanted. Way to be a team player, Mish!*

I found a tiny sliver of satisfaction in knowing that the PR director would probably be on his ass for that before too long. Twenty bucks said it would be deleted before our press conference was over. Not that it would matter, since screencaps were forever, and I had already seen it capped and reposted a few times. Lovely.

I kept scrolling even though I knew I shouldn't, and the collective message was impossible to miss.

What the fuck kind of player, fan after fan demanded to know, *abandons a team and fanbase who adore him just for a piece of ass?*

That had me on my feet and pacing back and forth

across the small office. I couldn't even count the ways it pissed me off and cut me to the bone.

I hadn't left Toronto for Jarek. But even if I had, he was more than a piece of ass. Couldn't they see that? Couldn't they tell by the way we'd been looking each other in those photos and in that video heard round the world?

Of course they couldn't. It could've been a goddamned wedding photo, and they'd still be reducing Jarek to a piece of ass.

Fuck. Fuck! I didn't care all that much that we were out, but this part was—

"Hey." Jarek caught my elbow as I was turning on my heel, and he faced me, worry etched all over his face. "You okay?"

Oh, yeah. I was fantastic. And there was no pretending I wasn't because Jarek knew me, my tells, and this whole bullshit situation. Did I want to lie to him anyway?

Shoulders sagging, I stared into the narrow space between us. "We're a fucking *joke*."

His fingers twitched on my arm, and a second too late, I remembered the nickname that had been chasing him for the last several years.

My head snapped up. "Fuck. I'm sorry. That's... God, that's not what I meant."

Jarek nodded, exhaustion radiating off him. "I know. And..." He released my arm and shrugged heavily. "You're not wrong. Everyone thinks it's fucking hilarious." He spat the last word like an epithet.

"We're not a punchline," I whispered, and I sounded more pleading than persuasive. As if I were trying to convince myself more than him, and doing a piss poor job of it.

His half-shrug spoke of even more exhaustion, but he

said nothing. Neither did I. What was there to say? This was humiliating. Violating. I was tempted to read through the team's group chat again just to cling to some support from people close to me.

And Jarek had taken no end of shit for things ever since his fateful final season in Toronto, so if this was fucking my head up, it had to be a nightmare for him.

Jarek had apologized for all of this, as if it was his fault, but now I was the one softly saying, "I'm sorry."

He met my gaze, deep crevices forming between his eyes. "For what? You didn't do anything. That—" He hesitated, jaw working, then continued, "You said yourself. It was that girl with the camera. Not you."

I sighed. "I know. But if we hadn't started seeing each other, and—"

"Don't." He shook his head as he wrapped his arms around my waist. "We didn't do anything wrong."

I held his gaze, searching for reassurance.

Jarek sighed. Then he pulled me in closer, and I decided his kiss was plenty reassuring. I put my arms around his neck and returned that kiss, hoping to offer up reassurance of my own.

Everything outside this room was beyond our control. What rumors and gossip were flying all through the simultaneously huge and tiny world of hockey—there was nothing we could do to stop it. Nothing we could do to change the minds of those who'd already decided why we were together, why I'd come to Pittsburgh, and what this meant about our loyalty to either hockey team.

But here, at least—in Rachel's office, just him and me—we could tell each other all the things neither of us knew how to say out loud.

I broke the kiss and held him, wondering how a long but

chaste kiss had left me so out of breath. "At least we know the team has our back."

A soft breath gusted across my lips. "I can't believe they do."

I drew back to meet his eyes, the words *"Of course they do"* poised on the tip of my tongue, but then I remembered who I was talking to. Who'd been a verbal punching bag for the whole damn League for my entire career. And why.

"We're on a different team now," I told him instead. "This isn't Toronto."

"Thank God for that," he muttered.

"I know, right?" I lifted my chin to kiss him lightly. "But seriously, this team is close. They support each other. Contrary to what everyone's saying all over social media, *that's* what made me sign here." I chanced a cautious grin. "My sometimes surly left winger just turned out to be a hell of a bonus."

To my great relief, Jarek laughed, if quietly, and some color rose in his beautiful face. "No pressure."

"None." I ran my thumb along his cheekbone. "I mean it."

He looked in my eyes, and he took a breath like he was about to speak, but a knock in the door turned both our heads.

Rachel leaned in. "You boys ready?"

Jarek scowled. "Is no an option?"

"I'm afraid not." She opened the door all the way and gestured for us to step out into the hall. As we followed her toward the media room, the sharp marcato of her high heels cracking alongside my heartbeat, she said, "I've briefed everyone on the situation, and the limitations we're requesting on questions. If there's something either of you feel is too personal, you can decline to answer."

"It's *all* too personal," Jarek growled.

I grunted in agreement.

"I know," she said without slowing her stride. "But this is the reality of having public faces."

Whatever Jarek grumbled under his breath, I probably agreed.

She let us into the room, and I tried not to think too hard about how many cameras and faces were pointed at us as we took our seats at the two microphones. At least I wasn't facing down the press alone. Solo media scrums were not for the faint of heart. Especially not when there was a "situation."

Situation, my ass. This is my personal life getting leaked without my consent to the public. This is bullshit.

The one saving grace was that there was always a black tablecloth draped over the media table. One that went all the way to the floor. I stole a peek just to make sure there wasn't so much as a sliver of light peering through, and then ever so subtly nudged Jarek's foot with mine. He pushed back a little—an acknowledgment, not an effort to shove me away. We stayed like that as Rachel introduced us (like anyone here didn't know by now who we were) and opened up the floor for questions.

Hands shot up.

I glanced at Jarek. He offered a shrug and a slight nod toward me, so I faced the small crowd and picked one of the local reporters I recognized.

"Question for both of you," he said. "How have your teammates reacted to this news? Or did they already know about your relationship?"

Jarek and I shared another glance.

I cleared my throat and leaned in to speak into my microphone. "They didn't know before today." I hesitated, then decided to be a little spicy, though I kept my tone professional: "We weren't ready to come out to anyone yet, so... we didn't get the chance to tell people, including our teammates, on our own terms. That opportunity was taken away from us."

A few reporters were writing frantically. From the corner of my eye, I caught Rachel giving us a look that was a mix of amused and annoyed. She liked the fact that we all knew how to toe the line of professionalism. She just sometimes didn't care for how close to that line we all liked to get without actually crossing it.

Beside me, Jarek held up his phone. "The team group chat is having a ball with it." He managed a soft laugh as he put the phone facedown beside his mic. "Like Hunter said, they didn't know until this morning, but they've..." He chuckled. "They've taken it with good humor."

If not for the cameras peering at us, I'd have stared at him and just basked in that nervous laughter and faint smile. He was so damn cute, even under pressure.

The best I could do was nudge his foot again. He did the same.

Jarek called on the next reporter—a woman off to the right with a tight blonde ponytail. She asked, "You said you were outed without your consent. Were you aware someone was filming or photographing you at the time?"

Jarek's smile was gone, and my stomach turned to lead. I wasn't sure if I was imagining him pressing harder against my foot, as if he were seeking as much contact as he could get for reassurance.

"No," I said to the reporter. "We had no idea."

"The club has a very strict policy against it." Jarek let his anger slip into this tone, though he was still measured and controlled. "That's why we felt safe enough to go there.

As a couple. Because it's understood that people who go to places like that might not be able to be out for whatever reason." He shook his head and added a bitter, "She broke the rules, and now we're paying for it."

I sensed Rachel fidgeting off to the side, probably worried one of us was going to snap.

Keeping my own voice calm, I said, "We don't hold it against the club owners or employees, by the way. They're all really good about enforcing it if they see someone photographing or filming someone else, but it's dark and crowded." I half-shrugged. "There's only so much they can do."

Beside me, Jarek nodded wordlessly.

An unfamiliar reporter raised his hand, and I called on him.

"Mr. Badura," he said, "I'd like to ask about the game in Toronto."

Beside me, Jarek tensed. My own stomach roiled, because I knew exactly which game they were talking about. And a second later, before he'd even asked his question, I knew with a sinking feeling why he was bringing it up.

"Was your fight with Aiden Evans a reaction to him attacking your boyfriend?"

Jarek didn't answer right away. His jaw worked, and he stared at the microphone for a long moment as everyone waited for him to respond.

The temptation to reach for his hand was almost overwhelming, if only to maybe calm him down a little, since my foot wasn't enough and I thought smoke was about to start curling out of his ears. The muscles in his jaw were so tight, his teeth had to be aching by now. And could I telepathically beg him not to tip my hand about knowing that my former teammates had it out for me that night? That we both had it on good authority that I'd had a target on my back long before we'd hit the ice?

Heart pounding, I gave in and put my hand on his forearm. I didn't look at the crowd to see if they reacted. I could sense it, even if it might've been in my imagination. Though the camera snaps—I didn't imagine those. Fine. I wasn't telling them anything they didn't already know.

Jarek closed his eyes and pushed out a breath through his nose. The tension in his jaw eased. Opening his eyes, he turned to me, and he put a hand over the top of mine. His expression was completely unreadable.

Finally, he faced the reporters, and he must've been calling on all the media training he'd ever had to keep his voice that calm and even. "It was a dirty hit. Boarding. Every hockey player knows that can cause a serious injury." He swallowed. "You've all covered this sport long enough to know that we don't let things like that slide. We stand up for our teammates, especially when someone tries to injure them. And when the refs won't do anything about it..." He gave a flippant half-shrug. "Then I will."

I had to fight hard against the laugh that wanted to bubble up. Not so much at the comment—at the startled expressions on the reporters' faces. What had they expected him to say? Yes, he'd valiantly come to his boyfriend's rescue on the ice and taken the suspension for it?

One of them cleared his throat. "But did your relationship with Hunter affect your reaction at all?"

Hand still resting on top of mine, Jarek said without hesitation, "No. We were not dating at the time." A chuckle broke through his icy mask, and he glanced at me. "We didn't even like each other at that point."

I laughed and leaned in to say into the mic, "Can confirm."

That prompted a ripple of amusement, which was a relief. Anything to break the tension in the room, even if it wasn't likely to last.

A third reporter ensured it didn't: "So, this means the rumors that you left Toronto to be with your boyfriend are untrue, yes?"

The laughter vanished.

Jarek's muscles twitched under my hand, and I gave his arm a gentle squeeze. To the reporter, I said, "He had nothing to do with my decision to leave Toronto *or* my decision to come to Pittsburgh."

Most of the questions after that were pretty tame. How long had we been dating? Did our families know yet? Did our teammates take it as well as their social media posts implied? What did we think of our teammates' social media posts about it?

That last question caught us both by surprise.

"I'm kind of afraid to ask," Jarek said, "but what *have* they been posting?"

Someone read off a screen, *"If Yars marries Mish and I'm not his best man, I'm knocking over the cake. #NotJoking"*

Jarek actually laughed for real. "That came from Meknikov, didn't it?"

The reporter confirmed that Dima had been the one to post it, and everyone chuckled.

Someone else read, *"This will put Mish in the running for the Kramer Memorial Trophy for sure."*

"Hey!" Jarek barked. "What the hell?" He rolled his eyes. "Ugh. That was Dolls. It had to be."

I snickered. "You don't think I deserve that trophy?"

He shot me a look. "You think dating me means you should get the trophy for perseverance and overcoming hardship?"

I batted my eyes and shrugged innocently.

Everyone in the room laughed, and I was pretty sure I heard some cameras more snap. Jarek muttered something, then let himself chuckle as he nudged my foot beneath the table. I nudged it back.

At least that broke the tension a little more. God bless our teammates and their online chirping.

The mood shifted back the other direction when a reporter asked if we thought this would affect our hockey, especially at tonight's game.

"I've played through worse," Jarek said dryly.

"Same," I said.

Every face in the room asked us to elaborate. We did not.

Then I decided, hell, the whole point of this press conference was to get ahead of rumors and gossip. Might as well get it all out there.

I folded my hands behind the microphone and leaned in a little. "One thing I do want to say is that I've already received a message from someone who wants to blackmail me with this information."

That prompted a murmur of surprise. Beside me, Jarek tensed, but he didn't speak.

I swallowed. "This person thinks they're going to out me as cheating on Jarek because we"—I hesitated, not sure how to word it tactfully—"met at up at a club not long ago. If he wants to say we hooked up?" I gave the most flippant shrug I could. "Let him talk. I won't deny it." Then I laced my fingers between Jarek's. "But anything that happened with him was before Jarek and I started dating." I turned to him and smiled. "I haven't looked at any other man since then."

He squeezed my hand, a soft smile playing at his lips. That prompted a few people to "aww," which made us both laugh.

Okay, being outed sucked, and I wasn't happy about how it had gone down, but it couldn't be undone. Now that we were out, I didn't mind at all that people were going to get shots of us looking at each other like that.

Let that hookup talk. Let people gossip. Let the cameras look.

I want the whole damn world to know how stupid I am for you.

At the side of the room, Rachel cleared her throat. "Unless there are any more questions or if Mr. Badura or Mr. Michaud have anything else to add..."

Jarek and I shook our heads.

No one in the crowd asked anything further.

We were, thank God, dismissed.

In the hallway, I wrapped my arms around Jarek and exhaled. "Well, that didn't suck as bad as I thought it would."

He leaned into me. "No. Still sucked, though."

"Yeah." I kissed his cheek before I loosened my embrace. "But now we don't have to hide. We can be out to everyone. It happened sooner than we wanted it to, and it didn't happen on our terms, but we can work with this."

Some of the tension left his shoulders. "We're going to have people gossiping about us. And I'm sure the fans will have opinions." He winced. "Especially fans of other teams."

"Let 'em talk." I drew him back in. "It's not going to

change a damn thing here." I paused. "Not unless it changes things for you."

Exhaling, Jarek shook his head and pulled me all the way to him. "Doesn't change anything for me."

I smiled and kissed him.

And I hoped to God neither of us was wrong.

CHAPTER 33

JAREK

"And now..." Hunter put his hand on the locker room door. "The really fun part."

I laughed uneasily. "You ready?"

"Eh." He shrugged, but he pushed open the door, and despite my nerves, I followed him into the familiar room.

"Hey, there they are!" Dima gave us a big shit-eating grin, then pointed a finger at me. "And *you*, my friend, are *liar!*"

I laughed as warmth rushed into my face and I put up my hands. "What did I lie about?"

Dima rolled his eyes and muttered something that was lost in the sounds of all our teammates joining in with good-natured chirping. He wrapped me in a bear hug and slapped my back before he said just loud enough for me to hear, "It's all good. And I'm glad you two are, um, getting along."

Chuckling, I playfully shoved him away. "Fuck you."

He just laughed again and gave my shoulder a squeeze.

"I can't believe you fucking lied to us!" Ferns smacked my shoulder. "You said you didn't have a boyfriend!"

I shrugged. "Not my fault you couldn't figure it out."

He rolled his eyes.

The reactions from the rest of the team were more of the same—lighthearted chirping and comments about "Well, damn, no wonder the two of you started getting along so well."

Even though I'd known all along that this team was cool with queer players, and that homophobia wasn't tolerated, the sixteen-year-old major junior player in me couldn't help but feel relieved with every teammate who showed their support. Whether it was a chirp about us having awful taste in men or something about how they'd *known* something was up lately, it was all soothing to the soul of that kid who'd been terrified of anyone finding out he was gay.

Yeah, our relationship had probably caught everyone by surprise. And no, I wasn't thrilled with how we'd been outed.

But goddamn, I loved this team.

As everyone started to settle down a little. Mayweather glanced around the room before he turned to the two of us. "Look, all joking aside—it wasn't right, the way you got outed like that. It should've happened on your terms."

All around us, our teammates nodded and murmured their agreement.

Our captain went on, "But now that it's out, and now that people are saying what they want to say, remember that no matter what people say, we"—he gestured at our team-mates—"all have your backs."

That prompted enthusiastic applause.

"What your captain said," Coach Henley broke in. "It caught us all off guard, including the two of you." He put an arm around my shoulders and squeezed gently. "But the Hornets stick by their own."

"Thanks, guys," Hunter said. "It means a lot."

"It does," I agreed.

"Man, when I heard we signed Hunter Michaud," Cole said, "I knew it would be awesome." He grinned and jerked his thumb at me. "Just didn't think he'd also soften up this prickly bastard."

Everyone laughed, and I flipped off Cole.

I seriously loved this team.

I felt all right after the morning skate. My focus wasn't as good as I would've liked on game day, but all things considered, I could live with it. The team wasn't treating Hunter and me any differently, though there was a little chirping here and there. That was to be expected. In fact, I'd have been worried if the guys didn't tease us about it; that was how you know you'd fucked up with a hockey team—when they *wouldn't* make fun of you.

So by the time we all returned to the locker room, the panic I'd had on the way to the arena was mostly gone.

Mostly.

Because in the back of my mind, I didn't imagine this was over. It couldn't be this easy. Not even these days when the League was chill about queer players. Though everyone had taken it in stride so far, the tip of the Sword of Damocles was still tickling the back of my neck. Was I just expecting this to blow up in my face because I'd finally gotten my career back on the rails? Or was there really something else coming?

Trust me to look at my club and teammates' acceptance of us, and instead of clinging to my relief, find a way to be sure that the real shit was yet to come.

"Hey." Hunter appeared by my locker. "You doing good?"

I nodded. "Yeah. Wasn't as bad as I thought it would be. You?"

"Same." He laughed, looking and sounding tired. "This was, uh... Definitely not how I thought today would go."

"No kidding." I tugged on my jacket. "I'm ready to head out. You want to stay at my place before we have to come back here?" I paused. "Wait, you have PT today, don't you?"

He made an unhappy sound. "Ugh. Yeah. I do."

I touched his back and guided him down the hall. "Let me take you home, then."

"Take—oh. Right." He fell into step beside me. "I totally forgot we came in your car."

"It's okay. Just means I get to spend a little more time with you before you go off to be tortured."

Hunter's laugh echoed through the concrete hallway. "Ass."

I just chuckled, and we continued out to my car. We kept the conversation light on the way out of downtown and up to Cranberry. The whole fiasco with us being outed hung in the air between us like an unwelcome passenger in my nonexistent backseat, but we ignored it for now. Probably best to let some dust settle for a while. Especially since we had a game tonight.

As my engine idled in front of Hunter's apartment, I said, "Well, I guess we don't have to hide me kissing you goodbye."

Grinning, he leaned over the console. "No, we do not."

And we didn't—indulging in a deep but not indecent kiss right out here in broad daylight. By the time we came up for air, I was seriously considering suggesting he bail on physical therapy.

But... no. He needed it, and I also needed a little time to myself. I needed to decompress and think for a while, and I didn't want to use sex with Hunter as a distraction.

Touching his face, I said, "I guess I should let you go."

"Yeah, probably." He kissed me lightly before settling back into his seat. "I'll meet you at the arena tonight." With a grin, he added, "Then we can figure out our postgame plans from there."

His wink once again had me wondering if I could talk him into canceling his appointment.

But I just smiled and slid a hand over his thigh. "I'll see you there. Have fun at PT."

He groaned and rolled his eyes. "Fun. Right. That's what it is."

I just chuckled, and we shared another quick kiss before he got out of the car.

As soon as he was gone, I headed home, and I found myself alone for the first time today. That... was unpleasant. Without Hunter's reassuring smile and our teammates' enthusiastic encouragement, doubts crept in.

How would this actually look when the dust settled? Because I couldn't help feeling like, on some level, this was going to end in disaster. Someone with a lot of power and little tolerance in the League would find some loophole and boot us out. Or the team's support would vanish the first time Hunter and I had a bad night on the ice; every player and every line had bad nights, but I had a feeling we didn't have nearly as much leeway as we'd had before today.

Or...

My blood turned cold.

Hunter would decide what we had wasn't worth the attention and gossip.

I shook that away.

No, we'd be fine.

I was just in panic mode because that was what I did when I was stressed, and I'd have been lying if I said this didn't stress me out. In panic mode, I gathered every worst-case scenario imaginable and *wallowed* in them until I couldn't function. Why should this time be any different?

A distraction. That was what I needed. Not sure what could distract me from this, but it was worth a try.

At home, I took out my phone, planning to look up something to do for the next few hours to occupy my stupid head.

I stopped, though, because I had a text from my sister.

You'd better call me, Kokot.

I snorted. Our mother sometimes sighed and said we'd still be calling each other terrible names and acting like children to each other when we were ninety. She was probably right.

I sent the call to my sister, and when she picked up, I said, "What do you want, Kráva?"

I could almost hear her rolling her eyes. "I want to know why you didn't tell me you have a boyfriend." She tsked. "Isn't this the guy you had a crush on? The one you *swore* you couldn't be with?"

Wiping a hand over my face, I exhaled. "Yes, it is."

She cackled. "Ha! I knew it! *I knew it!*"

"Oh, you did not. You were just guessing like—"

"Pfft. Whatever. I was right. And I don't blame you—he's *hot.*"

"Eliška. For fuck's sake. Don't ogle my boyfriend. Please?"

"Why not?"

"Because it's weird."

"*You're* weird."

"Fuck you."

She giggled. "Oh, come on. I don't get to tease you about boyfriends very often. Let me enjoy this."

"Ugh. Fine." As I said it, my humor drained away. Yeah, I could let her enjoy this, but how long would either of us really get to enjoy it?

"Jarek?" She sounded concerned now. "You still there?"

"Yeah, I'm... I'm still here." I leaned over my elbows on the kitchen island and pinched the bridge of my nose. "I can't help this feeling like this is all going to blow up in my face somehow."

Eliška was quiet for a moment. "Why?"

"I don't know. Maybe because everything in my life eventually does? But..." I rubbed my forehead. "I don't know."

As stupid as it was, I wished I was at her house right now. I wished I could channel my frustration and confusion into handling some tedious task on her endless home reno-vation. Or, I thought with an ache in my throat, I could sit on the couch with Boleslav purring in my lap. That didn't fix a damn thing, but it always made me feel better.

Eliška took a breath. "Listen to me, Jaromir."

I straightened. She only ever called me by my full first name when she *really* wanted to get my attention. Or when she was pissed at me, but she didn't seem to be this time. I swallowed. "Okay."

"I know you, all right?" Her tone was even and calm, but deadly serious. "And I know that when you get scared, when you think something is going to happen, you tend to accidentally *make* it happen."

"What?" I laughed humorlessly. "What are you talking about?"

She gave one of those *you are the stupidest brother in the world* sighs. "Don't you think I saw it with Marc-Yves?"

I flinched. "You weren't even there."

"No, but you sucked at hiding it, even on FaceTime. And when the two of you came to Kladno to visit..." Eliška pushed out a breath. "I could see it. That you were pulling away from him."

The sudden welling in my eyes caught me off-guard.

Of course, my sister kept going. "You were pulling away from all of us then. Your boyfriend. Matka and Táta. Me. I'm sure you weren't as close to your team, either."

"Why would I be close to that team?" I croaked, my voice raw. "I knew they weren't going to keep me any more than the last one did."

Her sigh was heavy with sympathy. "But the family wasn't going to trade you. And neither was Marc-Yves."

Anger surged to the surface, shoving the threat of tears aside. Well, mostly. "What are you suggesting? That it's my fault I lost—"

"No! Jarek. My God. No. But something was off between you two, and I know you were afraid you were going to lose him. And when you're afraid of losing people, you pull away from them. You run away because you're afraid you're going to be *chased* away."

The anger subsided a little, but I couldn't find my voice. I wasn't sure what I'd have said anyway.

My sister, of course, didn't have that problem. "Whatever was going on between you and Marc-Yves, you were scared. It's not your fault. Fear is—it's a strong thing. But so are you. And I'm telling you—begging you, honestly—to *not* let that fear win this time."

I gritted my teeth, not sure if I was holding back tears or fury. Both? "So just wait around for him to decide I'm not worth the bullshit?"

My own words slammed into my ribs.

Whoa. Sakra. Maybe Eliška was right.

I swore aloud. "Christ. Why am I such a mess over him?"

"Because you're afraid to lose him," she said softly. "Because he obviously means a lot to you."

I had to swipe at my eyes. Thank God we were talking on the phone so she couldn't see me. Not that she'd have chastised me or made fun of me, but I hated letting people see me get emotional. Even my little sister. "He does mean a lot to me."

"Then take a deep breath, and don't let fear you chase you away from him. Because I'm going to guess this is all bigger in your head than it is in reality. Or in his head."

I closed my eyes and slowly exhaled. She was probably right. Who was I kidding—of course she was right. Hunter hadn't made any noise about wanting to bail. He was stressed, but he hadn't pulled away from me.

Maybe that meant he wasn't going to.

Maybe the Sword of Damocles was all in my imagination.

We'd be fine.

Maybe.

CHAPTER 34

HUNTER

"All right, boys." Coach Henley stood in the middle of the locker room, ringed by the bench we were all sitting on. "I know we've had a lot of excitement the past few hours. And I'm glad we're all on the same page—supporting Mish and Yars."

That got a round of applause, and from the heat in my face, I was blushing as brightly as Jarek.

Coach went on, "But we need to focus now. We've got a hockey game to win tonight. I need everyone out there focused on the game, *not* on what's been going on in the media."

In that moment, I felt like I was listening to a teacher tell the class not to do the really dumb thing I'd done without saying *I* was the one who'd done it and necessitated the lecture. He knew it. I knew it. Everyone else in the room knew it. But as long as he didn't make eye contact with me or Jarek while he talked, we could all pretend this was just a generic pregame speech so we'd focus. I wondered for a moment if he'd pull me aside afterward to tell me I was staying in from recess, and the thought almost drove a conspicuous snicker out of me.

I managed to keep that to myself, though.

And like my teammates, I shifted my focus to the game.

Mostly.

Because before the game started, there was warmups. And warmups meant stepping out in front of the fans. We knew how the internet fans felt about it. Those who were ten feet tall and bulletproof behind a computer screen. And the trolls. Of course, the trolls.

But how would our *fans*—the ones who filled the seats at games—react?

Guess it was time to find out.

The sudden swell of cheers when we hit the ice for warmups made me smile even as it made my stomach twist into knots. So did the well-wishers and the people who thought we were a cute couple. It was heart-warming to see signs read *"We love #Michura"* and *"Badura + Michaud = Relationship Goals."*

I appreciated it all. I really did.

But it was also disappointing in a way. Over the years, I'd watched my teammates go public with their partners, announce engagements, all of that, and I'd secretly looked forward to being able to do that with someone. I was out and proud, and when I finally had a boyfriend, I'd wanted us to come out together, proudly and publicly, on our terms. I'd wanted it to be a happy occasion. The kind of thing where we ran it by PR so they knew what was coming, and the whole team already knew, and the token homophobic comments were impossible to hear over being that excited to say, "This is my man."

I couldn't shake the feeling that that had been taken

away from Jarek and me. Was it too much to ask for us to come out in *our* time and on *our* terms?

Apparently so.

Even the well wishes and smiles from fans couldn't elevate my mood. I appreciated their support. They just weren't supposed to know yet. Not now and not like this. Not with apologies and press conferences that felt suspiciously like the ones past teammates had done after they'd been suspended, tested positive for a substance, or—in the case of one past teammate—been arrested. Not getting grilled about why we'd kept it a secret and if we'd lied about anything else.

Damn it. As relieved as I was that we didn't have to fly under the radar, I couldn't lie—this felt somewhere between having someone catch me jerking off and having a meticulously planned marriage proposal ruined. Not the end of the world, but... it kinda sucked, what could I say?

Playing through it was tough, too.

After warmups were over and everyone's signs were put away, the whole arena was focused on hockey, but I was still off my game. I struggled to concentrate. It was like realizing too late that I'd arrived at a party with mismatched socks or an inconspicuous stain on my shirt—nobody in the room noticed or cared, but it felt so obvious to me it might as well have been on the Jumbotron. That relentless feeling like everybody was looking at me and whispering behind their hands even when I knew damn well they weren't.

Except this time, people did know. They'd acknowledged the mismatched socks. Loudly. Pointedly. And now we were all supposed to tuck that away and focus on hockey, and why can't you control the puck tonight, Hunter?

"Mish." Coach touched my shoulder as I took a seat on

the bench after my umpteenth shift. "You good out there?" He asked in that tone that said he knew I wasn't, and he was politely giving me a chance to unfuck it.

I twisted around to look up at him. "I'm good, Coach."

He held my gaze, then nodded and fixed his attention back on the ice, where Carlson's line was regrouping after the other team had iced the puck.

I stole a glance at Jarek. His mouthguard, hanging half out of his mouth like it often did, twisted between his lips, and his eyes and furrowed brow were full of worry. It reminded me a little of how he'd been when I'd first met him—distant and focused on anything but me or the game. No animosity, though—he was just distracted.

Around the time the 1A line's shift was almost over, I finally caught Jarek's eye, and I offered what I hoped was a reassuring smile before I slid my own mouthguard back in. He returned the smile, and we went over the boards.

We were better after that, but not a hundred percent. Thank God the rest of the team picked up our slack. That was the nice thing about being on a team with so much depth—if one player or even a whole line was having an off night, the rest could be counted on to make up the difference.

Though I didn't know if that would help tonight— Edmonton was kicking our asses and taking names, and they probably would've been even on a good night. Offensively, they weren't the best, though they had some young forwards who would be spectacular in a few years. One had managed to slip a puck past Dolls in the first period after swatting in someone else's rebound off the crossbar. Dolls hadn't had a prayer of stopping that one.

Unfortunately, their defense was solid, and not just in the net. I thought Mayweather was going to blow a gasket after being kept out of the offensive zone for an entire shift, despite an incredible effort with Cole and Williams. And then once we did finally make it past their D, we had to tangle with the netminder, who had been an absolute sieve in Toronto last season only to turn into a brick wall in Edmonton.

"How did he *do* that?" Cole shook his head as we sat on the bench. "They need to test him for performance-enhancers."

"Like what?" I said. "Octopus DNA?"

That got a laugh out of our teammates, but seriously—this goalie was impressive as all hell.

And maybe we'd have had better luck if our second line —our 1B line—had its shit together tonight. I stole some glances at Jarek whenever we weren't in the thick of things. He was playing well, but any time he was on the bench or the whistle had been blown, the exhaustion showed. As if he had to fight so hard to play halfway decently, it was draining the life out of him.

Admittedly, I could relate. The day had been mentally exhausting, and hockey was a mentally taxing game. We were only human, after all.

I pulled him aside on the way to the locker room during the second intermission. "Hey. You doing okay?"

"Yeah. Yeah." He rolled his shoulders under his pads and wiped some sweat off his jaw with the back of his glove. "Tough team."

"Tough *day*."

Jarek scowled, avoiding my gaze.

"Hey." I nudged him gently. "It's going to take a toll on us. It's okay."

Lips pressed together, he nodded. "Would've been a hell of a lot easier if that asshole had outed us on a day off."

"I know, right?" I took off my glove and touched his arm. "Listen, we've both been under the spotlight ever since this came out, but we haven't had any time to ourselves, you know?"

He tried for a laugh, but it just emphasized how utterly wrung out he was. "Well, we were in my car earlier."

"Yeah. But maybe we just need some downtime, you know? So we can talk about all this without all the..." I gestured around us. "People."

Jarek swallowed. "Okay."

"After the game?" I raised my eyebrows.

"Sure." He nodded toward the ice. "Let's see if we can get two points out there first."

"Sounds good to me. Let's go."

Another nod, and we started up the tunnel.

We ended up snagging one point instead of two. A win would've been ideal, but I could live with an overtime loss. We'd all fought hard, and our position in the standings wasn't so precarious that we desperately needed every single point.

Disappointed but not disheartened, I shed my gear and hit the showers. Now I could take off with Jarek and focus on us for a little while instead of hockey, the media, or standings.

But when I came back after showering, he was already gone.

CHAPTER 35

JAREK

There weren't words in either language I knew to describe the panic that had been swelling in my chest ever since Hunter had said we needed to talk. I tried to tell myself he just wanted to get on the same page, but deep down, I was terrified there was more. I was so sure about the inevitable outcome, I couldn't fucking breathe. Not even twenty-four hours after we'd been blissfully lost in each other, this was going to be over, wasn't it? Hunter was under enough pressure. Coach Henley had been on him several times during tonight's game, same as he had me. The last thing Hunter needed was a relationship that had barely gotten off the ground and had already become a professional distraction and a goddamned punchline.

I didn't know what he was going to say, only that I couldn't see any way this didn't end with goodbye. Everything good in my life ended in disaster. Why would this be any different?

I couldn't face him. I didn't care if that made me a coward. I *was* a damn coward when it came to the prospect of losing him, and it didn't matter that I probably already *had* lost him. I couldn't face him and listen to him tell me this was over and why.

So I did what I always did—I ran.

Not literally, but I did get the hell out of the arena as soon as I could slip away. Dima almost headed me off on my way out, asking if I was joining them to eat, but I bowed out and said I'd eat something at home.

That wasn't a lie. It just wasn't the whole truth.

At home, I was a restless mess. I made it as far as taking off my jacket and shoes, but I was too scattered for anything else. I opened a beer and tried to let that settle my nerves. It didn't help. Neither did sitting still. I *couldn't* sit still. I paced my condo, ignoring the texts and calls as they started trickling in. Some were from Hunter. Others were from teammates. A generic number. Eliška. God, I couldn't face my sister any more than I could face Hunter. Despite our earlier conversation, I was sure that this time, she was going to tell me what I already knew—that Hunter was going to walk—and she'd say it in that firm, non-negotiable way that meant I'd be smart to just make peace with it.

How the hell was I supposed to make peace with this? I'd let myself get close to someone for the first time since Marc-Yves, and now it was going to end—well, not the same way, but it was going to end. I'd be standing at the end of this relationship, shell-shocked and heartbroken and wondering how I'd ever imagined it would end any other way, and I'd—

My doorbell rang.

I froze halfway between my kitchen and the hall. He'd... Hunter was here? Because it couldn't be anyone else. Eliška had a key and wouldn't bother ringing the doorbell if she thought I was being a dumbass.

Gnawing my lip, I leaned against the wall. I should

answer the door. Talk to him. Hear him out. Let him go. He deserved that much.

I was just a fucking coward and didn't want to believe that the best thing that had happened to me in a long, long time was slipping away. Was it too much to ask to be in denial for a little longer?

I mean, I wasn't in denial. I knew what was coming. But as long as he hadn't said the words out loud yet, there was still a *chance*, however tiny, that he'd come here to talk about something *other* than splitting up.

Hunter's text tone pinged.

I closed my eyes. Fuck it. Fine. Delaying the inevitable would just drive me insane. Might as well rip off the bandage.

With my heart in my throat, I pulled out my phone. My screen was covered in notifications. The most recent was, unsurprisingly a text from Hunter:

Please let me in. We should talk.

I didn't want to. There was nothing in the world I wanted more than to let Hunter in and have him here with me. But tonight...

Well. It wasn't like I could avoid him forever. We had practice tomorrow. Better to do this here than have him corner me up in the locker room.

I pushed myself off the wall and went to the front door. When I turned the deadbolt, I grabbed on to a tiny glimmer of hope that while I'd been trying to decide if I should open the door, he'd given up and taken off.

No such luck.

"Hey," he said softly. "You, um..." He slid his hands into the pockets of his slacks. "You left."

"Yeah. I... Sorry. I needed to get out of there." Avoiding his gaze, I stepped aside so he could come in.

He did, and he paused to toe off his shoes. Because he planned to stay a while? Oh, fuck, how long was this conversation going to be?

In silence, I led him into the kitchen. "Coffee? Beer?"

Hunter shook his head, not quite looking at me. I still had half a beer on the counter, but I suddenly wasn't so sure I could keep it down if I drank any more, so I left it.

After a moment of uncomfortable silence, he opened his mouth to speak, but I cut him off:

"If you're here to say we can't keep doing this, then just say it. Don't beat around the bush."

Hunter blinked, mouth still open. Slowly, he closed it. Then he shook his head again. "I... No. No, that's not why I came here at all."

I stared at him. "It isn't?"

"No! What made you think... God, Jarek. What made you think I wanted to end this?"

I had to swallow a couple of times, and my voice still came out ragged. "Why wouldn't you?" I leaned against the kitchen island. "You said yourself that if we hadn't started dating, this wouldn't have happened, so if you regret it, then—"

"*No.* That was—I'm sorry. That wasn't what I meant. I don't regret us being together, just that it caused you all this..." He circled his hand in the air as if that could encompass the shitstorm that had erupted around us. "I'm sorry. I didn't mean to imply that I regretted..." He gestured at each of us. "I'm sorry."

I gnawed the inside of my lip. "So you... You don't think we should stop?"

"No!" Horror reclaimed his expression. "Jesus, no. I know it's going to be rocky for a while—all the public shit—but this? What we have?" Another shake of his head, this one even more emphatic. "I don't want to give it up. Not... Not unless you do."

"I don't," I said quietly. "But the shit we're getting..." My shoulders fell, and I sighed as I rubbed the back of my stiffening neck. "How long are you going to want to put up with that for the dubious honor of being with me?"

The confusion on his face made me wonder if I'd accidentally spoken in Czech. I rewound what I said, and... no, it *had* been in English. Pretty clear English, I thought.

But he was still staring at me as if none of the words had registered.

Before I could ask, Hunter said, "Do you really think it's news to me that people are going to have opinions about us?"

I blinked. "What?"

He laughed almost soundlessly. "Jarek. We're teammates. We're public figures." He threw up a hand. "There's a reason we were keeping it on the DL, you know?"

"But now it's not on the DL."

"No, so if anything, as much as I'm not happy with how it happened..." He offered up a cautious, lopsided smile. "I meant what I said earlier—this just means we don't have to hide anymore."

I stared at him. "You... really want to keep doing this."

The smile fell. "Don't you?"

"Of course I do. I just..." My words died away, and I leaned back against the kitchen island. "It's nice to imagine, you know? But how long before you resent me for all this?"

"What?" Hunter stepped a little closer, though he still kept some distance between us. "I've spent my entire career —hell, my entire life since I started playing hockey—under a microscope. People have scrutinized everything I've ever done. They've put tons of pressure on me to carry everyone and everything." He threw up a hand in a heavy, exhausted gesture. "If they think this *one* goddamned time that I did something selfish, or they insist on believing I left Toronto to be with you, then... Fuck it. Let 'em."

I stared at him.

"Jarek." He exhaled. "I'd have gone insane by now if I stressed that much about how people look at me. The only opinions I care about are yours, mine, and the team's. As long as everyone in a Pittsburgh sweater is on the same page, and they're cool with us together, then I'm not backing away. Not unless you want me to."

"No, I don't," I said quickly. "I'm just..." I sagged back against the counter. My throat was tight, and it took work to swallow. I had no clue how to put into words all this shit running through my head.

"Jarek. Look at me."

I didn't even realize I'd looked away from him, but I lifted my gaze.

His expression was full of all the same emotions crashing through me. Fear. The utter violation of having our private life made public. Guilt.

"You said you wanted this to be ours for a while," he said. "But the thing is—it's *still* ours. Yes, people know. Yes, they have opinions." His voice softened as his eyes pleaded with me to understand. "But this?" He gestured at the two of us. "This belongs to us and nobody else. And I don't know about you, but I'm not interested in letting anyone take it away from us."

My heart did things I'd never felt before, and I couldn't quite remember how to breathe. Since when was I something someone wanted to fight for?

"I mean it," he whispered. "My entire career—my entire *life*, honestly—has been about living up to other people's expectations. Doing what other people wanted me to do. The first time I ever made a selfish decision was when I signed with Pittsburgh." He swallowed hard, eyes locked right on mine. "And the second was being with you."

I didn't know how to respond to that.

Hunter went on, "I'm not saying I want to be selfish with *this*." He gestured at us. "Not at all. But if you think I'm going to let other people's opinions or professional pressures pull me away from you—think again."

"I'm..." I rubbed the back of my neck as I tried to process all of it. With a somewhat watery laugh, I said, "I thought you came here to break up with me."

"Not a chance," he said without hesitation. "Neither of us did anything wrong. I'm not going to break up with you because some drunk idiot posted a video about us."

I swallowed. "But it caused you a lot of—"

"I don't care." His voice was soft now. "We've already had other people interfering with us before we even got started. Everything you told me about why I went to Toronto and why you left—we were just pieces on someone else's chessboard. You paid for it professionally, and God only knows what we *both* missed out on because of their crap." He swallowed. "I don't want to lose any more time than we already have. Not just as hockey players, but as... *us*."

I couldn't speak. I knew Hunter understood the shit I'd been through, especially since he'd been through more than his fair share, but it caught me off guard that he saw the last several years as time wasted. Time that could've been ours.

He must've read my silence as still not understanding, because he whispered, "Let them talk. I'm not letting anyone take away the one thing I've ever wanted for myself." His voice softened and went a little ragged at the edges. "All I care about is not losing you."

I couldn't comprehend that. The words, yes—even if he'd spoken in perfect Czech, I'd have still been in this state. No one went to bat for me. Not like this. And Hunter had seen me at my worst. He knew the secret I couldn't tell anyone else. Somehow, he'd stuck around to see a side of me very few had ever known, and even now, he wasn't willing to walk away when anyone else would've been long gone.

No, I couldn't fathom why he was staying—what in God's name he saw in me that was worth all this bullshit— but I could understand well enough that, no, he didn't want to cut me loose. And somehow, I managed to whisper, "I want this. Us." I winced. "Even with the spotlight on us like that."

Hunter shrugged. "I didn't want the pressure of the spotlight on us, but I think the fear and stress of keeping it a secret took more of a toll than I realized."

"There is that," I acknowledged. "I wish we could've come out on our terms."

"Me too." He closed some of the space between us, and when his fingertips brushed my cheek, my knees almost dropped out from under me. "This... it's not ideal, how it happened, but maybe it's okay in the long run, you know?"

I nodded. "Yeah. Maybe? I hope."

"It is. And... look, I can't tell you I'm in love with you," Hunter whispered from way, way too close. "It's too soon. And it would feel like a desperation play right now. Some- thing to keep you from letting me go instead of because I just genuinely want to tell you. It... I don't know. It wouldn't be honest, I guess? Plus we already had our hand forced with coming out—I don't want to lose this, too. If we get there—*when* we get there—it needs to happen on its own time, you know?" He tipped up my chin so I'd meet his gaze, and his eyes were full of sincerity as he said, "I want to give us that time." He swallowed hard, and his voice came out thick but full of determination "We've already had a lot taken away from us. There is no way in hell I'm letting anyone take away my shot at falling for you."

I exhaled. I had no idea what to say, or if I'd be able to even get the words out before I lost it, so I did the next best thing.

And oh, God, the familiar brush of his beard against my chin and the softness of his lips on mine... It hadn't been all that long since we'd touched, but the last few hours had made time stretch out, and everything before we were outed suddenly seemed like it was on the other side of a giant canyon of time.

Holding him tight, I slid my hand up into his hair and opened to his insistent kiss. Even now, with his touch echoing everything he'd said, it was hard to believe this was real. I'd given this man every reason to want nothing to do with me, and he'd not only stubbornly stuck around, he wanted to *keep* sticking around. He wanted a chance to fall for me like I was pretty sure I'd long ago fallen for him.

I'd pulled away just like Eliška said I would.

And he'd come back.

Because Hunter, I could truly believe in this moment, wanted me.

CHAPTER 36

HUNTER

It was a solid minute or two before anything registered beyond relief. Jarek wasn't showing me the door—he was holding on to me for dear life. All the fear I'd had on the way to Cranberry and into his condo, it—it all evaporated in the heat of this long, languid kiss.

Little by little, though, an entirely different kind of heat made itself known. The kiss deepened and intensified. Relief gave way to a kind of hunger I'd never felt before—all the usual desire I had for him coupled with a deep-seated need to make sure this was all real. I needed to be as close to him as two men could get, both because I always wanted him and because I was still afraid that even a sliver of space between us would turn into too much.

From the way he kissed me and slid his hands all over my body... this was not a one-sided feeling.

Leaning against his kitchen island, kissing and rutting against each other, should've felt quick and dirty. It should've felt frantic and messy and primal—barely a step up from a men's room or the backseat of a car.

This wasn't what I imagined when I thought about

making love with someone, but that was exactly what this was. Still hungry, still greedy, still friction and gasps and sharp curses swallowed up by deep, demanding kisses. Still something that was absolutely going to devolve into a breathless and half-dressed fuck over a piece of furniture.

But it was pure lovemaking at the same time.

I couldn't explain it. I couldn't begin to figure out how all that could be happening simultaneously. Mostly because I was too busy holding on to Jarek, sliding my hands all over him and memorizing him as if committing his whole body to memory again would make this real. Because in that moment, it was surreal that we'd ever made it to this at all, impossible to comprehend that we'd danced along the edge of losing it, and fucking *mind-blowing* to believe that we'd landed back here.

"I want you so bad," I slurred between kisses. "Jesus, Jarek..."

"Me too." Some tension rippled through him. "I don't..." Jarek sighed, and when he drew back, there was some extra color in his cheeks that I didn't think was from being turned on. Avoiding my gaze, he whispered, "God, I don't even know if I can get off tonight. I've been so..." He closed his eyes and shook his head.

"I don't care."

He looked at me, brow creased.

Touching his face, I said, "Of course I want you to get off because I want you to be satisfied. But there's no pressure from me."

Jarek chewed his lip as uncertainty carved deeper lines in his forehead.

"Sex isn't what I need tonight." I ran my fingers through his hair. "It's you. That's all. The rest—we'll have plenty of nights." I held his gaze, and my voice threatened to give out as I whispered, "If you want us to."

Jarek exhaled and pulled me back into his arms, burying his face against my neck. His embrace was strong—almost too tight for me to breathe—but I returned it, closing my eyes as I drank in his familiar scent.

"I want us to," he murmured. "More than anything."

"Me too." I kissed his jaw, then loosened my embrace so we could see each other again. "We don't have to do anything tonight. I just want to be here. With you. That's all."

He studied me for a few heartbeats. Then, right as I was about to plead my case and beg him to believe me, he curved a hand behind my neck, lowered his chin, and claimed my mouth.

With the way he held me, and with the thick ridge pressing in next to my own hard-on, I didn't think he was going to have any trouble performing tonight. Maybe he'd just needed some reassurance. Today had been a hell of a roller coaster, and when I'd been on my way into his condo, I probably couldn't have gotten it up, never mind gotten off.

But we were okay now. We were us. And from the way he touched me now, I was pretty sure he had what he needed, too. Even if he didn't I'd make sure he felt good tonight. I'd make sure—

"Oh my God..." The words tumbled out of my mouth as Jarek's palm slid over my dick. I shuddered so hard it was a miracle my knees didn't go out from under me. Or maybe they did, but I didn't notice because Jarek was holding me so tight I *couldn't* have fallen. "Jesus, baby..."

He grinned. "We need to take this to bed," he mumbled between kisses. "I need you naked."

If my mouth had still been connected to my brain, I'd have pointed out that he could have me naked right there if he wanted. But when Jarek kissed me like that, when his hard dick pushed against me the way it did whenever he was two seconds away from grabbing a condom and going to town on me...

Screw words. And anyway, the bedroom sounded like a damn good idea, so I tugged him back a step. He got the message, and between us, we stumbled down the hall.

My hip bumped a chair as we crossed his living room, and a couple of brain cells lit up with a better idea than going all the way to his bed. With a handful of his shirt and a couple of decisive steps backward, I dragged him down on top of me on his couch. Jarek didn't protest; he growled from deep in his throat as he kissed me hard and thrust his clothed dick against mine. We weren't in his bed, and we weren't naked yet, but... to hell with it. I wanted him. Now. At least we weren't wearing jeans; these suit trousers were thin enough and soft enough to let me fucking *feel* him. I could barely breathe, barely think—all I could do was feel him as my head went light and my whole body hummed with need.

"Too many..." He nipped my lower lip. "Sakra, too many clothes."

"Then get out of the way," I murmured.

He lifted his hips a little, and we both fumbled with belts and zippers. There was nothing graceful about frantically shoving clothes out of the way, but graceful was overrated when I needed Jarek's body against mine. With some shifting and cursing, we managed to shove pants and underwear far enough out of the way to get to what we wanted, and we even managed to open some shirt buttons while we were at it.

Then we were pumping each other. Moving together.

Breathing together. Lips brushing but not quite connecting as we both panted and swore and pleaded.

God, he was hot. And he was here. And I was his. All his. The fear of losing him had cooled, but the remnants of it were still vivid enough to make me desperate for him, and everything my hands and mouth begged for, he gave me in spades. He had me so damn hot. So damn *high*. I wanted to come, and I wanted him to come, and—

I grabbed the back of his neck and kissed him hard, and then I was coming, thrusting up into his fist in search of all the friction I could find, and the way Jarek groaned into my kiss almost made me come undone.

In seconds, he followed me right over the edge, his hot cum mixing with mine between us on my stomach, and he broke the kiss with a moaned curse as he shuddered and trembled above me.

Then we were still. He slumped over me, panting and trembling, and I let my hand slide off the back of his neck.

Holy hell, we were an absolute mess. Both of us shaking. Cum all over us. Clothes rumpled and half pulled off.

It was perfect.

It was ours, too. No one here but us to see it and know about it. No one to out us. We'd never put the cat back in the bag, but maybe I could live with that moment at the club being tarnished when we'd still have so many other moments that would be ours and only ours. It didn't fix what had happened, but it did take out some of the sting.

Today was a bump in the road. The future was ours.

Yeah, I could live with that.

After a moment or two of catching our breath, Jarek pressed the softest, sweetest kiss to my lips. Then he lifted himself enough to meet my eyes. He stroked my cheek with his clean hand, and when he spoke, his voice came out as a ragged whisper. "I don't need more time. I've known for a while." He kissed me again, lightly this time. "I love you, Hunter."

God, my heart. I cupped his face and claimed a longer kiss.

He broke away first, and he pressed his lips to my forehead. "You don't have to say it. I don't want to pressure you. I just..." He held my gaze. "I just wanted to you to know, but I—"

"Baby. Shut up." I lifted my head to steal a kiss. "I do love you. I so fucking do."

The confusion written all over his face was adorable. "But you said—"

"I know. I know." I ran my fingers through his mussed hair. "I... Look, I was panicking, and also I didn't want it to be a hail Mary. Something I just threw out there to keep you from pushing me away. I wanted you to *believe* me when I said it." I had to swallow a couple of times as I stroked fingertips along his sharp jaw. "But we're both complete dumbasses if we can't see that I am stupidly in love with you."

Jarek blinked. "You... You are?"

"Yes," I said on a soft laugh. "Or hadn't you noticed how you couldn't chase me off even when you were being a prickly asshole?"

Color bloomed in his cheeks as he chuckled. "Okay. Okay. Point taken." He shifted a little on top of me, and his face took on a wry look. "Do you think Rachel would have heart failure if we told this story to the media?"

"What? Me telling you we're dumbasses because of course I love you?"

He half-shrugged. "And the part where we're..." He

gestured between us, reminding me of the somewhat messy state we were in.

I couldn't help it—I burst out laughing. He did too, and he buried his face against my neck as I held on to him and we both laughed like dorks.

After a while, Jarek lifted his head, pausing to kiss beneath my jaw. "Maybe we should clean ourselves up and go someplace more comfortable." He nodded toward his left arm, which he'd been resting most of his weight on. "My arm is falling asleep."

I grinned. "Your shower, and then your bed?"

Jarek's grin was pure magic. "Sounds perfect."

CHAPTER 37

JAREK

I hadn't thought anything could ever surpass the disbelief of having Hunter Michaud in my bed the first time.

I'd been so, so wrong, because lying here with him now didn't even feel real. For as much as I'd convinced myself he'd bolt now that our relationship was causing him headache and humiliation, he was here, warm and naked and holding me like *he* was afraid *I'd* let go.

Because I almost had. I'd almost shoved him away.

Stroking his hair, I pressed a kiss to his forehead. "I'm a lucky man."

He looked up at me. "Oh yeah?"

"Mmhmm." I smirked. "Because you're a stubborn fucker."

That startled laughter made my spine tingle. He was just so damn gorgeous.

"All right, fine," he said through his chuckling. "You got me there. I am a stubborn bastard." He cuddled closer to me. "When I see something I want, anyway." From the way he kissed me, even my disbelief over all this being real couldn't question that I was that something he wanted. I still struggled to imagine I deserved him, but he'd made it quite clear it wasn't up for discussion. Somehow, by some miracle, Hunter believed I deserved him. End of story.

"You're amazing," I murmured against his lips. "Just so you know."

"Oh, I know. I've seen my stats."

It was my turn for a startled laugh, and he chuckled too. God, I loved this man.

"So humble," I said, and claimed a kiss. We were both still laughing, but it only took a second or two for our lips to soften into something very, very nice. It had been a long time since I'd slept with someone who liked kissing as much as Hunter did, and even longer since someone who was as good at it. The fact that we were doing more than sleeping together—well, maybe that would sink in eventually. If this novelty decided to stick around, and my mind was still blown every time we touched or kissed... I couldn't complain.

After a little while, Hunter broke the kiss and settled back on the pillow, though he didn't let me go. Another thing I couldn't complain about—how much he loved to just hold me.

Running his hand up and down my arm, he said, "Okay, getting outed and everything sucks..." To my surprise, a grin spread across his lips. "But as long as we're stuck with it, I mean, it's not *all* bad."

I cocked a brow. "It isn't?"

"No. For one, we don't have to fly under anyone's radar anymore."

I considered it and shrugged. "Fine. I'll give you that."

"Annnd we're a positive queer presence for young queer fans. Plus the response to us has been mostly good. Like, not a ton of homophobia, you know?"

He did make a valid point, and I conceded, "True."

"Also..." Mischief suddenly lit up in his eyes. "I don't know if you've looked since this morning, but some of the memes that have come out of this are *gold.*"

My eyebrows had to be in my hair by now. "Oh, really?"

"Uh-huh." He grabbed his phone off the nightstand, then curled against me so we could both see the screen. "Check these out."

I was, to say the least, dubious. I'd spent enough of my career being the butt of jokes and the subject of memes, I really didn't relish giving social media comedians more ammunition.

It turned out, though... Hunter was right.

Under the hashtag #Michura—*really, guys?*—there were dozens of memes featuring us.

One was a photo of us on the bench. I was staring out at the ice while Hunter was furrowing his brow at an iPad, his glove off as he tapped the screen. The caption: *Michaud, googling: Valentine's gifts for hockey lovers*

"Okay, that's kind of cute," I admitted.

"It is. But how the hell did they see what I was typing?"

I chuckled, rolled my eyes, and kissed his temple.

He kept scrolling, and another meme showed the two of us reacting to a goal against. At the top of the image, it showed a tied score and about four seconds left in the third period. We were both exhausted and frustrated as our opponents celebrated behind us. I was scowling. Hunter had his eyes closed and his head tilted back in a look that screamed, *oh, fuck my life.*

And the caption? *Not us going into OT on date night.*

I snorted. "Okay, that's a good one."

"I know, right?" Hunter chuckled and scrolled down. "Oh, I love this one!" He shoved the phone at me.

This time, it was an image of me in that fight in Toronto after that asswipe had boarded Hunter. We'd already gone down, and I was looming over him, my face bloody and a ref trying to pull me off before I threw another punch into Evans's idiot face. Below it: *GIRRRL DON'T YOU TOUCH MY BOO.*

I barked a laugh. "Jesus."

"I should keep this one as my lockscreen."

"You would, too."

"Mmhmm." He tapped the screen. "Done."

I rolled my eyes. "Seriously?"

He showed me his phone as he flashed me a toothy grin. Sure enough, the meme was now his lockscreen.

"You're ridiculous."

His shrug was as unrepentant as his grin.

I laughed and leaned in for a light kiss. As I settled on my pillow, though, I sighed. "I'm still... The memes are funny. And I like that we don't have to hide. But it's..." I wiped a hand over my face.

Hunter watched me, his expression serious. Trailing the backs of his fingers along my forearm, he said, "Tell me."

I didn't immediately, and he didn't push. Maybe he sensed that I needed to pull all my thoughts together into something coherent, and from there, into my second language.

"I don't like the spotlight," I said after a long moment. "Not like this. Even when it's been something good—like when I hit a hundred points in a season for the first time after..." I waved a hand. "Whenever the cameras are on me, I'm afraid they're going to..."

"Figure out what happened earlier in your career?"

"Something like that. It's..." I sighed and rolled my eyes. "It's stupid. No one's going to see through me and figure out what I did, and... I mean..." I laughed nervously. "I know, it's stupid. It isn't like I committed a murder or something. But it's..." My humor faded, and I had no idea how to finish that sentence. How to explain the sick feeling that swelled in my gut whenever I thought too long about that awful season.

"Jarek." Hunter touched my face. "It's not stupid. It had a big impact on your career and your life."

"And yours," I whispered.

"Yeah. It did. But you were young and beaten down. I took shit from the same guys who did that to you, so I totally get why you did it." He paused, then softly added, "I was afraid of them, too."

The comment had my throat tightening around my breath. I didn't want Hunter to have been afraid of them—I didn't want anyone to know what it was like to feel that sick and terrified every time they came to practice or a game—but it was liberating, too. He'd told me before, but even hearing it for the second time—it was a relief to know it wasn't all in my imagination. That the man whose world had been affected as much as mine by what I'd done not only didn't hold it against me, he understood what had driven me to do it.

And he must've also understood that my silence was me trying to process all of that, because he just gathered me in his arms and held me against him. Eyes closed, I returned his embrace and buried my face against his neck. I didn't break down. I wondered if he expected me to. On some level, I expected me to, but... no. This was more like... settling onto solid ground. Like I'd spent so long feeling like the world was going to collapse under me, I just needed to take a moment to feel the safety of something firm beneath my feet.

Hunter knew about me, and he understood. The world knew about us, and the people who mattered accepted us. We'd been thrust out into the spotlight as a couple before we were ready, and if anything, we were better for it now. No more secrecy. No more fear of being outed. It was still bullshit that we'd *been* outed, but we'd be okay.

When I'd done exactly what Eliška had predicted I would, shoving away the people who tried to love me, Hunter had grabbed on and said we were going to weather this together. Despite my panicked efforts, I hadn't lost him. He was holding me close to him, letting the dust settle around us, not between us in the space I'd tried to create.

I kissed the side of his neck. "Anyone ever tell you you're stubborn as fuck?"

Hunter laughed. "It's come up a time or two."

Releasing him, I pulled back enough to meet his gaze. "Too stubborn to let me run away." I half-shrugged. "I'll take it."

Hunter's smile was the sweetest thing I'd ever seen. "I'd have let you run if you'd really wanted to. I wasn't going to force you to stay with me." He caressed my cheek as his voice turned more serious. "But I'd have made sure you knew I'd still be here when you finally came back."

I held his gaze, searching for insincerity even though I knew to my core I wouldn't find it. Then I exhaled and pulled him back in. "You're something else."

He murmured something I didn't catch, kissed my cheek and held me.

We stayed like that for a while before we let each other go, and as I sat back, I sighed. "I'm a fucking mess, aren't I? All fucked up in the head from everything that happened back then, and so quick to panic that my sister knew I'd push you away when things got..." I trailed off, shaking my head.

"You're not fucked up." He ran his fingers through my hair. "But you can always talk to someone, you know. Like a counselor." I stiffened, but before I could protest, he added, "They're bound by doctor-patient confidentiality. They can't repeat a word of what you've said to anyone."

I chewed my lip. "Is it irrational to not want to trust that after we got outed? I know Lanterns isn't legally—" I waved a hand. "I know it's not the same. But..."

"But you've got trust issues," he whispered. "Baby, anyone would after the shit you've been through. Especially when you're a public figure and your business can get a ton of exposure."

I shuddered. Even here, in my bed with Hunter, my skin still crawled over us being outed. Yeah, I probably did need some therapy. I was probably long overdue for it. Still, I wasn't sure I was ready.

"I'll think about it," I said with total honesty. "But right now..." I shook my head.

"Okay." He slid closer to me. "I'm not going to force you. It's your decision."

"Thank you," I whispered. "And thank you for not giving up on me when I convinced myself you were already out the door."

Hunter's smile melted me all over. "I don't know if you remember from playing against me, but I *am* a stubborn son of a bitch sometimes."

"You mean like when you get the puck and rudely won't give it up?" I chuckled. "That's a lot less infuriating now that we're on the same team."

"Exactly." He sobered a little and draped his arm over me. "Seriously, though—I want this. What we have. If we make it or if we don't, I want that to be *our* decision. Not someone else's." He touched my face again. "I want us to have a shot at doing this, you know?"

I nodded slowly, covering his hand with mine. "I'm not used to people fighting for me."

"Well, get used to it." He lifted his chin and kissed me softly. "Because you are worth fighting for, and so is this."

I was going to get a lot more emotional than I wanted to in that moment, so I gripped the back of his neck and kissed him instead. From the soft little moan, he was onboard with that. Of course he was. I loved how much this man loved kissing.

And my God, for all Hunter was spectacular at dancing around players and getting behind another team's defense, I hadn't imagined he would also find a way past *my* defenses. That he'd have let me leave in a heartbeat if it was what I really wanted to do, but he wasn't about to let this be taken away from us. That *I* was something he refused to have taken away from him.

It blew my mind and almost drove me to tears that he saw what we had—what I was—as something worth fighting for. He'd have let me walk away if I really wanted to, but he'd known that I was running scared when all I wanted to do was hold on.

And now here we were. Wrapped up in each other. Together. On solid ground.

It was perfect.

But...

Hunter met my gaze. "What?"

My heart jumped into my throat. "Huh?"

"You tensed up." He ran his thumb along my jaw. "What's on your mind?"

I chewed my lip. "The whole thing about what I did—the past. It wasn't just what I did. It was why."

Hunter swallowed hard. "Wilcox and Robertson."

The names made my stomach lurch. "Yeah. The thing is, before I told you, I didn't tell anyone anything. None of it. And... I'm tired of keeping this secret."

His eyebrows shot up. "Are you?"

"Yes. I can't go public about what I did, but... I mean, I always thought Wilcox and Robertson were just fucking with *me*. But it wasn't. And it sounds like they're still doing it to other players."

"They are," Hunter said. "I know for a fact they were doing it to some of my buddies, but I'd bet money there were—and are—others. Almost no one talks about it, but it's just... It's a vibe, you know? The guys—especially the younger guys—are terrified of him."

I shuddered as both shame and that ages-old fear roiled in my stomach. "They can't keep doing that."

"No, they can't." Hunter's brow furrowed. "Do you... Do you want to do something about it? Like, drop the hammer and take action?"

I considered it. Of course that had even more fear welling inside me, a ball of ice chilling me to the bone, but there was also something else. A surge of determination I hadn't had before. As many times as I'd fantasized about taking down those assholes, I'd never imagined actually going through with it, but the fire of determination this time was too strong to be cooled by that ever-present ice.

Because I wouldn't be facing them down alone.

I met Hunter's gaze. "Together?"

The fire burning in my chest was right there in his eyes, and he nodded as he took my hand. "Absolutely." He swallowed. "You in?"

"You better believe it." I chewed my lip. "How, um... What do you think we should do, exactly?"

"We've got time to think of something." He paused. "Though, we play in Toronto again soon. Couple of weeks, I think." He brought my hand up and kissed my palm. "If you're good with waiting that long, I think I might have an idea."

"I've been waiting almost a damn decade," I breathed. "I can wait another couple of weeks."

"Good." Hunter's grin made my pulse soar. "Because if we do it there, I don't think we'll have to do it alone."

CHAPTER 38

HUNTER

"Are you sure about this?" Jarek asked from the passenger seat of the rental car.

I reached over and took his hand. "I am."

He said nothing. In silence, I drove through the familiar streets of Leaside. When we reached our destination, Gonzo's garage was open, his car parked in the driveway, and I pulled into one of the empty bays. The other bay was empty as well, but it wouldn't be for long.

I parked, and as we got out of the car, Gonzo stepped out of the house, Potts on his heels, and the door started coming down.

I greeted them both with a quick handshake-hug. Then, although pretty much every hockey player knew each other on sight, and I knew for a fact that Gonzo and Potts knew who Jarek was, I introduced the three of them anyway. This was, after all, the first time they'd met outside of a game.

Gonzo let us in and offered us coffee, which we declined. I noticed he and Potts weren't drinking anything either. In fact, they both looked as uneasy and wound up as Jarek and I were. Not surprising. If their stomachs were as tied up in knots as mine, they weren't interested in eating or drinking anything. And we sure as shit didn't need the caffeine. Not with all the twitching and weight-shifting as we made uncomfortable small talk in the kitchen.

We all tried to be slick about it, but everyone kept glancing at the clock on the microwave and at our phones. Soon. Not soon enough. Entirely too soon. But... soon.

The Pittsburgh Hornets had flown into Toronto late last night. We'd practiced this morning, and we had a few hours of downtime before we all had to be at the arena for tonight's game. I'd worried about doing this now, but honestly, once we'd dropped the hammer, there was no other way to do it. I would be useless playing tonight until this was over, and I suspected my friends and boyfriend would be too. Especially if we had to hear *his* voice when we knew—and he didn't—what was coming.

Gonzo's phone pinged, and everyone stiffened. He looked at the screen, then all of us. "He's here."

Without another word, he headed for the garage, and the three of us stayed in the kitchen, exchanging nervous glances.

A moment later, Gonzo returned. With him was the man we'd all come here to see.

Graham Norwood, the Toronto Shamrocks' president of hockey operations, looked from one of us to the next. "This is, um... Unusual."

"We know," I said. "But we couldn't think of any other way to be discreet."

Norwood's eyebrows rose. "Discreet? What exactly is this about?"

A fair question—Potts and Gonzo had approached him and said that we needed to meet with him away from Toronto Shamrocks facilities, and that we needed to meet with him alone. All they'd said was that it was important and it couldn't wait.

Now that he'd come this far, the man deserved an explanation.

Potts folded his arms and leaned against the counter, probably trying to look a lot more relaxed than he was. "We've got a leadership problem. And the four of us"—he gestured at himself, Gonzo, Jarek, and me—"*need* to know that everything we say is going to be kept completely confidential."

I couldn't be sure, but I thought Norwood's complexion lost a shade or two. When his gaze landed on Jarek, his spine straightened. He'd known Jarek was here, of course, but when he glanced at him this time, something seemed to click in his mind. As if he might've had some inkling of what was going on. He sounded grim as he asked, "Am I to assume this is a, um... ongoing problem?"

Jarek nodded. "Doesn't sound like anything has changed since I was here. Not for the better, anyway."

Norwood breathed a curse and rubbed a hand over his bald head. "All right. Well." He looked from one of us to the next. "I'm here. Let's talk."

After some discussion, it was agreed that we would each talk to him one-on-one, which made me think all three of them had some things they needed to get off their chests without an audience. God knew I did.

I had no idea how much Jarek would tell him. He'd said a few times he might tell the whole story. Others, he'd balked and decided to keep it to himself. I'd promised to support him regardless of how many cards he did and didn't show. I wasn't even sure how many *I* would show.

Hopefully, between the four of us, we'd all lay down

enough cards for Norwood to see that there was a serious problem.

Gonzo got Norwood a cup of coffee, then took him downstairs to the rec room. There, one by one, we would each go down and talk to him.

Even after the guys came up after their turns, I didn't know how much Jarek, Potts, or Gonzo told him. That was between them and him. What I did know was that Potts needed a few minutes alone afterward. Gonzo sat on the living room floor and played with his kids, probably to decompress. I think it helped.

Every time someone came out, rattled and off-balance, I dreaded my own conversation with him even more. There were things I'd never told anyone, not even Jarek, and I still wasn't sure I could get it all out today. One minute I was determined to put it all out there. The next... not so much.

Finally, it was my turn to go downstairs.

Or, well, it would be in a minute. Jarek had just come up from the rec room, sweat darkening the edges of his hair. I touched his face and searched his eyes. "You all right?"

He rolled his shoulders and released a long breath. "Trying to decide if I'm going to puke or not."

From where he was still playing with his kids, Gonzo called out, "Bathroom's down the hall. Second door on the left." He wasn't being snarky or a jackass about it. If nothing else, he sounded sympathetic, same as he had earlier when Potts had gone straight in there to get sick after talking to Norwood. And Gonzo still looked a bit green himself.

"I think I'm good," Jarek croaked. "Well, I hope I'm good."

I chewed my lip. Norwood was waiting for me, but I didn't want to bail on Jarek.

He must've understood, because he rested a hand on my waist. "Go. I'll be fine."

"Are you sure?"

He glanced toward Gonzo, then met my gaze, and a small smile appeared. "I'll be fine."

I looked at Gonzo too, and he offered up a reassuring nod.

Okay, I could live with that. I wasn't bailing on Jarek and leaving him alone. I paused for a soft kiss, and as I headed downstairs, couldn't help smiling as I heard Jarek asking the kids, "Ooh, are those Lego?"

Yeah, he'd be fine for now.

Me, on the other hand...

Fuck. My own conversation with Norwood was cathartic, painful, liberating, exhausting, and fucking nauseating. I hadn't even realized how much it had all piled on over my seven long seasons in Toronto until it all came tumbling out in a single conversation. It was like my tenure on the Shamrocks had been death by a thousand cuts spread out over several years, and tonight I was feeling every single one of them again.

I laid it all out, too. The way Coach Robertson would scream at me in front of our teammates. The way he'd threaten me in private. How he'd constantly tell me the only reason I'd been so in demand during my draft year was because everyone wanted to virtue signal that they'd drafted a queer player.

"It was hell," I said shakily. "Just... Christ." I raked a hand through my hair, which turned out to be damp with sweat. "Every fucking time he took me into his office, I was scared shitless."

Norwood studied me. "What exactly were you scared

of? That you'd get released from your contract? Because Toronto would've rioted in the streets."

"No," I whispered. "I mean... yeah. There was that. He threatened me with it enough times. And no, the fans wouldn't have taken it well, so it was probably an empty threat, but it didn't feel like it in the moment."

Norwood deflated back against his chair, wiping a hand over his face. "Man. I'm sorry, kid. I had no idea."

"It's worse than that." My voice came out hollow. "Most of the time when I was in his office, I was afraid of..." My tongue tried to stick to the roof of my mouth. "I mean, I've fought on the ice, you know? I've taken punches. And no one's ever going to hit me harder than that puck that broke my jaw. But whenever he had me up against the wall like that, I—"

"You thought he was going to whale on you." The man didn't even sound surprised, which made me wonder if Jarek, Potts, and Gonzo had said something similar. I knew Jarek had been afraid of the same thing. I'd once run into Potts trembling badly after an encounter with Robertson, and the way he hadn't been able to look me in the eye or tell me what happened... I could guess. Shaken as Potts was that day, sometimes I still wondered if Robertson *had* taken a swing at him. Gonzo, I didn't know, but I wasn't putting anything past Robertson.

"He never touched me," I told Norwood, and I was a little embarrassed by the way my voice wavered as I finally said the words to someone other than my boyfriend: "But I was *absolutely* sure every single time that he was going to."

"Jesus H. Christ," Norwood muttered. He glanced down at some notes he'd been taking, then met my gaze. "What about Wilcox? Was it just Robertson, or did—"

"Oh, God, no," I said on a caustic laugh. "He was

always threatening me with my contract or a trade to some awful team. Or being sent down to the minors."

"You?" Norwood scoffed. "Every member of this team's management would've been fired in an instant if Hunter Michaud set foot on the farm team for anything other than rehab."

On some level, I knew that. It wasn't hubris—people fucking told me as much. "Tell that to a kid who's under that much pressure and is terrified of the people in charge." I swallowed. "And he knew I was scared of Robertson, because he would always threaten to bring him into our meetings so they could both talk sense into me."

"Talk sense—" Norwood pushed out a breath. "What were they even so upset with you about? You were a star in this city. Christ, you were the *last* member of the team who needed to straighten out or work harder."

"Maybe so." Fuck, my voice really was ragged now. "But they told me from the start they expected me to make this a winning team. They expected me to take them to the top. I..." I had to stop to clear my throat and take a breath. "One of the reasons I signed with Pittsburgh was that they *explicitly* told me the only way I could play there was if I understood I would be part of the team. This would *not*, under any circumstances, be the Hunter Michaud show." I looked him right in the eyes even as my composure wavered. "That's all I ever wanted. I carried this whole fucking team on my back for *seven seasons*, and it was never enough. All I ever got was shit for not singlehandedly hauling Toronto to a Cup win." I put up my hands. "I am one player. I don't care how good I am—I need a team around me. Not a coach and GM who expect me to work actual fucking miracles and then threaten me when I can't."

Whoa. Shit. That had all just come pouring out, and at

this point, I didn't even care that he could see me swiping at my stupid eyes with an unsteady hand. Show me someone who wouldn't get all fucking emotional after letting that out, especially after all this time *and* to a man with the power to do something about it.

Not that I had much faith that he would. On the other hand, he'd come here. He'd listened to us. Maybe...?

After a long moment, Norwood scrubbed a hand over his face again and sighed heavily. "To tell you the truth, I almost fired Wilcox when he couldn't get you to re-sign. Maybe I should've trusted that instinct. I definitely should've caught on that something was going on in the locker room."

"For what it's worth," I said, "he tried to get me to re-sign."

"There wasn't a chance in hell, though, was there?"

"Not as long as he and Robertson were still there."

He swore under his breath. Then his eyes lost focus, and he must've rewound what I'd said, because he admitted, "I never realized Robertson was homophobic."

I considered that. "I don't know if he really is, honestly."

He eyed me.

"I mean, he's not much an ally, but if I'd been straight, he'd have grabbed on to something else to use against me. I know he liked to lord people's visas over them, too, if they were only in Canada to play hockey. Like all he had to do was make a few phone calls and they'd be deported."

Norwood huffed. "That's... not really how that works."

I looked right in his eyes. "Tell that to a scared teenager who's constantly being threatened with losing the one thing he's worked for his entire life."

He deflated, and I though he lost a little color. "Jesus Christ..."

I shifted in my seat. "And this, um... This *is* all confidential, right?"

"Absolutely. He might put two and two together if he's only caused problems for a select few players, but..." Norwood's broad shoulders sank as he sagged back against his chair. "Somehow I don't think this was isolated to just the four of you. Especially not if it's been going on since Badura was a Shamrock."

I didn't want to be relieved by that. It wasn't right, finding comfort in the fact that Robertson had probably terrorized enough of us that he wouldn't be absolutely sure who'd ratted him out. He'd have his suspicions, sure, especially if Norwood took action sooner than later, like while Pittsburgh was still in town. But he'd never know for sure.

I felt guilty for my relief. It would've been terrifying, being the only one who needed to blow this whistle, but there were likely enough of us that my face would get lost in a crowd of other hockey players who'd also been scared to death of the man who was supposed to lead us. And shit, hadn't he coached in the minors before he got this job? Fuck. That was a thought.

Well, however many people Robertson had fucked with, hopefully it was stopping here. I was sure—maybe naïvely—that Norwood planned to do something meaningful about this.

If he didn't, then I guess people would know it was me who blew the whistle, because I would be telling a room full of cameras and microphones about something a hell of a lot more scandalous than my relationship with Jarek.

Norwood asked me a few more questions, mostly to clarify some timelines and make sure he understood a couple of situations. Then he dismissed me.

When we came upstairs, I wasn't at all surprised to see

Jarek sitting on the floor with Gonzo, Potts, and the kids. The guys got up for a moment to debrief with Norwood, who said he'd take everything we said back to the club— anonymously, of course—and that it wouldn't go unanswered.

"I appreciate you boys telling me all this," he said as he shook each of our hands. "I'm sorry you had such a shitty experience in this city. Hopefully we can make sure that stops."

We thanked him, and he left. All four of us exchanged looks, but no one said anything. We just rejoined Gonzo's kids on the living room floor. The kids were in seventh heaven; they had no idea what was going on in the basement or why their dad and Jarek needed a distraction. They were just happy to have Dad, Potts, and this new guy playing with them.

I didn't need my arm twisted to join them, and yeah, it helped. I was still rattled and queasy, both from feeling like I'd just pulled open all my old wounds and the fear that this would, despite Norwood's reassurances, blow back on us all somehow. A few times, I considered taking up Gonzo on the offer of using his bathroom down the hall to heave a few times, but the longer I sat here with my teammates, my boyfriend, the kids, and this pile of Legos... I mean, it didn't solve anything, but it cooled some of the acid in the back of my throat. Made me think I could keep my stomach where it belonged.

I must not have been the only one, because after a while, Gonzo said, "Anyone else feel like pizza or something? I swear I could eat a large by myself."

"How is that different from usual?" Potts asked. "You always eat—"

"You want pizza or not?"

"I do, but I'm just saying—"

"Oh my God." Gonzo elbowed him. "What about you two? Pizza?"

Jarek shrugged. "I could eat."

We did have a few hours yet before we needed to be at the arena, so why not? "I'm in."

Potts held up his phone. "I'll order. Gonzo, see if the kids want anything."

Right. Because kids were going to say no to pizza.

While they handled getting food on the way, Jarek and I stepped into the dining room for a moment alone.

He stroked my cheek. "How did it go?"

"It was tough," I said. "Tougher than I thought it would be."

Concern etched deep creases across his forehead. "You all right?"

"I'm good. It just sucked. I'm glad it's over."

"Me too. And I... didn't tell him everything. I..." He shook his head. "I couldn't. I can't."

I wrapped my arms around him and kissed his cheek. "It's okay. I think between us, we told him enough."

Deflating, Jarek nodded. "I hope so." He chewed his lip. "I can't decide if it's rational or not to be afraid Wilcox and Robertson will retaliate by outing me for throwing that season."

"It doesn't have to be rational." I ran my fingers through his hair. "And for what it's worth, I don't think they will."

An arched eyebrow asked me to elaborate.

"If they admit they knew what you were doing," I said, "they'll have to explain why they kept putting you in for first line minutes. Why they didn't discipline you or do... *something*. At best, they'd be confessing to incompetence. At worst, admitting they put you up to it."

Jarek's eyes lost focus, and little by little, some tension slipped out of his posture. He leaned into me and released a long, heavy sigh. "Thank you," he whispered.

I wasn't sure what to make of that. Though as I held him, the pieces clicked into place—one of the fears he'd had dangling over his head all this time was probably that if he stepped out of line, Wilcox and Robertson would make sure he burned for what he did. It likely hadn't occurred to him that they had something to lose, too. And even now, if Norwood took our accusations and sent those men down in flames, their credibility would be shot no matter what.

If I had to guess, Jarek was realizing that after all these years, Joe Wilcox and Hal Robertson couldn't hurt him anymore.

However this all shook out for them, it was over for Jarek.

Finally.

———

The fallout was swift to say the least. Usually, there were investigations into these things that could take weeks, if not months.

But when we played Toronto that night, Coach Robertson was conspicuously missing behind the home bench. The game was chippy, of course, and the team was snarly and spicy with us, but the checks weren't so rough and nobody was spoiling for a fight. Whether that was because of how bad things had gone last time or because Norwood had said something, I had no idea, but I appreciated leaving the ice on my own power rather than a stretcher.

The fans were also... kinder. I still got some token

booing, but there was a surprising amount of applause, too. During warmups, someone on our end had a sign that read *Hate That You're A Hornet, Glad You're Okay* next to my number. I tossed him a puck.

In the end, we won five-two, which broke a short losing streak we'd been on lately. Both the losses and the win had probably been at least in part because of today; Jarek and I had both been dreading our meeting with Norwood, and it was a huge relief for it to be over. The absence of Robertson's voice in the building definitely didn't hurt.

And speaking of that asshole, by the time we were dressed and eating after the game, the Toronto Shamrocks had announced that he was "taking an indefinite leave of absence."

I texted Gonzo to ask if he had any more info. He responded, *Norwood told me & Potts he didn't want Robertson around any players until this is sorted out.*

You think they're gonna fire him?

Don't know. But Cams said he saw Wilcox leaving in a hurry. Said he didn't look too happy neither.

I showed the texts to Jarek.

He swallowed hard as he handed back my phone. "Let's hope this means they're getting fired."

"I know, right?" I smirked. "Is it too much to ask for tarred and feathered, too?"

His laughter made my heart soar. God, it was good to see him with so much years-old weight off his shoulders. "Just making it all public would make me happy."

I agreed. As much as I valued privacy, these men had hurt too many people. They deserved to burn out in the open.

On our way out to the buses, we ran into Potts and Gonzo, and we chatted with them for a few minutes. They hadn't had much chance to talk to Jarek today since we'd all been otherwise occupied, and the conversation quickly shifted to the four of us getting together in Pittsburgh when Toronto came to town next week. Jarek was telling them about a couple of different restaurants we could consider, and I realized we were running behind to catch the bus.

I touched his shoulder. "I'm going to go down and make sure the bus doesn't leave without us." To Gonzo and Potts, I said, "I'll see you guys in town next week. And thanks again, man. For letting us do this at your place."

"No sweat." Gonzo pulled me into a bear hug. "Take care, all right? We'll all do something this offseason, too. Not just dinner when we're in town!"

"You got it."

While Jarek finished up chatting with Gonzo and Potts, I headed downstairs, and I couldn't help smiling. We did it. We'd won. Wilcox and Robertson had done immeasurable damage to countless players, but it looked like they were finished. Going down in flames like they so richly deserved to. I just hoped the League didn't decide to have them quietly retire or something.

Tell the world, or I will.

I continued down a flight of stairs and followed the familiar route toward where the buses parked. As I walked, I didn't think anything of it when another set of footsteps joined mine in the otherwise deserted hallway. We still had time to get to the bus, and I doubted Jarek and I were the only stragglers.

Thinking it was a teammate or a staffer, or that Jarek had caught up with me, I glanced over my shoulder.

And I almost stumbled.

"You little *bitch*." Coach Robertson strode right up to me. "It was you, wasn't it?"

"I..." Fuck. All that old familiar fear ripped through me, and I froze, suddenly nineteen and speechless. "What are you even—"

"Oh, don't play stupid." He stopped in front of me, giving me that look that always made me feel two inches tall. Stabbing a finger at me, he hissed, "It was either you, or that worthless asshole you've been screw—"

"I don't know what you're talking about." It was easy to play stupid and clueless in front of him. Even when I knew exactly what he was talking about, he sent me right back to the terrified rookie whose mind went blank when that voice barked at me. Showing my palms, I shakily said, "I didn't say—"

"That's a load of horseshit," he spat, and he drove me back a step. My shoulder blades hit the wall, and we were back in his office. Fear. Deep, cold, nauseating fear as Robertson tore into me. I couldn't even understand most of what he was saying through the sickening terror he'd instilled in me. "You're fucking useless, Michaud!" Yeah, I caught that part. Heard it plenty of times before. "A useless piece of—"

"Hey!" Jarek came out of nowhere and stepped in between us. The gap was narrow enough he brushed up against me, and Jarek—Jesus, he got *right* up in Robertson's face and hissed, "Step off, Coach!"

Robertson staggered back a couple of steps, clearly caught off guard. Jarek followed, opening up some space between us, but Robertson recovered fast and got right in Jarek's face, as if he might either send *him* back a step or goad him into taking a swing. "You were in on it, too, weren't you, *Joke?*"

I could feel Jarek's hackles going up. Oh, fuck. We did

not need him losing his temper. Not here. Not like this. I touched his arm. "Jarek…"

He shrugged me off and glared down at our old coach. "Why would I be in on it?" His laugh was even more caustic than mine. "You think I'm the only player who thinks you're an asshole who should've been fired years ago?"

"I was the only coach who ever had a shot at getting through your thick fucking skull," Robertson threw back. "You were as useless as *he* was." He pointed sharply past me, the gesture making both of us flinch, especially Jarek. Probably because Robertson's finger almost stabbed his shoulder. "I know the two of you are behind ruining my career, and I'm going to make sure—"

"Fuck you," Jarek snarled. "You didn't deserve either of us on your team." He gave Robertson a caustic laugh. "How's it feel, huh? Losing to two players you thought were shit? Seeing them on a team that's already this close to clinching a spot in the playoffs?" His voice turned even colder. "Guess all we needed was a competent coach so we could—"

Coach Robertson's fist sent Jarek stumbling back. He cursed as his hand went to his face, and I caught him by the shoulders, hauling him back before he retaliated. Every hockey player knew it wasn't the guy who threw the first punch who went to the box—it was the one who retaliated.

Robertson followed him, fist upraised again. "Come on, you worthless excuse for a hockey player. Show me you can actually fight for once!"

And that was when we learned that some security guards, having apparently heard the commotion, had joined us in the hallway.

Everything happened fast after that. Or maybe I was just too rattled and disoriented. The post-fear crash, the adrenaline dropping out from under me, the renewed spike of fear as I saw Jarek wiping blood from his nose.

"Jesus." I touched his arm. "You okay?"

He nodded, and one of the security guards handed him a wad of paper towels. No idea where they'd come from, but gift horse, mouth, etc. Jarek dabbed them gingerly to his nose and upper lip, almost muffling a string of curses.

In between mopping up the blood, he looked at me and raised his eyebrows. "Are *you* okay?"

"He didn't touch me," I said shakily.

Jarek saw right through me. "We both know he didn't need to touch you."

Fuck. The bottom dropped right out of whatever was holding me together, and I sagged against the wall as I tried to stop the shaking. Tried to catch my breath.

"Hey. Hunter." Jarek touched my face. "Breathe, baby. Breathe. He's gone. He's done."

But he wasn't. He was still here. His voice was still echoing through the hallway as he argued with security. Someone was informing him the cops were on their way down, and that he was probably going to jail tonight for both trespassing and assault and battery.

Robertson was still shouting, though. The voice. That anger. The echoes of him screaming at me. The blood on my boyfriend's face that was confirmation of my worst fear through seven miserable years on this team.

Except...

No.

Reality cracked through the cascade of panic, and steadily, the breaths I was taking were enough. The wall against my back was keeping me on my feet, not taking me back to my old coach's office.

Because, no, this *wasn't* my biggest fear playing out.

Because in all those worst-case scenarios, I'd been alone. Escaping with a bloody nose and maybe all of my teeth to someplace quiet and private to let the shaking subside. Puking a few times before pulling myself together while I came up with an explanation my teammates and friends would believe.

None of that was happening now.

And when I told Jarek I'd be okay, I believed it. I think he did, too, because after giving my arm a reassuring squeeze, he let himself be pulled away to be checked out.

I took a seat on a concrete step and let my head fall forward as I pushed out a harsh, ragged breath. The world around me started to slow down, and my heart came with it. I'd probably have nightmares about that confrontation, not to mention the punch at Jarek, but the real living nightmare was on its way to over.

Robertson had finally crossed that red line, and instead of having to face him alone, Jarek and I suddenly had people stepping in from all directions. A security guard— who turned out to also be an EMT—was checking Jarek over. Toronto police had been in the building already, and they were now frog-marching Robertson out of the stadium.

All this time, I'd been so sure that if shit ever hit the fan with Robertson, I'd be alone in the moment and in the aftermath.

But I wasn't. And neither was Jarek. And from the nod and the lack of urgency from the security guy, Jarek was fine. No one seemed concerned he was any worse for the wear. Shaken, bloody, and sore, sure, but he'd be okay.

The cops wanted statements from us, so Jarek sat beside me on the steps to wait for one of the officers to come back.

As we waited, I rested a hand between Jarek's shoulder blades. "You good?"

"Yeah. I'll probably be hating life tomorrow, but..." He dabbed at his nose and inspected his fingers. There was some blood, but not much. As he wiped it away on the paper towel in his hand, he muttered, "Should've known I wasn't getting out of Toronto without someone taking a swing at me."

I didn't know what to say to that. I just leaned into him, grateful for the comforting touch and the arm around my shoulders.

"Hey, you guys all right?"

Mayweather's voice turned my head, but it wasn't just him coming up the hall. Dolls, Dima, Cole, Ferns, Sawyer, and Coach Henley all had that look like they were ready to answer the bell and throw gloves.

"What the fuck happened?" Coach Henley demanded. "I heard Robertson went hands on?" His gaze locked right on Jarek, and I could tell when he noticed the blood beneath his nose. His expression hardened and his eyes turned colder than the concrete we were sitting on. "Fucking hell. You okay, son?"

"I'm good." Jarek turned to me, eyebrows up.

"I'm fine." My voice was still shakier than I would've liked, but it wasn't like Robertson had touched *me*.

Jarek ran a hand up my back. Then he pushed himself to his feet and motioned in the direction the Toronto police had escorted our old coach. As I got up, too, he said, "Cops took care of it."

Mayweather glanced in that direction too, then looked Jarek up and down. He must've taken Jarek at his word that he was all right because, he smirked, tapped his own upper lip, and said, "You got something here."

Jarek rolled his eyes and flipped him off as he chuckled.

Coach Henley scowled. "Graham Norwood told me

and the front office what happened. Said he wanted to give me a heads up in case there was any blowback on you boys via the media." He sighed and shook his head. "Didn't think he'd do... *that*."

"Wait, what happened?" Mayweather asked. The rest of our teammates had the same question on their faces.

I was grateful Coach Henley explained it. We filled in a gap here and there, but he carried most of it. I didn't think I could've.

"Shit," Cole said to Jarek. "I always wondered about that slump you had, especially since I started playing with you and saw how good you are." He swore softly, shaking his head. "I don't think I'd have been able to skate if that shit was happening."

Beside me, Jarek exhaled, some more tension leaving his muscles. "It was, um... It was hard. This?" He gestured at his mouth. "Kind of always expected it while I was playing here."

"Me, too," I admitted.

That got wide-eyed stares of horror from everyone.

I'd have bet money it was validating as hell for Jarek to see that horror in the faces of our friends and coach. It sure was for me.

Mayweather exhaled and clapped Jarek's shoulder. "Fuck, dude. You've always hated playing here, but... Christ. Now I get why." He shifted his focus to me. "And why you got the hell out of here the minute your contract was up."

I nodded, wrapping an arm around Jarek's waist. "Yep. There was a cancer in the locker room here, and it wasn't any of the players." Leaning into my boyfriend, I added, "And he's finally fucking gone."

"Wow." Mayweather squeezed my arm. "That took

some brass balls, blowing the whistle like that. I don't know if I could've."

I blinked. It was hard to imagine Chase Mayweather being afraid to do anything. Then again, it had been hard to imagine Jaromir Badura being cowed by a coach and GM the way I had, and here we were.

"Shit, Yars." Dima stepped around Jarek and pulled him into a hug. "I had no idea."

"I know," Jarek whispered. "No one did. Not until..." He drew back and tilted his head toward me.

"Then it's a damn good thing Mish came to Pittsburgh," Ferns chimed in. "Got you both away from that shit, and gave you the safety in numbers to do something about it."

My throat was getting tight, and I couldn't even say why. Maybe the lingering relief and crashing adrenaline. Maybe the solemnness of our usually irreverent friends. Or maybe just the realization that after so many years of thinking I was alone and there was nothing I could do, I wasn't. And I'd done something. We'd done something. Our team had our backs, the clubs were taking us seriously, and Wilcox and Robertson's reign of terror was *over*.

I smiled and cleared my throat. "I think coming to Pittsburgh was the best thing I ever did."

"Of course it was." Dima smirked and wrapped an arm around Jarek's shoulders, throwing him off-balance. "Because now he's doing you and isn't such a pissy jackass."

The guys all groaned, and Jarek gave him a shove, but he was smiling.

"All right, boys." Coach Henley gestured over his shoulder. "How about we get on the bus? We've had enough excitement for one night, and we've got an early flight in the morning."

Our teammates nodded and headed back down the hall, but Jarek and I hung back.

"We, um..." I motioned toward the Toronto cop who had returned and was waiting for us. "We have to give statements. We can take an Uber to the hotel when we're done."

Coach glanced back and forth between us. "Send me the receipt. I'm billing the Shamrocks for it."

Jarek and I both chuckled. After Coach left, I said, "Think he'll actually bill Toronto?"

Jarek considered it. "Maybe? But it's nice to have a coach who's on our side, so..." Trailing off, he half-shrugged.

I couldn't agree more.

And even as I rehashed everything in my statement, I felt lighter than I had in a long time. Like more weight than I'd known I was carrying had tumbled off my shoulders.

I had Jarek. We had an amazing team who had our backs. The men who'd made our lives hell were getting what was coming to them.

In that moment, I realized I really, truly meant what I'd said to our teammates.

Coming to Pittsburgh was the best decision I'd ever made.

EPILOGUE

Jarek

About a year and a half later.

The Pittsburgh Hornets had gone deep into the playoffs Hunter's first season with us—going farther than either of us ever did with Toronto—and we'd *almost* made it to the finals. We'd forced game seven in the Eastern Conference finals, and we'd held our own into double overtime, but New York had finally scored.

It had been heartbreaking to see our chance for the Cup dashed, but getting that far at all had been a victory for everyone, especially Hunter and me.

This season, though, the whole team had been determined to go all the way. We'd had a taste, and we also knew it was likely going to be Mayweather's last season. Our captain deserved to go out on a high. We all wanted that high for ourselves, too. From training camp on, we all knew we weren't going down without a fight.

We weren't, it turned out, going down at all.

When Mayweather hoisted the Cup, he cried. We all did. It was a fitting end to a fantastic career.

After we won, the team had given out prints of everyone's names engraved on the big Cup, and sometimes I caught myself staring at it. There'd been a time when I'd done things I wasn't proud of because I'd been—in addition to being beaten down and manipulated—promised that my name would be on the Cup someday alongside Hunter Michaud's. It was vindicating and liberating in ways I couldn't explain to see our names now... especially since that framed print was hanging between our two miniature Cups in the living room of the place Hunter and I had bought last summer.

In a couple of weeks, we'd spend his day with the Cup in Vancouver. Another week after that, we'd spend my day with it in Kladno, where he'd meet my extended family for the first time. We'd also be celebrating Eliška's graduation from medical school.

It was a great year, that was for sure.

And it wasn't just the Cup win and moving in with Hunter. Helping to get Coach Wilcox and Robertson ousted from the League had done a number for my mental health, but that karmic dick punch for them still hadn't been quite enough to help me let go of the past. Not even after I'd testified—alongside Hunter and several other witnesses—against Coach Robertson for hitting me.

The effect those two had had on the Shamrocks was plain to see after the team's first season under a new coach and GM. Coach Robertson's replacement had a hockey IQ that was off the charts, and he'd been well-known as a great leader during his twelve years as captain before he'd retired from play. Under his leadership, and with the prospects the new GM was bringing in, the Shamrocks were flourishing now. Still very much in a rebuild, so they'd missed the play-offs, but their performance was more consistent and their systems were, little by little, coming together.

Neither of us received nasty receptions in Toronto anymore. Several players had thanked us, and the fans had been incandescent with collective rage after they'd learned how their beloved hockey team had been treated. When they realized those assholes were what had driven Hunter out of Toronto, they'd been ready to almost literally crucify him, and we'd seen a number of fans wearing Hunter's Toronto jersey at games after that.

I think that was good for him, being redeemed in the eyes of the fans and the city he'd loved.

It had all been good for me, too, but there was a lot for me to deal with that was still taking a long time to unpack. I'd resisted seeing a therapist to talk about what had happened in Toronto, and lucky for me, Hunter understood why. After we'd been outed while visiting a supposedly safe space, and after I'd been fucked over by a team that had made me empty promises, I had trust issues. Who wouldn't?

But Hunter had convinced me, and I'd gone to see someone during the offseason. It was... not easy, especially at first. After *six sessions* with her, I finally felt safe enough to tell her the whole story. When I'd asked Hunter to come with me that day, I was so relieved—and somehow not surprised—he'd said yes.

"*This conversation doesn't leave this room, right?*" I'd asked my therapist for the fourth time, gripping Hunter's hand for dear life in her office.

"*Doctor-patient confidentiality is the law,*" she'd

patiently reminded me for the hundredth time. *"And even if it wasn't, it's sacred to me. Nothing leaves this room unless I think you're a danger to yourself or others."*

So, as reassured as I'd ever be, I told her the story. Palms sweating, voice unsteady, I'd told her everything from start to finish. I'd even let out some details I hadn't told Hunter before, like how Robertson had spent the latter half of the previous season verbally beating me down as if the team's lack of success fell squarely on my shoulders. Or how the GM had obliquely hinted and occasionally outright threatened for months to trade me, buy out my contract, put me on waivers—keeping me in a constant state of certainty that my career was one turnover away from done. By the time they'd sat down with me to explain their plan to acquire Hunter, I'd been terrified that I was hanging by a very thin, fraying thread.

When I'd finished telling my story, even Hunter had been sweating, visibly horrified by how badly the brass had treated me... and I felt even guiltier because the worst of it had happened in the name of acquiring *him.*

I'd gone on to explain to her, same as I had Hunter, why I couldn't go public. Why I was so scared of it getting out. As satisfying as it had been to take down the people who'd derailed my career, there would always be a part of me that wished *all* their sins could come out.

But there would be too much collateral damage. That was an unacceptable price, so I'd carried it by myself instead, and—apart from Hunter and my therapist—I'd continue to carry it myself.

"So you've carried all this shame, guilt, and anger for eight years," she'd said evenly when I was finished. *"You've carried it all by yourself. Because you didn't want to hurt*

*anyone else. Not even those who should've faced conse-
quences for their actions."*

My eyes had welled up all over again. I hadn't been able
to speak, so I'd just nodded.

Folding her hands on top of her notes, she'd said, *"I
think in order to let go of all that shame, guilt, and anger, you
need to revisit the narrative. Revisit who was the villain in
this story."*

I'd stared at her, startled and not sure I'd heard her
correctly

*"You told us what happened as if you feel like you did the
most heinous, shameful thing imaginable,"* she'd gone on.
*"You know you did things that were wrong, and you clearly
own them. But it sounds very much to me like you're taking
on far more than your fair share of the blame for a situation
where you didn't have nearly as much agency as you might
have thought."* She'd paused as if a few seconds of silence
was enough to let all that sink in. Then, voice softer, she
said, *"When we take a step back and look objectively at the
narrative, however, is this the story of a calculating co-
conspirator who got burned? Or is it the story of a kid who
made a mistake because he was led to believe a situation was
solely or mostly his fault, and that it was solely his responsi-
bility to fix it?"*

I'd just... sat there. For a solid minute, I'd sat there, my
eyes unfocused and lips apart as I replayed it all in my
mind. I'd known all that, I think, and Hunter had said as
much, but something about hearing it from an objective
third party had thrown things into focus in a whole
new way.

It seemed so obvious. It seemed like it had been
obvious all along, and yet had fallen out of the sky. I'd
known all along I'd been fucked over. That I'd been lied to

"No, we do." He kissed behind my ear. "We've just got a stop to make between now and dinner."

I furrowed my brow, eyeing him in the mirror. "What kind of stop?"

He flashed me a wicked grin. "You'll see."

Huh. Hunter wasn't usually one for quite that level of spontaneity, and he'd definitely piqued my curiosity. What in the world did he have up his sleeve?

I'd find out soon enough.

On the way out to the car, I double-checked that the box was still securely in my inside pocket. I was a little restless, knowing I'd have to wait longer before *finally* asking him, but it wouldn't be that long. A couple of hours at most, if I had to guess; otherwise most of the nice restaurants would be closed.

I could wait.

Maybe.

Are we there yet?

We rode in his car tonight, since I planned to have some wine and I'd driven last time. On the way, we talked about our upcoming trips, as well as some of our recent antics with Dolls, Dima, and Ferns at the practice rink. Last week, Dima had put Ilya in skates for the first time, and he'd carefully held his tiny hands as he guided the toddler around the ice. He was barely two, so of course he wasn't going to be *really* learning to skate for a while yet, but both sets of grandparents were going to love the video Chloé had taken of him giggling as he glided between his father's skates. I was pretty sure Dolls, Ferns, Hunter, and I had all melted watching the adorable family like that.

It had sparked another conversation later that day that brushed up against long term plans. Over the past year, "if I ever have kids" had been steadily shifting toward "if *we* have kids," which had more recently been turning to "our future kids." Maybe it would sound weird to anyone else, but lying in bed that night, musing with Hunter about how young was too young to put skates on our kids—for a video op and for lessons—had probably been one of the sweetest and most romantic moments of my life.

God, seriously—are we there yet?

Hunter turned off the main road, and I didn't think anything of it until a familiar neon sign came into view, and I had to do a double take. Then my heart skipped when Hunter slowed down and pulled up to the curb right in front of the door.

Right in front of Lanterns.

I turned to him, eyes wide. "You... You wanted to come *here?*" My therapist had suggested coming back, and Hunter and I had been meaning to for a while. I just hadn't realized he wanted to come here tonight.

He smiled shyly as he set the brake. "Is this okay?"

"Oh. Uh." I didn't know what to say to that, but managed, "Yeah, it's fine." I held his gaze. "Are *you* sure? After the last time..."

"I'm sure." He leaned across the console and kissed me. "I like this place. No time like the present to come back, eh?"

There was that. And truthfully, I had *wanted* to come back here since before my therapist had suggested it. The owners had fallen all over themselves to apologize, and they'd invited us to come back any time for free drinks and VIP treatment. We'd meant to take them up on it, but we'd both kept shying away. Even though it wasn't the club's fault, well... once bitten.

But we were in a good place now, so I smiled and shrugged. "Let's do it."

Given that it was a weeknight, there was no line outside. In fact, I didn't even realize they were open on Tuesdays. But the lights were on and there was a bouncer by the door, so... game on, I guess?

I got out of the car, and as Hunter handed off the keys to the valet, I checked my pocket again just to be sure. Yep, still there.

On our way inside, he rested his hand on the small of my back. No self-consciousness. No hesitation. We were together, and Hunter didn't give a damn who knew. Hell, he *wanted* people to know. So did I.

The music wasn't quite as loud tonight, thank God. I loved the thumping bass when I came here to dance, but I liked it like this too. Besides, there was a good chance I was going to run out of patience while we were here, and I didn't want to have to shout my question at Hunter. The whole getting down on one knee thing would probably get the message across anyway. I just needed to wait for the right—

"Hey, there they are!" A familiar voice broke through the music, and I did another double take, this time to see Dima waving us over to a large booth. There, he and Chloé sat with Ferns, Dolls, and their wives, plus Sawyer and his fiancée.

The hand on my lower back pressed gently, herding me in that direction. "There's our table."

"Our—" I turned to him. "We're meeting them?"

Hunter grinned and shrugged. "Why not?"

I... didn't have an answer. Or an objection. The butterflies in my stomach got even more active, both with nerves over doing this with an audience, and excitement at the prospect of our friends being here to share this with us. They—and Hunter—just didn't know about that part yet.

It turned out Lanterns had a dinner menu during the week. I'd only been here on Fridays and Saturdays, but on weeknights, the vibe was a bit more lowkey and they had a decent menu of sandwiches, flatbread pizzas, and even some pastas. We all let Dima and Chloé choose the beer, and they didn't disappoint, ordering an amazingly crisp, nutty lager for everyone who wasn't driving (or, in the case of Sawyer's fiancée, pregnant).

After an amazing dinner full of trash talking and laughing, our server collected our dishes and offered to bring around a dessert menu. I was about to seize that opportunity to ask that question that had been itching to come out, but then the deejay announced that it was karaoke night.

Everyone—especially Hunter, to my surprise—was onboard.

Eh, I could wait. I was going to lose my mind, but this would be fun, so I didn't complain.

Though as karaoke got going, I thought I was going to *die* listening to my teammates doing hilariously terrible karaoke. Though Sawyer and Lisa did a surprisingly solid duet of 'Islands in the Stream', and Dolls turned out to be a way better singer than I expected.

The rest? Good God. They were awful, and everyone was laughing so hard, we were all almost in tears.

"Sit down, Dima!" we all shouted through our laughter. "Sit the hell down!" He was chuckling too, and Chloé was laughing so hard she was wheezing.

Fortunately, a few other singers stepped up, and they were... mixed. Entertaining, to be sure. A couple were pretty good. More were very *not* good.

As an excruciating rendition of a Justin Bieber song ended, the deejay called out, "Next on the list—come on up, Hunter!"

My jaw dropped as my head snapped toward him. *"You're* doing karaoke?"

He smirked. "What? You don't think I can sing?"

"I..." Okay, I had no idea if he could sing. But getting up onstage and singing in front of our teammates? Yeah, this I had to see.

Ferns and Dima shouted for someone to take away the microphone, and Dolls begged someone to cut the power.

"Oh, fuck all of you," Hunter said when he had the microphone.

There were groans all around our table. I was laughing as hard as Chloé was now—not necessarily because I thought Hunter would be bad, but just the whole shitshow of all our various teammates getting up there. And... maybe from the three beers I'd had. One of which had been for liquid courage. I was pretty sure I had enough of that now; all I had to do was wait for Hunter to come down from the stage and for enough of a lull for me to get a word in edgewise.

Hunter pulled a chair from offstage and plunked it in the middle of the stage.

"Oh God," someone called out. "You're not going to break out an acoustic guitar, are you?"

"Your mom liked my acoustic guitar," Hunter said.

Dolls actually choked on his beer. Ferns slapped his back, which didn't help at all. I was pretty sure that was the point.

I fucking loved this group.

"All right, all right." Hunter cleared his throat. "If I'm gonna do something sappy and romantic..." He patted the chair and looked right at me. "I need someone to sing to."

The crowd broke into a chorus of groans and awws, and Chloé nudged me with her elbow.

"Get up there," she shouted over the noise. "The sooner you do, the sooner this is over."

"Oh my God," I muttered, and did as I was told, which only made our friends roar and chirp louder.

As I took my seat, I met Hunter's gaze, hoping he read my plea of, *Please either kill me or just don't do this.*

No such luck.

The intro for some ballad I didn't recognize started playing, but it was soft. Hunter cleared his throat, then said into the microphone, "I'm going to get sappy here for a second, and you're all going to deal with it."

There were some chuckles and groans, and he flipped someone off.

I pressed my lips together, my cheeks on fire as everyone in the room stared at us.

Then he spoke, and the snark in his tone was gone. "Jarek, I always thought I could learn a lot from playing hockey with you. And I have."

I fully expected someone to shout, "Learn more!" or "That's a start!" But the crowd stayed surprisingly quiet.

He put a hand on my shoulder. "I just didn't think I'd learn so much about myself. Or about what it's like to be happy." He swallowed hard. "Or how maybe it was time I thought about what I wanted in life instead of what everyone else expected of me."

I couldn't breathe. The whole room was silent except for that music still playing in the background, not to mention my pounding heart. No chirping. No heckling.

Hunter took his hand off my shoulder, and he pulled in a deep breath. "I learned how to be someone who sees something he wants, and goes for it." He reached for his pocket. "And in this case... asks for it."

Then, right there on the gaudy karaoke stage, Hunter went to one knee in front of me.

In front of the whole club.

In front of our friends.

He swallowed again, bringing up a simple gold band, and his voice wasn't quite steady when he spoke again: "Should we make hashtag #Michura official?"

The laugh that burst out of me was a mix of joy and surprise. I rose, taking his hand and tugging him up, and as soon as I threw my arms around him, the whole room exploded into cheers and applause.

I kissed him, and he grinned against my lips before he curved his hand behind my head and returned my kiss.

"Well?" someone called out. "Did he say yes or not?"

Rolling my eyes, I gestured for the microphone, and when he handed it to me, I said, "Just for the record—" I held up the ring. "I'm not a complete idiot. Of course I said yes."

That had everyone roaring and cheering.

When everyone had quieted, I said, "But *also* for the record..." I reached into my pocket, and as soon as I produced the ring box, the room was deafening with more cheers and shouts.

Hunter glanced at the box, then stared at me. "Were you..."

I nodded, shakily opening it. "I was going to wait until dinner. But you beat me to it."

His eyes were huge. "You..."

I took a deep breath. "I love you, Hunter," I said, the noise giving us almost total privacy even here at centerstage. "And one of the things learned from you is what it's like to believe I deserve to be happy." I took his hand. "I'm happy with you. And I want stay that way. I want to make you happy."

"God, Jarek." He threw his arms around me and kissed me. "You do make me happy. Always."

"So, is that a yes?"

He drew back and cocked a brow. "I just proposed to you, and you're asking if I'm saying yes?"

I gave him my best innocent look as I half-shrugged.

Hunter rolled his eyes. "You're a dork." He led me offstage so we weren't hogging it anymore, and as soon as we were out of the spotlight, he kissed me again. When he spoke this time, the teasing was gone. "For the record... yes. Absolutely."

I couldn't explain the rush that gave me. The relief, the euphoria—all of it. Yeah, he'd proposed, so I wasn't shocked by his yes, but hearing it...

Oh my God. This was real.

"I love you," I whispered as I held him to me.

"I love you, too."

"So, are we allowed to post about it yet?" Dima appeared beside me. "I've got the perfect meme and everything."

"What?" I squeaked as I drew back from Hunter. "You guys—you made *memes* already?"

"Well, yeah." Ferns shrugged. "We've been working on them ever since Mish told us about this."

I eyed all four of them. "Which was how long ago?"

"Last week," they said in unison.

I groaned and facepalmed. A week was way too much time for these idiots to get up to no good.

"So, can we post them or not?" Dolls pressed.

I rolled my eyes and took out my phone. "No, if anyone gets to announce this with a meme, it's me."

Hunter straightened. "*You're* going to make one?"

"No." I tapped the screen a few times before I showed it to him. "I had one ready since I was planning on proposing."

He stared at me, then looked at the screen. After he read it, he rolled his eyes and laughed. "Oh, my God."

Ferns, Dolls, and Dima crowded around to peer at it. I grinned—I was actually pretty proud of this one.

It was a shot of me handing off the Cup to him after we'd won it, both of us grinning like idiots with our bushy playoff beards. I'd captioned it, *Guess who doesn't have to wait until next season to get another ring?*

They all groaned, too.

"For fuck's sake, Jarek," Ferns muttered. "You're going to give us all cavities."

"Where did you learn to be sappy, anyway?" Dima asked. "What the hell?"

"Yes, do tell." Chloé slid her hand around Dima's elbow and grinned at me. "You could give him lessons."

"Hey!"

She batted her eyes and shrugged.

I just chuckled. Then I jiggled my phone. "So... should I post it?"

Hunter eyed me, but his expression quickly softened to a smile, and he wrapped his arm around me and kissed my cheek. "Yes. Post it."

My heart soared. "Let's put a selfie with it."

His grin made my knees week. We posed for a quick selfie, both of us holding up our left hands and showing off the new rings.

My hands shook a little as I uploaded the photos. I captioned them, *achievement unlocked—put a ring on it! #Michura*, and posted it.

"There." I slid my phone into my back pocket. "Done."

Hunter smiled. "Think I should give Rachel a heads up?"

"Hmm, probably."

While he did that, I stared down at the ring on my hand. Holy shit. Of all the ways tonight could've played out...

"God, I can't believe..." I turned my hand over and over, watching the disco lights play on the gold band.

"What?" Hunter put his phone away. "Were you that surprised?"

"Yes!" I met his gaze. "I mean, I was pretty sure you'd say yes when I asked, but I didn't think..."

His expression softened. "You didn't think I'd ask?"

"I..." Biting my lip, I trailed off, unsure what to say.

"Baby." Hunter pulled me in close. "Everything you said? You're right. You're *absolutely* someone who deserves to be happy, and you shouldn't be afraid to go for it when you see something that makes you happy." He swallowed hard, and his voice wavered a little as he stroked his thumb across my cheekbone. "But you're also that something for me. And you better believe I want you. Forever."

I exhaled, wrapped my arms around him, and buried my face against his neck. Closing my eyes, I held him tight and just let this moment be.

So much of my world had been controlled by other people who didn't give a damn about me, and I'd convinced myself I was no longer worthy of happiness, never mind love.

But tonight, the most amazing man I'd ever known... asked.

There was a part of me that wished I could've made my proposal first, but honestly, I was relieved beyond words that things had gone down the way they had. Because I'd been terrified. We'd talked about getting married and having kids. We'd bought a house together. I'd been absolutely sure he was onboard with the idea, but it had still been a leap of faith.

One I'd been determined to make tonight because I was *so sure* about us.

And I'd been scared shitless anyway, because those voices that had been telling me I was unworthy were still there.

Then he'd walked up onto that stage, and all the doubts I'd had coming into this evening—all that fear that Hunter wasn't as into me as I was into him—they scattered like an opponent's fans after we'd shut out their team on home ice.

This was real. I'd found love again, and I'd found peace, and somehow, I was going to spend the rest of my life with the man who'd been too stubborn to let me stupidly push him away.

"I love you," I whispered.

Hunter smiled and leaned in, and just before our lips met, he said, "I love you, too."

Running my fingers through his hair, I asked, "So, I assume we don't actually have a dinner reservation someplace else tonight?"

He laughed, shaking his head. "No, that was just a ploy to get you into a suit and out of the house."

"Baby, you don't need a ploy to get me into a suit."

"No, but it was the 'out of the house' part." He slid his hands up my back, drawing me in closer. "Because when you're in a suit, I just want to take you in the bedroom and peel it off you."

I shivered, and my knees wobbled as he kissed me. "We can still do that tonight, right?" I murmured against his lips.

"Of course we can. And we will." He kissed me again, lighter this time. "Eventually."

"Tease."

"Maybe." He grinned. "And you were right, by the way." He held up his hand. "I really didn't want to wait until next season for another ring."

"Neither did I. But maybe we can get another one of those big fancy rings again this season."

His eyes lit up. "Ooh, two Cups in a row—think we can do it?"

"With you as our number one center?" I touched his face and kissed him softly. "Of course we can."

"I know we can." Hunter smoothed my hair. "I'll have you next to me."

Yes, he absolutely would.

On *and* off the ice.

For more books by L.A. Witt, please visit

http://www.gallagherwitt.com

Romance * Suspense

Contemporary * Historical * Sports * Military

Titles Include

Rookie Mistake (written with Anna Zabo)

Scoreless Game (written with Anna Zabo)

The Hitman vs. Hitman Series (written with Cari Z)

The Bad Behavior Series (written with Cari Z)

The Gentlemen of the Emerald City Series

The Anchor Point Series

The Husband Gambit

Name From a Hat Trick

After December

Brick Walls

The Venetian and the Rum Runner

If The Seas Catch Fire

...and many, many more!

ABOUT THE AUTHOR

L.A. Witt is a romance and suspense author who has at last given up the exciting nomadic lifestyle of the military spouse (read: her husband finally retired). She now resides in Pittsburgh, where the potholes are determined to eat her car and her cats are endlessly taunted by a disrespectful squirrel named Moose. In her spare time, she can be found painting in her art room or destroying her voice at a Pittsburgh Penguins game.

Website: www.gallagherwitt.com
    Email: gallagherwitt@gmail.com
    Twitter: @GallagherWitt

Printed in Great Britain
by Amazon